PENGUIN CLASSICS

BEEN DOWN SO LONG IT LOOKS LIKE UP TO ME

Richard Fariña was killed in a motorcycle accident in Carmel, California, on April 30, 1966—two days after the publication of *Been Down So Long It Looks Like Up to Me*. Mr. Fariña was born of a Cuban father and Irish mother, both of whom came to this country during the 1930s, and he spent time with them in Brooklyn, Cuba, and Northern Ireland. At eighteen he worked with members of the Irish Republican Army but eventually had to leave the country. Much the same happened in Cuba, which he visited often when Fidel Castro was still in the mountains and again during the heavy fighting in Santa Clara and while the revolutionary army was entering Havana. From the time Mr. Fariña left Cornell University in 1959 until late 1963 he lived in London and Paris. The author wrote that he made his living from "music, street-singing, script-writing, acting, a little smuggling, anything to hang on. Lost thiry pounds." In 1963 Mr. Fariña married Mimi Baez and returned to California, where he finished *Been Down So Long It Looks Like Up to Me*. His shorter work appeared in such magazines as *Poetry*, *The Atlantic*, and *Mademoiselle*, and his plays were produced at Cornell and at The Image Theater in Cambridge, Massachusetts. Also a respected folk-rock singer and composer, Mr. Fariña appeared with his wife at the Newport Folk Festival and on tour, and two of their record albums were released. The first was chosen one of the ten best folk records of 1965 by *The New York Times*, and that newspaper called the second, *Reflections in a Crystal Wind*, "wild, imaginative, poetic, surprising." A posthumous collection of his writings, *Long Time Coming and a Long Time Gone*, was published in 1969.

Thomas Pynchon is the author of the novels *V*, *The Crying of Lot 49*, *Gravity's Rainbow*, and *Vineland*.

BEEN DOWN
SO LONG
IT LOOKS LIKE UP
TO ME

Richard Fariña

INTRODUCTION BY
THOMAS PYNCHON

PENGUIN BOOKS

PENGUIN BOOKS
Published by the Penguin Group
Penguin Group (USA) Inc., 375 Hudson Street, New York, New York 10014, U.S.A.
Penguin Group (Canada), 90 Eglinton Avenue East, Suite 700, Toronto,
Ontario, Canada M4P 2Y3 (a division of Pearson Penguin Canada Inc.)
Penguin Books Ltd, 80 Strand, London WC2R 0RL, England
Penguin Ireland, 25 St Stephen's Green, Dublin 2, Ireland (a division of Penguin Books Ltd)
Penguin Group (Australia), 250 Camberwell Road, Camberwell,
Victoria 3124, Australia (a division of Pearson Australia Group Pty Ltd)
Penguin Books India Pvt Ltd, 11 Community Centre, Panchsheel Park,
New Delhi – 110 017, India
Penguin Group (NZ), 67 Apollo Drive, Rosedale, North Shore 0632, New Zealand
(a division of Pearson New Zealand Ltd)
Penguin Books (South Africa) (Pty) Ltd, 24 Sturdee Avenue, Rosebank,
Johannesburg 2196, South Africa

Penguin Books Ltd, Registered Offices: 80 Strand, London WC2R 0RL, England

First published in the United States of America by Random House, Inc., 1966
Published with a new Introduction by Thomas Pynchon in Penguin Books 1983
This edition published in Penguin Books 1996

30 29 28 27 26 25 24 23 22 21

PUBLISHER'S NOTE
This is a work of fiction. Names, characters, places, and incidents either are the
product of the author's imagination or are used fictitiously, and any resemblance to
actual persons, living or dead, events, or locales is entirely coincidental.

Excerpts from the following are reprinted by permission: "General William Booth
Enters into Heaven" from *Collected Poems* by Vachel Lindsay; copyright 1913 by
The Macmillan Company. "Good Mornin' Blues," new words and new music
arranged by Huddie Ledbetter and edited with new additional material by Alan
Lomax; copyright © Folkways Music Publishers, Inc., 1959.

LIBRARY OF CONGRESS CATALOGING IN PUBLICATION DATA
Fariña, Richard.
Been down so long it looks like up to me.
Reprint. Originally published: New York: Random House, 1966.
I. Title.
PS3556.A715B4   1983   813'.54   82–15090
ISBN 978-0-14-018930-8

Printed in the United States of America
Set in Times Roman

INTRODUCTION

In a dim way, I had been aware of Richard Fariña before I actually met him. It was the winter of 1958, toward the end of the school semester, and I was a junior editor on the *Cornell Writer*, which was the campus literary magazine. At some point these stories and poems began to arrive. It was a radically different voice, one that seemed to come from the world outside, surer, less safe, of higher quality than the usual run of submissions. Not many of the staff could tell me much about this "Fariña" character, except that he'd been away from Cornell for a while, out traveling around.

Soon, in the back spaces of classrooms I happened to be in, I would sometimes detect this dangerous presence, not wearing a jacket or tie, more hair than was fashionable, always sitting with the same group of people. Quiet, but intensely *there*, checking things out. Eventually I connected him with the other, literary presence.

We ran with different crowds, so our paths only crossed now and then. One day in the spring I was crossing the Arts Quad and spotted Fariña, reclining on the green grass with an open book. We nodded, said hello. "Listen," Fariña said,

"I'm having a party Saturday night at my place on College Avenue, if you want to fall by." Which was how I first encountered his remarkable gift of civility. As we chatted, a strange thing was also happening. Coeds I had lusted after across deep lecture halls were actually altering course, here, out in the daylight, to stop and talk to Fariña. He was inviting *them* to his party too. Oboy, I thought to myself, oboy.

1958, to be sure, was another planet. You have to appreciate the extent of sexual repression on that campus at the time. Rock 'n' roll had been with us for a few years, but the formulation Dope/Sex/Rock 'n' Roll hadn't yet been made by too many of us. At Cornell, all undergraduate women were supposed to be residing, part of the time under lock and key, either in dormitories or sorority houses. On weeknights they had to be inside these places by something like 11 P.M., at which time all the doors were locked. Staying out all night without authorization meant discipline by the Women's Judiciary Board, up to and including expulsion from school. On Saturday nights the curfew was graciously extended to something equally unreal, like 12 midnight.

Curfews were not the only erotic problem we faced—there was also a three- or four-to-one ratio of male to female students, as well as a variety of coed undergarments fiendishly designed to delay until curfew, if not to prevent outright, any access to one's date's pelvic area. One sorority house I knew of, and certainly others, had a house officer stationed by the front door on date nights. Her job was to make sure, in a polite but manual way, that every sister had some version of a Playtex chastity belt in place before she was allowed out the door. Landlords and local tradesfolk were also encouraged to report to the Administration the presence of coeds in off-campus apartments, such as Fariña's. In these and other ways, the University believed it was doing its duty to act *in loco parentis.*

This extraordinary meddling was not seriously protested until the spring of 1958, when, like a preview of the '60s, students got together on the issue, wrote letters, rallied, demonstrated, and finally, a couple of thousand strong, by torchlight in the curfew hours between May 23rd and 24th, marched to and stormed the home of the University president. Rocks, eggs, and a smoke bomb were deployed. Standing on his front porch, the egg-spattered president vowed that Cornell would never be run by mob rule. He then went inside and called the proctor, or chief campus cop, screaming, "I want heads! . . . I don't *care* whose! Just get me some heads, and be quick about it!" So at least ran the rumor next day, when four upperclassmen, Fariña among them, were suspended. Students, however, were having none of this—they were angry. New demonstrations were suggested. After some dickering, the four were reinstated. This was the political and emotional background of that long-ago spring term at Cornell—the time and setting of Richard Fariña's novel *Been Down So Long It Looks Like Up to Me.*

Not that this is a typical "college" novel, exactly. Fariña uses the campus more as a microcosm of the world at large. He keeps bringing in visitors and flashbacks from the outside. There is no sense of sanctuary here, or eternal youth. Like the winter winds of the region, awareness of mortality blows through every chapter. The novel ends with the death of a major character.

Undergraduate consciousness rests in part on a set of careless assumptions about being immortal. The elitism and cruelty often found in college humor arises from this belief in one's own Exemption, not only from time and death, but

somehow from the demands of life as well. It is Exemption
—in a sense which Fariña interestingly broadens here—
that so perplexes and haunts the novel's main character,
Gnossos Pappadopoulis.

For Gnossos, Exemption is nothing he can either take
for granted or have illusions about. His life is a day-to-day
effort to keep earning and maintaining it. In the course of
the book, Gnossos looks at a number of possibilities, including Eastern religion, road epiphanies, mescaline, love.
All turn out to have a flaw of some kind. What he's left
with to depend on is his own coherence, an extended version of 1950s Cool. "Immunity has been granted to me,"
thinks Gnossos, "for I do not lose my cool." Backed up by
a range of street-wise skills like picking locks and scoring
dope, Cool gets Gnossos through, and it lies at the heart of
his style.

There was a similar element of reserve to Fariña's own
public character. When he spoke, one of the typical expressions on his face was a half-ironic half-smile, as if he were
monitoring his voice and not quite believing what he heard.
He carried with him this protective field of self-awareness
and instant feedback, and I never did see all the way through
it, although I got to know him a little better during the '59
school year. We were never best friends, but we did like
each other, and each other's writing, and we hung out some,
at parties, at beer outlets on campus like the Ivy Room,
or at Johnny's Big Red Grill (called Guido's in the book),
which was the usual nighttime gathering place.

The eats and atmosphere at Johnny's were pretty much
as Fariña describes them. From time to time there'd be live
music. Peter Yarrow, later of Peter, Paul and Mary, had a
standing gig there, maybe one of his earliest. He alternated
with a rock 'n' roll group, all of them related, from the

grocery across the street. In a few years these same two currents, modern folk and working-class rock, would flow together in what we remember now as the music of the high '60s. Fariña's ear was taken not so much then by pop music as by more traditional American forms like jazz, and especially blues, both country and black. To the now canonized Buddy Holly he listened with some ambivalence— evident in the novel—but he did pay close attention to "Peggy Sue." It seems now that in the guitar break of that recording he may have caught something others didn't, some flash of things to come—but this could also just be my own retro-fantasy. Two albums of the period I know he was crazy about were Mose Allison's "Back Country Suite," also mentioned in the novel, and the English version of Weill and Brecht's *Threepenny Opera*.

When it came to dancing, Fariña went for Latin music. He was blessed, and knew it, with a happy combination of heritages. His mother was Irish and his father Cuban. He had relatives in both countries and had visited with them. It happened that in '58 and '59 there were a number of students from Latin America in the School of Architecture, and their circle was one of several that Fariña could move in with some intimacy and ease. Their weekend parties were regarded as the best around. Fariña danced a strange *paso doble* I've never seen since, and whose authenticity I can't confirm. But the women he danced with, though now and then puzzled, were certainly enjoying themselves, which was the whole point.

Each year on St. Patrick's Day, the tradition in the Architecture School was to construct a giant, what seemed like hundreds-of-feet-long, Chinese dragon, get as many folks under it as possible, and go running around the campus, in and out of classes and lectures, hands emerging from underneath the critter to grab and fondle the nearest coeds, many of whom had their hair tinted green. Everybody whooped it up all day long with oceans of beer dyed the same color. This was the one day, close to the Spring Equinox, when Fariña's two ethnic sides swung into balance, and he could indulge both. He would end the day with a crowd of dragon personnel, all spattered green, down at a venerable bar called Jim's, standing up on a table with a mug of green beer, quoting García Lorca's "*Verde, qué te quiero verde. . . .*" This would produce a long series of toasts to everything green, *cervezas verdes, coños verdes.* "*El barco sobre la mar,*" Fariña hollered, "*y el caballo en la montaña!*" Years later, in California, around sunrise on the morning of his marriage to Mimi Baez, we happened to stagger into each other in somebody's front yard, both hung over. It was somewhere out in the country, in the hills near Palo Alto. We then managed to have one of those joint epiphanies. Fariña was staring up one of the slopes nearby. A white horse was standing out on this very green hillside, looking back at us. Of course Fariña and I were both thinking of Lorca's horse on the mountain.

Sometimes at college we also succeeded in getting on the same literary wavelength. We showed up once at a party, not a masquerade party, in disguise—he as Hemingway, I as Scott Fitzgerald, each of us aware that the other had been through a phase of enthusiasm for his respective author. I suppose by then I was learning from Fariña how to be amused at some of my obsessions. Also in '59 we simultaneously picked up on what I still think is among the finest of American novels, *Warlock,* by Oakley Hall. We set about getting others to read it too, and for a while had a micro-cult going. Soon a number of us were talking in *Warlock* dialogue, a kind of thoughtful, stylized, Victorian–

Wild West diction. This may have appealed to Fariña partly as another method of maintaining Cool.

The first time I read *Been Down.* . . was in manuscript, an early draft, in the summer of 1963. I remember giving him a lot of free advice, though I've forgotten what it was exactly. But fortunately he didn't take any of it. He must have wondered if I thought we were still back in writing class. Later, having rewritten it, ten pages from the end of the final draft, his hand went out on him. "Did you hear about my Paralyzed Hand?" he wrote in a letter. "Why Tom old boy"—*Warlock* talk—"I woke up this here otherwise promising morning with a clump of inert floppy for a hand. Lentils. Lentils and some kind of exhaustion known only to nits in sedentary occupations. Me, the once hunter after restless game gone to seed in a J. C. Penney armchair covered by a baby blanket. . . . But the hand came back by pins and needles after a month and I got done. . . ."

When I first read the book, I was comparing it with my own experience of the same place, time, and people. It seemed then that Gnossos and Fariña were one and the same. It was also great fun recognizing the real-life counterparts of the other characters, being tickled by what he'd done with and to them. Now, nearly twenty years later, seeing a little further into his method, I think maybe it wasn't so simple. He didn't just take things that had happened and change names. He really worked his ass off, but the result is so graceful that the first time around I was fooled completely.

For many of the characters, Fariña seems to have begun with the key traits that in their Cornell originals appealed to him most—Drew Youngblood's decency, Juan Carlos Rosenbloom's manic bravado, Judy Lumpers's build—and then from these cores gone on to develop each of them more fully. Presently, as characters will, each took on an inside-the-novel life, separate from whoever they'd been outside it. There isn't much point Naming Names here—they know who they all are and they walk among us, even today.

Gnossos himself is not Mr. Perfect, by any stretch. He has a short temper and a low tolerance for organized religion, national mythologies, incompetence, resignation, anybody from the American South, racist or not—the list of resentments goes on. He is susceptible to the thrill of vendetta or karmic adjustment, an impulse I suspect isn't entirely absent from why Fariña wrote the novel. Gnossos uses drugs and alcohol injudiciously, and gets publicly abusive with women, something I never saw Fariña do. His own approach to women was never less than courtly and sensitive, though not without perhaps one or two jiveass moments.

The wolf story, for instance. This is one of Gnossos's encounters with homicidal animal life, the other being the monkey demon of Chapter 14. In the book, Gnossos tells the wolf tale to Kristin McCleod, a young woman he's falling in love with. He puts it in the form of a dialogue, in which Kristin, and we reading, are asked to provide the sense data—the cold, the squeak of the snow, the Adirondack visuals. It is Fariña's most perfected version of a piece whose early tryouts many friends first heard at Cornell, some more repeatedly than they really wanted to. He was in fact dismayingly successful with the wolf story, which he was using then mainly to hustle coeds, often those on whom one had sort of had one's own eye. Most of them, as I recall, went for it. Each time he told it, of course, he rewrote, so it got better and better.

The monkey demon or mandrill-at-the-window story didn't play as well. Some only thought he was being dramatic, others thought temporarily insane. When winter boredom set in there was always a chance of entertainment in sneaking up to Fariña's window at unlikely hours and making what we imagined to be mandrill faces and sounds, in hopes of some reaction. But he would only half-smile, and shrug, as if to say, if you don't get it, you don't get it.

But it remains one of the most effective of the many dark scenes in this novel. The darkest of all, and I think the best written, is the sequence that takes place in revolutionary Cuba, in which Gnossos's best friend is accidentally killed. Although a few pages of campus rioting come later, the true climax of the book is in Cuba. Back in his Hemingway phase, Fariña must have seen that line about every true story ending in death. Death, no idle prankster, is always, in this book, just outside the window. The cosmic humor is in Gnossos's blundering attempts to make some kind of early arrangement with Thanatos, to find some kind of hustle that will get him out of the mortal contract we're all stuck with. Nothing he tries works, but even funnier than that, he's really too much in love with being alive, with dope, sex, rock 'n' roll—he feels so good he *has* to take chances, has to keep tempting death, only half-realizing that the more intensely he lives, the better the odds of his number finally coming up.

Close to the end of his last term at Cornell, Fariña seemed to grow impatient. He had a job waiting in New York, and they didn't care, he said, if he got his degree or not. There may also have been some romantic disaster involving Kristin McCleod's original, though we never talked about it and all I heard was vague gossip. We were in one class together that term, and studied for the final at Johnny's Big Red Grill over bottles of Red Cap ale. Next day, no more than half an hour into the exam, I was scribbling away at an essay question, caught a movement, looked up, saw

Fariña handing in his exam book and leaving. He couldn't have been finished. As he came past I raised my eyebrows and he gave me that smile and that shrug. This was the last I saw of him for a while.

He went to New York, to Cuba, married Carolyn Hester, got a career in music going, toured overseas, lived in London, Paris, got divorced—then it was back to California, Boston, California again. Sometimes we wrote letters, sometimes—not often enough—we'd run into each other. We talked on the phone the day before he died. His book had just come out. We arranged to connect in L.A. in a few weeks. The next evening I heard the news over an AM rock 'n' roll station. He'd been riding on the back of a motorcycle on Carmel Valley Road, where a prudent speed would have been thirty-five. Police estimated that they must have been doing ninety, and failed to make a curve. Fariña was thrown off, and killed.

I called his house—no answer. Called the AP in Los Angeles—they couldn't confirm anything for sure. It never occurred to me to call the hospital up there. I didn't want to hear what they'd say. The only person I found in that night was a long-distance friend who'd also known him at Cornell. She didn't have any more solid news than I did. Both still hoping, hope fading, we talked for a long time, into the middle of the night, about Fariña and the old days, in our voices the same mixture of exasperation and love most of us had always felt whenever his name came up. Finally, toward the end of the conversation, she laughed. "Just thought of something. If *that fucking Fariña*," she said, "has only been seriously hurt—if he goes up to the edge of It, and then comes back, you realize—we're *never* going to hear the end of it."

—THOMAS PYNCHON

This one is for **MIMI**

This one is for Milton

"I must soon quit the Scene . . ."

Benjamin Franklin
in a letter to George Washington
March 5, 1780

CONTENTS

CHAPTER 10

A Dream before Dinner. The Virgins Two:
a Confrontation. A Paradox in Indelible Ink.

CHAPTER 11

Oeuf. The Plot persists in Thickening.

CHAPTER 12

Yea, Hooray, the Happy Couple.
Madness through Pragmatic Method.

CHAPTER 13

Blacknesse, Birds, and Bees. Midshipman Fitzgore
on the Bathroom Floor. The Epiphanal Defloration.
David Grün Explains the Third Dimension.

CHAPTER 14

Gnossos becomes Further Involved.
A Theory of Cosmic Origin, Differing Points
of View, and an Undesired Guest.

CHAPTER 15

The Bower of Innocence Lost. Beth Blacknesse
and a Contradiction in Terms.

CHAPTER 16

Seeds of Doubt are Sown.

BOOK
THE FIRST

1

To Athené then.

Young Gnossos Pappadopoulis, furry Pooh Bear, keeper of the flame, voyaged back from the asphalt seas of the great wasted land: oh highways U.S. 40 and unyielding 66, I am home to the glacier-gnawed gorges, the fingers of lakes, the golden girls of Westchester and Shaker Heights. See me loud with lies, big boots stomping, mind awash with schemes.

Home to Athené, where Penelope has lain in an exalted ecstasy of infidelity, where Telemachus hates his father and aims a kick at his groin, where old, patient Argus trots out to greet his weary returning master and drives his fangs into a cramped leg, infecting with the froth of some feral, hydrophobic horror. Oh welcome,

for home is the madman,
home from his dreams
and the satyr
home to make hay,

whether or not the sun shines, for in that well-hilled land of geological pressures and faults, there is always much rain.

Banging up the steepest slope, shoving away mounds of cinder-spoiled snow with his hobnails, smelling of venison and rabbits, the anise odor of some Oriental liquor on his breath. No one has seen him (or if they have, there has been no acceptance of the impossible sight, for rumors have him dead of thirst, contorted on his back at the bottom of Bright Angel Trail, eyes gnawed out by wild Grand Canyon burros; fallen upon by tattooed pachucos and burned to death in the New Mexico night by a thousand cigarettes dipped in aqua regia; eaten by a shark in San Francisco Bay, a leg washed up in Venice West; G. Alonso Oeuf has him frozen blue in the Adirondacks), he stumbles back from its lakes now (found sitting on a bed of tender spruce boughs, his legs folded under him in the full lotus, a mysterious caste mark where his third eye would be, stark naked with an erection, discovered by the St. Regis Falls D.A.R. out on their winter bird walk).

I am invisible, he thinks often. And Exempt. Immunity has been granted to me, for I do not lose my cool. Polarity is selected at will, for I am not ionized and I possess not valence. Call me inert and featureless but Beware, I am the Shadow, free to cloud men's minds. Who knows what evil lurks in the hearts of men? I am the Dracula, look into my eye.

Shuffling up an insipidly named Academae Avenue from the pea-green walls of the town's Greyhound station, wrapped tightly in his parka (the blanket of Linus, the warmth of the woods, his portable womb), the rucksack packed thickly with the only possessions and necessities of his life: a Captain Midnight Code-O-Graph, one hundred and sixty-nine silver dollars, a current 1958 calendar, eight vials of paregoric, a plastic sack of exotic seeds, a packet of grapevine leaves in a special humidor, a jar of feta, sections of wire coathanger to be used as shish kebab skewers, a boy scout shirt, two cinnamon sticks, a bottlecap from Dr. Brown's Cel-Ray Tonic, a change of Fruit-of-the-Loom underwear from a foraging at Bloomingdale's, an extra pair of corduroy pants, a 1920's baseball cap, a Hohner F harmonica, six venison loin chops, and an arbitrary number of recently severed and salted rabbits' feet.

Flipping through the ads of the unbought Athené *Globe* at the bus terminal, he had come across the number 109 in the list of apartments available for the spring term. He hovered before it now, panting from the climb, evaluating, doing the geometry of escape routes, counting windows and doors. The house was a red frame structure, American Gothic, freshly painted, white trim, Swiss drolleries carved around the window boxes. Touch of the pastoral, pleasant to wake in May with a scalding hangover, lean back your head and breathe forget-me-nots.

He knocked timidly and was greeted by the thinnest bone of a girl he had ever seen. Terrycloth robe with kitty-fluff on the collar, long brown pigtails tied with yellow rubberbands, no eyebrows.

"You came about the flat?"

British. Murderess of Cypriot peasants; innate antagonist, be careful. Lie: "My name is Ian Evergood, miss, you're quite correct. Could I have a look?"

"It's a mess; we're just moving up over Student Laundries, you know where that is?"

My God, wearing high heels with the robe, anything under? Be discreet. "I'm not sure, I've been away for over a year, they're always shifting things about. Splendid flat, this."

"It does me."

Devilishly clever, flat in there instead of pad. She's looking at me. "Been on a bit of a hunting trip. The Adirondacks. You'll have to forgive my appearance."

"Hunting? You mean animals?"

"Rather."

"How appalling. Killing small things that can't fight back?"

"There was a wolf, you see. A marauding bear."

"A bear? Really? Won't you come all the way in, no sense standing in the hall."

"Quartered three children before I got him. Ghastly business. Made a topping shot, though."

"Are you British?"

"Greek."

"Oh."

Too late, could have said anything. Have another try, "Mountbatten blood in the family. Is the place furnished?"

"Two of the bucket chairs belong to them," she said, nodding at the bolted French doors that led into the neighbors' quarters. "One is mine, and that butterfly thing. I could sell it if you really wanted, they're not comfortable; at least not for sitting."

For what, then? The flesh over her eyes arching the way her eyebrows might have arched. Worth a try. I hear water boiling, free food. "I'd need it, all the same. Here, you're not making tea? I only came by to see—"

"That's quite all right. Take a look 'round, you're the first to come." Going off into the kitchen, Jesus, wearing stockings as well. "You take cream and sugar?"

"Everything." There was no bedroom but a section at the far end of the room had been partitioned off with bamboo shades, a bad sign. Still, everything else looked good, rice-paper globes on the lamps, white walls, a Navajo rug, roomy couch, fireplace. Have a look at the kitchen.

"My name's Pamela," she told him, pouring through a wooden sieve into handleless cups. The robe open slightly at her throat, kitty-fluff parting enough to reveal a blond chest hair, which caused a spasm of lust.

"What school are you in?" between cups.

"Astronomy," he lied. "Theories of origin, expanding galaxies, quantum mechanics, that sort of thing. You?"

"Architecture."

"How come you're not living in the dorms?" Hopefully.

"I'm fifth-year. Do you like the kitchen? There's an enormous fridge, and they give you all your silver. Is your name truly Evergood?"

"Took Mother's name when Father entered the Benedictines."

"Ah. I didn't mean to pry."

"Not at all. Sends me brandy, monk-bread, you know. Smashing tea, this. Pamela what?"

"Watson-May. But did you really kill a marauding bear? I mean, isn't that rather a dangerous thing to have done?"

Just so. And doesn't your thigh-down tingle to think about it? Shame it's afternoon, never much on matinées. Good to have the parka covering or she'd see. Hardly care for them skinny, but those high heels and that hair. Push it a little: "Not necessarily dangerous. A lot depends on the man and the first bullet." Ho ho.

"Of course."

"You either kill them straight away or turn them and make a heart shot. Gets me edgy to discuss, though. You wouldn't have a drink around the house?"

"Isn't it a bit early?"

"Not today, no."

"There might be some gin and a little Scotch left."

"You don't carry Metaxa?"

"Which?"

"Scotch is fine; just pour it in the tea. Have one yourself, takes the edge off moving, I always say, ha ha."

She poured the drinks and sat straddling the butterfly chair. The robe was up over lumps of knees, a phthisic hand clutching the collar against her throat. Gnossos feeling the need for a paregoric Pall Mall—filter the pain on the way to his brain. But the Scotch did part of the trick.

"Do you like the flat all right?"

"What does it go for?" was the question, sipping.

"Seventy dollars, thirty-five of course if you're planning to share."

"Of course. What about utilities?"

"Everything's included but the phone, which I can leave if you cover the deposit."

Sure thing. "Who lives over there?" nodding, "behind those doors?"

"Only the Rajamuttus, George and Irma. From Benares, I believe, but very nice, just the same. They drink gin and tonic all day long, with grenadine, they'll never bother anyone."

Possible connections? "What's their interest, at school, I mean?"

"I think George is hotel administration. Factotum studies, master bartending, something of that sort."

Cordials at the Punjab Hilton. Pappadopoulis poured himself the last of the bottle. "I just might take it, old girl. Do I have to see real estate agents?"

"You sublet from me. The landlord lives in the country."

And the mice will play?

There came a feeble knocking at the door, Pamela calling, "Just a moment," setting down her drink, pulling the kitty-fluff closer together. The police? An angered father? A familiar voice just the same.

". . . ad in the paper; I wonder, could I look—"

"I'm sorry, there's a Mr. Evergood seeing it now, I believe he's taken it."

"Is it Fitzgore I hear?" The carrot-red hair and freckled nose peering around the door, going pale with shock.

"Sweet Jesus Christ."

"Come on in, man."

"But you're dead! Frozen up north someplace. God above, Paps."

"I'm resurrected is all. And choose your words, paps are the dugs of an old crone."

"I feel sick."

"Is there any gin in that other bottle, Pam, for this thin-blooded cabbage? Come sit in my new pad, sport, look around." He stood and shook the tentative hand, clapping the smaller man on the shoulder, guiding him to one of the wicker chairs, where he collapsed with a half smile.

"Wow, no kidding, what a hell of a noise. There was even some Grand Canyon story, but you were spotted in Las Vegas."

"Only heat exhaustion, man, searching for sun gods at Phantom Ranch. Have you met Pamela here?"

Fitzgore gave a desultory nod and took the offered drink, looking curiously at its cherry-soda color. "Grenadine," she explained. "A custom in Benares."

"And San Francisco Bay, they said—"

"That was the cop who saved me. He lost a leg to a hammerhead shark; crushing irony, rescued by the law."

"Mother of God."

"Hardly deified. A fuzz like all fuzz. They gave him a

ribbon, a Mickey Mouse stamp, I can't remember. Where's Oeuf, anyway?"

"Recuperating from mono in the infirm. There was some rumor about the clap, too."

"No imagination, Oeuf. We've got to visit him, though. Drink up your gin, we'll tour the campus."

"I've got a lab this afternoon, Paps, classes have started, you know. Are you back as a student, or what?"

"Little of everything," grinning wickedly. "Is it too late to register?"

"They'll probably fine you five dollars," said Pamela, slipping a record on the player, catching some sort of party mood. She has possibilities, came the oblique thought. Fetish?

"Oh what the hell," said Fitzgore, "I may as well cut."

"Are you of Irish descent, Mr. Fitzgore?" she asked. The record was Bach. Man, the oneness of them all. Identity implicit in half a dozen LP's, the usual books, eighteen punched cards run through a Univac, carried in a turquoise wallet next to the picture of your favorite sorority sister. Beethoven, Brubeck, selected symphonies, *The Prophet*, assorted anthologies, *Now We Are Six*. "Call him by his Christian name, Pamela. Hardy is devout, he invokes tradition."

"Hardy, is it?"

"Goes a long way back," said Fitzgore. "Salem Irish, Back Bay antecedents."

Mustn't waste time. "Miss Watson-May," from Gnossos formally, standing, "we really have to flee. The flat will do nicely, and it's only fair to warn you, I'm a bit of a bore about noise."

"You don't like it?"

"He makes it," said Fitzgore.

"All the time. Very little reserve, Greek marrow wins out."

"Quite all right with me, actually."

"Pappadopoulis is the name, in fact. Call me Gnossos if you want, silent *G*, okay? We'll dig you later." She turned down the Bach, looking slightly disappointed. Because we're leaving? "You stay home nights?"

"I'll probably be packing."

"Might fall by. Give the word to the Rajamuttus. I'll be, whatever you called it, sharing with Fitzgore here."

"Hold on," came the protest. "I wanted a place by myself, to study—"

"Haa!" bellowed Gnossos, "to be sure. To be thoroughly sure."

They went down the icy steps into the street, up the rest of the long hill toward the campus. Mounds of heavy, bulky snow everywhere, the Mystic Lakes breed of winter, swooping early out of the north; the sky swollen, portentous, dumping huge, carpetlike flakes incessantly, neutralizing each extreme of spectral color, sterilizing shapes, muting sounds, holding out against the first torrential thaw, the first blinking of the unclothed sun. I am not ionized and I possess not valence.

But breathes there a soul
with man so dead
who never to his head has said,
"Is there anything happening, Fitzgore?"

"What do you mean?"

"Is there any shit around?"

In a whisper, the red head dropping down into its overcoat like a turtle's, eyes searching up and down the crowded

avenue, windows and doorways, any one of which might en-
close some ovarian doom waiting to be fertilized: "You
mean *narcotics?*"

"What about Oeuf, you can't tell me he's straight."

"Nothing. Not a thing since you left. And speak softly, I
want to graduate. Only six months left, you know."

"To be sure. What about the Black Elks downtown, Fat
Fred?"

*"No*body white goes in there."

"We'll see. I brought some paregoric with me, just in
case. Anyone have an electric fan?"

"Holy Ghost, Paps, you're really the kiss of death."

"That's Thanatos, but also Greek."

All about them the golden girls, shopping for dainties in
Lairville. Even in the midst of the wild-maned winter's chill,
skipping about in sneakers and sweatsocks, cream-colored
raincoats. A generation in the mold, the Great White Pattern Maker lying in his prosperous bed, grinning while the
liquid cools. But he does not know my bellows. Someone
there is who will huff and will puff. The sophomores in their
new junior blazers, like Saturday's magazines out on Thurs-
day. Freshly covered textbooks from the campus store, slide
rules dangling in leather, sheathed broadswords, chinos
scrubbed to the virgin fiber, starch pressed into straight-
razor creases, Oxford shirts buttoned down under crewneck
sweaters, blue eyes bobbing everywhere, stunned by the android synthesis of one-a-day vitamins, Tropicana orange
juice, fresh country eggs, Kraft homogenized cheese, tetra-
packs of fortified milk, Cheerios with sun-ripened bananas,
corn-flake-breaded chicken, hot fudge sundaes, Dairy
Queen root beer floats, cheeseburgers, hybrid creamed corn,
riboflavin extract, brewer's yeast, crunchy peanut butter,

tuna fish casseroles, pancakes and imitation maple syrup, chuck steaks, occasional Maine lobster, Social Tea biscuits, defatted wheat germ, Kellogg's Concentrate, chopped string beans, Wonderbread, Bosco, Birds Eye frozen peas, shredded spinach, French-fried onion rings, escarole salads, lentil stews, sundry fowl innards, Pecan Sandies, Almond Joys, aureomycin, penicillin, antitetanus toxoid, smallpox vaccine, Alka-Seltzer, Empirin, Vicks VapoRub, Arrid with chlorophyll, Super Anahist nose spray, Dristan decongestant, billions of cubic feet of wholesome, reconditioned breathing air, and the more wholesome breeds of fraternal exercise available to Western man. Ah, the regimented good will and force-fed confidence of those who are not meek but will inherit the earth all the same.

He remembered the previous Christmas with Heff. Mexican grass and birdbath martinis, stealing the D-Phi car at a purple passion party, both of them going to the imported manger in the Ramrod, staring for almost half an hour at the yard-high figurines around the crib, listening to the peals of Gregorian celebration from the speakers overhead. One of the shepherds too obviously cross-eyed.

Hey, Heff man, you dig Sebastian?

I what?

The cross-eyed shepherd cat. Behind old Saint Joseph.

Oh yeah. Look at him, he's cross-eyed.

That's poor taste, right?

Who's to say?

He sees double, dig?

Yeah.

He sees two little baby Christ Jesuses.

I'm with you.

Then it's no good.

Yeah?

Two little Jesuses, I mean, Christ, that's a Roman paradox right there.

I'm hip, Paps.

We get rid of one, set the whole thing straight.

Pappadopoulis picking up the plaster statue of the child and tucking it under his parka as if it were a bottle of vintage champagne; the two of them turning casually, ambling out to the illegally parked car. Then sitting with the motor running.

You know what, Heff? The Virgin Mary-Mother dug the whole snatch.

She's hip?

We're in trouble.

Let's get her.

Heff picking up the Virgin's statue back at the manger, returning clumsily to the car, then tripping with a clatter on the steps, the figure flopping into the air, making a bottom-heavy arc, crashing against the stone, its head flying off and rolling down the street.

She lost her cool, Paps man.

Yeah, put it in your pocket.

Driving across the blanketed campus toward Harpy Creek, Pappadopoulis fondling the statue of the child, tucking it under the chin, poking his pinky in its navel, feeling its swaddling clothes for poo-poo. Stopping at the bridge and strolling across.

Tradition, old Heffalump.

Check. Mustn't collapse the bridge.

They kissed the statues in turn and threw them out into the snowy void, where they fell tumbling against the frozen gorge below. Listening for the sound of impact, two muted crunches.

We go back for Sebastian, Paps? Liable to say he dug four kidnapers 'stead of two.

Let's get him.

The kidnaped shepherd stood on a pink Formica tabletop in Guido's Grill, everyone standing around singing Christmas carols, toasting the cross-eyed image. Heff giggling the words to his own song:

Holy Infant,
So tender and mild,
Sleep in heavenly pieces . . .

Heavenly pieces. Speaking of which:

"Have you had any ivy league ass, Fitzgore?"

"Jesus Christ, you ask the most disarming questions."

"I've been on a voyage, old sport, a kind of quest, I've seen fire and pestilence, symptoms of a great disease. I'm Exempt."

"There's some nympho in Circe III who's screwing everybody since Heff left her, but she's got warts."

"Splendid Heffalump, always loving the disfigured. Was she any good?"

"I don't really want to think about it. Got her drunk on grasshoppers and she barfed all over the back seat of the car. This Pamela girl kind of interests me, though."

"Car? You don't have wheels?"

"My dad got me an Impala for senior year."

"Oh splendid. Splendid, splendid illness and decay."

"Hey look, Paps, really. I've *got* to hit the books this semester. I'm carrying eighteen hours and I'm on pro."

"So?"

"So I've got to get through."

"Maybe sometime, you rat-bastard traitor to your ancient blood, I'll ask you why. But not today, right? Let's go to Louie's."

"They're tearing it down."

"What?"

"Building a thing called Larghetto Lodge. Things have changed, for Christ's sake, you can't go stomping around the country for a year and expect to come back to the same lousy landscape. C'mon, let's get a beer in the Plato Pit."

Plodding along, backs angling at sixty degrees to the never-leveling hill, Gnossos thinking of the students at their left and right, ears deaf to doom. Little shops and businesses springing up to court the passing generations. A new photographer's, specialty in dramatic pose from the look of the window, black backgrounds, faces lit from beneath, pipe smoke, passionate intensity: stare at me, I am the bust of Homer. At Student Laundries the ambitious, short-haired young men scrambling about, mixing everyone's wash, student drivers jumping happily into student vans with student routemen, muddy fruit-boots squeaking in the snow, everyone with a share in the business. How to con them, worries Gnossos, remembering the roulette wheel he ran with Heff in their cellar. A sudden sign creaking on its hinges: MENTOR UNIVERSITY, FOUNDED 1894. Visions of mustached juniors, celluloid collars, evolving undergraduate vocabulary, making tradition. Give me the Victorian for "how's your ass, ace?" Cow pastures then. Jove Dormitory a gabled sign of the times.

Past the law school with its university Gothic. Mock-Yale really, pleasant courtyard, splendid for a duel. Odd heads turning to look at him, not believing, who's that weirdo with all the curly hair? New faces, incredible bodies of young American girls, beckoning even under wool. Avoid my gaze, ladies, for you read the wish well enough. Care to mount a maniac before you marry your lawyer? Some

Gnossos seed, in case your man goes sterile from martinis. That one with the green knee-socks. Seen her once.

"Who is that one, Fitzgore?"

"Where?"

"The green knee-socks, loafers."

"Don't know her, some kind of genius in government, I think."

Incredible legs. If they knew how long it's been. The Golden Fallacy. What the hell, its worth saving. "And that thing over there?"

"New engineering building. They're planning a whole quad of sorts around the chem school. Wasn't it up when you left?"

"Certainly not." Tinted aluminum plates, long sheets of weatherproofed glass, dymaxion torsions: the synthetic contents of a collective architectural grab bag. Clean, well lighted, cheap to heat, functional, can be torn down and replaced over a long weekend or transported to Las Vegas by helicopter, demolition incorporated in the structural design. A nod to mortality.

Heffalump the quadroon was waiting at one of the varnished picnic tables in the Plato Pit next to the jukebox, under a pathetic plastic pot of ersatz ivy. His thin, quarter-spade body gathered over his Red Cap, in case it should get away. A girl next to him, Joan of Arc hair-do and men's clothes. Creep up slowly, let him know.

"Is it truly a Heffalump, Fitzgore? Brooding with its snout in foam?"

The spidery form uncoiling in an explosion of arms and legs, the Red Cap clattering over the table, spilling in an effervescent pool. "Gaaaaaaa!" His eyes, moons of disbelief.

"Then why does it retreat? Home from the great adventure and no one takes my hand. Philistines."

"Jesus and Mary! You're not dead!"

"So Fitzgore's already told me."

"Pachucos in Texas or somewhere, Oeuf told us you were murdered——"

"Oeuf's projected death wish, baby. Anyway, it was New Mexico, some boy scout they burned in Taos. Me, I was in jail."

"No shit, man," Heff giggling nervously, "we thought you were down." People beginning to stare. Fitzgore, embarrassed, fed the jukebox and disappeared into the line for beer. The Joan of Arc girl stuck out her hand and said, "I'm Jack. You must be Paps." Her voice a husky baritone.

"Gnossos, man," finding the strength of her grip excessive, then sitting. Heffalump's mouth still hanging open between giggles, huge teeth jutting forward like a beaver's.

"Wow," he said.

"You really hadn't heard?"

"Something about the Adirondacks, but nobody knew for sure, and anyway the time sequence was always screwy. We didn't know if you were coming or still going."

"Neither did I. Flew back is where it's at. Had an epiphany in North Beach, dug my reflection with all the other faces. Threatened my Exemption status, right? Had to flee."

"Why?" from the girl called Jack, her brow furrowed, looking a bit too serious.

"Who knows? Keep a jump ahead of the monkey-demon. The signs were there." Fitzgore returning, glancing about, placing the three cans of ale on the table, then going back for something else. "The time was right, mostly." And disaster hovering behind the last silver dollar in the rucksack. "You still run the wheel, Heff?"

"Shhhh! My God, they'd bust me as soon as look at me if they got into that."

"New administration?"

"Some woman called Susan B. Pankhurst. Vice-President for Student Affairs."

"Virgin?"

A moan from Heffalump, who looked down at the same time to find the spilled ale dripping on his jeans. Jack laughed and slapped his back, making him cough. Dyke from the pelvis up. "What're you doing for a pad?" she asked.

"Just found one on Academae Avenue with Fitzgore. British chic moving out."

"British?"

"Fitzgore?" said Heff. "He's in a fraternity."

"There is what Memphis Slim once called the rent situation. And he has wheels."

The words to Peggy Sue blaring from the jukebox, Buddy Holly with hiccups.

Fitzgore setting down a cup of tea, poking the dissolving lumps of sugar. "When are we moving in, Paps? I'm still at the house, and this is what, the second day of classes?"

Heff was licking the puncture in his can. "I'll check to-night," from Gnossos. Maybe get that splendid hair on her chest. No bosom to speak of, but it's been a long time. Legs the important thing. Maybe have a midnight cook-'em-up, dolma with vine leaves, little egg and lemon sauce on the side, moussaka. Need some Metaxa. Where to feed later? Fitzgore's fraternity?

Peggy Sue grunting into a chorus.

"Is your house rushing, Fitzgore?"

"All week. Probably fine me for moving out," pressing the teabag against his cup with a fork. Ask him.

"Is there any clause against Greeks?"

"I don't think so."

Catching on suddenly, dropping the cup from his lips, peering over its rim, hint of wrinkle in the forehead, "Why? What do you have in mind?"

"Oh, a little purloined Harris tweed maybe, some Daks, a challis tie—why, I'm choice cut for the best house on the hill."

"We did it two years ago at D-Phi," from Heff. "He's good at it."

"I'm topping. Witty conversation, parlor games, charades, recite the Greek alphabet, impress the troops. What house are you in?"

"D.U. But—"

"Dikaia Hypotheke. Splendid motto. Inspiring, I might say." Quick drink of ale, feel it already, stomach churning, anxious acid. "Non-secret house, if I remember. No hand-shakes, hocus-pocus, ritual shelved in favor of the Square Deal. Who knows, Fitzgore, I might dig it and pledge. Wear a propeller-topped beanie during Hell Week, pull a quack-ing toy to class."

"Jesus, Paps, you'd only be coming for the free meal. Some of them might know."

"What are you having? Filet mignon? Buttered lobster tail? Something groovy to impress me?"

"You don't have any real clothes, to begin with."

"Heff?"

"I've got a Brooks suit from Student Laundries."

"There you are, then." Jack laughing her baritone laugh again, rubbing her hands together. Good-looking, all the same. Wonder, does she have a roommate. "Why not pick me up at Heff's, say six."

"Jesus, Paps, I don't know."

"They'll love me," into the rucksack for a blessing on the moment, a silver dollar and some feta, having to burrow through moist rabbits' feet, underwear, around the vials of paregoric. He screwed open a jar and broke off four pieces of white, chunky goat's cheese, holding them over his head and mumbling solemnly:

"Confiteor Deo omnipotente,
Beatra Pappadopoulis, semper virgini,
Beatra Pappadopoulis, semper paramus."

Little transubstantiation. "This is my body, gang." Then, sliding a can of Red Cap forward, "This is my blood." Goat cheese, the cookings of a copper-plated vat, symbols for the silly cells of being. With sanctified fingers he placed a piece of cheese on each of the proffered tongues before him.

"I'm redeemed," said Heff.

"Amen," from Jack.

Flipping the silver dollar to Fitzgore, Gnossos said: "A sizable percentage of my fortune, that, to purchase more blood."

"Okay, if I can have tea instead." Fitzgore going obediently to the line, resigned to the dinner ahead. Jack staring wildly, smiling. Careful, she might be Heff's. Trouble enough with friends' women. Fitzgore returning from the line almost immediately.

"They won't take it."

"What?"

"Your silver dollar."

"Won't take it?"

"She says she's never seen one before, the woman at the checkout."

Up at once, eyes flashing, the parka over his large shoulders like a magician's winter cape, his hair tumbling on his ears. Stomping up to the line, walking ahead of two coeds buying corn muffins, who jerked their sneakered toes away from the clang of his boots. The woman at the cash register, with a potato for a face, complexion like Wheatena. He has seen her in a hundred roadhouses and side-street hotels, in countless supermarkets and bargain basements, squatting in a print dress, wearing hobheels, smelling of purchased secrets from Woolworth's, lips puckered, passion plucked or pissed away some twenty years before. The resigned are my foes.

Three opened Red Caps and a cup of tea were waiting by her side. He snapped down the silver dollar with a weighty click.

"That ain't no good," she said. "I just sent one back."

"What?"

" 'Sno good."

Placing the flats of both palms on the counter and leaning so far forward that she had to change position and back away: "I beg your sublimely idiotic pardon, but it IS good and YOU are taking it."

"I'm awful sorry, sonny, but—"

"Sonny? SONNY? DO YOU KNOW WHO I AM?"

The entire length of the Plato Pit falling silent, heads at each of the picnic tables turning in the direction of the bellowed cry.

"I am King fucking MONTEZUMA, that's who, and *this* is the coin of my kingdom."

The woman looking around her for help, compulsively fingering the keys on the cash register, her mouth open, her elbows seeking balance.

"And if you fail to honor the symbol of my realm, I will

have your heart torn out, right?! OUT OUT OUT of your
body." She gasped. "At the top of a pyramid." She reeled.
"And I will eat it RAW!"

The two girls dropping their corn muffins and retreating
from the maniac; the woman's blood draining from her
head.

Gnossos picked up the ale and tea, and hissed, "Keep the
change, baby. Buy yourself a hot-water bottle." Returning
to the table, where they drank quickly under a veil of cautious murmurs, then departed into the already darkening
evening with snowflakes gray against the sky, the chains on
the tires of passing cars making muted jangles on the roads.

2

All across the blue-tinted campus, circling the illumi-
nated tall Clock Tower, up and down the many sidehills
scored by trails of the afternoon's tray sliders, the cars were
shuttling back and forth between dormitories, fraternity
houses, and Lairville. An electric atmosphere hovering
above the primeval silence of the winter's end, odor of
ozone, bright-eyed rushees everywhere, giving measured
ground to this latest complexity of social intercourse, nervous and excited over moratorium's end; free to mingle with
the suave elegance of upperclass brotherhood. The best of
them in Thunderbirds and Corvettes, MG's and Austin Hea-
leys, occasional white Lincoln convertibles, top down for
windy adventure. Chi Psi's fire engine loaded full, clanging
down Labyrinth Avenue. All part of the tactical wizardry

conceived in the previous weeks, long hours between terms in the dovetailed dissection of collected intelligence, identities summed up and catalogued on index cards: name, hometown, school, extracurricular activities, position of father, family income, antecedents, race, religion, salient personal characteristics, tailor (if any), nuances, likes, and dislikes. The Class-A essence of superficial cream spun centrifugally upward by the silently churning forces of a blue-eyed society. Gnossos cruising meanwhile in the back of a charcoal-gray four-passenger Aston Martin, wedged between two freshmen football heroes with android heads, from Alexandria, Virginia, mouths mumbling in taut, athletic fashion as if they have unopened Brazil nuts packing their cheeks. How's your ass, ace?

No index card for me, I'm Exempt. Secret identity mortally guarded, for I am the Plastic Man, able with an effortless shift of will to become a bowling ball, a pavement, a door, a corset, an elephant's contraceptive.

"Got an extra Brazil nut there?"

"What's that, ace?"

"Brazil nuts."

"Ha ha ha. Not with me, ace."

"Ha ha ha. I didn't think so." A stiff finger to the Adam's apple and he eats death. Okinawan karate more aesthetic. He fails to know his Enemy.

Swinging into the D.U. driveway, house officers in Harris tweed gathered around the open front doors, hands ready to wring, smiles frozen on their jaws. Heff's suit uncomfortable, pinching my balls. God help me if they see my St. Louis socks, give the whole thing away. Feel lushed but shouldn't. Paregoric making little lumps in side pocket. Good of Heff to let me use his lamp. Have to find a place though, maybe men's room in the house. Turn Pamela on later. Wouldn't dig it probably, first time. Fitzgore coming over. Oh, see the concern in him. Easy now, stick to vernaculars: "Hello there, Gorzy, how goes it?"

"Pretty good, Paps," glancing around, uneasy grin, too many roles to play. Going to be intimate, getting ready to whisper, "Listen, go easy, okay? They think you're a transfer student. The idea is to get around, meet some of the guys, make noncontroversial small talk."

"When is dinner?"

"Jesus. There you go already. In about half an hour. But you've got to mix a little first, feel things along."

"I have to go to the bathroom."

"Oh my God. Upstairs, second door on the right." Calling after him, "First floor, Paps."

Two brothers already closing in behind, just made it. Interiors all walnut paneling, leather chairs, brass. What was it about Tudor? Comfortable-looking, all the same. Ah, nobody in the loo.

Gnossos opened a window, closed the stall door, and sat down on the pot. Both joints were still a bit damp, having been only partially dried from the heat of a lightbulb in Heff's mildewed room. He waved them in the air to hasten evaporation, then lost patience and lit the first one, taking as long a puff as possible, keeping the saturated smoke in his lungs for thirty seconds. A delicious respiration, almost nothing coming back. Oh yes.

Yes.

Another puff, this one not quite as long, then a series of short ones, carbureting the air, sucking at it noisily. Exhaling again.

Ummmmmmmmmmmmmmm.

He finished the first one. All right. Absolutely all right. Hold on to the second, low tolerance out tonight.

He stood slowly and opened the door to find his face in the mirror. Very funny eyes. Most peculiar. Ought to do something about them.

Oh.

Wouldn't it be nice to have a drink of good Greek wine? Whose room is this?

He tiptoed quietly. The walls covered with bullfight posters and a large Utrillo print of Montmartre. A Belafonte calypso record displayed above the turntable of the machine, quaint Chianti bottles, all empty, hung from nails, some with candles inserted in the necks. Try the bedroom.

Playboy Playmates tacked on the ceiling, neatly made beds. No sign of nectar, though. Oops, someone coming. Into the closet. Eeek, bottle of Cutty Sark. Ho ho ho.

He opened it up, tipped against his lips, and poured. It was altogether glorious. A little provocation for my opiated cells. Listen to them:

". . . is the bathroom here, Harry babes? We don't go in for the dorm setup like some of the other houses. Makes it harder to party, if you see what I mean, ha ha."

"Yeah. Guys waking up all at different times for class, one big room like that . . ."

"Sure thing, ha ha . . ."

Gone. Take some more, good long one, pulsing, there. He put the bottle carefully under a pile of shirts, then eased out of the room. I am invisible. Must remember this place for after dinner. Downstairs. Oh ratshit, someone coming over, looks official, dig the smile, gargles with Lavoris.

"I don't believe we've met, Nooses, my name is John Mayke. The guys call me Maykes," shaking hands like a piston. Makes what? His pillow every night? Careful, play the game, he smells the lush. Can't see my brain, though.

"Gnossos is how you pronounce it, Makes, but old Gorzy calls me Paps."

"Oh sure, old Gorzy. A great guy. Done a whole lot for the house. Said you were a transfer student."

"Quite right. Got tired of Princeton, no girls. To speak of, ha ha."

"Yeah, never thought of it like that. You're here on scholarship, he said."

"Little astronomy action, pays everything, spending-money under the table, you know." Head going higher, might need to flee.

"That right? Couple of guys in the house took that one-o-one course for their science requirement, said it was a real gut."

"Sure thing. It's the advanced courses give you trouble. Relativity principles, spiral nebula in Coma Berenices, that kind of hassle. Really keeps you on your toes. Got to grind all the time. No picnic."

Two more coming over, been hanging on the edge of the talk. Be gregarious: "Howdy," folksy touch. "My name's Paps." Conical hilltops side by side.

"Al Strozier, Ohio."

"Mike Peel, Chicago."

"Paps here was just telling me about astronomy."

"Real gut," said Peel, brush cut, tab collar, cordovans, Skull and Dagger pin in his paisley tie.

"Chicago?" from Gnossos, the opium creeping still higher, "Mister Kelly's, the Loop, Adler–Sullivan Auditorium—"

"What was that last one, Paps?"

Philistine. "Breed of opera house. Acoustically perfect. Closed down. Used as a bowling alley during the war, USO and all. You know. A genius, old Sullivan. Maniac. Died alone."

"They're like that," said Strozier, twist of suspicion in his viscous tone, looking at Gnossos' hair.

"Why are you looking at my hair?"

An uneasy flush in all three faces. "Ha ha," from Strozier, looking around, "ha ha ha."

"You were staring at my hair. You find it peculiar?"

Fitzgore, sensing disaster, coming over just as the dinner chimes were sounding, "Let's go eat, Paps."

"He should see my socks if he thinks my hair is weird—" hiking his tight trousers, revealing a flash of chartreuse that caught the eye of everyone in the room.

"Food, Paps, remember? C'mon."

They entered the dining room in slightly better order, each rushee flanked by selected brothers, deployed and maneuvered to the seat he thought he had chosen himself. They remained standing behind chairs until the president of the house gave the signal to sit. All-ivy lacrosse type, probably from Chevy Chase. A great clatter of dishes, silver, pouring water, busy conversation. The two tables long and rough-hewn, period chairs, stained blocks in the windows, wagon-wheel lamps, gamboge shades. Mead? Dancing girls? Barrels? Tankards of ale? Pappadopoulis closed his eyes briefly, willed himself into a Mediterranean olive grove, a sandaled sprite of eighteen at his side, light cotton dress blowing in the warm breeze, nothing on beneath, unshaved legs and underarms, hammered artifacts dangling from her ear lobes. In his palpebral vision, she beckoned. He raised his lids, hoping to find her sitting cross-legged before him on the table, but found instead a bowl of alphabet soup, a piece of toast sloshing on top. Fitzgore was at his left and a stranger with horn rims blinked assiduously at his right. He wolfed down the saturated toast with one enormous sucking gulp and sopped up half of the bowl's remaining contents with a Parker House roll. Surges of laughter.

At me? Dodge the paranoia. Symptoms and disease often dovetail. The opium still working. Fitzgore saying something, Peel and crowd eying from the end of the table. Fall on them in the night with cyanide spray. Woosh, breathe death.

". . . been wanting to meet you, Paps. Byron Agneau; Gnossos Pappadopoulis."

A limp hand offered from horn rims, "How do you do, Paps, Gorzy here's been telling me about your stargazing. I'm a lit major myself, minor in theater arts."

So you are. And who's the Chinese dwarf at the next table? Hallucination? Watch for the monkey-demon. Behind me? No. Agneau still talking: ". . . mentioned that you enjoyed telling, well, tales on occasion. Just what kind of tales is it you do?"

"No tales. No more tales at all, if you see what I mean."

"Well, not exactly."

"Subversive art form, archaic distortion of the passions, dig?"

"Subversive?" asking seriously. Fitzgore with nervous droplets of perspiration on his upper lip and brow, afraid I'll slice away this twit's ear.

"Taletellers always making trouble, Agneau, leaving mess-piles behind, right? Social schizophrenics, dying in the alleyways, jumping off trestles with anvils tied to their feet, making a terrible scene, most of them queer. Michelangelo queer, even."

"Michelangelo? But wasn't he an artist, ha ha? A painter?"

"A taleteller, baby. *Dear to me is sleep,* right? You don't mind if I quote?"

"Oh, not at all, really."

"Where was I?"

"Something about sleep being dear."

"Sure thing. *While evil and shame endure, not to see, not to feel is my good fortune.* Dangerous shit, that. The cat was into a stone thing, dig? Do you have any idea what's taking them so long in the kitchen, Agneau? Terrible hunger in me. Ought to serve wine with meals, slake the pauses."

"Ha ha. That's true enough. No liquor allowed during rushing, though. An I.F.C. ruling. Only at exchange dinners, the other usual functions we run."

I.F.C. The police all around us. Careful, there may be microphones in the lamps. Or the soup, even. One of the little alphabet pieces, a transistor pickup.

"What do you exchange?"

Nibbling uneasily at his roll, looking at my stained teeth: "Ha ha. You know. Tri-Delt or Kappa sends some coeds over here, we send some guys over there."

Drink purple passions, run upstairs and fumble in each other's underclothing. Rehearsal for the real thing, come in your pants, pretend they're not wet. God, I'm hungry. Moan.

"Mmmmm."

Fitzgore jerking around, asking in a careful whisper, "What's the matter with you?"

"Pax. Only the sound of an alimentary canal. Mmmmm-mmmm."

"For God's sake, some of the guys are looking at you."

"MMMMMMM."

"Oh Jesus," Fitzgore biting his glass.

"You don't tell tales any more then?" from clever Agneau, trying to distract, "that right, Paps?"

"Pornography. I do some gigs I call the Sally Sisters Chronicles. Currently working up the stalled-freight-elevator episodes."

"Really? Episodes?"

"Nymphomaniac oud trio, South American band, Siamese twins. Mmmmmm."

A sharp, hoarse whisper from Fitzgore, beginning to despair: "Paps!" Astounding how Agneau seems not to notice. Almost British in reserve. Try it in his face, cloud his horn rims: "MMMMMMMMMMMMMMMMM-MMMMM." Little better, anxious murmurs stirring, heads turning to see who.

"Siamese twins? Really?"

"Joined at the left diddly. Everyone making everybody else. All plugged in, stuck together, the Ultimate Machine, dig? The twins try to pull out without breaking down the machinery."

Hint of saliva at the corners of the Agneau mouth: "How could they?"

"Whatever they take out, they plug into someone else. As long as there's an opening. Momentary pause but the machine keeps going."

"Mmmm," said Agneau. Everyone staring at them, the upperclass brothers conferring rapidly just as the T-bone steaks were carried in. Mushroom gravy, fried onions, baked potatoes with sour cream and chives, string beans and white sauce, endive salad, bottles of ketchup.

"Ommmmmmmmm." The Chinese dwarf still there, I'm

not mad. "Fitzgore, excuse me a minute, but who the hell is that Chinese dwarf?"

"Shhhh! Holy Christ, Paps, that's Harold Wong."

"Number-one son?"

"He's coxy on the Olympic crew."

"Oh splendid, splendid."

Agneau leaning forward confidentially: "Is it a very long tale?"

"Are you queer?"

"What?"

"I just want to know where you're at. If you have homosexual tendencies?"

"—Me?" A finger at his heart.

"He's drunk," explained Fitzgore, bending over in a desperate whisper, trying to keep the others from hearing too much. "I thought you were hungry, for God's sakes."

Pappadopoulis picking up the steak in his hands and tearing away a huge chunk with his incisors. "Mmchhnmm." All around the room attention shifting to the main course. Perhaps they'll try to maim me before coffee. Eat well first.

He devoured the food on his plate, refilled it, ate again, refilled and ate. Long silences, clattering dish noises. He wet the tip of his forefinger and moved it smoothly around the rim of the half-filled glass, making a high-pitched whining sound that was barely discernible, then drank some of the water and did it again, altering the pitch. "What's that noise?" asked Peel from the head of the table. He drank off another inch, dipped his finger and tried again. "E. Above high C." Fitzgore paling, unable to eat beside him.

Hot fudge sundaes for dessert, anything to impress the rushees, Gnossos having two, saving the fudge for last. Might have to spend the night in jail, bread and water, maybe get hit by a truck going home. Always eat well. Nutrients squirming in the marrow of Anglo-Saxon foodstuffs. I'm in a room full of robots. Be careful. You are what you eat.

He reached into his jacket pocket and took out the second lamp-dried cigarette, lighting it before Fitzgore could take notice, burning half away with a single inspirational puff, holding the smoke down, adding little sips of sharply sucked-at air. His shoulders hunched, his eyes bulging, the house officers beginning to mumble uneasily, someone coming over to talk to Fitzgore, report me. Exhale. Beautiful, no smoke. Another puff, almost gone, weee. Fitzgore sniffing.

"What's that you're smoking, Paps?"

No time to talk, saturate lungs. All that spongy fiber swilling. Listen to your nerves hum. Yes.

Oh yes.

Fitzgore telling them secretly he'll get me out. Not quite, babies. Fifty to one, but they don't know the Shadow. Disappear.

"Woooooooooooooooo . . ."

Fitzgore jumping up, "Okay, Paps, let's go, that's enough—"

"Wooooooo-HOOOOOOOOOOO!"

"PAPS!"

"SHAZAM!" He was up on the table, making a noise like a thunderclap, then with a bound into the middle of the dining room, pointing a finger at Harold Wong. "Beware the monkey-demon, Wong." Then to all the startled faces, their every expression chilled stiff, interrupted: "Lock your doors, gang. Bolt your bedroom windows. He may be the house mascot now, but in ten years, zoom, back to Peking, a commissar. Swoop . . ." He was out the door, flapping his wings like a bird trying to fly. Steps behind him.

Flee. Where? The Cutty Sark. Swish, up the stairs, three at a time. Voices following. Which room? Here. Into the closet, ho ho.

He found the bottle beneath the pile of shirts, drank it down a full third of the way, and tucked it upside down into his belt, forgetting to put the top on, the cold whiskey running over his leg, into his sock and shoe. What a waste. Carnage. Should be more. Under the shirts? No. Cheap bastard. Take some clothes instead, box of cufflinks. Old Spice toilet water, kill the liquor smell. What's this? Holy God, an enema bag! Take it, one never knows. Voices closer, searching for me. Footsteps in the next room. Wait for the whites of their eyes. Just outside the closet now.

Bang! The door flew open, three strange faces and Peel. Scare them. "HAAAAAA!"

They fell back with shock, knocking into each other. He was past them, swinging the enema bag over his head like a lariat. On the stairs again, through the Tudor living room, where little groups were gathering in front of the silver samovar, chattering like gelded contralto chipmunks.

"Zaaaap, you're all sterile." Out the front door, into the street. Ho ho. Where to? Sanctuary. Portable womb. Preferably with a view. Up, up, and awaaaaay.

Superman winging over Metropolis, cape fluttering in the wild wind. Safe as long as no one pulls any Kryptonite out of a lead box. Wheeeeee, down the cinder path behind the law school, people passing, jumping out of the way. And a good thing too. The Man of Steel infallible, X-ray vision, sees your every move. Out on Academae Avenue now, blinking lights, neon gases in fragile tubes, chart your viscera in the tiny ion chains. Left foot sloshing from the liquor. Holy shit, the police. Doorway.

He hovered back in the secure entrance to a photography shop until the swiveling red light was safely gone. Not too many people in the streets. A half-familiar figure strolled casually by, turning the corner from Dryad Road, peering into the closed shop windows. Her hair bound by a brass clasp, wearing green knee-socks, loafers, humming to herself, complete. She walked away, toward the campus, arms folded in front of her. Who?

But beware the monkey-demon when your interest shifts.

He turned and looked sharply over his shoulder, ready to surprise the waiting assassin, and found instead a photograph of Heffalump blinking at him in the reflected red light from Student Laundries, Humphrey Bogart pose, cigarette dangling off the lower lip, one eye half closed in haze, smoke polarized in the photographer's clever lamp. Beaver teeth. Blink, blink, blink.

Down the street then, down the hill, fuzz all gone, flee from whatever follows, looking left and right, where the hell was it, anyway? There, white Swiss drolleries, 109. Up the steps to the door. Straighten tie. Ring. Feet coming.

"Yes, please."

My God. Yellow-eyed Benares face peering at me. Say something. "What's happening?"

"I beg your pardon, please?" Long hair, cherry soda in the bony hand? Dressed in a gauze coat. He's drunk.

"Must've rung the wrong bell. Looking for Pamela is the thing."

"You are Mr. Pappadopolum, of course, yes?"

Of course. Nearly. Also the Dracula. But how did you know? Guard your jugular. "You're Mr. Muttu?"

"Rajamuttu, to be sure," in the clipped, liquefied sing-song accent. "When you move your belongings, you must come and pay to me and my wife a particular call."

"Sure thing. Perhaps—" the door closing in my face?

"Goodnight, then. Miss Pamela is assuredly no doubt at home." Gone. Jesus.

He tiptoed around the porch and peeked in through the bamboo shades. She was sitting alone on the Navajo rug next to the fireplace, eating a TV dinner. Spooning the thawed, reheated food out of its partitioned aluminum tray. Creamed corn, beef with gravy, whipped potatoes. Eyes like a water spaniel. Tap on the pane. She's looking up. Can't see me, too dark out here. Press nose against glass. Don't be afraid, ducks, it's only Rubberface.

He went to the door and waited.

"Why, Mr. Evergood, hello again. Whatever do you have with you?"

"Little gift is all," handing her the Old Spice toilet water, trying to hide the box of cufflinks and the enema bag. Her missing eyebrows penciled on.

"Well. Thank you. Coming in, are you?"

"Just passing by, thought I'd see how your packing was getting along." Ooof.

"You smell rather like a distillery," letting him pass. Turn around slowly, smile; for Christ's sake, don't breathe on her. "Coming from a party?" was her question.

"Always. Part of my condition. And my name is Pappa-dopoulis."

"Yes, you said something like that earlier; I thought you were joking, surely."

Five syllables, too many for a proper-sounding name. Three appeals to the conditioned ear. Buckingham. Bolingbroke. Butterball. Man, chaos all over the pad, boxes, books left out, ladies' things. That photograph.

"Your husband?" he asked slyly, pointing.

"Fiancé. He graduated last year, from the ag school." Spoken with little enthusiasm. Still wearing that kimono thing, kitty-fluff, high heels.

"Listen, just go on and eat, don't mind me. Nothing like a little energy." Ought to have a fire in here, make it cozy. White bear rug. Black Mass.

Between beef bites, the Japanese robe falling open slightly so he could see the single hair on her chest.

"Are you really a student here, Pappadopoulis? I trust you don't mind my asking?"

"As soon as I register. Why?"

"You hardly seem the type." Looking at me. Ho ho, edge of the wedge.

"I'm not. Can't be classified is where it's at. Certainly better than screwing around out there, though," with a nod to the void, marking time beyond the Athené city limits. The Scotch pure ambrosia. Paregoric less groovy after eating.

"I'm not sure I understand. How better?"

"Everything all Orgone Boxish. Little microcosm thing happening."

"No responsibility, you mean."

"Check."

"Rather fascinating, all the same."

Be humble. Lie. Intense Brando look: "Umm, when are you going to be married?"

Hesitating with a spoonful of creamed corn halfway to her mouth, looking vacantly over her shoulder: "I'm not terribly certain. He has a farm, you see, hybrid Iowa corn. Depends on the rainfall and that sort."

"Jesus."

"Why Jesus?"

"That part of the country, is all. Man-eating sows and B-47's. Walked across half the state last August, no one gave me a ride."

"You were alone?"

Look sad: "Always. Made the same mistake continually. Got hung up in the provinces, had a couple of beers, walked too far out on Forty, the cars won't stop. You have to walk to the next town, right? Bombers over your skull, seas of chemical grain is where it's at. Supposed to be very fertile, they tell me, but it all looks barren. You know. Too rich. Creamy. Exploited, wasting with fat. God Bless America. Cheers." Toasting her, have another sip. She's interested.

"What's it like, running about like that?"

"It doesn't matter."

"Surely it must, if you do it. Dispensing with bears, hitchhiking."

Finished her last spoonful, whoopee. Never thread anyone while they're eating. "Can I make a fire?"

"Yes, go right ahead. You may as well pour me a drink while you're up, if you don't mind."

And another one for me. And wouldn't you like to be carried off to Margate or Brighton, some whitewashed cottage with British roses in the window boxes, wood and iron doors six inches thick. Turn off the lamp.

"What did you do that for?"

Careful now. "Takes away from the firelight."

"Ah." Then, "You're not truly an astronomer, are you? That was all part of the Evergood business, yes?"

"Stargazing is all."

"I thought so, you're far too lyrical."

"The conscience of my elusive race gives not a fig for me, baby. But I endure, if you know what I mean."

"Must you be so cryptic?"

Always present a moving target. "Define a thing and you can dispense with it, right? Come here."

"No. Not yet, I mean. I want to know more about you."

"Sure thing. But you have a hair on your chest and it has me up-tight."

"Ohhh. What a horrible thing to say." But the flash in her expression not repelling. Move closer. Touch her arm. There. Put down the enema bag.

"Your skin is creamy. Jergens Lotion and all."

"Please, I asked you not—" Neck, try neck with finger-tips. Ho, see her eyes close, what did I tell you. Knee?

"Please—"

"You'll like it."

"You're too sure."

"Practice."

"Really, how awful—"

My Christ, no boobs at all. Not a goddamned thing. But that hair. What a glorious flaw. Try the thigh.

"Oh please, you don't even care about Simon."

"Simon?" Going religious?

"My fiancé."

"Check." Kissing her throat: oh, feel the squirm.

"You're so terribly vulgar."

"I'm going to *move* you, baby."

Take a sip of Scotch, push her back. I knew it, I just knew it.

"No."

"Yes."

Oh so drunk. Kimono away, nothing to her.

"What are you doing?"

"Mmmmmmm."

"Ohh."

"MMMMM."

"But my heels are still on."

"Ahhhmmmmm."

"Ohhh, you're disgusting."

But you love it. Jesus, I'm still dressed. Maneuver carefully, keep her on the floor. Jacket tight. There. Hell with the shirt. Pants.

"Wait, do you have one of those things?"

My God, in the parka pocket. Lie: "Yes." Pants down, too tight to get over shoes, ivy league fashion. Leave them.

"You don't have any underwear on?"

"Never use it."

"Are you circumcised?"

"Look."

"Oh, you're not."

"Catholic."

"That's horrible."

"Why?"

"I read something once, about cancer."

"I'm Immune. Here you go."

"Ohhhhhh . . ."

"I'm going to move you all over, baby."

"Oh!"

Climb up. Her eyes wild. Maybe insane. No such luck. Easy there. There. There.

"Ummmm."

Take a sip of lush, don't hurry things. "You want a drink?"

"What? Now?"

"Here."

"No. No, just hurry along."

Little sideways action. Oh, feel her legs. Heels need spurs. Easy, easy easy easy. Going to be fast.

"Ohhhhhhhhhhhhhhhhhhhhhhh."

"Mmmmmm," what rhythm? Night in Tunisia. Charlie Parker. Timpani. Close now. Wooooo. Faster . . .

"Oh God . . ."

No invocations, baby, Gnossos right there. Closer now.

easy

easy

easy

unh.

Unhh.

UNH!

"Ooooo."

"There."

"God."

"That's right."

"Did you—get it on all right?"

"What?"

"The thing."

"What thing?"

"The contraceptive thing."

"I didn't really have one."

"What?"

"Lust overcame me."

"WHAT?" Pamela lurching away from underneath, rolling off to one side. Seed thick with lush and paregoric, better say something sweet.

"Paregoric."

"What?"

"Too much shit in me, you'd never fertilize."

"Oh, what an ugly word that is. What will I do? I feel it inside of me."

"Here," handing her the enema bag. "Emergency douche for your peace of mind."

"You pig."

She snatched it away from him and ran to the bathroom. Gnossos sitting there with his pants collapsed around his shoes, shirt and tie still on, erection wilting slowly. He drained the glass of Scotch and poured another. Through the wall, the sound of anguished moans and squirting water. Talk to her.

"Do you need any help?"

"Oh, go away."

Gratitude. So to speak.

He scuttled over to the record machine and flipped through her collection, finding little of value, settling finally on a Brubeck. Footsteps coming. "Did it work?"

"Oh, I suppose so. I feel sick."

"Original sin."

"You're some help, you are. And why are you sitting there with your pants down? Oh, couldn't you go away? For a little while, please?"

Standing up, pants all wet. From her? No, the Cutty Sark. Jesus, forgot about dinner. Poor Fitzgore. "Can I move in tonight?"

"No! Oh, I feel awful. Poor Simon."

Got to piss. Better wait until I get someplace else. "Okay, baby, dig you later."

"Take this thing with you," holding out the damp, deflated bag.

He slung it over his shoulder, shrugged, looked at her

sadly for a brief moment as she stood shivering by the fire, her arms crossed in front of her belly, then turned and wandered out the door and up the street.

He hesitated once as a peculiar figure danced out of the shadows, limp wrists dangling, eyes leering in the moonless, overcast night, then vanished. He blinked at where it had been. Bald skull? He hunched his shoulders against the cold and continued walking through the snow. What the hell.

Semper virgini.

Without commission the membrane was still intact. Soon, he told himself again, soon: there must come love.

A black and swollen depression closed down around him and spilled heavily through the blood and marrow of his night.

3

A tarantula.

Eyeless and hairy, squatting thickly in his mouth, a brown prickly leg twitching between closed lips.

How did it get there? He turned his head to one side and tried spitting, but it squirmed and remained. What if it bites? Smoldering greasesticks impaled in my neck.

He rolled over with extreme caution, feeling for the pillow, but there was only the dusty rug on the floor. He had been breathing lint throughout the night and the tarantula was not a tarantula but his tongue.

"Water?" came the feeble try.

A brief stirring in the adjoining room, sounds of someone

dressing, then silence. The effort expended uttering the weak request had driven a sliver of caustic, nauseating pain from temple to temple and he lay as still as a closed book until it went away. Move very slowly.

His chin was on the rug and he opened one eye to find stray hairs, nail parings, spent staples, little dustballs, cat fur, dried flower petals, onion peel, and a dehydrated wasp. He closed the eye. Attacked in the spine by some species of burrowing, parasitic worm. Easy now.

"Heff?" Again the sickly throb.

The door to the connecting room opened and Heffalump walked over barefoot, in jeans, a towel around his neck. He carried a glass of fizzing Bromo Seltzer in one hand and two fingers of umber horror in the other.

"Drink it," came the unsympathetic order.

"Gggggg," from Gnossos, gulping down the chilly effervescence.

"Never mix shit and booze," came the reprimand.

"Oh crap, a mother."

"Here," handing him the whiskey, which went swirling spasmodically through his blood, jarring the terrified will of nerves and blood cells. Then a warm calm. "Better?"

"A little. You wouldn't believe my tongue."

"You look very near death."

Remembering. "He passed me last night. On Academae Avenue."

"Oh yeah?"

"Kind of a bald cat, looked like a teenager, though."

"You should have asked him in for a nightcap, save him the trouble of looking you up in a year or two, when you overdose on horse or something."

"Will you *stop* being a mother! Jesus, man, there's a growth in my frontal lobe. Oooo."

"Have it cut out."

Not a bad idea. Be a vegetable, no emotional response. "Why am I on the floor?"

"You wanted to be. You were worried about low-flying planes. You even called Monsignor Putti, he'll be here any minute. You need something to eat?"

"Jesus, no. You wouldn't have a strawberry frosted? What's Putti coming for?"

"You wanted Extreme Unction. Come on, try getting up, we'll find something in the Plato Pit.

"Ooooohhh—"

"It's not that far, man—"

"Those Red Caps, that's where it started."

"How'd it go at the fraternity?"

"Ohhhhhhh."

"We figured. They might bid you just the same, make you the house maniac," swilling a can of Donald Duck orange juice. "Let's go, don't you have to register?"

"Hey, how about a little orange juice? That British chic said I'd be fined, registration takes bread, I'm nearly clean."

"No citric acid on a twisted stomach."

"Mother Heffalump."

"Your rucksack is full of silver, anyway."

"From what, man, green stamps?"

"The wheel, Jesus, you don't remember?"

A smoky recollection. "What wheel?"

"You won over a hundred bucks. Proctor Slug's probably got a warrant out."

"You're not serious? Roulette? From who?"

"What does it matter who? Some spic in a cowboy suit and a guy from the Mentor *Daily Sun*. Now try getting up, man, you look like spoonfuls of warmed-over death."

"Hundred bucks? Ohhhh."

"Now what?"

"That woman at the checkout."

"Hey, all this expiation is a drag," Heff pulling on a pair of stiffened socks from his laundry bag. "Why don't you go to Confession or something."

"Penance the wrong sacrament, baby, only add to the pain. Need myrrh for the injured cells. You're putting me on about Monsignor Putti, right? I mean, what would I do that for?"

"You even left an instruction note. You want to see it?"

"Prayer is all. Fasting, Satyagraha. Out of the depths I cry unto thee, O Lord—"

"Look man, would you please get up, I want to find out if I'm still in school."

"De Profundis, semper hangovum—"

"Oh shit," Heff dropping into a rocking chair, socks collapsing on his ankles. Long bone of a quadroon body gangling with the remnants of Watusi blood, almost close enough to pass, not quite. But blue eyes, unlikely, gets the girls.

"You're beautiful, Heffalump, I ought to marry you."

"Ugh."

"Ohhhh, my neck. Always worst in the neck, have you noticed? And the left eye."

Heff flipping idly through the *Anatomy of Melancholy,* whistling some Randy Weston, asking casually:

"You going to make Cuba with me over spring vacation?"

"Please no mother-organizing. You should have grown out of that adventure syndrome, anyway. This is '58, not 1922."

"At least things are happening down there; talk about a revolution, getting rid of this Batista maniac."

"You couldn't grow a beard, where's the percentage? Ohh, this is all too much for the head. Will you play a little Miles? You got any Miles? Something to mollify my bruised cortex? Oof." He scrambled to a sitting position and found his swollen reflection in a cracked mirror on the other side of the smelly room. Don't look. Mortality. Mornings always hardest. Heff was dutifully settling a record on the spindle of his borrowed turntable, fondling the Heathkit preamp knobs with a free hand. Next to the lamp which had been used to dry the previous night's joints were a half-empty vial of paregoric and the eye dropper.

Gnossos stood unsteadily and aired his tongue. He removed the slovenly remains of the lint-coated suit he'd slept in, then shuffled naked across the room to the sink, scratching his scrotum. He flicked some cold water from his fingernails to his eyes, blinked painfully, and set about replacing everything criminal in the rucksack. Got to cool Mother Church, too much irony in getting busted by a priest. As he turned toward the speaker, snapping his fingers, he found the image of a wrinkled penis looking back at him. Only after it moved did he recognize the reflection as his own.

"Jesus, put some clothes on," from Heff, who also saw, tossing him a black terrycloth robe. "Your body is obscene after a debauch."

"Meaningless word, man."

"Lewd, then. How the hell you ever get women to make love to is way past me." Traffic noise from the street, a world functioning on.

"I don't. I bang them is all. I'm still a virgin. Have yet to make love, right?"

A polite rapping at the door.

"Jesus, the Man."

Heff leaping up from his rocker, "Lie down somewhere,

quick. And for Christ's sake, keep that robe closed!"

Pappadopoulis pulled the terrycloth around him and jumped onto the pathetic leather couch, its skin peeling in jagged strips. Heffalump threw an army blanket over his knees, tucked him in, and waited until hands were locked in reverence before going to the door. Monsignor Putti was waiting nervously, carrying a black pigskin satchel in stubby fingers. He entered and stood to be helped with his heavy coat.

"Is this the patient?" he asked with a twitching smile. Wound around his splendid frock was a scarlet sash. Swollen belly, balding scalp, hair combed back to front in a foppish attempt to conceal. Eek, a concave sternum.

"He finds it difficult to speak," explained Heff cautiously.

"God help us. Has the doctor been here already?"

"He refuses all medical assistance."

"Dear me, is that wise?"

"He has faith only in, well, you know."

From the couch a hand groping weakly into space: "Father. Father, is that you?"

The monsignor bending curiously toward Heff, "Perhaps you'd better ring the infirmary, after all—"

"And movements, you see, sudden movements give him great pain."

"Yes, yes . . ." shakily opening the pigskin bag and removing the delicate cruets of holy oil. Plump pink fingers. Jesus, that Miles.

"Father?"

"Yes, my son?"

In a whisper: "More treble, we're losing the highs."

"What's that? What's he saying?"

"He wanders now and again, Father. It happens every

half hour or so," Heff going over to the amplifier and adjusting the controls.

"Better," from the figure on the couch.

"My son, I'm, well, I'm moved that you sought the blessing of the Church first in your infirmity; but perhaps a doctor—"

"BUTCHERS," called Gnossos violently, thrashing under the army blanket, "ATHEISTS!"

"Oh dear."

"You see, Father, that's how he becomes."

Then, in a lower tone, inviting them closer to hear, clutching the monsignor's retreating sleeve and staring at him with one eye closed, breathing Bromo Seltzer, whiskey fumes, and hangover in his face: "I know what they do, Father. These doctors, these men of learning, I know what they do, all right. They cut open your belly and look inside for a soul, that's what. They look inside for a soul and when they don't find any they say, 'HA! No soul! Pancreas maybe, but no soul!' " Releasing the sleeve, falling back against the couch with a gasp, "I've got one though, haven't I; I've got a soul, tell them I have a soul."

"Yes, my son, yes," brushing his sleeve unconsciously, glancing for support at Heff, who just in time suppressed a choking giggle.

"Fix me, Father, I'm a sinner. I've done wrong. My mortal soul is in danger."

"Yes, yes, of course, try and calm yourself, I'll be only a moment." With shaky gestures and an odd glance around the mildewed room for security in some familiar object, the priest annointed the senses with holy oil. He squinted as he prayed hurriedly for the sins each perceptive organ had under its jurisdiction.

There was a pause, then a startling, erotic sensation on the soles of his feet. Looking down, he was astonished to find them being annointed and prayed over.

"What are you doing *that* for, man?"

The priest was silent until he had finished, then answered with a weak smile, "The sins of the feet."

"Of the feet?" Big toe right in there. Blakean fetish.

"They carry one to sin."

"Ah." He stared down at his great paddles, the ankles jutting out absurdly, Mr. Right and Mrs. Left, the hermaphrodites. Introduce them again, annointed sinners. Hello there, you handsome thing. Hello there yourself; wanna tickle?

"Well then." The priest stood and replaced the cruet in his bag. "We'll certainly remember you in our prayers. It's so seldom we're called out to administer this lovely sacrament. So many think it's reserved for the dying, you see."

"Ohhhhh," pressing both forefingers to his temples.

"What is it, my son?"

"The dregs of the pain, ohhhh."

"My, my. You really must not negate the value of secular medicine," looking to Heff for corroboration.

"Symptomatic claptrap, Father; they fail to treat the disease. But here . . ." he motioned for his rucksack, fishing out two of the silver dollars, "here; for the poor."

"Oh. Well, thank you. My. But what are they?" Turning them over cautiously in pink fingers.

"Silver, Father. Sow and ye shall reap."

"Yes, well. Well then, I'll just be going. When you're healthy again you must come along to the Newman Club. There are so few members."

"I certainly will, man. And may I bring this fallen angel as well?" Heffalump twitching at the reference.

"Of course, you might even be interested in the little choir we're getting up. Well then, I'll just be on my way. Lovely sacrament, this. Pleasing to give." He squirmed into his heavy coat and turned to the door as Heff rose, "No no, I'll let myself out. Thank you." And was gone.

"Weeee," squealed Gnossos when the footfalls had faded, "Dig me. Dig where I'm at. Annointed, cleansed, purified."

"Your feet are all greasy."

"Infidel. Know ye not the fury of the Lord profaned?"

"I do, man, but it sure looks like you don't. C'mon, get out of the sack. You want another drink?"

"Only sacramental wine. Oh, listen to that Miles. I'm cured, right?" Creeping off the couch, hobbling to the speaker on all fours. "Dig how pure, how clean. Dig the control." His hangover still tapping.

"Dig it later," said Heff, turning off the turntable. "It's the middle of the goddamned afternoon. You've got to register and I've got to see if my appeal did any good—"

"What appeal, man?"

"They busted me out at midterm, I already told you, but I appealed."

"They can't bust you, Heff." Gnossos rolling over on his back. "That puts you out in the world."

"Cuba."

"Yeah, I heard you once. It's the wrong generation, baby, you'll be purged. Anyway, your spade blood is where it's at."

His face flushing. "Bullshit."

"Don't put it down. Twenty-five parts out of a hundred itching for the white-man's scalp. You've got problems."

"They ain't your problems, gumbook. And moving out is one hell of a lot better than chewing cud at Guido's Grill."

He picked up an envelope of forms and appeal material, then wheeled around, pointing a finger. "If I stayed, I'd end up like G. Alonso Oeuf, ten *years* on the academic scene."

Gnossos blinked at the name and sat up. "Oeuf? You've seen him?"

"In the infirmary is all. Scheming to take over the university, from the look of his little headquarters. Talk about short-sighted vision!"

"Anyway," from Gnossos, finally pulling on a pair of crumpled corduroys, "you don't have enough bread to make New York, let alone Havana. Did you show anything on the wheel last night?"

"Your buddy Aquavitus will set me up, don't worry."

"Who?"

"Aquavitus, man, you heard me."

"Giacomo? From the Mafia?"

"I used your name; he's operating out of Miami now. And let's not make a big thing out of it, I'm not exactly free to talk."

"Oh intrigue, Heffalump, beautiful. I saw your picture in some photographer's last night. Very dramatic. And what about that little dyke chic with the Joan of Arc look?"

"Goddammit, I'm in love with her."

"No."

"Oh shit, I'll see you later," and he stomped out the door for Anagram Hall. Has it bad, all right. Conjures up cafés with back rooms full of anarchists, smoke thick over crowded tables. Dens for impregnating rebel minds, conceiving attitudes, ferment, brush-fire wars. *Heff,* he hears his khaki commander telling him, an arm clasped to his own, *this is no longer a time of waiting. Take this zircon to Foppa and tell him we move tonight.* One fourth of his blood

French. Corpuscles of his reason. Needs some Greek plasma. Feed him dolma, more goat cheese. Biochemical transfer. Alter his mind. Must find a hothouse, plant pot seeds.

Hours later, at the end of a tangled spool of red registration tape, Gnossos was in the office of the dean himself. A roomy, leather-chaired kind of library, filled with mineralogical specimens. Obscure varieties of limestone, quartz, shale from the gorges, chunks of coal from Newcastle seams, spongy layers of igneous Hawaii, silica, granite, semiprecious stones. All the wrack and refuse of a ridiculous career interrupted by colleagues who sensed incompetency. Instead of dropping him into Maeander with a slab of Carrara marble tied to his leg, they made him a dean. Molder of men.

But they forget me.

"Yes sir, mister," Dean Magnolia was saying, "that is correct. Five dollars."

"Extraordinary amount of money. You realize that being trapped on this ice floe I was telling you about, it was difficult, to say the least, to get back to Athené on time."

"I understan' your situation, naturally. But nevertheless the administration has its regulations, an' we must abide by them."

"I'll have to give you silver dollars."

"I beg your pardon?"

"United States silver dollars. Good at any Federal reserve bank."

"I don't understand—"

"Where they can be given in exchange for silver."

"Ah yes, of course."

"I trust you'll take them?"

"Don't you have any paper money, Mr.—"

"My last employer never used it. Germs."

"Is that right?"

"You'd be surprised the amount of parasitic corruption gets spread through the handling of dollar bills. Osmosis. Still a theory, of course."

"You seem to have a great interest in medicine, Mr.— uh—"

"I am going to be a cancer surgeon."

"Ah."

"Dig down, find a little disease, cut it out."

"I'm pleased to see you've come to a decision so soon. Many of your fellow students, they—"

"Oh, I understand. They take so long making up their uncertain minds."

"Precisely."

"Drifting aimlessly down the many separate trails of youth, irresponsible, failing to choose the Proper Path in time. It must be frustrating to men such as yourself, having to put up guideposts, show the way, and all that."

Dean Magnolia swiveling in his chair, fondling a piece of petrified Saratoga Springs, "It is refreshing to have someone understand my position. Why, you'd be surprised, truly surprised, the number of unsympathetic young boys pass through this office year after year."

"I am not surprised, sir." Distract the cat, cool the five bucks. "It is the symptom of the times. Unrest. Indecision. Waiting for Things To Happen. What the first Dr. Pappadopoulis called the Largesse Syndrome."

"First Dr., um—" rimless spectacles slipping down on the potato nose, leather chair creaking with shifted weight.

"My father, sir. Died in the steaming jungles of Rangoon. UNESCO experiment. You read about it, perhaps, in the special *Times* supplement dedicated to his memory."

"I remember it well. Must have been a blow to you and your mother."

"She died with him, sir." Look at the floor. Blink.

"Ah. I'm certainly sorry to hear that."

"Quite all right, I was prepared. May I go now? Ought to be hitting the books, really. Time is money."

"Course, my boy. You drop by sometime. Whenever you want to talk about your future again. That's why I'm here."

It sure as hell is. "Thank you, sir." Walking across the room, rucksack slapping against his shoulder, almost to the door.

"Oh, unh, Mr. Pappadopoulass . . ."

"Yes sir?"

"We, unh, forgot the matter of your fee. The one fo' late registration."

Be cool, you'll get revenge. "Of course. Terribly sorry, must have been distracted."

Look at him. Benevolent smile. White hair of the sage. Actually looks the part. Playing with pebbles. Wonder will his penie calcify, break off?

4

But at quite another level, marking an entirely different breed of university time, right there on the listing top floor of Polygon Hall, he found the lean, ever-esoteric figure of

Calvin Blacknesse. Gnossos discovered him where perhaps he'd been waiting all the while, posing beneath a grand mansard skylight in his lambent whitewashed studio, the very walls of which were impregnated by the odors of linseed oil, turpentine, paint, sizing, incense, and rosewater. Old Blacknesse, the only advising buddy who had paused, then failed to give his teacherly blessing on the voyage out across the asphalt seas; who had cautioned against the plotting friendship of G. Alonso Oeuf; who alone had warned him to beware the paradoxical snares of Exemption. In failing to subscribe or bear approving witness, he had become Gnossos' only ear, the single object of introspective phrase. To him alone could the wanderer speak secrets.

Now he stood with serene but ambiguous late-afternoon patience, wearing his linen mandarin jacket, sketching an eye in the hand of the dark goddess. Out of many thousand lines of light and gloom emerged small heads and skulls absent of some otherwise requisite feature: a mouth, or a nose. Here and there fanged monkey-demons hovered, the Eastern brethren of the gargoyles, who had been driven screaming, holding their horns, from all the celestial majesty of the Christian West. Around him were his stacked canvas, never static, always in flux, sections being painted out and annihilated with the same pitch and rhythm as the ones taking on substance. The demolition of self. A sucking vortex, Gnossos always reasoned, the diameter of which narrowed over the years, pulled closer to the pinpoint when creation and destruction were one. Then, with any luck, he'd die.

"You're all right?" came the easy question.

"Hung, man. And constipated. How come you didn't answer any letters?" Gnossos taking a seat on a fish-shaped stone. Its pocked surface was dappled with dyes.

"They were more epistles than letters, yes? And we knew we'd see you again."

"Come on, you didn't think I was dead? Along with the rest of Mentor?"

Blacknesse laying the delicate graphite sticks on a piece of dried cobraskin: "No, Gnossos, not really. Your end could hardly have come in the rumored manner. A little at a time perhaps. By your own hand?"

Sucking the barrel of a double twelve. Slugs or birdshot? "Thirty below when I got lost, man, can you imagine?"

"No. By fire perhaps, but never by ice. I don't need references for that one." Blacknesse smiling the smile he had learned in India, setting a saucepan on his mauve hotplate for tea. Mauve, of course. No object so totally defined that it should elude decoration. One day, no doubt, the hotplate would shudder, shake off its stasis, stand up, stumble out the door, and flop into Maeander with a violent, sputtering sizzle.

"I've got some cinnamon sticks, if you want." Feeling around through the hodgepodge of contents in his rucksack, coming against the jar of pot seeds, "Oh hey, you don't have a greenhouse, Calvin? I've got something to plant."

"David Grün has one, I think. Some kind of cactus?"

"Just Mexican grass. How's old David doing, anyway?"

"Coming out with more disturbing music than you'll remember. But potent and red-faced."

"He was always a pretty lyrical cat." Pamela calling me that. Not altogether correct.

"More atonal now." Pouring the tea over the cinnamon sticks. "You'll have to hear for yourself. He had his fortieth birthday last week, you know; a sixth daughter born when you were looking for Motherball."

"Sixth?"

"Robin, they call her. A bird's name like the other five."

And me a spiritual virgin. How many unborn children flushed in rubber balloons. Name them after insects, even if I had them: how do you do, like you to meet the twins, Locust and Centipede.

Jesus, that eye in the hand. Wink at it. No don't, it might wink back.

They drove into the country, along frozen Harpy Creek. A faint gurgling under metallic ice. The painter's black Saab, its two-cycle engine puttering with a hypnotic whine, Pappadopoulis slouched down in the seat, his eyes on the padded lining of the roof, remembering his quest in Taos, looking for the Connection who might tie all the loose ends of vicarious experience into a woven sign or pattern, some familiar rebus. A triangle, perhaps. A fish. The symbol for infinity.

But now he sat with Blacknesse, whose slender dye-stained fingers were closed gently around the wheel. Their vision was focused arbitrarily on the rippling white hyphens that danced back under the car whenever they passed a melting stretch of road; both of them taking pleasure in this sensation of shifting surface, having to deal with different mediums, different textures in the same plane.

"You were starting to tell me something. In the studio."

Gnossos collecting various thoughts, his attention having drifted to the sound of the tires. "New Mexico, man, I finally found him, right where every hophead in the country figured he'd be. But no sun god or anything, just tacos and shakes. It's enough to bring you down."

"We figured."

"We?"

"Beth and myself."

A lazy sigh, a sound of marrow-bone weariness, hoarded, stored for precisely this moment. "If I'd been into the Middle Ages, man, you *know* I would've gone looking for the grail or whatever it was got them hung up. And so would you, so don't come on cocky. Everybody's got his little search and yours happens to be internal, but I'm just not cut out for meditation, right? Don't have the time, for one thing; this is a nervous little decade we're playing with."

"Exactly."

"Exactly nothing. And come to think of it, you were among the first people to mention the cat, apart from Aquavitus."

"My error, and I apologize. I'd heard he was a mushroom-warlock from Mexico, not part of some narcotics syndicate. You were looking for visionary enlightenment, if I recall, not just a chance to get high."

"Well, you take what comes along. Maybe next time I'll cross the border and avoid hangups. Let me tell you, man, you can't move in this country without catching your heel in a hangup. Mousetails in your root beer, grubs in your Hershey bar, always some kind of worm in the image, munching away." Shifting his glance to a drop of water that had worked its way through the sealed glass and begun breaking apart from the vibration of the frame. "Even the desert. Maybe I'm naïve or something, but I *did* expect a little dune here and there, *some*thing besides the Arapaho Motor Inn, ninety-two units, all Polar Bear Cool. And the lights! Pink, chartreuse, Congo ruby, magenta, baby blue, you've got to pack a mule to get away from the glare, man, believe me. Even the sand is full of hump-trash. The only thing you get to know about is hot wind and dry, see, you really get involved with dry." The broken drops on the windshield lurched together, formed a single stream, and ran back up into a shivering ball. "Old Pluto's got his dirty claws in the landscape, all right. Try to groove behind the daytime cosmos and you get a faceful of whipped cream and Betty Crocker pastry. They *could* hit you with a lightning bolt but that wouldn't be comic enough. I mean, somebody'd have to send the little pile of ash and hair back to your mother and who'd get the joke?" He crossed his fingers to guard against any possible hex.

"I was ready to throw in the towel when I Tried Taos, let me tell you. It just didn't seem the likely place to find him, little town full of getups, serapes, silver talismans, jade rings, all like that. But sure enough, this Indian comes out of the shadows, wrapped up in a flannel blanket, everything hidden, even his face, nothing showing but the eyes. And stitched across the back of the blanket, Calvin, one word. One word, right?"

"Motherball."

"What else? That's how he reaches people. Sends out his boys with these blankets, you follow one and there you are. If you're fuzz they probably nail you, they all look like assassins out of *Four Feathers,* thuggees with piano wire; but they've got some way of knowing how to pick out the junkie types. He took me to a bar with a rainspout over the door, kind of adobe place, in an alley. I remember the spout because there was never any rain. And Louie Motherball, sure enough, waiting inside, just like that." Gnossos drawing an *M* on the moisture of the windshield. "Just standing there behind the bar, wiping glasses. Sydney Greenstreet. Fat, hairless, fuchsia suspenders, no shirt, sweat lines all over his ɔelly—like a hogshead, no fooling—and chewing sen-sen. Some starving Pueblo chic sitting next to him, his wife I think, wearing a maroon dress, drinking out of a gallon bowl through a surgical tube. You should have seen them, man, the whole thing was very gross. You know what he said? I wasn't in the door a full minute and he said, 'You're of course familiar with the works of Edward Arlington Robinson.' Talk about the Mushroom Man, baby, I really thought I'd found him. Lord Buckley out doing the Gauguin or something, ready to straighten my head once and for all, right? But what he was doing the whole time was mixing up this juice he calls Summer Snow. White Bacardi from Cuba, shredded coconut, crushed ice, milk, orange sherbet, the whole thing whipped up in a Waring blender. Then he serves it in chilled bowls, and wipes the rims with cactus heart. He chops peyote buds into the froth with chocolate jimmies." Gnossos erased the *M*. "So I stuck it out, you know what I mean, two, maybe three weeks, just lying around digging these recitations he gives, talking to light-bulbs, and like that. Man, he had it all down, line after line of that Mickey Mouse verse, coming on like the March of Time, and all the time his old lady so wiped out of her skull she couldn't hobble as far as the head without getting hung up by the candles on the way and forgetting what she wanted. And no food, either. Just Summer Snow and Moth-erball's voice day and night, whenever he wasn't busy whip-ping up new juice. 'Bout every four hours or so, these shifts of Indians fell by in flannel blankets and lushed it around a little. It really got euphoric, man. A couple of them would start out by giggling when the session was halfway through and finally the whole place would go to pieces, everybody rolling into weak-fits. Edward Arlington Robinson, man, you'd have to hear it to believe it. And every year he picks someone else. Year before, it was John Greenleaf Whittier or James Whitcomb Riley. His plan, the way he laid it out, was to do a cyclical rendering, starting around the Wife of Bath and ending up at Pooh Corner. What I didn't know until the end, of course, was how he was taking the Indians. Lock, stock and barrel, man, life savings, government checks, silver mines, jade stashes, everything for a suck at the surgical tube-thing."

"But he never showed you the sun god."

"He got busted. I went back one evening with supplies, and everything was gone. Windows boarded up, no trace of them. Just some old cactus hearts, fertilized egg shells. Some kind of rumor that he did in his old lady too, torture chamber in the cellar or something, pliers and acid, fishhooks. Oh yeah, and the rainspout, it was spilling out a regular torrent of water. Eerie."

Blacknesse relaxing the weight of his accelerator foot, giving the pause its proper measure, both of them again momentarily listening to the sound of the tires on the road.

"Any connection with the pachucos? Your epistle was unclear."

"No connection with Motherball, really, it's just that I hung out in this boy scout camp after the bust. Seemed like the last place they'd look for cohorts. And actually it was the only part of the desert without old Kleenex and beercans. There was also the chance the scouts might have been into something, merit badges for enlightening the troops and so on, but mainly it was just groovy cover. Or until the pachucos moved in, anyway." This time he drew a *P* on the windshield. "They came in Packards, two of them, they dig big white cars; twelve, maybe thirteen chucs in all. Hybrid physiognomy, weird little pig-eyes, colliding bloods, none over five-three, top-heavy with hair, tattooed rebus behind their thumbs, three little dots. A feeling of evil, you know, sublimated."

Gnossos pausing, shifting his weight, looking now at nothing in particular, his senses afflicted only by the lower whine of the engine as it droned behind his tale.

"Who can say where they're really at, Calvin? They came into the camp lushed, but nasty lush: ethyl alcohol cut with Gallo sauterne and tequila, some shit like that, coming on like the sleeping bags weren't there, you know? Just paring fingernails with stilettos. Oh yeah, and moving in time to the music, keeping rhythm while they walked. The radios in the Packards were turned up all the way, both on the same station, a Buddy Holly side. Peggy Sue, I think. Then all of them standing around this one particular boy scout, blond, the one with the most garbage on him, merit badges, patrol-leader bars. They didn't look at him, they just stood there all the way through the song. And three of them, no two maybe, came over to my roll and said something like 'You stay put, mother, or we cut an ear.' "

"Just you."

"Just me, all alone, individual, right there. They said it and went back to the circle around this scout. Who was of course building a fire with sticks. And when the music was right, they stripped him down, the patrol-leader one, right down to the pubes, man, they peeled him. Oh, and was he shitless with fright, whimpering, making little sounds. They staked him to the ground, see, with tent pegs, then burned him all over with butts. Even his thing."

Blacknesse closing his eyes briefly but not shifting his expression. Gnossos failing to notice: "And all that Peggy Sue heat on the radios. The one who did most of the actual burning, he kept on saying soothing things. The way chics speak to puppies, you know? Telling him how everything was all right, how he was a sweet kid, even stroking his forehead while he put out the last butt in his ear."

"Jesus, Gnossos."

"He threw up finally. Almost choked on it." Pappadopoulis lying, adding a little relish. Keep the story straight and you'll get involved. Blacknesse grunting, about to say something, looking around to check Gnossos' expression, then easing off the main road in the direction of his house. The rain was clattering heavily on the hood of the car, and in the rapidly falling darkness the green blinker light on the dashboard changed the color of their complexions. It seemed to flash them in and out of a bonus, middle-frequency dimension.

Gnossos turned to watch the familiar rises and shapes of the countryside through the side window, then pulled a strand of hair down to touch his nose, staring at it cross-eyed for a moment before glancing back out the window. "I blew it after that. I mean, I really packed it up. You go looking for something simple and the whole cancer of your country gets in and infects it. You know, I couldn't even manage a goddamned sunset without a little competiton from the Firebird Motel sign. Which, relatively speaking, was bigger to begin with and stayed lit one hell of a lot longer."

"You tried at least."

"Bet your sweet ass I tried, but I got busted anyway. For vagrancy, of all the idiot raps. Fuzz, man, they want to bust you, they bust you, doesn't matter what the charge, that's the whole fuzz syndrome right there. Smug, repressive bas-

tards, they followed me out of town, just creeping along behind me, keeping their cruiser in first, trying to get me to
look around. What did it, naturally, was my smiling at the
goddamned sign. If you smile or laugh, you're automatically
laughing at the cop in question, supposedly putting down his
baggy pants or his missing buttons. So right before I get to
the town-limit sign they pull around in front of me and say,
'How much money you got, boy?' I looked at him, you
know what I mean? I put down my roll and leaned on the
sign and looked him right in the nose." Gnossos making a
sound as if he were vomiting, "Bloooouaughh!"

"Go on."

"Shit, man, I didn't dig them playing with me. I just
climbed in the cruiser and told them to hang me. It killed
them. They hated me. If I were darker they would have
ruptured one of my kidneys or something. If I were Heffalump they would have broken ribs. As it was, one of the
pachucos pulled him in about three in the morning and they
wiped him around with belt buckles out of sheer frustration.
But he kept his cool, let me tell you, in some bitter, insidious
way. Even though he cried a little, he never lost that cool
they have. So I just crept right back into my Immunity
thing, no valence, no nothing. Old inertness is where it's at.
You're not about to join *that* kind of shit."

"And fighting it?"

Gnossos became conscious of toying with his hair and
shoved it back. "Not Greek enough, man. Too Coptic." The
leak in the window had begun again and the drops were
beading up heavily, falling regularly onto his pants. "They
just put me out of town in the morning; the sheriff doing a
John Wayne, thumbs looped in his belt, telling me to move
west. Anyway, I came back in across the desert in the after-

noon, when the sun was good and hot, I mean, all the fuzz asleep, and figured I'd check out the pueblo, see what the Indians were into, now that Motherball had gone. But no pueblo, man. Nothing but this ridiculous Victorian mansion perched right up there with the sage. Painted vermilion. Dead magpies hung from wire loops in all the rooms, red velour furniture, Kerman rugs, stuffed Algerian ottomans, portraits of Boer War types. And an odor, let me tell you, couldn't have been anything but death. I dug it all through the windows, by the way; I really wasn't about to wander in. I'd expected something a little more celestial."

"Not demonic?"

Perceptive bastard. "I don't know, maybe. There was a name washed over on the mailbox, something like Mo-go, but I couldn't make it out. I had a dream that night too, after some chic from Radcliffe, kind of a muse, picked me up on her way to Vegas. The pachuco I was telling you about, his tears were turning into feathers, sticking to his cheeks. Something to do with his mother tearing him away from breast feeding 'cause there were too many others on line. Then the nipple turned into a piece of surgical tubing and she hung the kid on a hook in the Victorian house."

"Were you in the dream?"

"On the line, man, last one. Where else?"

They turned into the leafy drive of Calvin's somber clapboard house. Each heavy, hedgelike shape on either side of the entrance surrendering a vestige of anonymity as the rain weakened the great bulks of snow. Here and there, huge lacquered masks leered out of the trees, dangling from the branches where they'd been hung. After the first thaw, the decorated stumps in his swamp would appear, their hollows stained mauve and violet. On the porch in back, above the path of flagstones that were arranged and painted in the fractured image of a tiger, were Calvin's wife and daughter, waiting in saris. Half a dozen cats with bangles twisting and purring around their legs.

Just before opening the car door to greet them, Gnossos felt a restraining touch on his arm. Blacknesse's lips fixed in the suspicion of a smile again, his dark features blended in an expression of intensity and affection.

"Listen, Gnossos, you needn't try this tonight." A pause. "You understand me?"

"Sure thing."

"I mean, there might be better times, yes?"

"Come on, man."

"If you want to talk instead"—hesitating—"to tell some more . . ."

"Hey really, you know my manic thing with boo. If I start seeing spiders, you can always slip me a little niacin." This last word, with its easy intimation of goodness and health, spoken as he was stepping free of the Saab, already preoccupied with the people on the porch. Old friends, look a little changed.

Beth came forward, Middle Atlantic States heritage all but vanished in the Eastern bearing of her grace. She plucked a fold of the sari away from her thigh and said:

"Gnossos," extending a jeweled hand from the yellow silk, her eyes flashing. "How grand to have you back."

" 'Lo, Beth . . . Kim."

The young girl blushing, her color changing through a softer echo of her father's darkness, brooding hands locked behind. Eleven now, perhaps twelve. See the excitement in her.

"We have curry for supper," she whispered quickly, "an' Mommy's rice cakes."

"Hey, no kidding," touching the tip of her nose with a finger.

"Go on in, Gnossos," from Calvin, behind him, his feet banging off loose snow on the porch. "It's in the living room, if you're rushed."

Who me? Talk to the ladies. "Come on, you guys, you'll catch cold in those nightshirts."

The house as he remembered it, alive with fauna, grafted species of creepers and vines, wild tulips, potted umbrella trees, banked Irish moss. Set close along the orange and saffron pillows, which formed a pallet on one side of the room, a group of carnivorous plants looped out of the belly of an inverted brass centipede, little clawed pods pointed in the air, waiting to be sprung by whatever settling creature. Each wall entirely covered by a painting, from floor to ceiling. Countless images, liquid metaphors dipping away into neutral depths and planes, looming forward again, threatening the surface of the canvas. That one with the tapestry look, a beheading. Must have it sometime.

"Some sake with it?" The steaming drink on a ceramic tray from Beth, her long gray hair belying the youth in her dancer's body. Gauzes and silks billowing as she strides.

"Hey, there's no real hurry, man. Let's talk awhile."

"There's time, Gnossos, you'll be here. Civilities are such a nuisance, anyway. Like showing slides after a trip." She produced a toad carved from cypress and pressed a catch, which lifted the lid of its skull. "It's just here." The capsule was in the tiny compartment. Hello there, little fellow.

"Well, if you insist. Just trying to be polite is all."

"I'd rather get the story in pieces. Like a jigsaw, you know?"

"Put them together yourself?"

"Precisely." Pausing. "Especially in your case. Here, you'd best get this down."

"I'd rather mix it."

"Is your stomach empty?"

"Ummm." Gnossos separating the sections of the capsule carefully and squeezing the white powder into the sake, where it lumped and fell, then dissolved. He poked at it with his pinky and threw it all down like bourbon. "How've you been, anyway?"

Beth looking to see where Kim and Calvin were, picking up the toad and ceramic tray, "A trifle confused, since you ask. But that can wait too. Why don't you lie down, I've got to see after the curry. Kim will be here, if you feel badly." Smiling, fondling one of the cats with her free hand, looking into his eyes for a moment as if they were a photograph, then going to the kitchen. Where to lie? Those pillows. Kim coming in, talk to her.

"Getting much these days, kiddo?"

"I don't know. Getting what?"

"Oh, anything. Snowmen, late Christmas presents?"

"You're still silly."

"Silly Willy, you see me."

"An' your name is all funny."

"So's yours."

"Kim's a pretty name."

"How come you're so skinny, then?"

"I'm not skinny, either."

"Lumpy knees and funny pigtails."

"Mommy!"

He he. Beth calling from the kitchen, "Yes, Kim?"

"Mommy, Gnossos is making fun of me."

"Let him, then."

"If it's fun," he asked, touching her knee through the sari, "why worry?"

"Are you only teasin'?"

"Just look at your knees."

"I don't like you any more. Even if you went away."

"Look at them."

"What for?"

"They're lumpy is why."

"*Momm*—"

"Shhhh," he interrupted, "Now stop that. Everybody's are lumpy, secretly."

"Are yours?"

"Look," pulling up his corduroy cuffs.

"They're hairy."

"Maybe when you grow up, *yours* will be hairy."

"No they won't, only men's are hairy, so there."

"Maybe you'll have a mustache, how about that? Ha!" Quite suddenly, the first numbness stunned his extremities. Fingertips. Necessary to touch them one against the other. Nose, and the temples. The temples.

"Girls don't have mustaches at all, they're not supposed to, and everybody knows that."

A vague nausea hinting, maybe put my head down. "I know one who did, in Chicago "

"That's a fib."

"Maybe it was St. Louis."

"How's it going?" called Beth. "Are you all right?"

"Woozy, man."

"Why?" from Kim, looking down at him.

"Woozy, that's the snowman. Didn't you make any this winter?"

"I don't like the winter."

Staring at me like a lamp. Kids turned on all the time. Kids and pussycats. "Why don't you?"

" 's cold. I can't talk to the mushrooms."

Wooooooo. She can't talk to the mushrooms. "What else?"

"There's that turtle in Harpy Creek I once told you about. I think. Big snapping one."

"What do you say to him?"

"I don't *talk* to the turtle, silly."

Of course not.

"I want to kill him."

Wooo-hooo. "Why?"

"I don't know."

Ziiing. The colors of these cushions. Even through peripheral vision. Why so cold? Nasty nausea. Hold it down, though, no puking. What talking about? Turtles. "You don't know why?"

"Nope. Gonna kill him with a spear. After the snow's melted."

Pliers and acid. Fishhooks. How much in the pill? Big one is five hundred, this a third or so, say half is two-fifty, subtract a little, say one-eighty milligrams. Two hours, maybe three. "Three hours."

"Hunh?"

"No, no, I was talking to your father."

"Silly, Daddy's thinking now. In his painting room."

Meditation. Worthless alone, he says. In conjunction with some discipline, perhaps. In conjunction. Conjure. Conjuration. Conjugate. Conjugal.

What damp? My forehead, yes, Beth. "Beth?"

"It's all right." Calvin behind her, looking down. Jesus,

the height of him. I'm on the floor again. Ohh-ho-hooo, be careful, sonny boy, you're flyyyyyyyyying . . .

Calvin's voice: "Kim said you were pale and shivering. How is it?"

Beth wiping forehead with a cloth. Soooothe me. "Unh, how long—you know what I mean, she's not here now, right? He he. How long has, uh, Kim been gone?"

"What do you mean, Gnossos?"

"Kim, man, you know. She was just here, you dig, talking about turtles and all."

"An hour ago, maybe more."

"Oh yeah? You're not serious?"

"Try sitting up," from Beth.

All right. That's easy, no challenge there. Careful of the backbone, though. Could snap very easily. Easy, up. There. What's that? Over there, you idiot. WHAT'S THAT? "ANHHHH!" Dark.

"It's just the painting. You looked at it before, you can open your eyes."

"No. I saw him. He cut his head off. All by himself."

"It's just the painting."

"Don't lie to me."

"You saw it when you came in. On the wall."

The tapestry one. But it didn't move then. The blade it used. Careful of blades. Razors. Watch them, watch them all, they may want to kill themselves while you're here. Razor blades. "The bathroom."

"You want to go to the bathroom?" Calvin holding me up. Mustn't let him know. Nod. Right, old sport, right you are, got to wee-wee, la la. Beth gone. Never saw her leave. Careful about that. Must really be careful about that. They'll get you sometime, if you don't keep track. Step out of the room and make a phonecall. Tap tap tap at the door.

A gaunt woman in a robe, no features on her face, paralyzes you with a touch. Always be careful. Lock all doors. A.B.C.

"Here's the bathroom, Gnossos. Are you all right by yourself?"

"Sure thing. Right." Inside, shut it tight, slide the old bolt. Now then. What? Oh, razor blades. There, a loose one on the sink. Gather them all up, medicine cabinet? Yes oh yes, nice, a whole package. And in the shaver, a used one. Hairs on it. Ugh. Any more? Got to be more, use reason. Tub, cabinet, sink, towel rack, scale, window ledge, ha—one there. Commode, no, what for? Circumcision. Castration. Zip, slip it out. White, I read somewhere. What color's a spade's? Castration complex. That Mississippi cabbage, taking my five bucks. Vendetta. Oh, another one on the ledge. Any more? Looks good, got them all, now where to hide them. Not in here, too obvious. Feed them to that plant, one at a time. Ecch no, tear up its insides. Under the tub. There. Now. Oh wait, flush the toilet, make them think. Slosssssssh. Slosssssssh. Careful now, open . . . They'll thank me some-day, all safe from suicide—

What's that? He he, an orange cat. Looking at me, re-member her name. Apricot. Apricot the cat. "What do you want, Apricot?"

"Rrrrnneow."

"You know something, right?"

"Rrneow."

Maniac beast, following me. Some kind of scent we hu-mans leave, invisible glands in our hoofs, eluding animals out of the question.

"Do you think you'll be able to eat?" asked Calvin. "Say, in ten minutes?" Jesus, sitting next to me. Don't remember sitting. Food—of course, man. "Yes, I'm, you know, hun-gry." All staring my way. Quiiiet. Shhhhh.

"When Kim left the room that first time—"

"That's right."

"—did you see anything?"

"See?" The woman without any features on her face. No, that was later, not really seeing. Wait. The feathers on—no, some other thing, primate creature, gnarled, tell him: "Some kind of gnarled thing, short—"

"The pachu—"

"Nononono." Wait now, behind me the cat is going to *Jump.*"

Gnossos swung around, pointing at the place where Apricot had just gathered strength in her legs and lifted herself off the floor, into the air, down on a saffron cushion, front paws trapping the scuttling spider, which had been making for the wall.

"You see. You see him. I *knew* he was going to jump. I felt him wanting to—"

"What kind of gnarled thing, Gnossos?"

"No. Nothing. Nothing there." Get the spider from the cat. Easy now. Still alive, see the legs going. Black widow to sting me? Wrong shape. Kills her mate. Preying mantis, female eats his head while he screws her. There, the plant. Pod waiting. Better to feed it with something. "Tweezers."

"Just a minute," from Beth, rising beside him. How did she know? That music. "I hear sounds, Calvin."

"I just put it on, Gnossos."

"Raga?" Sitar hunting a scale. Me on the tamboura, droning, wire in the wind, easy undulation. Soft.

"Here."

"What?"

"The tweezers." Beth holding them in front of him. For what? The spider. Right. Okay. By one of its legs. Gently now. Wonder, can the plant smell? Oh, the drone talking.

Concentrate now. Conjugate. There. There. It's closing.
Apricot watching too. Afraid? Feed it the cat? Too big, ugly
mess. Other cats seek revenge, come after me in the night,
smell the gland in my antic hoof. You killed our brother.
Die, infidel.

"C'mon," said Kim. "Dinner's all ready."

Kim. Her father's brooding. But her body, whose?
Mustn't think that. Oh look. The foods, the glorious foods.
Blue pears.

"Blue pears?"

"Daddy stains them."

"Hey, I want a blue pear."

The meal was divided all about the table, stacked in anthropomorphic serving dishes, cupped in the hollow backs
of sloe-eyed ceramic creatures, ready to pour through contorted clay mouths: mounds of steaming brown rice, unpolished, starchy to the smell; bowls of yellow curry, chunks of
lamb falling tenderly apart; roasted almonds sprinkled with
sesame; organic okra; glazed pineapple sticks; cruets of
rosewater; cups of melted butter and oil; mango chutney;
scented dal; carafes of dark wine; sweet and sour peppers;
blue pears in minted syrup; Gnossos wanting it all, antic-
ipating each exotic taste, every foreign flavor.

"Here," Beth told him, "at the head of the table."

"For me, man? The place of honor?"

"The returning warrior," said Calvin.

"Wow," sitting down, playing with his napkin, sniffing the
goodies, watching his plate being heaped with magnificence.
"Dancing girls, man, that's all we need. Bangled sprites,
wriggling sylphs."

"You can have them," said Beth, pausing with a ladle like
a wand in her hand. "Close your eyes and look."

Try it.

Sure enough, they were there, blinking at him above their silent veils. Oh la.

After dinner Gnossos sat stuffed in the full lotus beneath one of the shedding Australian umbrella trees, munching on a carob-covered cashew nut. "I'm coming down, Calvin."

Blacknesse sketching him roughly with a broad-nibbed pen, delineating features, unable to prevent the emergence of satyrs and nymphs from the tangle of hair. His own brow curled and wrinkled, dark eyes searching, hinting vaguely, as always, at the uncertain, the nearly defined. "You only think that. It was over a hundred and sixty milligrams, there's still time left, even if you don't hallucinate."

"Yeah, well other cats get all the heat, man. Me, I'm beginning to think it won't happen." Swallowing the cashew nut with a mealy effort, realizing he'd been hung up, chewing its pulverized meat for perhaps fifteen minutes.

"You want it all without the discipline, Gnossos, you can't exactly expect the revelations of Saint John."

"That's cool, man, no visions, no sun gods, no anything, right? What do you think, I'm a junky or something, what's it all about?"

Calvin's pen tracing the simple Greek nose, a line dropping vertically from the forehead. "Whatever it's all about, it would be senseless, in the real meaning of the word, to try and tell you."

"Yeah, that's right, I'm supposed to tease out the old synthesis on my own. But I'm just not about to go squatting on a nail carpet or something, man, you know what I mean." Shifting out of the lotus, the implication of which distracted him, and finding a cramp in his calf, which he rubbed vigor-ously while going on, "Look, I talk to you, at least. I confide in you?"

"Probably because you think I know something."

Swinging a forefinger up to the painting of the man cutting off his own head. "That little mother, for instance. Now what's that all about, if you don't know something, man?"

"I gave you the mescaline, yes?"

"You did. So you did. Point well taken. But no vision things happening. What alternative? Ratiocination like Oeuf? I mean, *any* old vision would do it. That one of yours from fasting and whole grains last year, that woman with the flaming pubes, striding over a cloud; man, I'll take seconds on that one."

"Ah, you'll forgive an intuition, then?"

" 'Swhat I'm here for man, I'm up-tight."

"The immortality worm has been chewing."

"What if it has?"

"Try chewing back."

Beth saw them off at the door, her bearing full of question, something not concluded. Kim by her side, hands again locked behind her, failing to wave goodbye as the car backed out on the slushy driveway. The rain had stopped.

They drove into Lairville without conversation, no sound but the tires and the occasional clicking swish of the wipers when they cleared splashed snow. A blue-gray tint to the night, bizarre purple lips and gums as they passed through distorting pools of mercury-vapor light. They slowed down on Dryad Road, Calvin asking finally, "Where to?"

"Guido's'll do. Just on the right there," Gnossos zipping up his parka against the cold, fondling his rucksack. "You want a drink?"

"I think not. You don't mind?"

"No, man, that's cool, I just thought you might have wanted some time, you know, away."

They eased over against the curb and Calvin left the motor running. Gnossos opened the door to get out but hesitated. A mammoth red neon bear blinked on their faces. No tension scenes, what the hell, say thank you. "Thanks, Calvin."

"That's all right. Come out again soon, for whatever reason."

"I'll wait awhile, I think. I'm a little down just now."

"It doesn't really show."

"Euphoria. Adrenalin. Upbeat metabolism, and all."

Putting the car into gear. "That beheading picture; I'll have it for you at the studio tomorrow."

"Hey no, you don't have to—"

"It'll be there anyway. It's my decision, yes? And be careful, Gnossos."

"Right," his hand reaching nonetheless into the side pocket of the Saab and removing a small hammer, which as soon as he touched it took part in a plan of earlier revenge. "Later."

And bang, he was through the swinging doors, inhaling the familiar fumes of Guido's Grill. Odors always able to hang you up, lay bare the honeycombed cells of nasal memory. French-fried onion rings, pizzaburgers, bubbly cooking fat, Breath-O-Pine disinfectant.

Students were meanwhile packed together in polyethylene booths, most of them independents, an odd minority of slumming fraternity types, ending their collective day over plates of late-night swill, mistaking the knots of academic anxiety for hunger. Coeds in mohair sat nibbling, watching the clock for curfew. Through the cacophonic murmur of extracurricular chitchat, plots to collapse the administration, talk of Caribbean gunrunning, and kneesie games among the graduate queens, Gnossos heard the Saab out in the street turning around and puttering off. Oh well.

"Hey, Paps!"

Heff in a blue-striped French seaman's jersey, calling from a mobbed booth. Voices suspended above the din of talk for a brief moment, heads bobbing up from ale and strawberry shakes. Here and there an occasional expression of shocked recognition, then embarrassed shifting away. Only one of them with enough hair to call my name. Go over, why don't you. Man, seven of them. Break the ice, choose your words. "Pax."

"Sit down, Paps," Heff's arm slung limply around Jack's shoulders, a knuckle toying with her cheek. "Little celebration thing going on. You know these people, these undergraduates, these old university cats?"

Jesus. Four empty martini glasses in front of him, fifth half-dead. "You're smashed, Horralump."

"Old-timey celebration happening, Paps, they threw me out."

"No, man, don't say that."

"Out out out on my ass, bump bump down the stairs, dig?"

Lord, Fitzgore, didn't see him. Four others, no three, that horn-rim type, where? Pimples. Oh Jesus, the D.U. dinner, flee.

"Old-timey Agnoo here's buying up the Red Cap supply, man, kind of cornered the market, you know? Have a little Red Cap, veal scallopine, you hungry? You know everybody atta table? You know the Lumpers chic here, you know Agnoo, you 'member Rosenbloom an' friend from the wheel?"

"Agneau," came the nervous correction, an uneasy, bespectacled glance at Gnossos, pinching motion to the knot of his tie. No cool. Fitzgore glaring, being too quiet, Condition Red, man. Christ, the dubbies on Lumpers.

"My name is Juan Carlos Rosenbloom," said the one in a sequined rodeo shirt. "From Maracaibo." He strained formally over the red plastic tabletop, stretching out a minuscule, hairy hand. Not more than five feet tall, Saint Christopher medal tight on his throat, grease mat for a head. All I need. "An' my freng Drew Youngblood, the editors of the *Sun*."

"We weren't introduced that night," said the editor.

"What night, man?"

"The roulettes," explained Rosenbloom, spinning his tiny finger around the table to mimic a wheel. Yes, of course. Want their bread back? May have to bust noses.

"The appeal failed, y'know," from Jack, her hand going up and down on the inside of Heff's bluejeaned thigh, a third of her attention on the Lumpers breasts. Fitzgore too quiet.

"I will buy you something to drink," said Rosenbloom, signaling for the waitress.

"Wha'd you like?" asked Youngblood.

Gnossos shrugging his shoulders, lush not exactly right for the time, pointing to his head for Heff's benefit, who saw and understood the reference but made a blubbering sound with his lips just the same. Lumpers sliding over. Ought to flee, really, use tact. Lobes still not straight, waitress looking at me. Ahem. "You have any Metaxa?"

"I can't unnerstan' you." A blob of gum in her jaw.

"It's Greek."

"It's what?"

Control. "Rye, then. Any kind of rye. Four Roses even, and a little ginger ale."

"I'll see 'fthey got any. You have a draft card?"

"Look, baby—"

"Jus' answer the question. Y' never know who's gonna be checkin' up. Y' want Guido t'lose his license?"

Do the Gandhi. "Yes, I've got one. You'd like to see it?"

"No, as long as you got it. Why don't you make life simple, have a beer?" Going away. Fat legs. I'll have her mutilated, so help me . . .

"My round," said Youngblood, still serious in expression.

"No, plis," from the South American, flashing a twenty, "I'm insist."

"Hey, Paps," said Heffalump, putting down the fifth martini glass, empty, "I want it verified who was Tonto's horse. Old Jack here, she says Scout, and Fitz says Tony."

"My *God*," said Lumpers, in angora, "I used to listen to that on the *ra*dio. Every Sunday afternoon."

"Get 'em up, Scout," said Jack, sadly. Her free hand extending from a man's blue buttondown Oxford shirt, fingers drumming hoofbeats on the table.

"I was hoping I'd catch up with you again," said Youngblood intimately, motioning Rosenbloom's twenty into obscurity and struggling to get his own wallet free of his chinos, away from the press of bodies in the booth. "There's this Susan B. Pankhurst thing I wanted to talk to you about, although you probably never heard of her."

"I'm insist," continued Rosenbloom.

"Really, it used to be on every Sunday afternoon, the *Lone* Ranger and Tonto," Lumpers' attention given to Heff, who was trying to contain all his martini olives under a single inverted glass. "Although sometimes we called him the *Long* Ranger, he he ha."

"Susan what?" Gnossos with his eye on the Lumpers dubbies.

"It couldn't've been Sundays," said Jack, stopping her finger-drumming, licking her Red Cap. "It was Thursdays, brought to you by Cheerios. And Tony was Tom Mix's horse, anyway."

"B. *Pank*hurst. A new Vice-President for Student Affairs. She's putting through a bill about coeds in apartments."

"Sundays was Nick and Nora Charles," said Heff, not looking up from his project, "with that crazy dog they had. What the hell was that dog?"

"Do you realize I'm being fined TEN DOLLARS for that dinner, you *maniac?!*" yelled Fitzgore, lurching over suddenly, shoving his carrot-colored hair away from his eyes. "Ten goddamned bills?!"

Pretend you can't hear him. Lost his mind. What to do? Return the enema bag.

Gnossos reaching into his rucksack and handing over the rubber bag and tube while looking casually for the waitress. Highball, the near-perfect drink, la la. Defines social status. "Heff—excuse me a minute, would you, Youngblood?—they didn't truly throw you out, did they?"

"An' the House of Mystery, that was Sundays too."

"And Sky *King,*" said the Lumpers girl with delight, shifting weight, nudging Gnossos accidentally with her left breast.

"Sky King was Saturdays," from Heff. "With Bobby Benson and the B-Bar-B Riders. And you bet your rosy buns they threw me out, man."

"Look, Gnossos," insisted the editor of the *Sun*. "We

have to talk over this Pankhurst thing, if you follow me. I mean, what she's after is to keep unchaperoned coeds out of apartments."

"In Maracaibo we have chaperones, ha ha." Rosenbloom giving up the twenty to a sequined shirt pocket and fingering his Saint Christopher absently.

"Listen," Agneau was whispering to a broiling Fitzgore. "Don't get excited. Why get excited, really?"

"I don't mind the ten bills, it's only this embarrassing a whole damn house for a lousy T-bone steak, or whatever the hell it was. Who wasn't embarrassed, for instance? Tell me you weren't embarrassed?"

"Who?" continued Heff, ignoring them, "was the Green Hornet's faithful Filipino companion?"

"Kato," answered Gnossos casually, taking his highball from the passing waitress. "Who by the way was a Jap to begin with, but they had to cool it after the heat at Pearl Harbor."

"Check. And Hop Harrigan's ace buddy?"

"Oh. Hop *Har*rigan."

"Tank Tinker," from Gnossos, sipping.

"Listen," insisted Youngblood. "You don't realize that if she gets this chaperone thing through, you won't be able to have *women* in your apartments!"

A subtle collective pause in everyone's breathing. "I beg your pardon?" asked Gnossos and Fitzgore, almost simultaneously.

Another pause.

"No women." Youngblood leaning back.

"Townies, even?" Agneau twisting his cuticle-free pinky, smiling falsely at the two coeds, who froze him right out.

"She said," continued Youngblood, sensing his time, "this

Pankhurst actually said that male apartments, if you follow me, are conducive . . . to petting and intercourse."

Silence.

"She's only doing her duty," from Heff, pulling himself up, "as God gave her the right."

"To do her duty," added Jack.

"Who sponsored Jack Armstrong?" asked Heff.

"Wheaties," said Gnossos. "She's down on humping, is she?"

"Intercourse," corrected Fitzgore in despair, "for goddamn Christ's sake."

"An' who was responsible for bringing you Captain Midnight?" asked Heff.

"Ovaltine, man. Now if you could get her to come out and say it again—"

"Don' bother leetle things," said Rosenbloom. "Have a revolutiong. Smash her, how you call her, Panghurts."

"Somebody's getting involved," warned Heffalump slyly, across all the jumbled conversation. "Somebody better be careful, he gets himself infuckingvolved."

True. Proceed with caution: "What's the ploy, man?"

"You had it figured. We want her to say it again. In public this time."

"Have a revolutiong," said Rosenbloom.

"Only we're not certain how to go about it." Pausing, leaning forward. "We thought you might have something in mind."

Gnossos looking around the table. "Me?"

"Captain Midnight's archenemy?" Heff winking.

"Ivan Shark," said Jack, her hands on the table now, most of her attention on the Lumpers breasts.

"What, are you serious; *me,* man?"

"If she said it all publicly, this petting and intercourse thing, maybe we could *do* something. The issue would be *moral*. I mean, she'd be opposing P and I as *entities,* as *concepts* having nothing to *do* with Lairville apartments. We could take her *on.*" There's even talk about her becoming Mentor *President*, but that's too horrible a prospect to consider just now."

"Smash her," said Rosenbloom.

Gnossos looked at Youngblood. He was wearing a plain white Arrow shirt, no buttons on the collar, open at the throat, and even had an honest face.

"That's your plan, then, you want to take her on?"

Youngblood leaning in closer, lowering his voice and looking at the table: "We want the President."

"Kill him," said Rosenbloom.

"Don't get involved, Paps."

"Listen," said Judy Lumpers, turning away from Jack's gaze, *"I'm* a government major and I know that it doesn't *really* have very much to do with what you're talking about, I mean God, but if you want the President out, that can be extremely tedious. Not to say *dif*ficult."

"We gotta get back to the dorms," said Jack, looking at the clock. "You going to Jove, Lumpers?"

"I mean, the President, *really.*"

"Some other time, man," said Gnossos, rising, gulping the last of the highball. "But later. Up, old Heffalump, I want words with you. Got a little mission to accomplish."

"Who designed the Captain Midnight Code-O-Graph?" from Heff, struggling to his feet. All through Guido's a shift in movement, in inflection, as the Coed Curfew Hour became apparent.

"C'mon, Lumpers baby," said Jack, "we'll be late."

"I can drive you back," from Fitzgore.

"Nobody's paying any attention to me," said Heff, reeling slightly as he stood. "Who designed—"

"Ichabod Mudd," said Gnossos, reaching casually into his rucksack and producing a small rusted device with letters and numbers on its side. Everyone stopped talking and stared at the object with stunned admiration.

"A Code-O-Graph," said Heffalump, after some awed moments. "A Captain Midnight Code-O-Graph!"

All of Guido's collapsed into total silence as every head in the place, including the waitress', turned to gaze reverently at the artifact, which Gnossos fingered proudly, then elevated like a communion wafer so tribute might be offered. They all remembered.

In the marble vestibule of Anagram Hall, deserted except for the echo of their hoarse whispers, Heffalump and Gnossos crept along on hands and knees.

What the hell are you doing, you madman? Where'd you get that ball-peen hammer?"

"From Blacknesse's car. And shut up, there might be a watchman. There'll be enough noise in a minute."

"Jesus Christ, Paps."

They inched away from the vestibule, along the main corridor, Gnossos lighting matches and checking office numbers, the glow giving eerie definition to the white busts which stood against the wall.

"Here, this looks right."

"Where?"

"Shhh."

He kneeled and examined the lock, dipping into his rucksack for a long nailfile, which he inserted in the keyhole.

Feels like a single tumbler. Too far in. Back a ways. No. No good. "You have your knife, Heff?"

"Shit, man," feeling the pockets of his jeans, fumbling, then handing it over.

Gnossos pulled out the awl and inserted it as he had the nailfile. Much better. Left, I imagine. There. The tumbler turned over with an audible clack and he twisted the brass handle quickly, motioning Heffalump inside. He closed the door behind them and for a moment they stood silently on the carpeted floor. Easy as that.

"Well, here we are."

"Shit, Paps."

"Stay loose, man. The cat kicked you out, right?"

"Yeah."

"He hit me for five, right?"

"Right."

They crawled across the office, ducking under windows, Gnossos lighting two more matches on the way, finally stopping before a large glass cabinet.

Open, he ho. The sweet saliva of retribution.

He lifted out each of Dean Magnolia's mineralogical specimens, crystal, shale, semiprecious quartz, igneous delights, and laid them all on the rug in the shape of an equilateral triangle.

"What the hell are all those things, Paps?"

"A whole lot of doodley-shit," from Gnossos, bringing the hammer down ferociously on the first of the stones, smashing it violently into dust and sand.

5

March came fumbling in like the *Wizard of Oz* lion, winds shifting the surge of their northern force, padding around the horizon, creeping further and further west as the still invisible sun climbed nearer the zenith each day, warmed the gorge-crawling clouds, and loosened the first of the spring rain.

On this damp and leaden morning Gnossos sat in his narrow bed by the recently installed, hermetically sealed window, legs crossed under the monster eiderdown, scanning the editorial page of the Mentor *Daily Sun*. The paper had appeared, as usual, after mysterious, delicate rapping. Whenever it happened, he would tiptoe over the Navajo rug, wait a moment—his fingers poised on Fitzgore's pewter latch—then pull the door open, hoping to surprise Jimmy Brown the Newsboy or the yawning little toddler from the Fisk tire ads, candle in hand, tire slung over his shoulder. But always there was no one there. The hallway, the front steps, the avenue beyond were empty. On the odd wide-awake mornings, when his brain was clear, or dawns following all-night sessions with polar co-ordinates, he would crouch against the door, with a hard-boiled breakfast egg in hand, waiting for footsteps, ready for the rapping. But when he waited, the paper never came.

Now he kept his place with a middle finger while glancing through the two-ply glass in the window to see if the rain had stopped. He grunted and continued reading. Fitzgore was snoring on the other bed, perpendicular to the wall at the foot of his own. The apartment looked much the way it had when he'd seen it that first afternoon, with the single, pub-emulating exception of Fitzgore's pewter, copper hunting horns, and hammered brass plates. The rice-paper globe had been lowered so that it hung not three feet from the floor over a circular piece of black plywood, which rested insecurely on a cinder block from the construction site at Larghetto Lodge. The globe advertised a single, complex Chinese ideogram, inked by Gnossos' trembling hand while he waited one evening for Beth Blacknesse to fill a paregoric prescription. The character signified that the rucksack was holy and the rucksack was not for sale. Harold Wong, coxy on the Olympic crew, had done the translation.

There were marks on the wall from strips of masking tape, where he'd torn away the landlord's quaintly familiar Degas, Renoir, Soyer, Utrillo, and Mary Cassatt prints in a narcotized rage. A nail had been driven into the French doors that separated him from the alcoholic Rajamuttus, and on it was hung the rucksack. It emanated a faint odor of month-old rabbits' feet and Oriental goods from the Greco-Turkish supply company in the Negro section downtown. Two rubber plants stood by the fireplace, still in the dappled, plastic pots he'd meant to disguise with flat-black spray. And spilled textbooks everywhere, notes scrawled in the margins, faces drawn on the covers. All horizontal surfaces were occupied by at least one open beercan stuffed with cigarettes saturated in some reeking liquid. And dominating the entire white-walled living room, hanging over the mantel by the number-fifteen housewire anchored to the molding, was the tapestrylike Blacknesse painting of the man cutting away his own head.

Before turning to the editorials, Gnossos had finished the rear-page release on the demolished stones. *Vandalism*, read the headline. *Still No Leads on Smashed Magnolia Specimens*. The subhead told how Proctor Slug Suspects Drunken Prank, Discounts Psychological Motive. Oh la. In the body of the story there were vague references to the last incident of its kind, the disappearance of imported Italian statues from the Christmas crèche at Hector Ramrod Hall, the amazing springtime recovery of the Virgin Mary's head, found intact by bathing coeds in Harpy Creek gorge. A miracle.

There came quick, clattering jangles. Gnossos sprang from the bed, pounced on the vibrating alarm clock next to Fitzgore's ear, muffled the sound, found the switch, then shuffled back to bed. Fitzgore tossing only slightly, altering the pitch of his snore, failing to wake.

Wrapped again in the eiderdown (a gift from Pamela Watson-May), knees against his chest, munching on a chunk of dried-up feta, sipping at the last of the Schweppes she had also left behind, he continued the editorial by Drew Youngblood, a public warning to faculty and students that Susan B. Pankhurst

> was merely one personified facet of a cleverly conceived plan on the part of the present administration to shift the responsibility of certain highly significant student affairs into the hands of Minotaur Hall. In addition to the already proposed, and highly speculative, ruling on coeds and Lairville apartments—a ruling certainly improbable, had the faculty committee not been dissolved by the President at the end of its tenure—

there has occurred yesterday's failure to reappoint the Architectural Advisory Committee, an extremely eminent authority, whose permission and advice have hitherto been mandatory before construction *or demolition* of new campus buildings could commence.

Crusades, thought Gnossos. Jehads and holy wars. Youngblood with that unlikely combination of honest expressions folded in his face like stiff-peaked egg whites in a batter. Truthsayer, his white shirt without a buttondown collar, no tie. Sew a cross of Saint George on his back, tie a maiden's scarf in his sash, point him at the Tigris and Euphrates. It's somewhere out there, lad, in the hands of the pagan Turks. I know we can count on you.

Still, he may be into something.

Gnossos shifted weight uncomfortably, one aspect of his mind quietly furious at the constipation which continued unrelieved despite cautious doses of mineral water, lemon juice, olive oil, and Carter's Little Liver Pills. Good for little livers; mine as big as a strawberry shortcake, reconstitutes its spongy self, adding volume each time around the bilious cycle. Me like Prometheus, no bird needed. My spiritual old man, kicking determinism in the head. He turned the page, ignoring "Pogo" (something insipid in political possums) then went carefully through the frames of "Peanuts." He studied each line of Snoopy's self-indulgent countenance as the dog lay on top of his little white house, nose up, ears down, gazing fondly at the universe.

He was saying the word "sigh" along with the balloon in the last picture, when the front door opened without a knock and two peculiar-looking men wandered in.

They were making sniffing sounds.

The police?

From recent experience with Pamela, and light in the room, Gnossos realized they could see neither Fitzgore nor him through the bamboo-reed curtain that isolated the beds from the rest of the apartment. But he had no difficulty seeing them. He crouched down into the eiderdown and watched their curious, halting gestures as they nosed about. Something subtly familiar in their manner. He moved his hand under the sheets, searching silently for the hammer he had taken from Blacknesse's car and kept in bed ever since. Who? Proctor Slug's men? Impossible, man, they move like potheads. Nudge Fitzgore with toe.

The two strangers paused, one on either side of the table, the rice-paper globe with the Chinese character at thigh height between them. Mutt and Jeff. The little one pudgy with an inch-thick tweed jacket, patches on the sleeves, blue shirt, white bowtie. Carrying a yellow briefcase. His hair like Hitler's, patch combed forward, plastered on his brow, heavy Kitchener mustache, ends waxed, pointing straight out; little eyes glancing about, mole-nose twitching, the palm of one hand going up and down on his belly. Beside him was a bald man in black from head to toe, a turtleneck jersey covering only a sixteenth of his windowpole throat. Mary, no, not a man, a kid! Gnossos watched him stroke his head, then dangle his fingers in the air, snapping at dust. Seventeen, maybe. Why grinning? Up, Fitzgore, up up, there's a zombi in the room.

"Eminently casual," said the mustached man, kissing the end of a Robt. Burns cigarillo and looking at the Blacknesse painting. His hand hesitating on his belly as he realized simultaneously what was occurring on the canvas and that other people were in the room.

Gnossos gripped the handle of the hammer and tested it for balance. Find the temple first, tap swiftly. Wait, though. Maybe seraphim sent to test.

"Pappadopoulis, assuredly," said the stranger, inching his head around the curtain, his gourami lips parting in a smile that was shy one tooth. The teenager oozed across the distance between him and the shorter man, his feet never seeming to leave the floor, and said, "Wha's happening, baby?"

Jesus. "Nothing much, man. Who are you?"

A pause.

"You don't know?" asked the fat man. He turned to the teenager with a resigned gesture: "I knew he wouldn't mail the letter. What did I tell you before leaving the city, Heap? He wouldn't mail the letter."

Nudge Fitzgore with big toe. Wake up, mother, stop snoring. Talk to them. "Was I supposed to get a letter?"

"Aquavitus. You didn't hear from him? No letter?"

All a morning dream, no correlation between events.

"What letter, man?"

The teenager with the shaved skull shook his head sadly, in slow motion, his left eye opening and closing. Not a wink but a lazy, muscleless drooping of the lid. His fingers kept snapping casually at the air.

"I couldn't call him an especially close friend," continued the pudgy one, lighting his cigarillo and offering another to Gnossos, who neither refused nor accepted, "but I visit with him when I'm in the city, have a little sweet-and-sour pork at Hong Fat. You've been there, you're familiar with the place?" The cigarillo going back into his outside pocket.

"How do you know Aquavitus?"

"The Buddha, of course."

"Check," said the bald one. "We're all of a family."

"From Havana?"

"We have a business deal, an arrangement," smiling, touching one of the lumpy forefingers to the tip of his waxed mustache, as if testing for a lethal point.

The Cuban connection with an opal in his forehead. Seven-foot spade in silk robes, Motherball once said. No one had ever seen him. These guys, who? The eyes on the kid, like a runt water spaniel, stoned, flying.

Leave Fitzgore alone. "And who are you?"

The two creatures looking at each other as if to find out, the pudgy one turning back slowly and saying, "Mojo," setting his briefcase down on the floor and unraveling the long swiveled leash that attached it to his wrist. Extending his left hand backward, Gnossos shaking it carefully, his stomach shrinking at the soft, boneless feel. Like a rubber glove stuffed with putty. "Oswald Mojo. This is my assistant, Heap. So old Giacomo didn't send you the letter? We predicted that, of course. He's such an in*tense* kind of Sicilian, all work, all, how shall we say, intrigue. But you know that, you realize how he is."

"I haven't seen him in two years, I thought he was in Alcatraz." Heff talking about him recently. Cloak-and-stiletto shit, take this zircon to Foppa. Mo-go. The Victorian house?

"Ha ha," said Oswald Mojo. "Ha ha ha. No. No, not old Giacomo. That's why he's so beautiful, so, how shall we say, ob*scure*. He volunteered for a gout experiment at the Mayo Clinic, got paroled."

"He's beautiful, baby," agreed Heap, his eye drooping. Mojo said: "But you know me anyway, you've heard of me? It would have helped for you to realize I was coming, of course, it's always pleasant to be ex*pect*ed, not to cause surprises."

"Oh, I like surprises."

"Mojo," repeated the man, going into his briefcase, his face flushing, swelling as he leaned over to fish something out. "Oswald Mojo."

Gnossos shaking his head, not recognizing the name, turning his back to the wall, always cover your flanks. Leave the flanks exposed, they'll tear right up the middle, nail you with a howitzer or something. What's he getting, Luger? Stay loose. Aquavitus, man, of all people. Sicily ox-shit. Ersatz Mafia Capo coming from South Brooklyn, has eyes for the heavyweight heroin crown, still district distributor for Cuban grass.

"Here," said Mojo, "some of my work," tossing a number of political periodicals on the eiderdown. *Foreign Affairs Quarterly, Partisan Review,* back numbers of *The Reporter, The New Leader.* You probably didn't know I completed the treatise in *F.A.Q.* when I was twelve. The irony there, you see, the aesthetic injustice, as it were, was that Madame Pandit's translation achieved so much more fame than my original. But that's, well, how shall we say . . ."

"Show business," supplied Gnossos, flipping through the pages and actually finding a number of essays by Oswald Mojo, the paragraphs laced with Italian and Latin expletives.

"The monographs, baby," said Heap, smiling, also showing a missing front tooth, the same one in fact, "that's where it's all happening."

"Form, the significant variable. Contains the elocutionary passions."

"Double-crostics, myself," said Gnossos, looking one to the other, not getting response, "little haiku now and then, ha ha." Laying the magazines aside, figuring the geometry of the room, Heap an easy target, too stoned to move quickly. Feel them along: "I'll read the stuff later, if you don't mind, classes to go to and all, lecture in twenty minutes. So if you'll maybe tell me what it is you'd like?"

A pause while Mojo sucked at his cigarillo, nervously twisted the swivel of the leash on his wrist. Looking at Heap. "Your, how shall we call it, repu*t*ation, Pappadopoulis, being the kind of thing one can't help noticing, being attracted to—" The man broke off, not satisfied with his start, twisting the leash in the opposite direction. It was then that Gnossos noticed the braiding of the leather leash, thick at one end, tapering away at the other, exactly like, oh wow, a bullwhip.

"Events of an ex*ci*ting nature get communicated," he went on, "wouldn't you say? All this elusive talk about communication being lost in our—how shall we put it—era of abeyance. Boring circumstances, of course, are forgotten, but significant bits of information, *preg*nant facts, people of a dynamic bent, these things get talked about, one might even say, praised."

"Yes," said Gnossos, knowing no more, picking up the uneasiness in the room, "but this important lecture; my roommate—"

"Beautiful, baby," from Heap, his eye drooping in the direction of the slumbering Fitzgore, approving.

"Given individuals being more ad*ven*turous than the, oh, call them peasant stock, come to be thought of as, ha ha, sources of *en*ergy. Even more so if they travel a great deal, function in large urban, well, communities, such as, well, Las Vegas. People take *not*ice, want to par*take*—"

"He'll be late, old roomie, hates being tardy—"

"Yes," continued Mojo, seeming to ignore, still twisting

the leather, "par*take*. Come to enjoy the same little *things*. As a kind of example—were we looking for one—and I could phrase this more eloquently, were you not so seemingly pressed in your studies; I say, as a kind of example of this person there is the, well, example of yourself. Yes. Could you, all *things* considered, for instance, have failed to attract the attention of Werner Lingam in St. Louis or Alexander Jelly in Venice West, both connoisseurs in their own right? Even Giacomo, with his quaint Sicilian manner, has heard much in a different way about you; quite apart from the little jobs you've done for his, well, company. So of course, knowing as we did last week, Heap and myself, that we'd be coming in this direction, even stopping over, as it were, for the week, and looking a*round,* our mutual friend Giacomo said to me—you know how he likes to keep track of his former clients and employees—he said, 'Atheené, Atheené, shoo I got a fren'dere.' " (Heap chuckling at the imitation, murmuring just under his breath, "What a gas.") " 'You look 'im up, you look up Agnossos, I write 'im an introduction, he fix you up fine, ha ha,' and I remembered your name in particular from Richard Pussy, another very *dear* friend from Vegas, who never stops talking about that very *tall,* long-legged girl from Radcliffe you were making it with, the one who used to go around, ha ha, *bare*foot, if you recall. And of course, Louie Motherball . . ."

The pudgy fingers were going up and down on his belly again, and the momentarily forgotten cigarillo had grown a heavy ash, which inclined toward the floor. For a moment, in the pale reflection of the light through the sealed window glass, Gnossos saw a trickle of saliva at the corner of Mojo's mouth, a curling, needle-thin bead of tiny, adhesive bubbles half an inch in length. The glimmering thread existed barely a fraction of a second before it was dissolved by the tip of a fat, pink tongue. His eyes blinking in twitches.

"*Bare*foot, you see, if you'll understand my intent," he continued, fixing his gaze on a piece of polarized dust suspended in one of the light shafts, "and that *Negro* girl in North Beach, she used to wear *white* silk stockings all over her legs, which were, ha ha, black so to speak, *very* long. She was nearly six feet tall, from what we heard, communication being what it is and my knowing such an extraordinary number of people, a very *great* many, most of whom I meet after my readings. Although I *do* try to confine them to the women's schools, it's not always easy and you often take what you can get, don't you? Depending on your particular frame of reference, the species of habit you cultivate, a certain amount of bravado, which you, for example, Pappadopoulis, don't seem to be wanting, even in matters of *taste*, ha ha, that chic for example, wearing silk stockings, and those shoes with the extra long heels, even if the skirt wasn't, wasn't—"

"Leather," provided Heap, snapping his fingers for punctuation.

"Or a given grade of suede," said Mojo, the concept of the word stopping him suddenly, triggering some other degree of thought, causing him to come aware of the cigarillo, flick the ash on the Navajo rug, and take a noisy, sucking puff.

Gnossos stared at him.

"Your good friend Heffalump being another case in point, apart from his exceedingly *quaint* name and mulatto blood. That girl on the tabletop at Duke, that cheerleader, booster, whatever she was, wearing her *boots*."

"Quadroon," corrected Heap, snapping.

"Assuredly. And there was someone else too—who was that, Heap, the Côte d'Azur, at Pablo's place, somebody knew Gnossos here, his scene?"

"Pablo?" asked Gnossos, suspicious.

"Yeah, Picasso."

"The Buddha?" from Heap, not certain.

"No no, someone else. No matter, really."

Gnossos looked at both of them again, the palms of his hands perspiring, the hammer forgotten. Heap was nodding curiously, his left eyelid drooping, his hair barely beginning to grow back, a gray shadow of prickly fuzz. Mojo said: "Make some coffee, Heap—no, you stay where you are, Mr. Pappadopoulis, don't go to any trouble on our account, that's all right, that's perfectly fine, Heap makes an excellent cup of coffee, nice to have in bed, such a long time it's been too, since Las Vegas probably, that, ha ha, *bare*foot, long-legged girl, if I'm correct."

The morning after the atom bomb, the Radcliffe muse bringing him coffee at their motel.

"You sure you don't want a cigarillo, Robbie Burns, I'm sorry, they didn't have anything else at the campus store. Prefer Between-the-Acts generally, an Aquavitus recommendation. You need any shit?"

Oh ho.

So there it is. At ten-thirty in the morning. Into his briefcase again? Holy cow, look at the thickness. It couldn't be—

"Grass," said Mojo. "Mexican Brown. Very clean quality, I can assure you. Numbs the extremities. Certain percentage hash, about two to seven, you dig. Tangier hash. The kind they put in those chocolate bars."

Gnossos unfolded the wrapping paper carefully, looking

up at Mojo's contented expression, the cigarillo pressed delicately between the kiss of puckered lips. He sniffed first, then looked down and examined.

It certainly was interesting-looking shit.

"My own mixture," said Oswald Mojo, "I have it prepared by a musician acquaintance in Nashville, chap who blows electric oud, calls it Mixture Sixty-nine, very popular in certain *cir*cles, if you follow me."

"What a beautiful kitchen, baby," called Heap, "garbage and vine leaves all over the place. Where's the coffee?"

Lie. "Don't use it. Caffeine bad for the head."

"Uuuunmphhf," said Fitzgore, stirring as the word coffee filtered into his subconsciousness.

"Consider that a gift," said Mojo.

"It's nearly two ounces."

"Yeah, baby," said Heap, gliding back across the rug, "it's beautiful."

"Wha'timesit?" asked Fitzgore, looking up with his swollen redhead's eyes. "I gotn'eleven o'clock."

"Cool it," said Heap.

"You'll be late," said Gnossos. "Up up up, time for school."

"Uuuunmphhf. Who're these guys? Wha'timesit?"

"Perhaps," said Mojo, wrapping the bullwhip leash around his wrist and snapping the briefcase closed, then pausing with a thumb-flick, which meant Gnossos should follow him to the door and which he very nearly felt the physical force of, "perhaps we could get together later. You'll be at the party tomorrow night, that goes without saying?"

"Party?" he whispered. Heap's snapping fingers had abruptly stopped, one of them going to his lips in a hushing gesture. All three of them paused by the dangling rice-paper globe, looking at each other around the suspended white wire. The rucksack is not for sale.

"I've arranged a loft in Dryad, that very *quaint* village near here, you know the place well of course, the farm adjacent to the Dairy, ha ha, Queen." Mojo leaned forward, an expression of intimate confidence in his pig-eyes: "I try to keep these spaces available for little get-togethers in university towns. Space, after all, is such a significant *con*cept, so highly—we might call it—aes*thet*ic."

"Space is beautiful, baby," said Heap, whispering, his fingers snapping again, but with less force. At this closer distance Gnossos quite suddenly became aware that the eye under the drooping lid was made of glass and looked always through your head.

"There is a great *deal* of space in this loft, Pappadopoulis, but you must understand my position clearly when I say that this is my first, well, how shall we say, *soirée* in Athené, that I can't be relied upon to produce *all* the people I'd like to have there. While of course I *will* provide refreshments and a certain amount of my Mixture, ha ha, Sixty-nine, if you follow me. Ummm."

"He follows you, baby," said Heap.

"Wha'TIMEsit, anyway?" called Fitzgore from behind the curtain, everyone ignoring him.

"I don't know anybody," said Gnossos.

Both of the men stared.

"I beg your pardon?" from Mojo.

"You want to get laid, go get a pimp."

Heap ceased snapping his fingers again.

"A pimp?" asked Mojo after a moment of silence, pronouncing the word as if he'd never been aware of its exist-

ence, or if he had, that it lay at the outer reaches of some
other untouchable experience. "A pimp? Oh no. No no
nonono, Mr. Pappadopoulis, you must be careful not to
misunderstand me; very careful not to misconstrue my purpose. A pimp, really."

"Anybody can get laid, baby," said Heap, the glass eye
suddenly as rigid as a moonstone in the head of an idol.

"The *theme,* dear boy, is, how shall we say, open to the
public. It is the varia*t*ion, you see, the addition of given dec-
orations, as it were, which my friends and I—"

"Friends?"

"Yes. Yes, of course. Have I failed to mention our traveling companions? Outside. Waiting in the microbus."

"Minstrels, baby," explained Heap, playing with a string
on one of the bamboo window shades, "Poets. Beautiful
cats."

Gnossos went to the window and looked out. Parked at
the curb was a Volkswagen bus full of zombis. Glass fogged
from the inside, shape of bodies moving. Oh bad-ass scene,
get them out of here.

"Look, man," he said finally, pointing the forefinger of
each hand at the noses of the men opposite, "I cool it here,
dig? You never knew anybody so cool. I'm Emir Feisal in
Constantinople in 1916, dig, that's how cool I am. This
whole scene," with a gesture to include the Lairville complex as well as the university itself, "I keep at thirty-seven
degrees Fahrenheit. Average."

"Jeeschris'," yelled Fitzgore, still half asleep, "whyn'hell
don' somebody tell me wha'timesit?"

"You see *him?*" asked Gnossos, leaning across the black
plywood table, plucking the dangling wire to one side so he
could be closer to Mojo's twitching face. "You see that in-

nocent mother with the red hair; you see him waking up in that bed?" With an exaggerated, lying whisper, "He is the nephew of J. Edgar Hoover."

Heap's hand was suddenly on the doorknob, Mojo's was going up and down on his belly.

"And *I* am very, very cool, if you dig. Boy, am I cool."

"Naturally," said Mojo, hanging on, "I don't want to jeopardize whatever little things you have going here, but if at the same time you could in any way manage to fill out this party with what you might call *our* kind of people, after all, Richard Pussy was very impressed—"

"JEESCHRIST!" yelled Fitzgore.

"Let's split," said Heap.

"It would be worth your while, so to speak—"

"Later, man," said Gnossos, letting the lamp swing back, winking at them, jerking his head at Fitzgore, who was stumbling to his feet.

"Yes, of course," said Mojo, "later. And my monographs, feel free to peruse—"

Gnossos closed the door firmly behind them, slid the brass bolt, and watched through the window as Heap slithered to the bus and got into the driver's seat, Mojo waddling behind him, some mysterious figures in the back stirring with the activity, rubbing pale, puffy fists against the fogged glass in order to see the outside world. Here and there a face, white as a mushroom, wrinkling in the light.

"Holy Jesusmotherchris'," complained Fitzgore. "What'n hell kinda roommate you, anyway, Paps? Guy's gotn'eleven o'clock, roomie won't tell 'im the right Jesuschris' time."

"Get dressed."

"Wha'TIMEZIT?"

"Nearly eleven, c'mon hurry up, I want a ride to class."

"Why'nhell did'n you wake me up inna firs'place?"

"Let's GO, man," stepping out of his fraternity-stolen sweatpants and shirt, walking through the kitchen, closing his eyes to the piles of unused vine leaves, moldy egg-and-lemon sauce, empty jars of feta, and sticky coathangers that had been used for shish kebab skewers. He paused in front of the bathroom door, stared at it for a moment, then sighed and went in. Got to keep plugging, so to speak.

"Who were those guys?" called Fitzgore, dressing.

"Selling vacuum cleaners."

"Jesus."

Gnossos had the brown package of Mixture Sixty-nine in his hands. He turned it over absently, sniffing at it now and again as he sat on the pot. How did they find me? That talk about the Buddha. Suppose they really know him? Oxshit. Suppose anyway. And Motherball. Worth it for the connection?

"Paps?"

"What?"

"How's it going in there?"

"How's what going?"

"You know."

Sadistic wart. Still hates me for that dinner. Asking me every morning. Don't answer.

"Paps?"

Restraint, think of something else. Mojo, ugh, almost an odor of evil.

"Paps?"

"What the hell do you want, anyway; and hurry up, it must be after eleven already."

"I just want to know about your, unm, condition."

"No, I haven't shit yet!"

"Oh."

"What the hell do you mean 'oh'?!"

"I just thought you might have. I'm almost ready. What's taking you so long if you're not moving your bowels?"

"Oh gaaaaaaaaaaa . . ."

Gnossos wandered naked back through the kitchen, jumping wildly as his foot squashed a slimy lichee nut and his mind mistook it for a snail. He was pulling on his heavy corduroy trousers when Fitzgore asked, "When are you going to do something about that hermetically sealed window of yours? Let a little fresh air in here at night, place smells like a bluemold factory."

"The window stays."

"It's too stuffy this way."

"Got to seal out the boogiemen, keep it moist and warm."

"You're just spooked 'cause the English girl came and tapped at it one night."

"That's right, man, simple as that. Now come on, get your jacket."

"I mean, she doesn't have to make an *issue* just 'cause you made love to her."

Gnossos stopped while zipping up his parka. Measuring his words, he said: "You and Heffalump, no shit. I wasn't making love to her, I was FUCKING her. The difference is kind, not goddamned degree."

"Semantics. Anyway, I think she's still hot for you. Was she any good? I'm secretly kind of hung up on her."

"Why oh why," asked Gnossos, his eyes imploring the ceiling, his arms extended in supplication, "do I have so many innocuous crosses to bear?"

He spent the remainder of his distracted morning doing implicit differentiation in the company of twelve blooming engineers with brush cuts; then sacrificed a silver dollar for a bowl of bland chili, a Red Cap, a Brown Betty, and a cup of tea. The cinnamon stick was his own and nobody questioned the color of his money. A good thing too. The afternoon slipped by in the Quonset astronomy lab, where he made mud pies on the pretext of reconstructing the craters of the moon. Gets one out among the wandering galaxies, frees the mind from terrestrial concerns. Blooey.

After dark he looked through Ramrod Hall, checked the billiards room, stopped at Larghetto Lodge, trotted across the swaying suspension bridge, stalked the courtyards of the girls' dorms, and searched all over Lairville, trying to find Heffalump, who was only now beginning to shake off the shock of being busted out. Wise mother, though, hanging on in Athené, existence through academic osmosis, eluding the asphalt seas outside.

Gnossos left a note at Guido's, telling Heff to go to David Grün's the following evening. Share the spoils of the day's hunt, get the word on Mojo. Make the party?

There was no one in the pad when he returned, so he made a fire, undressed, and mixed himself a paregoric cocktail with Schweppes and bitters. He also played some easygoing eight-bar blues on his Hohner F, and rolled a slender joint from Mixture Sixty-nine, with an eye to a later nightcap. Study break, he ho.

But Pamela came in the after-dinner hush, sobbing and moaning down Academae Avenue, an Italian switchblade, abalone handle, tucked cleverly away in the folds of her muff. Gnossos, lying awake with L'Hopital's Rule, had paused with a finger at the expression:

$$\lim_{x \to a} \frac{f(x)}{g(x)} = \lim_{x \to a} \frac{f'(x)}{g'(x)}$$

"The relation holds," he was saying again and again in a susurrant murmur, "whether a is finite or infinite." Let a be Gnossos. Then what's the catch, baby?

The last limit, teased his reason, must first *exist*, the word becoming manifest just as he heard a spasmodic whimpering outside the sealed window and felt a chill from groin to scalp. He peered carefully and saw Pamela's slender form silhouetted against the snow. She wore only a flimsy peignoir and seemed to have tossed the muff into the air. Her bony arm high like the Statue of Liberty. Torch, he wondered, still involved with the calculus. But then he scrambled off the bed with a shriek, his hands over the crown of his head, as her sudden change of position revealed the object in her hand. A brick from the Larghetto Lodge pile. He heard the grunt of effort, then a thick, splintering crash, the window shattering into the room, the brick flopping ahead of it, thudding against the wall, knocking the Blacknesse painting from its precarious nail. Gnossos rolled away from the toppling canvas, terrified as the nearly decapitated profile rushed at his own. He banged against the foot of the bed, another whimper reaching his ears. Pamela's switchblade was clacking open through the devastated glass, her hand wielding it potently in a search for his flesh. He leapt to his feet, tripped over the painting, and fell on his back. She had vanished from the window.

The door.

He sprang across the room, cocked his heel against the plywood table, and sent it sliding over the floor as the handle turned and Pamela thundered in, cleared the obstacle with a bound, clutched the peignoir against her throat, and holding the knife by its blade, got ready to throw. Her hair was set in pincurls and pulled the brow away from her face, so her skin looked polished and hideously taut. Her feet clad in silk bedroom slippers, wet and filthy from the melting snow. Another grunt and the knife sang across the long room, Gnossos going over backward again, this time voluntarily, the blade hissing a path over his chest and sinking into the dangling rucksack, pinning it to the French doors.

"Oh," she said in frustration, looking for still another weapon, glancing about furiously, not seeing Gnossos' body flying through the air toward the middle of her own, the fingers outstretched like a dive-bombing Captain Marvel's.

"Ahhhhhhhh!"

They crashed together over the table, against the front door, and rolled to a stop, Pamela's knee thrashing, pumping in a wild attempt to cleave his manhood.

"What's the matter?!" he screamed, ducking her nails.

"OH," she grunted instead, driving the heel of her hand against his stubbly chin to throw him off. He reached around her neck from behind and pressed the ball of his thumb against her nose until she bellowed and ceased.

They lay back, each of them panting, Gnossos stealthily shifting his grip to a hammer lock, Pamela belly to the floor, face buried in the Navajo rug. "Now look—" he began, but the audacious imposition of his even daring to speak sent a jolt of adrenalin rushing through her blood. She kicked free with a snap that went the length of her body, then sprang to the wall, removing one of Fitzgore's just-delivered copper hunting horns. It had no mouthpiece and she ran it at him like a lance, again looking to castrate. Gnossos seized the end and pulled it, deciding what the hell, giving her a choppy left hook in the belly, which stopped her immediately. She sat down on the floor with an oomph sound.

He watched her for a moment, the way he might have watched a simmering tin of nitroglycerin, then shoved his hair over his ears, pulled the knife out of the punctured rucksack, and sat down opposite, pointing the tip of the blade in the direction of her mouth, speaking softly: "Now look, I know you'll probably find this very difficult to believe and all, but if you now try to so much as get up once from where you are or especially to come after me again, I'm going to cut off your lower lip. You got that?"

"He's killed himself!" she shrieked wildly. "He's dead, you lousy son of a bitch, he's killed himself!"

"Who?" asked Gnossos. His stomach suddenly swam with dread. "Who killed himself? What are you talking about, man?"

"Oh, Simon, you bastard, my fiancé, oh *poor* Simon."

Gnossos relaxed the grip on the stiletto. "Are you putting me on?"

"Ohhhhh, Siiiiimon . . ."

"Hey, for God's sake, *you're not serious?*"

She choked and was silent.

"Why, man? What for? What did you tell him?"

"About you," she screamed. "Oh, you lousy son of a bitch, about *you*, that I was in love with you! *OH, SIMON!*" She sprang and this time her knee got him. She picked up the knife and raised it above her head just as George and Irma Rajamuttu stepped into the room, each with a gin and grenadine, their jaundiced eyes calmly inquisitive.

"We thought you might be having a particular party," said George.

"Si*monnn,*" she wailed, collapsing on the butterfly chair.

But the door opened again, almost immediately, and Fitzgore stepped in, books in hand. He looked around the apartment and his jaw fell open. "What the hell's going on? Who broke my new copper hunting horn?"

Gnossos shrugged his shoulders, still on guard, not really

knowing what to say, nursing his groin. The Rajamuttus grinned insanely. And Pamela, in a moment of embarrassed anguish, bleated like a lamb and stumbled to the door.

"Hey," Gnossos said, but she was gone. He tried following but his testicles were having none of it and he groped toward the couch.

Later that night, while roaming the streets in a hopeless attempt to pace away an oily guilt, to purge the accusing picture of Simon sucking an exhaust pipe, he looked into his rucksack for a vial of paregoric to soothe his agitated nerves. But instead he found the Code-O-Graph, neatly sprung in two where it had been sitting, with all innocence of inanimate purpose, in a bed of rabbit's feet. While he was turning it over in his hands it discharged its secret little Captain Midnight spring with a sudden boing, shuddered, and lay lifeless forever.

6

The broad, low-ceilinged gambling hall of a Las Vegas hotel, sour with the predawn odors of stale smoke and all-night people, cigarettes doused and floating in abandoned tangerine cocktails. Here and there snoozing bodies exhaling fumes, crushed paper hats dangling off their ears by rubberbands, lips parted, pressed adhesively against imitation pigskin sofas. Vast muffled silences. The telltale rumble of some not very distant air-conditioning brain, its throbbing pulses muted in the pastured expanse of viridian carpet.

Mammoth crystal chandeliers poised over the deserted gaming tables, never threatened by the rustle of a wind, never to sway or tinkle. The weary group at the blackjack board, alone except for slumbering bodies and early cleanup men, who carried vacuums across the carpet, miles of wire trailing behind them, unplugged.

Eighteen, said the drunken movie star, how's that? His queerly familiar face pale against the splotched green of his dinner jacket, stained by the grasshopper he still held loosely in his hand.

Show him, honey, said the Radcliffe muse.

Why not?

The Oklahoma oil-cowboy watching intently, white Stetson down over his eyes, pausing a moment with his hands beneath the dress of the first strawberry blonde, fingers under the elastic of her lace panties, on her ass.

Hurry an' show him, said the second strawberry blonde, there ain't much time.

Gnossos with a bottle of Metaxa and a plastic magenta straw in his left hand, cards in his right; tennis sneakers, no socks, summer corduroys, stolen boy scout shirt, rucksack over one shoulder; leaning forward as if to guard from an overhead blow, flicking his four cards down on the aqua-felt tabletop, and saying as gently as possible:

Nineteen.

Pausing to check for capitulation before bringing the last stack of three hundred silver dollars from the movie star's side of the table. Grinning as his ear was licked by the approving tongue of the Radcliffe muse. He tucked his chin against her shoulder.

Jus' like in the movies, said the movie star, smile paralyzed in place by decades of exposure to high-frequency arc spotlights, ultraviolet lamps, Las Vegas sun. The Oklahoma oil-cowboy laughing an appreciation for the all-night diversion, his strawberry blonde squirming back against the heavy palm for a little more.

'Sthe game over, Sylvia? asked the other one; we gotta hurry up, there ain't much time.

Gnossos questioning the movie star with an easygoing gesture, waiting for the loser to end the game. The star, in turn, popping the maraschino into his mouth for effect, shrugging, saying, Game's over.

Okay, from Gnossos, telling the drowsing waiter at the bar: Six martinis, birdbath, chilled glasses, Gordon's gin, cocktail onions. Wipe the rims with lemon peel. Big tip. Grinning again as the Radcliffe muse licked his other ear.

Hurry, urged the strawberry blonde, we only got five minutes.

Shut up, Harriet, from the first one, squirming. There's a whole ten minutes to go.

They were standing on the perimeter of an expansive, seemingly endless salt flat, its parched surface cracked and fissured. Each of them staring at a single point on the horizon, delicately poising chilled martinis in their hands. The oil-cowboy with his Stetson eased over on the back of his head, a thumb hooked in a tooled fiesta belt; the strawberry blondes fingering bracelets and rings; the movie star cocking a well-trained eyebrow, striking a pose; the barefoot muse twisting the ends of her long, freely falling hair; Gnossos trembling, lips quivering, trying to control his voluntary muscles, tugging against the weight of silver in his rucksack. From the east, the ocher and orange sun bleeding profusely, steadily, into the semidark transparence of the dawn.

They waited, not speaking, standing line abreast, staring. They all knew it would happen, they had shuffled into the night's end to be witnesses, but when it occurred they were nonetheless surprised.

The sky changed, the entire translucent dome stunned by the swiftness of the shimmering atomic flash. The light drove their once tiny shadows to a terrifying distance in the desert, making them seem like titans. Then it shrank, the aurora crashing insanely backward, like a film in reverse, toppling, swimming into a single white-hot bulge, a humming lump, a festering core. It hovered inches above the horizon, dancing, waiting almost as if it were taking a stoked breath, then swelled in puffing spasms, poking high into the stratosphere, edging out the pale skyrocket vapor trails at either side, the ball going sickly yellow, the shock wave releasing its roar, the entire spectacle catching fire, blazing chaotically, shaming the paltry sun.

In the echo, there was silence.

Then the movie star said, Cheers, raising his glass by the stem in a reverent toast.

It's absolutely *fab*ulous, said the first strawberry blonde.

Gorgeous, said the second.

Show like that costs money, said the oil-cowboy.

God, said the Radcliffe muse, meaning it.

Gnossos watched the flaming sky, his mouth contorted in a twisted grin he could no longer bring under control, his shoulders hunched, teeth chattering, rucksack gone weightless, the stem of his glass clamped perilously in a needle-thin vise of thumb and forefinger.

God Bless America, he thought finally, clamping his eyes shut, unable to do anything physical about the demonic, possessed expression in his soul.

"And all the ships at sea," he added now, out loud. He was standing in the saddle of a small sidehill, high on the main slope above David Grün's farm, the composer's sixteen-gauge shotgun resting with its stock balanced on his shoulder, barrel closed in his gloved hand. Somewhere on the rim of the saddle, Grün's beagle was swinging in a wide circle, calling back hoarse, snappy barks.

The rabbit broke free and skipped down into the saddle, powdering up snow as it jumped, fur still white from winter. Hopping along, ears up, straight at me, not seeing, thinking only of the dog. Where? Shit, too close behind. Turn it.

Gnossos stamped his foot and the rabbit heard the sound, paused, and leapt to the right, the beagle closing fast, yapping furiously, big nose whipping back and forth over the ground. Lead wide, better in the head, meat for the morrow, full choke, David said, squeeeeeze.

The gun whomped, the dog slammed to a momentary halt and the rabbit flopped into the air, its hind legs thumping spasmodically at nothing. There was a single, joyous bark, then the dog sprinted again and continued sniffing, even though he'd seen the animal tumble to a halt. Gnossos let him poke it after he'd done the location by scent, then watched as he tossed it over his end. "Okay, beagle," he said aloud, "that'll do."

He used Pamela's abalone-handled stiletto for the gutting, wincing again in guilt, thinking of his own hair-lined belly, cutting away a front foot for his rucksack. Placate all the gods and demons, finger in every mystical pie. Finally he passed one rear leg through the other at the hock, picked up the carcass with a finger, and stood while the beagle pranced around for a new scent, coaxing the command that would send him off again. Gnossos failing to give it, looking instead at the gray and tepid innards he had scooped out.

They steamed in the cool air and melted in an ugly, uneven pile, down into the snow.

Heffalump was waiting in his stripey French seaman's jersey and faded Levis, rolling with three of David's six daughters before the open, hissing fire. The house was warm and cozy, giving off an odor of children and good food. Gnossos setting the gun, rucksack, and rabbit by the back door just as Grün and Catbird shuffled in from the kitchen with trays of coffee, shortbread, and apple-crumb delights. Everyone smiled.

"So?" asked Catbird, teasing, her hair rolled tightly in a black bun, "you got a bunny?"

"Where where?" squealed the girls, jumping up in pigtails, abandoning the disheveled Heffalump, running to him.

"Goodness' sakes," said David, "such a convention of noises, such a commotion. By the back door, look." The girls scampered away to see as he set his tray by the fire, holding his thick glasses against his nose with a pinky to keep them from falling as he leaned over. Old master of the beer hall, all right. Those sloppy, rummage-sale trousers; always the orange shirt and red suspenders. Catbird slicing the apple strudel, handing out spoons, being efficient, smoothing her flowered peasant dress, padding about shoeless in white ankle socks.

"So?" asked David, "how was young beagle here? He behaves himself properly, comes when you call?"

"He's okay, man, little independent maybe, but we knew things together."

"Ha," murmured Heffalump, cynically.

Grün winked. "So?" looking up while pouring, cheeks red and shiny. "Next fall you use him, then. Come often."

"Next fall?" asked Heff. He'd been testing the texture of a

woolen scatter rug, with twisting fingers. "Who's going to be here next fall, I want to know?"

"Me, baby. Ten years, like Oeuf. Safe and warm."

"Oh yeah?"

"Please," said Catbird, "not like Oeuf. And have some strudel, good and tart."

Gnossos taking the plate from her, asking Heff, "Why 'oh yeah'?"

"I got an insight is all."

"Well save it, you'll need the energy for Cuba."

"It'll keep, don't worry."

"Sugar?" asked David. "Cream?"

The high-ceilinged living room of the old house papered with children's crayoned drawings: improbable long-legged horses wearing happy grins, pumpkins making scary faces, David and Catbird in a sailboat, the house itself, each member of the family waving a flag out his window. All manner of mobiles dangling from the ceiling, Gnossos recalling last year's Halloween, balancing unsteadily on a ladder, roll of masking tape in his hand, brain awash with wassail, willing himself into the childhood that never was, superimposing pictures on his gloomy Brooklyn beginnings: the shifting image of a stocking-capped Greek farmhand boy puttering about in a Grandma Moses seasonal celebration, head in a sky of bottlecap mobiles, boxtop mobiles, mobiles made from seashells, straw flowers, paper rooks and storks, cutout dolls in printed undies, spools of thread, hatpins with rhinestones, earrings, brooches, rice-crispie necklaces, popcorn clusters, dolls' coathangers, miniature mandolins with pegs that turned.

The real instruments were hung around the wood-paneled walls wherever there was an open space, upside down, sideways, right side up, every which way: zithers from Austria, autoharps with painted roses from Sears, plastic ukeleles, guitars, one with twelve strings that David got from Leadbelly, fretless banjos, five-string banjos, banjos with Scruggs pegs, Appalachian dulcimers, lutes, bazoukis, a contra bassoon, two oboes, an alto saxophone, four flutes of different lengths, an Irish harp next to the piano, bongo drums on the mantel, Nigerian talking drums, tablas that Blacknesse had sent from Bombay, a colonial snare drum with peeling, gilded eagles, and a foot-long chromatic harmonica. Children's shoes scattered everywhere, tiny mirrors and combs, dolls by the score, toy baby carriages, building blocks, five colors of edible modeling clay, finger paints, nail polish, pastel beads with holes for stringing, lacquered gourds, dehydrated pomegranates, toppled tricycles, and special jars which could only be meant to contain all the millions shapes, contours, facets, and hopelessly lost memories of juvenescence.

My heyday never truly known, stolen away when my tomtit back was turned, stuffed in a cheesecloth sack, weighted with lead mortality sinkers, sunk in the fetid Gowanus Canal. Offspring the only chance, little Gnossi, but without love, the membrane holds. How long? Unborn children congealing, opiated brain cells whispering "waste," bowels thick with constipated horror. Oh, Thanatos baby, come give your easy kiss, old steel tongue into my mouth, taste the sweet oxide, bury me on a bunny-rabbit sidehill, Grün's pigtailed daughters sprinkling petals on my cindered grave. But nothing grows.

After coffee and strudel David led them on a little walk, nearly a tradition now, old owl knows I need it. Catbird to the kitchen, pots and pans all day, eight mouths to feed, water boiling, formulas brewing, puddings cooking up, meat marinating, lentils soaking, cider aging, things to do.

The greenhouse was moist and warm, smelling of musk and botanical secrets. They entered slowly, David letting Gnossos go first, Towhee still clinging tightly around his neck. There was a feeling of sudden movement among the plants, then nothing. Inside, the floor was a cushion of Irish moss, gleaming with moisture.

"What moved?" asked Gnossos.

"Snakes and frogs," said Tern, squirming ahead now, leading the way into her private domain. "And a toad we got from Fall Creek, me and Kim."

"For insects," explained David. Heffalump had quite suddenly gone pale and was looking over his shoulders, lifting each foot carefully to check what he'd been stepping on. "Geep," he said nervously, looking for an ally, "snakes. Not nice at all."

But fig trees grew, and poinsettias. Wild tulips, windflowers, jasmine, foxgloves, bearberries, pink carnations, sweet sultans, marsh mallows, Syrian mallows, fuchsias, candy tufts, tiger lilies, rhododendron, St.-John's-worts, mimosa, lavender, half a hundred buds and genera Gnossos failed to know. "What's that one?" asked Heffalump, pointing, trying to distract the attention of Sparrow, who was intrigued by the kinky texture of his hair, making a tunnel with her finger.

"From the *Papaveraceae*," said David. "A herb really, with bristles, if you look closely. A poppy."

"Poppy?" asked Gnossos, peering.

"From the corn poppy," he answered, smiling, lifting Kiwi from his shoulders to the ground, picking up the red-flowered plant, and bringing it under each nose for a sniff. "See? Not the dreamy one, the Eurasian flower. That has white petals, sometimes purple; they give, with a capsular fruit, a milky kind of juice."

Motherball's Summer Snow. "Capsular fruit," said Gnossos. "That's where it's at, babies."

"Unh!" yelled Heffalump, leaping into the air. An obese black snake had wormed its way across the space left by the poppy plant, pausing to lift its head and look at them. Tern picked it up, allowed it to glide in a coil around her throat, and said, "Don't be afraid, he won't hurt." Sparrow picking the moment to try and unravel a particularly tight kink of hair. "C'mon, Sparrow, it's only my head!"

"What about my grass?" asked Gnossos, "how's it doing?"

"Ah. Miraculous, you know. Here, see?" David picking up a long-stalked dark green plant with tiny buds on the ends. "Three weeks only, and in such poor soil."

"From little acorns," Gnossos said.

"Under the light, you see, sun in the day, very little water, zoop, it grows."

Gnossos running the palms of his hands around the moist clay pot, gazing with satisfaction. Not too long before harvest, have a country feast, invite the local farmers, do the Brueghel.

"You sure have funny hair," Sparrow finally told Heffalump. He blushed furiously and put her down, pretending interest in a creeper vine.

"Look what I've got," said Kiwi with a wicked smile, walking forward on tiptoes, cupping her hands together in a suspicious ball. She lifted the top hand off and a brown toad croaked, belly bulging in and out. "He eats the nasty worms. And the slugs."

"Eccch," from Heff.

Gnossos looking happily at the flowers again, setting

down the pot of blooming marijuana, running his fingertips along some of the leaves. The girls returned the snakes, frogs, and toads to their secret hiding places and gathered around Heffalump, who was trying miserably to escape out the door without losing face. They teased him with imaginary spiders and crawly things, giggling, sneaking glances at the other men. "C'mon," he tried, "let's go have some ice cream. Anybody want Eskimo pies?"

Catbird joined them on the balustraded porch, holding the new baby, Robin, wrapped in a patchwork quilt. Bobwhite was at her side, clutching her dress, holding a security pillow against her cheek, and sucking a thumb. The sight left Gnossos suddenly delirious. An old dinner bell hung from the side of the house, painted black, the size of a monster pumpkin. He danced up to it, head spinning, legs clearing the heads of the girls as he passed, and swung the clapper with a joyous lunge. The clang was deafening and everyone held his ears.

"David baby," he yelled happily, throwing out his arms, "you old benevolent motherjumper, I love you!"

But the harsh, reverberating noise of the bell woke the baby. She surprised them all with a startling scream of protest.

"There there," from Catbird, soothingly, "it's only Gnossos."

And Tern, acting as spokesman for the other girls, looked at her father—who was adjusting red suspenders so his rummage-sale trousers wouldn't fall down—and asked, "Daddy, what's a motherjumper?"

He wondered, on the way to the town of Dryad, but only a single image occupied his mind's eye and he turned it away. Can't exactly win them all.

They walked together along the moonless road, close against the roadside fence for company of the nighttime traffic, cinders crunching under their boots. Now and again they heard the grunt of an insomniac cow, the sinister croaks of invisible crows flying low above their heads. Gnossos with his rucksack slapping his back, the parka hood around his head giving him the air of a shuffling Carthusian. Heffalump with an army jacket borrowed from David, long skinny hands tucked under his armpits for warmth, squinting ahead of him in the dark, readying a question:

"Why don't we cool this whole thing and go to Guido's, Paps?"

"Guido's is debilitating, man, nothing ever happens at Guido's. You need an Equanil?"

"Skip the crap, what are we even bothering for, parties come cheap."

"Masochism, baby. Little evil."

"Jesus."

"It's an alternative. Got to step up and talk to it, see what it has to say."

"To you, maybe."

"The cat's probably out to make home movies of you and your old lady, different positions, variations on a theme, who knows? Did you see his microbus around town? Those zombis in the back? Creatures of the night, man, blooming in the moonshine."

Heff ducking as a surprised crow flew directly at them and veered away. He nodded silently, hands going into pockets. "Zombis."

"They've got it all down, Aquavitus man; even the cat with the opal in his forehead, from Havana, whatever they call him."

"Buddha," came the snappy reply, then a frown as he began walking faster. "C'mon, you think I got all night?"

"Stay loose, man."

"Loose, that's right. Ha," spitting. Something wrong?

"Little meprobamate, just the thing for your head."

"Take gas."

"What's up, man?"

His head shaking, foot kicking at the road.

"Heff?"

"What?"

"Something bugging you?"

"Nope."

"It's only that I thought something might be bugging you."

Heff stopping suddenly at the sarcasm, turning to face Gnossos in the dark. "Look, Paps, you're my ace buddy and all that but I've already told you about Jack, so cool it, okay?"

"What?"

"I dig the chic, I'm in love with her."

"Hey, man, I don't know what you're talking about."

"Jack, I'm talking about Jack."

"So?"

"So it's bad enough she fools around with other chics without you talking about her and me and positions, that's what."

Gnossos catching on, booming out a surge of laughter, poking Heffalump forcefully in the stomach, making him double over and cough. "Oh, splendid Heffalump, decadent old boogie."

Heff uncoiled at the word, hissed, and took off after Gnossos, who was bounding away, yelling back, "Help help, a heffable horralump; horr horr—"

Two cars came speeding around the turn at their backs, horns blasting, one passing the other, tires on the shoulder of the road. They had to leap out of the way, arms flying, both of them landing in a plowed but virgin snowdrift. They lay panting until the sound of the cars had vanished, Gnossos giggling to himself, chin tucked against his chest.

"Oh, you're bad-ass shit, all right," said Heff, raising himself momentarily out of the drift, not wanting to be there, then sinking back resignedly as his elbow slipped. Gnossos rose, still giggling, and strolled back the ten yards between them, flopping down again.

"Okay, baby, where's the insight?"

Silence. Then, in an annoyed voice: "Don't provoke me."

"I'm straight, I want to know whatever you meant at Grün's."

Heff checking for facial expression, inflection. "You're provoking me."

"No, man, I'm the soul of nonviolence. Dig me lying here in the wet, at peace."

"You said you'd be around next fall, that's all."

Gnossos giggling again, making a wet snowball, tossing it out on the road. "Oeuf does it, no reason why I can't."

"No, I guess not."

"C'mon, wise-ass."

"And what about all these maniac hangups you've got— secretly, mind you, but got all the same—with Morality and Conduct, and like that?"

"Hangups?"

"This whole neurotic *syn*drome about love. What's going to happen is you'll get dosed, as if I'm telling you something you don't already know. And you can't just say you're making this party tonight because of some clinical interest in

Mojo and his weirdo helper. That's a lot of crap too. You'll fall by just on the off-chance you'll meet the absolutely A-number-one apocalyptic love of your life, and walk off into a field of cherry blossoms or some shit. Man, you *know* you're pulling for the big one and don't tell me different."

"Oh come on, Heff."

"Or maybe not cherry blossoms, maybe Oriental poppies with that corpuscular fruit."

"Capsular."

"All the same junk. So why couldn't you get hung up on this Pamela chic and save yourself a lot of dosing? Least you can do, a little expiation for the blood on your hands, Seymour, Simon, whatever the cat's name was—which you can't pretend you're not a little paranoiac about. Fitzgore'll grab her while you're waiting."

"Hey look—"

"Probably you're not able to, excuse the expression, love her any, 'cause you're worried that your *approach* was too crude to begin with—stomping in on her the way you did. And what the hell are you going to do for a living when you get out of here? You don't have a dime, sweetheart, and you never did, outside of those scholarships you somehow conned—"

"Won, baby," corrected Gnossos, "in competitive exams—"

"—and nobody," continued Heff, barreling right over him, "nobody's going to give you squat, and you know it."

"Stipend. Grants. The Ford Fruit, the Guggenheim Vine."

"Tell me about it."

"What for, man, where's the percentage?" Gnossos falling silent momentarily as another set of headlights glowed dully on the horizon, grew brighter, then poked away into the night. "You're out to bring me down. You have any grass with you, by the way?"

"And that's another thing, that escapism syndrome. You watch and see, you'll be mainlining, man, in a year and a half you're gonna have trackmarks right down into your fingertips. Lying around on old newspapers in a Detroit hotel, with a neon sign blinking in the window on your collapsed veins, with a poppy pipe in your mouth."

"Stimulates the soul."

"Don't talk to me about soul, Paps. You go out and roll it around so it gets all dirty on U.S. Forty and then flee back to Athené to get purified. That poor monsignor didn't know what he was getting into."

"My senses, man, he cleaned out my senses, not my soul. Greek senses need reawakening every so often. And anyway, he was accomplishing his function."

"So what?"

"So he at least knows what his function is, and that puts him one up on you and me."

"Jargon."

"Vision, baby, that's all I'm after. Having a night light on all the time so's I can see."

"Be satisfied with the sun."

"I want to *be* the sun, schmuck. Particles, wave, and source."

"Yeah, and where do you fit it all in, Pythagoras?"

"You bet your ass where. Tight in the old womb-bag, if I could get one big enough to creep into." Gnossos reaching into his rucksack and pulling out a piece of strongly smelling goat cheese from Greece, old rabbit hairs and pieces of lint stuck to the mold. "Right here, baby, look at what

comes out, examine the texture. You smell it? Not very idyllic, true? A piece of old cheese with Saltine crumbs, that's
about the best I can do."

"So split for Athens, Mykonos, someplace groovy."

"With what? About as much heart as you'd have getting
on the British steamer for Nairobi? No thanks. Exemption,
baby. Walk among the diseased with Immunity. A little
knowledge-in-the-abstract is all. With any luck, a vision
every seventh day or so. Keep your senses hanging out, dig a
little."

Heff nodding, but without much assurance.

"Of course there's a rule of thumb that goes along with
that."

"Yeah?"

"Skip the Small Shit."

"Yeah."

"You know what I mean?"

"I heard you."

"You ever dig Washington crossing the Delaware?"

"All's I want to do is get to Havana, man, I don't want to
know anything about George Washington. I mean really,
who is that, George Washington?"

Gnossos popping the goat cheese into his mouth, shrugging. "Enough said. Let's go to this party."

They lifted themselves, wet and shining from the drizzle,
stomping their boots, just as a truck lumbered by and fixed
their forms in the conical glare of its lights. They watched
their shadows roll along the falling mist behind them. Then
Heffalump, after a moment's hesitation, gave Gnossos a
perfectly dry, solidly packed paregoric Pall Mall from his
wallet. "Pax," he said. "Before I have to punch you in the
mouth."

"Thanks, man, you're so sweet."

They shared the joint while walking, speaking not another word.

Oobop shebam.

7

The rain fell in sudden, torrential sheets, barreling out of the low-flying clouds. Gnossos and Heffalump breaking into a run to escape it, sprinting the last few yards from the road to the protection of the barn, glancing around through the lashing wind to make certain the place was right.

They stood shivering in an arched doorway, stamping their feet, wiping their faces free of the wet. The windows of the loft glowed above them, a soft orange color through the burlap squares strung across the panes. Lamps burning on the floor, no doubt, pointed at the walls, indirect hipster decor, always the same. The barn was next to the Dairy Queen, as Mojo had said, wispy thread of irony there, proximity to frozen-custard machines. A squat, angular building with a mammoth vanilla cone balanced on its sloping roof, entrances all boarded up, looking inert and functionless. A deformed glass egg abandoned the instant after laying, dropped unceremoniously to the earth by some huge, clattering aluminum bird.

"Ground zero," said Heff, shaking out his soaking jacket.

Gnossos nodded, looking for something to dry his hair with. He indicated the large number of cars parked by the road: no care for their placement, look of a party to them.

The microbus had been moved to a patch of dry ground under a dense grove of sycamores, secure position, half hidden from sight, snow shoveled away, ready to flee. Exercise caution, old sport, the furies are never asleep. Who to be? Green Arrow, Billy Batson? Plastic Man still best, do the metamorphosis, be a Mingus side, feel the crystal vibration in my grooves, spindle poking through the brain, reincarnation of a lovebird, three-four time, funk in a rocking chair.

They climbed the worn, surprisingly well scrubbed wooden stairs to the loft and paused before a heavy oak door. Everything too clean-looking for a barn, smell of disinfectant, no farmy odor, no snatches of old hay. Murmurs from the party within, sudden surges of laughter, glasses tinkling through the hubbub. A faint, then increasingly stronger, scent of smoldering pot. Heff made a sniffing sound. "Hey, man."

"Yeah," said Gnossos, "I just got the breeze myself." A comforting nutlike aroma, smoky, autumn leaves.

"Lot of cars down there, where'd he get all the people?"

"Who knows, Celebrity Service maybe."

The oak door was built to slide sideways on heavy-duty casters and it took both of them to roll it back. On the other side was a small vestibule, built for protection against winter, and another door, more conventional, opening into the party. Gnossos put his ear against it, waited for another surge of laughter, shrugged, and went in.

For a moment he could barely see through the smoky, polarized haze. Heff stepped in behind him, colliding, blinking, fanning his hand in front of his face. "Wow," he said.

The place was full of zombis.

One wall of the loft had been cleared of plaster, wirebrushed, and taken down to the ancient brick. Gnossos paid brief attention to what might have been a piece of frontal sculpture, a lumpy frieze, then shifted his cautious gaze. Above him was a skylight, its glass panels surfaced with different-colored sheets of translucent plastic to make it appear stained. Beams across the ceiling, antique, but too antique, blowtorch no doubt, knots and burls chiseled in, clever atmosphere. A hairy little man squatted on a silk pillow in the middle of the floor, wearing a V-necked teeshirt, holding a guitar limply in his hands. A bubbling narghile rested on a brass platform at his side, one of its many mouthpieces pursed in the man's lips.

Pallets on the floor, covered with Indian prints and burnt-sienna burlap, zombis on the pallets. Japanese bamboo mats, here and there a foam rubber cushion stained with spilled liquids, crushed fruit, spent love. Zombis on the cushions, each of them from the back of the Mojo microbus; leaning on the brick wall; lounging against a masonite collage; hovering by the narghile. Twin vampires with Egyptian eye makeup knelt by an icebox-size polyphonic speaker, digging sounds too muted to distinguish. Couples dancing on the bare floor, but not exactly dancing, more like shifting their weight around the common focus of their welded navels, rubbing.

"Very domestic little scene, wouldn't you say?"

"Lovely," said Heff.

But something out of key, in abeyance. Jaded energy only potential in the smoke-filled air. Too many students, straight as arrows, smoking legit cigarettes. Surely they know? That one with the boobs, dancing with what's his name, the editor. Lumpers, Judy Lumpers. And that South American ring-ding with his sequined rodeo shirt, they couldn't be heads. The orgy?

"Where's it all at?" asked Heff, picking up the thought.

"I don't know, wrong party maybe." But then he knew. Mojo, dressed in the same clothes he'd worn the previous morning, still carrying the bullwhip-fastened briefcase handcuffed to his wrist, was leading a girl through the haze, into a doorway at the far end of the loft. The girl had already stepped over the threshold when he noticed them, too late for Gnossos to recognize her. At that precise moment the record changed and the zombis paused with a collective hush, their voices falling silent in the absence of diversionary sound. Mojo failed to realize the quiet in time, retained the volume of his inflection, and offered a delicate joint from his tweed jacket to the girl on the other side of the small metal door. Her phthisic hand reached back across the threshold, and his faltering, anxious voice became clearly audible in the hush: "Like a kiss is how, dear girl; wanton lips against the flesh, then suck."

There were snickers and a quick, interrupted laugh. Mojo grinned nervously, showed his missing tooth, and stepped inside with a quick, weasel-like shifting off of weight. The door closed as the next record began, and conversation resumed its earlier level. Nonetheless Gnossos was able to distinguish a particular sound, unmistakable in intent: the clacking of a bolt jumping securely into place.

He turned to speak to Heff but Heff was staring at the brick wall in horror. Gnossos looked as well, and a scalding chill swam through the viscous fluids of his bowels like an evil fish. The frieze on the wall was not a frieze.

It was a spider monkey.

"Proust," said Heap, who had materialized at their side. They both jumped at the name. "What?"

"That's his name, guys. The monkey."

"Proust?" asked Heff.

"He's asthmatic, digs being alone. Has a weak bladder. Don't get too close."

Not a chance, sweetheart, came the thought, Gnossos clutching his groin to hex away the dangers of the under-world.

"We turn him on," whispered Heap, snapping his fingers leisurely, picking up the rhythm he'd abandoned the day before. "But only by stages, slow degrees. He's beautiful, baby, you really can't touch his head with the mixture any more. Digs lysergic shit, you ever make that? Mix it with a little banana purée, never know the difference. Eats horse for breakfast, sprinkles it over his Kix, so to speak. Can't sniff it though, bad for the bronchial tubes. Next week we shoot him up." Leaning closer, lowering his whisper, "He's gonna get a flash, let me tell you." The glass eye looking directly through Gnossos' head.

"He likes it all right?" asked Heff seriously, staring at Heap, whom he'd never seen before that moment.

"Little shit never hurt nobody," said the teenager, his good eye drooping, snapping his fingers extra loudly for emphasis. "Specially Proust, man."

Gnossos pulled up on his scrotum one last time for cosmic insurance. He edged away from the wall, trying to widen the distance between himself and the monkey, then smiled idiotically at one of the vampires who looked back at his groin-clutching hand. He put it quickly into his pocket, checking all the walls and shadows for possible mandrills. One never seems to know, does one?

In a dark corner Jack was prone on a couple of pallets. Gnossos checked to see whether Heff had found her, but Heff was still staring at Heap, trying to figure out what he was. Jack, on the other hand, was somewhat out of her mind, eyes glazed over, a matchstick-thin joint burning down in her fingers. She wore brine-shrunk Levis, a man's yellow Oxford shirt, and loafers. Her Joan of Arc hair was messed and her hand lay casually on another's girl's thigh.

It was the girl in the green knee-socks.

"Proust," said Jack, picking the word up from Heap, who had just whispered the name again. She started to giggle. So stoned, man, old euphoria factory. Selective ears, the sounds of certain words shifting senses, becoming delicious, rolling, tumbling through the Eustacian tube, tapping at the pharynx, pronunciation palatable.

But the girl in the green knee-socks.

Beware the monkey-demon, came the entirely undesired thought.

"Ppppprrroust," said Jack again, blubbering the *P*'s, holding the giggle deep within her chest, pulling for the resonance. Swing, sweetie-pie, you're the only one who knows.

"P-p-p-prooooooooooooooss . . . t."

The spider monkey was dangling upside down by the tail, hanging from an iron rod sunk into the brick wall, playing with itself, rolling its eyes, lifting its thick upper lip high above the gum linc.

As it turned out, the girl in the green knee-socks had also seen. She had been clasping her throat gently, shielding it, seemingly, from razors or teeth. But when the monkey again turned its back and curled into a harmless ball, she let the hand fall delicately between her legs, in a position of repose. It was a dancer's gesture.

She looked directly at Gnossos and said, "It does the same to you, I can tell. It's evil, you know."

He nodded, staring. I wouldn't exactly call it a cherub, either.

Jack took a last puff from the roach and laid it carefully on top of an unopened Red Cap at her side, letting the fingers of her free hand trail over the girl's thigh. Detached look, no sex in it, feeling for the texture alone, making touch a separate thing. A raga was playing through the huge speaker, people were trying to dance to it, keep the rubbing going, but Jack listened only to the tabla:

dum . . . budoom . . . duuooum . . . bum-douym-dooom . . . scscscsciiiinnnng.

"Mmmmm," she said, forsaking the thigh, transferring the beat to her pallet.

Satisfied that she was no longer the object of this other attention, the girl in the green knee-socks stood up, looked once at Jack's drumming fingers, and wandered over, just like that.

"Hey, what's up with Jack?" asked Heff, suddenly between them, hands in his pockets.

"Stoned, it looks like."

"Oh *shit*, Paps, what the hell for?"

"How would I know, man? You tell me."

"She didn't mean to," said the girl, a glass of white wine going to her lips. "She got impatient waiting for you."

"Oh wow, you see? What the hell did I say? We should've hitched a ride."

Looking at me over the rim. Could it be?

"Hey, Jack," said Heff, stroking her brow. "Jackie baby?"

"Ooooo," came the answer.

"She's beautiful," from Heap, materializing with one of the Egyptian-eye-makeup vampires, "leave her be."

The vampire played with the zipper on Gnossos' wet parka and asked, "Who're you?"

"Ravi Shankar," he said.

"Hey," from Heap. He had a stained forefinger on the shoulder of the girl in the green socks. "You feel like dancing, maybe fool around a little?"

She looked at Gnossos while she spoke an unmodified "No."

"I dig foreigners," said the vampire. "What kind of name is that? Ravi. So exotic."

"Armenian," answered the girl.

"I was talking to Ravi," said the vampire.

"Oooooooooo," said Jack, coming around, looking into Heff's concerned face. She giggled, threw back her head, and pulled him over so he crashed on top of her.

"She's a real groove, baby," said Heap, abandoning the girl momentarily, tapping Heff on the back, referring to Jack. "You wanna make it somewhere else, go someplace quiet?"

"Let's dance," said the vampire to Gnossos, toying with his collar. "Maybe fool around a little."

"Look—" he started.

"There's another room," she said.

"Hey, Jack," yelled Heff, squirming, imprisoned, "for Jesus Christ's sake!"

"I like it in here," said Gnossos, looking at the girl, openly this time, from top to bottom, letting her know, covering every inch of it, brown hair bound by a brass clasp, blue denim shirt rolled to the elbows, black skirt, green knee-socks, no shoes for the moment. When he came back up, there was a tolerant smile waiting, head tipped to one side. Too good, much too good.

"*Oh,*" said Judy Lumpers, skipping over in tennis sneakers. "You *fi*nally came. Juan said you were *com*ing and I couldn't wait to tell you how *real*ly great that night at

Guido's was, I mean *God*, all those radio programs, I'd practically forgotten all about them."

"Evening," said Drew Youngblood soberly, his white shirt open at the throat.

"Soon," said Juan Carlos Rosenbloom, "there will come a revolutiong."

"There's another room, baby," Heap was whispering to the embarrassed Heffalump. "Awful lot happening there." He was snapping the fingers of his left hand and holding out a joint in his right. Gnossos took it and struck a match without ceremony. Whole thing's falling to pieces, cool it, liable to be conflicts. Do the Gandhi.

"Listen," said Judy Lumpers, eyes agog, nudging him, tone confidential, "that's not what I think it is, is it, that, well, *ci*garette you're holding?"

"I don't know, baby, just a little mixture my tobacconist throws together, ha ha."

"Ha ha."

"No nicotine," explained the girl in the green knee-socks, sipping from her wine.

"Ha ha," continued Judy Lumpers, not going for it at all, lowering her tone, winking, "what does it make you *do?* Does it make you do anything?"

"Beautiful things, baby," said Heap, abandoning Heffalump, smiling at her, showing his missing tooth. With his good eye drooping, he held out the fattest tapered joint Gnossos had ever seen.

"Oh, I *could*n't," she said, holding up her hand, looking at Gnossos for the word. Why not?

"Make it," he told her, winking back. "It's a gas." He took a drag from his own, no carburetion, and held it down.

"We'd kind of like to unm, talk with you," interrupted Youngblood, "before you get too, well—"

"This Panghurts," said Juan Carlos Rosenbloom. "We smash her, you watching."

"Should I *really* try it?" asked Lumpers, Heap leading her away to one of the empty foam rubber cushions as she asked, the battle already won, "I mean, can't it make you do something you don't *want* to?"

Jack was wrapping her still-clad legs around Heff's back, pinning him above her. "I wanna get laid," she said, grinning madly into his bulging eyes. "Lay me."

Another drag, maybe flee, steal someone's car.

"Good shit, ain't it?" asked the vampire.

"Dynamite, baby, but get your paws out of my pocket."

The monkey uncoiled and leered at them.

What in my hand?

He looked down at his side and found his fingers entwined with others. They belonged to the girl in the green knee-socks, who was looking not at him but at the monkey.

She was actually holding his hand.

Finally she looked at Gnossos and asked in a gentle, but preoccupied tone, "Could you get me out of here a little?"

At the far end of the loft an anonymous couple had just stepped over the body of the hairy little man with the narghile and entered the chamber with the metal door. Again there was the sound of a clacking bolt.

The quarter tones of the sitar rose and fell across the drone of conversation. The spider monkey emitted a sharp, shattering squeal and urinated on the wall.

Judy Lumpers had the joint in her mouth, drawing. She looked up at him, shaking her head to indicate that just yet, nothing much was happening. He touched her brow with a thumb and zipped up his parka.

"If you have a moment—" Youngblood began.

"Maybe later, man."

The editor looked at the South American, who nodded and said, "We wait."

"Don't hold your breath," he told them. Then to the girl: "C'mon, man," taking her by the hand, bringing her out into the night.

Mustn't ever let a chance go by.

8

At the Black Elks downtown there was nobody else white.

They went there directly from the loft in a stolen Anglia, pausing only for traffic lights and every other stop sign. Test the odds, keep your hand in play. Gnossos had been away for over a year, but they remembered him at the door and made a show of his return. Everybody gave some skin all around and the menace went out of the night like bad-egg fumes through a bleeder valve in a gale-force sea breeze. He gave a little of the Mojo mixture to Fat Fred Faun, who took care of the peephole; a little to Spider Washington, who blew vibes, and a little to Southside, who checked hats whether or not you wore one. Saint Nicholas feeding the pussycats.

"Groovy chic," he explained in a whisper, "keeps a razor in her brassière."

"What about you?"

"She digs me, baby, I'm all right."

And the Elks who didn't know him knew him soon

enough. They came over, saying, "We heard about you, man" and "What's happening?" And he'd say, "This is Kristin McCleod; she hasn't been around here before," giving out the grass as he spoke; and they'd look over her green knee-socks and say it was all right, everything was cool, have a sweet time with Sophocles, their name for Gnossos. But Pooh Bear was what she called him, just the same, ignoring his uneasy protests, not going for the keeper-of-the-flame business, saying no, she wouldn't have it, vestal virgins fed the fire, and he didn't get the part. Fat Fred Faun at the peephole, who had once listened to an eighty-minute monologue on membranes, giggled and told her, "You talkin' to the right head all right, if you talkin' flame-keepin' an' like that to Sophocles." Gnossos trying to cover it up by asking Spider Washington for Night in Tunisia, being careful how he put it, since Spider had cut the lip off a blonde Deke in a white seersucker suit three years before and still wanted the club black.

"He doesn't look mean," Kristin whispered.

"Baby, there's just no such thing as a bad boy."

So Spider played it for them and they danced, Gnossos showing her how but coming on no stronger than he had to.

"Not a bad fit," she said, pressing cautiously against him.

"That's right," he answered, trying to do something with his maniacal, toothy grin, feeling better every minute.

And Kristin, who was also grinning, said, "I like your friends. Better than the crowd at the barn, I mean." She was smoking a straight Philip Morris, keeping her arm around his neck, having to bring her mouth over his shoulder, close to his throat, whenever she wanted a puff. Gnossos had stopped smoking anything but was still high enough for a rolling buzz. "Bad-ass scene, that loft. Monkeys, baby, monkeys and wolves, I'll tell you all about it sometime." The clapboard room was dark except for a single neon tube that glowed against the purple ceiling, angular chromatic designs splayed over the fissured surface, reflected there from the crumpled yard of aluminum foil that served as indirect-exposure motif. Twice a train rumbled by the downstairs window, not six feet from the building, Lehigh Valley going nowhere, whistle blasting its ominous discord with the alto sax. The Elks and their women were dressed in narrow suits and pug bowties and high heels and chukka boots and Mother Hubbards and short skirts, and little hats like Fat Fred's, brims down against the ears, everybody dancing or sitting around taking it easy.

They took a table finally, letting their knees touch beneath it, ordering drinks. Kristin clasped her hand around his forearm, the same hand she had used at the loft when the vampire had had her hand in his pocket, then tried bringing him closer so she could whisper again. But he went over too quickly and they bumped heads, crashing against the space between each other's eyes. Fat Fred looked as if he would roll on the floor and Spider Washington lost so much control he had to give away his solo.

"Ouch, man," came the chuckle.

"Oh, I'm sorry—"

"It's like an anvil, wow—"

"I didn't mean—"

Rubbing the spot, "That's okay, only our heads."

"Really, are you sure?"

"It's all right. Dry your tears, can't bear to see women weep."

She laughed, and wiped her eyes with a sleeve. "I'm glad they thought it was funny, anyway."

Gnossos watching her carefully, listening for a hint, an

echo of something insipid in the inflection, hoping in fact to find it, wanting the flaw. But there was nothing. Sow a seed of cynic, pocket full of lye. Her eyes were marble-brown and confounded his attempts at metaphor. Pictures instead, animated in gilded baroque frames. In bed, wearing a flowered muslin nightdress that buttoned to her throat, her loafers tumbled sideways on the floor. Satin sheets, a monster of a goosedown quilt for snuggling; her grandmother's patches looking like the loamy fields out the window. Old pennies tossed under the pillow for luck, features rubbed smooth, good for finding in the morning, copper warm from her body. Mustn't let them fall on the rug, luck would run out, perish in a vacuum cleaner.

"You like it here okay? No menace?"

"With you, no. I mean yes, no menace."

"It's all in front, man, they have a heart thing going for them, comes from having the Man around all the time, too many enemies. Heffalump's the cat to talk to, not me. C'mon, let's dance some more, I like the way you move around."

"We fit," she told him again.

And without unreasonable effort they slid into Wednesday Night Prayer Meeting, Spider playing it in lazy three-four time, Gnossos' particular preference in tempos, keeping the blue chords under the whole while, letting Murtagh on cornet tease the melody into what sounded like the southeast end of Nashville and all the way home again. They danced throughout the entire trip, their heads describing syncopated arcs.

Drinks were waiting at the table, and recognizing them Gnossos said: "Man I don't believe it. Rye and mother ginger, too splendid." He sat down satisfied, slapping his leg;

Kristin not seeming to understand but seeing his pleasure, coming around to him, putting her arms over his shoulders, and appreciating the finger he dunked into one of the glasses. He tested the drink with his tongue, remembered the taste from his childhood in Brooklyn, shrugged away the memory, and took a sip. She flicked his hair back from over his ears, and Southside came over with a card that read Compliments of the House. He could see from her eyes where she'd been.

"Some powerful grass," she told him.

"It's a mixture, honey, you won't believe it, they call it Mixture—"

"Sixty-nine," she cackled, then repeated it, "Sixty-*nine*," pointing at him with a long, bangled finger, shaking it, making them all laugh together. (At different things, he tried to remind Kristin with a glance, all at different things. Her hands were still on his neck and she squeezed, perhaps reading his meaning. Too good, it's all too good.) "Southside," he said, "you know who this is?"

"No, man," she said, looking lazily at Kristin, who was still not sitting down.

"This is Piglet, honey, you know who Piglet is?"

"Piglet?" she asked. "What's Piglet?"

"Right here," using his thumb to show.

"That there?"

"That's Piglet."

"What's happening, man?"

"You want to know?"

"Give me the word."

"I'll tell you true."

"Lay it right down."

"She turns me on."

"Yeah?"

"She turns me *on*, man."

"Yeah," said Southside, "you know what's happening, all right. This boy here," talking to Kristin, "he lay it down, we pick it up. He got the mixture—"

"Sixty-nine," said Kristin, still standing behind Gnossos at the table, pressing her stomach against his back through the slats in the chair.

It came up like a periscope. "Let's dance again," she said.

Jesus, impossible to stand, getting longer. "Have some highball, relax a little." Southside, in a white linen dress, belted out a sudden, high-pitched laugh, the squeal soaring right over the threshold of hearing, then stood and pranced around them both. "Daynce?" she asked finally, "daynce? Man, that Sophocles ain' gonna be able to *walk*." She pranced right back to her chair and sat down, sipping once from each of their glasses.

Change the subject, think of Santa Claus, baseball, someone will see. "Sixty-nine," he began but as soon as he spoke the name, Southside shrieked again and fell over backward in her chair. She lay on the floor, giggling, her high-heeled shoes sticking up in the air, her hands on her stomach. Spider was playing Lonesome Avenue and couples were dancing. Gnossos picked her up with the assistance of Fat Fred, whose huge, oil-barrel belly was hanging over his belt. "No, honey," he tried again, laughing with her, "I only wanted to know how you knew the name."

"Name, man?"

"Of the mixture, baby."

She fell over again, screaming with delight, and this time they all left her there because she looked as if she wanted it that way.

At the peephole, when they were putting on their coats to leave, Fat Fred wrapped his heavy arms around them and asked, "Gnossos man, this is some powerful shit you got goin' here. You mean to tell me," lowering his voice, pulling them closer, "that this here's the article?" His little maroon hat was pushed over on his eyebrows.

"Like I said, Fred."

"Man, you're the lily of the valley."

"Amen," said Kristin, surprising both of them.

"You've had it before?" from Gnossos, fishing.

"Man, ain't nobody round here ever got none of this since Spider's baby brother made it in Cuba. They got a cat, man, you wouldn't believe, call him the Buddha, somethin' like that."

"That right?"

"Ain't nobody ever seen that one. He got the opal in his forehead. He wear the robes, he has the gold chain on his neck from the Masai, man. An' he big. Come on like King Kong, they talk about him. But ain't nobody seen him is the thing. He cruises in the night, man, he got secrets, he never out of the shadows. Some say that what he does, he meditates."

"He's the rosebud," said Gnossos.

"That's right," said Fat Fred, "maybe the last one of the bunch too. An' this here's his shit you laid on us tonight, don't tell me no different. All's I know is who's the lily of the valley. Little skin, man."

They shook hands again, Gnossos holding a flap of the parka in front of him with an elbow, the erection having only slightly wilted. Fred checked the peephole and opened the door, everyone waving a lazy so-long except for Southside, whose feet were still sticking straight up into the neon-colored air. Once again they stepped through the night, feeling their way.

The only light in the burnished room came from a damp, sizzling fire. It shone just brightly enough to throw their shadows over the Navajo rug, across the floor, past the plywood table, and up against the door. But still he hadn't touched her. Now and again a coal hissed out of the fire with a crackling pop, arched through the air, and bounced on the rug. Whenever it happened, they took turns scooping it up with spoons and tossing it back. Their faces flickered in the warm coral, yellow, white, violet, blue, and black. Gnossos lay on his spine for temptation, hands folded under his head, nose not eight inches from Kristin's knees. She sat on her heels, and the length of firm, nearly hairless skin between the top of her socks and the hem of her skirt drove him to quiet distraction. He bent a leg to cool the old scope. Ambivalent ploy, he'd never hidden it before. The Radcliffe muse bringing his coffee to the magenta motel room the morning after the bomb, wearing her flowered muu-muu, padding in barefoot, long black hair brushing the tray. Zoom, up it had gone, propping the sheet like a mizzenmast: Ship ahoy, she had said, what's that? her guess entirely correct.

"What are you thinking?" asked Kristin.

"Who, me?"

He looked at the fire just as a coal popped onto the rug. Kristin leaned over his chest to get it. He could have held her there but he hesitated. Then she was out of reach and it was too late. "That wolf I mentioned once, that's all."

"The fantasy kind?"

"No, baby, the Adirondacks."

She smiled. "Judy mentioned something about that. All your friends thought you were dead."

"Who's Judy?"

Kristin making a sign of huge breasts, blanking her face to look like the Lumpers girl.

"Oh yeah. Trying to will me out of the picture." Maniac Greek safer as a legend.

"Will you?"

"They all want me down, dig? Give them something to talk about at Guido's."

"But you sound bitter. You're supposed to like taking chances."

"That's right. Makes the nights better. Like when nothing else is happening, you court the doom-beasties, you know?"

"Not exactly. How could I?" she asked. Three fingers of her right hand went to his shoulder, then back to the rug. "How could anyone really, when you love talking in ciphers? Couldn't you just *tell* me?"

"Show you, maybe. Pooh leading Piglet through the Hundred Acre Wood, and all like that."

Her eyes reading the implication, letting only part of it in. "But tell me anyway, can't you?"

Gnossos looking down, being silent for a long while, what the hell, no time for anything else. Old teller of tales. He traced the pattern of the rug with his spoon. One direction, then the other. "There was a lake, for one. That's where it's really at, the lake. But you've got to have it out in front. You're sure you want to get all involved?"

"Probably. A little at a time."

"Yeah, okay. Close your eyes."

"My eyes?"

"That's right." He checked and she had. "Now, it's winter

to start with, like Christmas cards, pine trees, everything gray-white and hazy-looking."

"Is it snowing?"

"No, man, it's too cold. Everything is quiet, kind of gloomy, nothing moving at all. You don't even suspect motion, it's so still. You know about still?"

"I think so."

"Okay, the lake is frozen about four inches, maybe more, strong enough for a horse and cutter, if you dug that. You could make a run three miles, easy, to the north, and a mile, oh, three quarters of a mile, across. Now, right in the middle, very erect, like a natural fortress of some kind, there's this pine island. The trees are really spectacular, they go up ninety feet, and all the branches are on top, sagging from the weight of the snow."

"Yes, it's getting easier."

"Only, don't let the island idea throw you. You can walk out to it, right? The lake is frozen, you can step up on one shore and down off the other. In the mornings, this is providing you get up, you can watch the mink, sometimes ermine, run out and disappear. You have to keep your eyes closed now, no peeking, it's all in the palpebral vision if you want a buzz."

"I promise."

"Think of the snow on the lake then. Powdery, light, high, good for snowshoes. Sometimes the wind dips in and spins it off in these giant swirls, like the runners on an alpine sleigh. Can you make the lake at all? There's a cabin with wood smoke coming out of it, just on the shore there, smoked-up windows, tracks around it, a woodpile, and like that."

"Umm," she answered, grinning, her hands holding her elbows. "What kind of sky is there?"

"Gray, very low. If you have a nose for this kind of thing, you know there's snow in the clouds. But it can't come down because of all the cold out in front. You make the lake, for instance, to chop through the ice for drinking water, and the snow under your boots is squeaky. That's where the cold is at. Below zero, but you don't know how much. All right, for a long time you're into rabbits, sometimes birds, partridge, they're all in the trees, the partridge I mean, from the cold, it's too frozen to find food on the ground and they have to eat buds, mostly spruce buds. When you cook them, unless you use a lot of salt, they taste like trees. And the deer are moving around, but they're all still young, and anyway there's plenty with the birds and rabbits, and you've got a pantry: creamed corn, hash, zucchini, codfish cakes. A lot of the time you read, or watch things out the window, or walk on top of the drifts with snowshoes."

"I can see it a little better now."

"Okay, you're bundled up cozy one night, good fire, little bit of lush, Coltrane on the machine, and it's getting darker, no twilight or sunset, because of the low overcast. But darker just the same, and something's happening on the other side of the lake, a big dog poking around maybe. Then he's gone, just as you take notice. So you forget it and have a little more lush and eat dinner and later mention how you saw this thing going on. Now, the person you're with says it sounds unlikely. Unlikely, right? I mean, a dog would know about people staying in the cabin from the smell, and come to sniff around. There's nobody else living in that part of the country, and he'd be hungry or lonely or something. So the next morning you check it all out and the tracks are way too big for a dog's. But just the same, you don't come out and say what you're thinking because it would be too soap-opera and who knows, maybe it was a Saint Bernard. One other thing you notice though, and that's the deer beds. Where the snow is pawed away and they lie down on the moss after nibbling for a while. It's the only warm-looking place in the woods."

"I like that part."

"It's pretty groovy. It's because of the weather. Otherwise they'd never fall by the lake, where it's all so exposed. But look at the connection. The reason you notice the deer beds is because the dog tracks, or whatever, are into the same thing.

"There's this feeling you get every evening, extrasensory goosebumps, and all. At first it's only a mild distraction but it begins to drive you up the wall, so you finally pick a time when you're having trouble reading, and you go after it, even though there's not much light left. But the person you're with—"

"A girl?"

"Oh yeah, from Radcliffe. It's her place, see? Second cousin."

"Oh."

"She says to be careful because she's got the same feeling you have. Spooking at the shadows, like that. Anyway, you make it, and the snow under your boots almost shrieks. It hasn't sounded quite that way before, and it really doesn't do very much for your head. The ice starts cracking too, not splitting open or anything, just little cracks, needle-thin, from all the contraction going on. They zip all over the place, like out-of-control buzz saws, and they make this weird roaring sound, like a huge gurgle. Then something happens that's really astounding. This deer, this young buck, breaks cover and takes off over the lake right at you.

It's as if he's been doing it all along, like he's running on an arc that somebody's plotted for him, and you're walking on your own, and that's where they're meant to intersect. It's as if the whole time, you'd already been thinking that when he did it you'd take him, then and there. So you do. You bring him down, I mean."

"You shot him?"

"That's right. There are reasons for that, though, things that make it back on top of other things, salt flats on the desert, movie stars, martinis, and crap. But that's not tied up with the wolf part yet. All I knew was how the deer went down and after the shot there was this commotion, this panic sound in the cover he'd broken out of. I saw a gray tail flashing around, right? Well, that's where it was all at, and both of us knew the score. Only, he was gone, zoom, like that, before he had eyes to leave. I had to track him, see, screw around in all the swampy parts."

She made a face.

"No, man, these are different swamps, just pine areas, depressed land, they get all the drainage is the thing."

"Not the icky kind?"

"Just dark. So in about the fourth one I put up a whole family—buck, doe, and two fawns—just like that, standing there looking at me, not knowing what the hell I am."

"Wait now, I want to understand. The one on the lake?"

"He was something else, baby, all hung up with other events, part of my karma, so to speak. But these guys just stood there looking; I mean, I thought they were digging me, until I heard that panic sound again. They were terrified, see? They were frozen with mortal fear, they couldn't move their noses to sniff the breeze. They were so up-tight it wasn't true. When I looked to see why—I'm telling you straight, now—it was like the different components of your head talking all at once. Like one part said, 'Now what's a German shepherd doing in the woods?' Twisted, right? But the inflection, the syntax, was already cynical. I mean, another part knew perfectly well what it was. I'd surprised him. Coming out of the wind, and all. And by that time, figuring that he'd foxed me after the lake business, he was looking out for more deer. I mean, I was supposed to be behind him, on his other side, the way he figured."

"Oh, Gnossos, how could you know that?"

"I don't know, baby, but that's certainly the look he was wearing. Then, to cool the whole thing, to make it seem as if he hadn't screwed up, he arched his gums and snarled. You know those little half-moon curves of the lip that tremble and show fangs? And he started crouching, man, like the way a cat does, really coming on, only he wasn't a cat, and he didn't look as if he wanted to be there crouching at all. Okay now, there were three slugs and two birdshot in the gun, a Marlin, an automatic, and this other head component had already arranged for all the safety business, and the trigger, and fingers, right? It was *like* that, it's true, the different ideas coming on at once. I was up-tight, myself, enough so that I missed the first two slugs, and really wide. The range was close, to make it worse, but he was moving out by then and I had to be cool; boy, did I have to be cool. The third slug took him from behind, straight from the rear, and tore through him and tumbled him over. Now close your eyes again. Tight. Now can you see him starting to tumble? Make it slow motion if you have to. He's just been hit, right in the ass."

"Almost."

"And his front legs collapse for a minute and he skids.

His nose plows up the snow ahead of him, that's the thing."

"Yes, I can see that."

"But then he got *up*. I mean, that was the insane thing. He just got up and bounded away, no limp, no dragging. And another head component was raging, oh I mean *furious*." Gnossos turning over from watching the fire, moving his weight to an elbow. Kristin sensed it and again opened her eyes. "I hated him. Baby, I *really* hated him. He disgusted me, he made me nauseous. And there was nothing rational about it. I just wanted him dead. No, more than dead, really, I wanted his gums all squashed, and his fangs broken, and his head cut off, and his insides pulled out for the weasels, and all kinds of terrible things. But even *there,* it was only one component doing the talking. Another one had me off running after him doing logical things, checking out patches of blood here and there. Sometimes there were deep impressions in the snow, where he'd rested; but he always jumped up again, you could tell from the tracks, the way they started a good way off. And I followed him like that for a *long* time. Nausea things, blood things, tracking things, cold things; man, it was too serious. Finally, in this last swamp, everything fell on my head. I mean, it finally came to me that it was much too dark even for the pines and the sun was probably down. And no matches, and I hadn't watched directions and no compass. And then the wolf, wounded, see, jumping around in the darkness someplace, and I couldn't feel my toes, and my fingers hurt, and everything was a colossally mortal drag. It was all of a sudden over. Absolutely all over."

Gnossos pushed the hair out of his eyes and swallowed. His throat was becoming dry.

"So at first I took it very easy and followed my tracks. But that didn't work; it was too dark, and there was no way to tell my footprints from the patches where lumps of snow had fallen out of the trees. Anyway, I ended up in the same swamp after about an hour, and for no reason at all I fired the other two birdshot into the air. No reason. I needed them in case the wolf came by, but I fired them off anyway. Clever, right? Then, in maybe another half an hour, I couldn't see anything. I mean, *any*thing at all, even if it were close enough to lick my forehead, and my fingers were numb at the tips, so you begin to get the picture."

Kristin's hands reached for his, but he had them tucked under his armpits. A little too tightly, he realized. She touched his shoulder instead and let the touch linger, her eyes searching his expression. But she remained silent.

"Stomach feenies," he said. "Loose bowels, baby, you know the scene. The smelly sensation when your own body is really capable of doing you dirt. *Betraying* you, man, moving out on its own, nothing to do with your will. Adrenalin has a high, that's where it's all at to start with, a jolt, little flash-connections it hits all the way down your nervous system. Then your lower intestines, all ready to unhinge like a trap door, make you crap in your pants. Think about that for a while; I mean, people finding you frozen, bringing you back to civilization, maybe laying you on a slab, and sooner or later, when they take off your pants, finding all this frozen shit. But then, when the adrenalin gave out, there was a calm. You become half a spectator, you watch symptoms like a doctor with a Rolleiflex. Except that you're making the action at the same time. So I broke off a lot of spruce boughs, a dozen or so, feeling around in the dark, the soft ones. I just wanted a little pad thing, to be off the ground, have a little distance between me and the enemy. That's when I thought about the two sets of tracks; remember, when I'd first checked the thing out? Another one, a female, dig, coming out for a little revenge. You want to know what you think of, naturally, I mean, when there's things jumping around that can see in the dark. You think: What part is he going to eat first? You're wearing a parka and boots and gloves, so there's only your face. The rest is cool, right? So what part will he start with? The nose? Chomp, no nose, just two holes, drip drip. Or your cheek, munch, like that."

Kristin making another face.

"That's right, but there's more. The calm business, it suddenly occurs to you, has nothing to do with your being cool. It's because you're freezing to death. It's just what happens. It's another lousy symptom of the cold, another body betrayal. There's nothing even unique about it. Everything's numb, especially your nose. But what the hell, the wolf gets it anyway, little bit of frozen nose might give him indigestion. Okay. Next you get sleepy. So in a little while there's nothing you can do to keep awake. There's even a weird odor starting to move in, sort of crowding out your perceptions, but it doesn't matter. That's where it's finally at. It doesn't matter what you smell or hear or anything. You can't be touched. Bang, it's all over. Now close your eyes again, and I'll tell you what you see right before you fall asleep. No, really, close them."

Again she did, keeping her hand at his shoulder.

"Everything is dark, almost like any sleep-dark, only the medium isn't just in front of you like a plane, or a wall. It goes off to both sides, it wraps right around your peripheral vision. You can actually feel it behind you; maybe under you, only the 'under' part isn't too clear. Little tingles of blue at the edge, but it's not exactly an edge. Then it's as if you've just thrown a pearl into the sky."

She blinked.

"You didn't really throw it but it's as if you did, because it came from you and it's small and white, phosphorescent. You see a kind of minuscule meteor trail behind it as it goes. It loses inertia, though, it stops climbing, it arches over and starts to drop. All the while gleaming. And the darkness, like I said, all around you. One thing has changed, though. When you threw it, or seemed to throw it, you were standing on something. Now it's as if you were about not to be, and everything is the pearl, and there's nothing underneath it. It's going to keep on falling. Underneath it, see, is an abyss."

There was a little sound of recognition in the back of Kristin's throat.

"Ah, but you hear something else. You've been hearing it for quite a while; in fact, even before the pearl went up. The thing is, you can't get away from it any more, it's become too clear, too recognizable. Just as the pearl starts to drop, baby, you dig it, it's the sound of your name, and you open your eyes."

She did.

"That's right. You wait a little, and it comes again; but nearer this time. There's a shaft of light poking through the trees, and now there's no way to get away from it. The only hangup is, you think you're making it up. Then at one point, which of all the screwy sensations to have at the time actually embarrasses you, you decide to call back. You're sure about it by then; I mean, you recognize the voice."

"The girl."

Gnossos nodding lazily, looking into the fire. "The girl, sure. All the same, you tell her to come to you instead of the other way around, just on the off-chance you really are making it up. She thinks your head is twisted, of course, but she comes and there you are, all flat on your back on top of these spruce boughs, with your hands folded and nothing missing but the lily. Pretty funny, right? Only, there's this uneasy expression on your face, and she's just seen it and nobody laughs. So instead she gives you a little lush she's thrown together in a thermos: whiskey with hot water and butter. It goes down, Piglet, believe me, like nectar and ambrosia."

A coal splintered and popped onto the rug. They both watched it momentarily, allowing the wool to burn, then reached for it simultaneously. Gnossos got there first but gave her his spoon and let her flick it back.

"That's all?" she asked.

"There ain't no more," he said.

She sighed audibly and for quite some time smoothed the material of her knee-socks against her legs. "This is stupid," she said finally, "but it's made me thirsty."

He watched the fire again, then answered, "That's all right. You want some wine? There's only wine."

"Please, yes." Another long pause, during which neither of them moved, until they became aware of the clock ticking in the next apartment. "Is it terribly late?"

"Yeah, probably. For curfew, I mean."

She took her hand from her ankle, waited a moment, and asked, "Where do you keep it?"

"In the rucksack, just on the wall there. Everything's in the rucksack. It's resin wine, Greek stuff, nobody else likes it around here."

"I'll like it, I think."

"That'd be nice."

She stood and crossed the room, pausing at the bag, which was fixed to the wall with Pamela Watson-May's replaced stiletto. "I'm sorry I have to get back," she told him. "It seems senseless. Especially tonight."

"That's right," he said. "Hey, would you like a little goat cheese with that?"

They were sitting in the stolen Anglia, the windshield wipers swishing back and forth, parked in the courtyard of Circe III, the girls' dormitory. Kristin turned to him and asked, "What time tomorrow?"

"I don't know, any time's good, figure something out. You go to classes, right? After classes sometime."

"Can we have dinner at your place? That *is* your place, isn't it? Where we were tonight?"

"Sure thing. Little dolma. Vine leaves stuffed with goodies. Egg-and-lemon sauce. You liked that resin wine all right?"

"I loved the wine."

"Yeah," he smiled.

"Are you preoccupied?"

"Who me, baby?"

"You look so serious, even when you smile."

"All façade, all role. Little forehead wrinkle makes for intensity, you know."

Fingering the strap on his rucksack, watching the wipers, always preferred the electric kind, predictable rhythm, something to lean on. "Having to take you back: it's a real drag." Moving around from the wheel to watch her. "Usually it's not, there's no sense telling you otherwise, because I don't get involved. But with you, man, it's all of a sudden a drag. What can I say?"

"I'm sorry."

"Right, what the hell." He looked at her again, measuring the intent behind the expression, but she seemed serious enough. And still beautiful. The brass ring had been removed and her hair hung down across her cheeks. Touch it, man, what's the matter, she's not the Virgin Mary.

But he couldn't quite.

"I'd better get in," she said.

"Hey, wait a minute," putting his parka over her shoulders for the short run to the dormitory entrance. Kristin closed her hands on his fingers for an instant as he did this, then got out his side and ran with him to the door. A light was blinking on and off and couples were clustered everywhere, clutching, whispering, mooning goodnight. All in white raincoats, pastel slickers, golf hats, tam-o'-shanters, pressed jeans, chinos, red and white school scarfs. They tried to find a dry, vacant place to stand but there was none available. At the main desk a line of just abandoned coeds was signing in pathetically for the night.

"A drag," she said. "Okay, I'll buy that."

"Tomorrow, Piglet," he answered, to be away from the scene, "fall by any time."

"I've got a seminar," she called after him, but he was almost through the doorway, waving back all right.

In the courtyard a crush of student cars, headlights crisscrossing in confusion, horns blowing anxiously, brake fluid heating, drivers itching to buttonhook the evening's frustration with quickie tidbits. Peanut butter and jelly on rye toast. Warm apple turnover. Pizzaburger with hotsauce from Guido's kitchen. Home to a Playmate tacked on the ceiling. Masturbation in a wet-strength Kleenex.

He cut off a convertible, white Lincoln Capri, and the driver leaned on his horn, protesting. "Shut the fuck up," he screamed back, a homicidal bellow.

There came immediate silence everywhere, a number of cars stalling as if the sudden malediction had mortally stunned the little rotor-hearts in their distributors. During the pause Gnossos gunned the Anglia out of the driveway, swerved onto the dormitory lawn, and accelerated through a complex of footpaths and dormant flowerbeds. A police whistle blew in his unmistakable direction but he ignored it, continued along the middle of the sidewalk at forty-five, and watched the pedestrians fleeing to the left and right like startled giraffes. He drove into the street, between two narrowly spaced elm trees, kissing their barks with door handles, then bounced over the curb with a couple of stiff bumps and flashed across Harpy Creek Bridge, driving on the wrong side of the road.

As he approached the desolate Dairy Queen, he cut the motor and let the car freewheel into its old space. There were only a few automobiles left, a motorcycle and two Lambrettas. Probably a six-state alarm out for the Anglia, fuzz combing the countryside. See them swarming into Mojo's little lair with searchbeams, he-ho, what have we here? But the loft was nearly empty, coeds safely home, only the vampires for possible partners. The hairy little man with the narghile was blowing eight-bar blues in the middle of the floor, snoring between measures, being ignored. Juan Carlos Rosenbloom was unconscious on one of the burlap-covered pallets, oblivious of the vampire who tested the gold of his Saint Christopher medal with her teeth and fondled the sequins on his rodeo shirt. Drew Youngblood sat sober in the corner, reading *The Foreign Affairs Quarterly*, looking up as Gnossos sauntered in. A yellow, caustic haze hovered in the air, lingered among the smoke fumes like hydrogen sulfide or some yeasty reagent. Through the metal, clandestine door at the end of the brick wall came occasional, muffled whimpers and moans. Regular little Gomorrah.

"Where you been, baby?" asked one of the vampires, pupils adrift in a sea of mulberry blood vessels, "it's all been happening since you split."

"Talking to the mirror, man, you ever try it?"

"Don't put me on."

"Dig it sometime. Dig your mouth."

"You're putting me on."

"Lip-synch goes off just a hair, slips ahead. Now be a good chic an' get me a Red Cap, would you? Who's the hairy cat with the ax?"

"Locomotive. And get your own goddamned beer."

Gnossos picked a piece of her leotard between thumb and forefinger, hissed, and whispered, "Your life is in danger." Youngblood at the same time gave him the high sign, and Locomotive sang:

> M is for the Methedrine you gave me,
> O is for the Opium we knew . . .

"What's up?" from Gnossos.

"Nothing much, really. Maybe something in that other room, from the sound of it."

"I'm hip, but they're choosy about guests."

"So it seems. I'm glad you came back, anyway, we wanted to talk to you."

"Hey listen, that girl I split with, that Kristin chic, you know anything about her?"

"How do you mean?"

"Like I said."

"She's a friend of Jack's, I think. Why?"

"Nothing, man." The vampire arriving with a tray of opened Red Caps, potato chips, and a bowl of creamy dip. She set it down next to the stoned Locomotive, who continued to sing with his shirt open, chest like a bear rug, thick lumpy glasses staring at the floor. "That's all's left," said she timidly.

"Have a nightcap, Youngblood," from magnanimous Sophocles.

"What else you want, baby?" the vampire taking a new tack, folding up next to them, blinking back runny mascara.

"And old Rosenbloom over there," said Gnossos, ignoring her. "What's his story? All those names."

"I'm available," said the vampire to her amulet.

"He's German."

"No."

"You didn't know that? Parents shipped him to Venezuela, got scared the war would spread and had him converted."

"Catholic?"

"He picked up on it, that's the weird part. He's very devout."

Poor old Jew. Saint Christopher keeps him safe in his wanderings. Me without a rebus, too vulnerable. "Oh, and another thing, Youngblood. This Pankhurst deal you keep in front. I'm a-political, right? No girl scout cookie campaigns, P.T.A. meetings, anything like that. I assume it's what you wanted to talk about. They start moving in on my pad, I'll deal with it all privately. But this committee-style setup; wow, really."

"You don't *have* to be so stand-offish, Paps. All the other independents—"

"Truly, man, you'd be wasting rhetoric, it's not my pattern. Dig the Crusades. Lots of guys got hamstrung and staked out. The rest got the Turkish clap. Nobody got the old grail."

> T is for the Trip to Coney Island
> H is for a Heroin Ragout . . .

"I got a little mixture left," said the vampire, "you wanna make some movies?"

"Just the Red Cap, ducks."

"Lush does your head, baby."

"Ain't lush, it's Red Cap."

"You?" she tried Youngblood, pointing an ebony fingernail.

Youngblood shook his head, then pressed for a last-minute advantage. "It's not all as Mickey Mouse as you might think."

"Please, man, I'm just not having any," Gnossos glancing at the gurgling Locomotive, then at the forlorn vampire, who was giving up and crawling away on all fours. A sudden, colossal weariness blew through his bones as he watched her go. He yawned and slouched down, afraid that Youngblood was searching desperately for something significant to say. He waved him into casual silence and offered a benevolent smile for recompense, then stretched out on one of the Indian prints. "Later," he said, closing his eyes.

The lids stung with soothing, soporific warmth.

E is for the Ether in your nosegay,
R is the Reward of sniffing glue.
Put them all together . . .

Unh. What sound?

He was awakened by the squeak of unoiled hinges, the shuffle of tired bodies. He rolled over sluggishly, his night torn open, and with one eye watched a lumpy apparition in a silk dressing gown, emerging from the door in the brick wall. The figure was murmuring to itself, and an odor of evil swam biliously through the loft.

Mojo. Lie still. His hair mussed, mustache-ends drooping. From the shadows of the chamber within came sounds of wet flesh. A phthisic hand reaching, a girl's, that same one. Whose? But before he could remember, Heap joined his master on the threshold and closed the ominous door. They moved along on tiptoes. As they passed the coiled, sleeping pile of unused vampires, the monkey jumped from the press of bodies and chattered a protest. Ugh, wake up.

All at once a semidark transparence glowed through the skylight. Dawn. Gnossos watched it for a moment, and when he looked again, Heap and Mojo were gone. He stood, stretched painfully, lost his balance, regained it, and found the monkey squatting on the floor, glaring. He tried glaring back, but the sight revolted him and he had to look away, taking deep breaths. The odor was overwhelming, like spilled ammonia. Finally he checked the rest of the loft, looking for an ally, but his friends were gone. Only the sleeping Locomotive remained, collapsed on the narghile. He struggled with his parka, threw it over his shoulders cape-style, and shuffled to the exit on wobbly legs. The monkey shrieked and struggled furiously against the chain as Gnossos, in a jolting rush of fear-inspired energy, jumped the last six steps to freedom.

Outside, the twittering whistle of morning birds, a wild, cleansing cacophony of tiny cries.

But after a moment he became aware of still another sound, a malevolent, slapping rhythm driving away the wings. What?

He made his uneasy way through the chilly morning mist, rubbing his eyes as he went, scraping the ale taste off his tongue with his teeth. The slapping was colored by a metallic ring, the kiss of leather on steel. Then a quick inspiration of breath, a sensual sigh, nearly a moan. It made the skin crawl along his thighs. It was coming from the Dairy Queen, not twenty yards away.

He stepped more cautiously now, not wanting to be seen, padding through the snow, pausing to pick up a handful for his headache. Eeeeeee, coldcoldcold. He wiped it off with his sleeves, ceasing all motion as the weight of the nearby slap became more forceful. He crept to the edge of the clearing, then stopped as if struck, his heartbeat crunching in his ears.

Heap was poised in front of the microbus, the bullwhip gripped in his bony fist. He raised it high above his head, swung it in a sinister circle, and flashed out, grunting, at the fenders and grill of the car.

Ten feet away, leaning with his back against the aluminum of the Dairy Queen, his silk robe fallen open, his legs apart, was Mojo. Beneath the robe he was naked and his pulpy knees were slightly bent. His penis was in his hand, his transfigured gaze was on Heap, and his rhythm was steady and forceful. "More," he whispered, groaning, as the yellow bullwhip cracked again and again against the enamel of the microbus. "Please, harder."

Gnossos stumbled away, perspiring the moisture of mortal dread. He paused for a moment, breathing deeply, then ran back to the highway, mind's eye awash with the electrifying scene. At first he cantered, hands in his pocket, later he walked, and finally he ambled.

After an hour the birds had stopped their song of celebration and the dawn had lifted. He reached into his rucksack for the Hohner F, put it to his lips, and thought the day's first tangible thought as he played along.

> Good morning, blues,
> Blues,
> how do you do?

9

But the day became a new one.

He awoke at noon, the sun exploding under the lids of his eyes like silent-film incendiary bombs; ears ringing with the drip and seethe of the thaw. Through the slats on his bedside window (boarded up with plywood and gypsum since the night Pamela Watson-May had tried to kill him), he could see the swollen Swiss drolleries on the porch. The snow had melted and slipped away, saturating the wood. The fat icicles were gone as well, patches of lawn miraculously green after months of entombment, walks and porches clear but for the wet; beams and timbers creaking with the sigh of shrugged-away weight, stretching back into place. All the parts and parcels of the winter that had been were sliding down the gullies of the hill, plunging into gorges, swelling streams brown and gurgling, creeping through fissures and corridors of shale in the glacial countryside, skimming over tops of fallow fields, across slopes like ducks' backs, seeking a level: the broad, steel-blue plain of bottomless Maeander, where if you listened carefully you heard the French and Indian cannons booming as some monumental piece of earth or stone was shouldered loose from a cliff face by the swelling lunge of ice beneath and dumped into the flawless, pregnant surface of the lake.

He bellowed like a Cretan bull. "Fitzgore! Where the hell are you? I'm in love!"

But Fitzgore was nowhere to be seen. The apartment was silent and his tidy bed was still unused from the night before. The only sign of him was implicit in a partially unpacked shipment of Victorian hot-water bottles, copper and brass. "In *love*, Fitzgore," Gnossos tried again, then leapt from the sack with an arabesque bound. He was wearing only a black motorcycle teeshirt and khaki socks. He hopped across the room on an imaginary pogo stick, and pounded heavily on the French doors, shaking the walls, jarring loose the hunting horns. "Rajamuttus!" he roared in celebration of the impossible event, "lotus, rosewater, Ravi Shankar!" Then zoom, away to the kitchen for a quick wash in the sink. (The basin in the bathroom was beyond use, swimming with waterlogged underpants, ammonia, and Listerine.) He tossed his teeshirt and socks on the mound of egg shells and cheese rind festering in the corner, and a small cloud of lazy bugs rose with the smelly disturbance. They settled again, sniffed at the new additions, and gasped off into cracks. Gnossos sitting in the sink, back to the faucet, washing his pits with a diluted mixture of liquid Lux, his feet in blue, lukewarm water, old vine leaves awash, blobs of poached egg white, puffy all-bran crumbs, and rice. This, the first ablution in weeks, humming Yerrakina under his breath, massaging his chest with a pink cellulose sponge, dehydrated and scratchy, good for circulation. He considered disinfecting his pubes, then decided to abandon body and soul to a later, evening bath. Take it just before she comes, salt and oils, little bit of scent. Max Factor bubbles?

drun droon droon droon-droon-droon-droon

He dried with a gray and tepid towel, flung it into the corner when he was finished, glanced hurriedly about the cupboards, and made mental notes on supplies that needed laying in. Then he ran around abandoning hermetic discretion, opening all the windows, some of them going up easily, others—like the one with the plywood and gypsum—needing a screwdriver. When the wood was too wet, he used Calvin's hammer: must remember to return it someday, Exhibit A for Dean Magnolia's case. Maybe melt it, have it cast as an evil eye, hurl it through the Mississippi cabbage-head with a sling.

On Academae Avenue, across the street from his house, an anonymous couple strolled hand in hand, colliding clumsily as they tried keeping step. He pointed a deliriously happy finger, forgetting his nakedness, and screamed, "YAAAAAAAAANH!" They leapt apart and ran away, but nothing could stop him. He'd felt the potent surge of warmth in the new air, smelled the shifted wind. Mean Mother Winter, man, poof, all gone. He jammed the heavy parka into a drawer with mothballs and lifted a damp, crumpled pair of lightweight corduroys from the rucksack. They had come from the same cornucopia of a forgotten laundry bag in San Francisco's Coexistence Bagel Shop that had yielded the 1920's baseball cap he pulled down now

over his hair and ears. The cap was a white dome with faded
gray pinstripes, a little black button on the zenith, a pale
orange peak. Om, zup goes the soul straight through the
button, grand slam for the old gods, over the center-field
bleachers.

He wriggled into his undersized boy scout shirt, relic of
Taos, and admired himself in Fitzgore's gilt-framed baroque
mirror. Five-year pin, assistant-patrol-leader bars, wolf
patch on the shoulder, ready to go. He laced up his boots
(no socks), tilted the baseball cap over his eyebrows, and
crash, he was out the door. He ran head on into George and
Irma Rajamuttu, who had materialized spooklike in the
hall, no doubt responding to his cry. They were cloaked
in gauze wrapups, eyes jaundiced, and they held tinkling
glasses of gin and grenadine. "Goodness gracious me," said
George, jarred sideways.

"The Vale of Kashmir," yelled Gnossos, flying past.
"Curried duck!"

"Orange dal," called Irma after him, the first words he
had ever heard her speak. But there was no time. He was
climbing the hill in seven-league bounds, flapping his arms,
trying to fly. Past the law school, with its Tudor courtyard
for duels; the student union, where students hovered with
May flies already buzzing in their blood; the high Clock
Tower sounding the half-hour in its pointed head; the arts
quad with sweatsocks and sneakers everywhere, faces turning to catch the apparition that galloped by; over the Harpy
Creek Bridge, where he made whooping sounds; down the
footpath by the still-incomplete Larghetto Lodge.

The shores of Maeander Lake were trapped high on the
hill, held in manmade place by the partially concealed hy-
droelectric dam, where the thaw had sure as hell begun.

Massive blocks of ice had heaved up from the surface, tumbled over the shore, and knocked trees flat against the ground with the unbridled force of their motion. The first muddy waters were beginning to pulse through the dam flues, heave against the concrete abutments, spout at the waiting gorge a hundred feet below. He ran around the muddy path, ankles sloshing, stopping to tug on a half-defeated tree and help it to the earth. Better all at once, might be suffering, get a stethoscope, listen to its agonies. He halted once, his breath taken away as one of the enormous iceblocks slid effortlessly past his nose. There were no trees to obstruct, and it moved a full ten feet before it stopped. "Whoo-hoo," he yelled, and swung up on its tilted, slippery surface, using a dangling branch as if he were Tarzan. He scrambled to the ragged peak and jumped up and down, driving his weight solidly into his bootheels as he landed. He did it with three successive blocks, finally cracking the third one, leaping free before it lumbered apart. Then at the bridge, where the young creek was struggling through the narrows, he paused and listened. Yes. Can you hear the blood soughing? Wind in the lung's leaves? So many million fibers and cells, surely their collision and tug must have a murmur. The seepage of bile, fluid trickling in the spine, the frequency of growing hair, high and piercing like a nail scratching on a pane of glass.

For a moment there seemed to be silence. But under the still-unbroken surface of the narrows he heard the gurgling roll of new waters. Here and there he could see beneath a transparent, brittle sheet of ready-to-collapse ice, frothy bubbles skimming along on the underside, seeking a path, collecting strength. He climbed to the outside of the bridge, balancing on the thin field-stone lip that ran along its perimeter, then leaned over cautiously and found a grip, first with one hand, then with the other. Kicking off his weight, he swung free; and thirty feet above the lake he hovered like a pendulum. Now giggling quietly, he inched along until he sensed an area where the snow and ice might be strong enough. Oh, sweet Mortality, I love to tease your scythe, and he let go, just like that, feet apart, arms high in the air, a forefinger holding down his baseball cap, rucksack aflutter.

He was flying.

His feet struck and he sank, spreading elbows to brake, stopping only when he was in to the nose. His toes had failed to touch water. Up, up, old Pooh Bear, the body bears heat. He twisted his way loose, stretched flat out, then crawled to firmer snow. He kneeled, stood, walked, hopped, and finally ran across the chunky, broken surface, bounding from block to block, keeping his stride, forcing a rhythm, figuring if he kept the proper pace and failed to find a foothold, he'd make the next one. Drun droon droon.

On the far shore of civilization a bus was approaching the Harpy Creek stop. Gnossos waved his cap and sprinted the final fifty yards, just squeezing through the doors, chilly beads of perspiration running into his eyes. He gave the driver a silver dollar and got a dirty look for change. Poor man, no nose for the spring wind. "Thaw," he whispered as explanation, grinning madly.

"Saw?" asked the driver, nervous, mistaking a lisp.

"Caw," said Gnossos, still whispering, opening and closing the fingers of his left hand like a flying crow.

"Sure," said the driver uneasily, letting out the clutch with a chop, glancing in all the mirrors, handing him quarters for the fare machine. Gnossos answering, "Seesaw."

"Marjorie Daw," from the driver, shifting gears, gripping the wheel.

Gnossos goading him to distraction, pocketing the bread,

sliding into a seat, not paying, the driver failing to notice, nearly colliding with a covey of coeds. They scattered like quail, and Gnossos chuckled, wiping his palms on his base-ball cap, turning it backward, Yogi Berra sliding down the window by his side. "Fresh air," he explained to the woman with a prune-whip face. Her hat had nearly blown off in the sudden blast. "It's spring," he tried. "Look."

But she couldn't.

Downtown in Kresge's he bought a bottle of Revlon bub-ble bath, two giant-size Yardley lavender bath soaps, a tor-toise shell comb, and a back brush for stray pimples. He had to try four drugstores before he was able to find oils and salt, and then only after he'd cornered and confused the teenage salesgirl. She had Jean Harlow hair and was lost behind cardboard displays of nail polish, dentifrice, chewing gum, and hairnets. Violet by a mossy stone. "Bath oil," he re-peated, pushing the baseball cap down over his eyes, flirting, leaning forward with his elbows in a counter of Tums and other reliefs for the rigors of acid indigestion. "Oil for the bath, if you dig." Her platinum hair shimmered in pharma-ceutical fluorescence, her lips glowed with the color of ionized muscatel grapes.

"I heard y'inna first place, but what do you mean, like Nivea for in case y'skin dries out, or what's she want it for, anyway?"

"What's who want it for, baby?"

"Y'mother, whoever y'get it for."

Gnossos seeing his problem, thinking a moment, then crooking his finger to motion her closer, winking. The girl looked around, leaned forward with an uncertain frown, a lump under her lip where she was rolling her tongue. "It's for me," he murmured.

The tongue went back into place. "What are y'kidding?"

"To make me lovable is why."

"What? Hehe." The girl looking for an ally.

"Velvety to the touch, man, smooth; you dig smooth?"

"Now *look*. Hehe."

"Ancient custom is all, balm for warrior, makes you good to feel, right?"

"Oh go on."

"You got any?"

"Hehe. What?"

"Bath oil, man."

"That you put right in the water?"

"You get the picture."

"I'll ask the manager." The girl skipped off, ears deaf to her doom, and talked to an old bone of a man in wire glasses at the soda fountain. See her in a year, straddling some pump-jockey in the front seat of a '46 Ford, knocked up. Watching Gunsmoke in their underwear, cans of Black Label, cross-eyed kid screaming in a smelly crib. Ech. Immunity not granted to all. Be Christian, help her.

She came back with a small carton and handed him a bottle of highly viscous, umber-colored Charles of the Ritz bath oil.

"Two," he said, getting the silver dollars ready. "Don't wrap them, I've got a thing," pointing at the rucksack, taking both bottles, then handing one back.

"What are y'doing? Y'just paid for that."

"I know, man. It's for you."

"What?"

"To make you smooth. Lovable."

"Oh go on. Hehe."

"You're one of God's chosen creatures, baby, I can tell. Do you know who I am?"

"Go on."

"I'm the Holy Ghost. Maybe look you up sometime, who knows, give you a ride in my Maserati. You dig Maserati?"

"What are y'kidding?" rolling her tongue under her lip, twisting a strand of shimmering hair, suddenly winking at him. Hey nonny no.

By the time he shouldered his way through the apartment door, the rucksack was bulging with cosmetics and foods. More vine leaves, unpolished brown rice, marinated olives, ground round, fertilized eggs, organic lemons, tarragon, bay leaves, garlic, Spanish onions, okra, resin wine, cruets of orange extract, and a new side. Heffalump, Drew Youngblood, and Juan Carlos Rosenbloom were lounging around the pad, drinking Dairy Queens out of wax cups, half listening to a Brubeck. "Gaaa," gasped Gnossos, "Dairy Queens."

"Just opened today," said Youngblood, who stood and helped with the rucksack. An onion had already wobbled over the floor. Rosenbloom, sucking his straw, peering over the strawberry froth, said, "Delicious. We dong get them in Maracaibo."

Gnossos picked up the onion and pointed at the record player. "And burn that Brubump crap, man, I've got new sounds. What are you doing, starting a Mickey Mouse club or what?" He handed the side to Heff, who took it and wandered over to the spindle, reading the notes. "Who's Mose Allison?"

"Trust me," from Gnossos, trying Rosenbloom's froth with a finger.

"Never heard of him."

"Not so loud, man."

"An' I don't dig names like Mose, Paps. It's Uncle Tomming."

"He's white, baby, don't lose your cool. And put on side one, thing called New Ground." Heff grunting as Gnossos walked into the kitchen to unpack his rucksack. But while he was putting away the fertilized eggs he remembered he had failed to inform the troops of the day's revelation. He sucked in his constipated stomach, sighed, and returned to the living room, where they all sat studying the cover photograph of Back Country Suite. "Ahem," he said. He was standing perfectly still, a hand on his head, waiting for silence. They put down their Dairy Queens and looked at him.

"Just thought I'd pass the word, babies, before legend distorts the fact. The voice of the turtle is in the air? Hey ring-a-ding-ding, and like that? Well, this spring has the blessing of the gods. The Daughters of Night are banished, zippo-bang, no more. Pappadopoulis, in fact," he lowered his voice and raised a hushing finger like Toscanini, "is in love." He said it again to confound any possible error. "Love. Dig it."

Boom went the percussion of New Ground, boom fell the silence in the room, down went the Dairy Queens, and up went their eyes to look at the place where Gnossos had been but was no longer, since with the cathartic announcement he had felt an unmistakable, long-absent urge in his lower intestines and gone in a flash to the bathroom, where he had barely sat down before his bowels found their exquisite relief.

One hour after this extraordinary visceral event all the dust had settled, and Youngblood had finally completed a list of anxious phonecalls. He had been attempting to incite diplomatically polite insurrection among the faculty. Rosenbloom was on the Navajo rug, wearing a new red and yellow rodeo shirt, tight white Levis, and jodhpurs, tracing diagrams from his volume of Clausewitz: strategic deployment, tactical flanking maneuvers, logistical supply techniques. Heffalump was curled in the fetal position on the butterfly chair in his blue-striped French sailor's jersey, faded jeans, and heelless bucks, making notes for their twice-weekly anthropomorphic word game. Gnossos was flying back and forth across the apartment with indomitable energy, wielding brooms, dustmops, vacuum cleaners, oil rags, Lysol, Oakite, and Mr. Clean. "Up up," he'd chatter if a body got in his way, flicking a section of cheesecloth or chamois, polishing, cleansing, rubbing, wiping. "You're going to get ulcers," warned Heff, "hives or something." Then to Youngblood, who was drawing a line through one of the names on his list, "You nearly finished, man?"

Youngblood nodded, tapping the sheet with a pencil, "It's really picking up, you know? Philosophy, English, architecture, all with some kind of commitment. Government's giving us a little trouble at the emeritus level but I think they'll go."

"We smash him, crack," said Rosenbloom, dropping an ink blot in the eye of the university President, whose picture was on the front page of the *Sun*. The man had announced the coming demolition of another old campus building. The paper had appeared under the door after the usual mysterious, gentle rapping at dawn. "Up up," said Gnossos, gliding past with the vacuum cleaner, eagle eye on the lookout for nail parings, dustballs, hairpins, and Oreo creme sandwich crumbs.

"Is there anything left to drink around here?" asked Heff by way of distraction. But Christian Pappadopoulis foxed him and flew to the icebox without breaking his stride, returning a six-pack of Ballantine ale and a church key with a synthetic ruby on the handle. "No stains, you guys, no spilling, little taut-ship action."

"Hey wow," said Heff, "where'd this compulsive house-cleaning come out of?"

"Order from chaos, babies. Art, if you dig."

In time a bloodshot, disheveled Fitzgore wandered in, followed eventually by Agneau, who carried his fraternity newsletter under his arm. But Gnossos managed to gather up all the fetid vine leaves, lichee nuts, lemon peels, and sordid bits of ugly from the kitchen, and he stacked them in a huge polyethylene bag, which had once contained Fitzgore's suit, while everyone else began work on a new six-pack. He slung the bag over his shoulder, turned up the final band of Back Country Suite, and went outside to find the landlord's garbage cans. While there, he paused for some time, sniffing at the new fragrance of warmth on the southerly wind.

When he returned, whistling arpeggios with Mose Allison, the large living room was mysteriously empty. He stepped out on the front porch but there was no sign of them. Youngblood's Anglia and Fitzgore's Impala were still parked in front.

But inside, he detected whispers from the bathroom. He tiptoed carefully across the freshly waxed kitchen tiles. Everyone was gathered in a semicircle around the commode, peering down. Their mouths were open. Heffalump and Youngblood held drinks, Agneau and Fitzgore leaned on each other, and Rosenbloom scratched his rump.

"Man," from Heffalump finally, putting his beer on the sink. "I don't believe it for a minute."

"What is it?" asked Gnossos, suddenly uncomfortable.

They all turned their heads from the commode and gazed at him, lips still parted. "Ech," said Fitzgore.

Gnossos nudged his way between them, peering down. When he glanced up, they were all waiting for his reaction. Then he looked again.

Floating in the water was the largest turd he had ever seen in his life.

Ever.

"Mine?" he asked, a finger at his heart.

They all nodded in sympathy.

"Bullshit," he protested, "I refuse it. It's somebody else's."

"Nobody's been here, man."

"You just came in to piss, Heff, it was you."

"No," said Agneau softly. "He saw it and screamed. When you were outside."

"But I flushed it."

"It's too big. Won't go through."

"Hell it won't," said Gnossos, reaching for the handle.

"No no," protested Youngblood and Rosenbloom together. "Save it."

"We can have it cast, man," said Heff.

Gnossos reached again, but they stopped him. "Hey, let go, goddammit, that thing's been trying to creep into the ground for months. You can't *leave* it there. Have the gods down on you in the night. Monsoons."

"Casting," said Youngblood respectfully. "The perfect solution, really. Just look at it."

Gnossos stared down again. As he did, a small eddying current in the water lolled it over on its side. It was astonishingly well formed, here and there a minuscule design. Cuneiform of the bowels. Secret cellular knowledge etched by the insides, trying to tell us something.

"It is sort of splendid," he admitted slyly, and lunged for the handle. But they stopped him again, Rosenbloom blocking the front of the pot.

"What is this, anyway? If it's mine I can do what I want with it."

"It belongs to the people," said Heff solemnly, gazing down.

"Like any other work of art," added Youngblood, agreeing. "You no longer have the right to destroy it. I'm sorry."

"How do we lift it out?" asked Heff.

"Ech," said Fitzgore.

"Nobody else gets it!" yelled Gnossos at the ceiling.

"One of those shirtbags," suggested Agneau, "those plastic things."

"Anybody got some rubber gloves?" asked Youngblood. Fitzgore went out reluctantly and returned with a plastic shirtbag, Heff coming up with an ebony salad fork and spoon.

"Hey," said Fitzgore, protesting, "my mother sent me those."

"For art," said Rosenbloom, rubbing his tiny, hairy hands together. Heff handed him the salad set and he knelt next to the bowel, implements poised.

"I want it left alone! Do I have to bust heads?"

"Shh," said Heffalump gently. "A little Satyagraha, please." He also knelt, spreading the top of the bag. "This is a very delicate operation." Then, to Rosenbloom. "Maybe we should put a little water in first, keep it fresh and all."

"Ugh," said Fitzgore, but he was grinning, fascinated.

Rosenbloom lifted six spoonfuls of water from the commode into the plastic bag. Heffalump tested for watertightness and signaled to proceed. Gnossos gazed spectatorially, like an anaesthetized catatonic. Rosenbloom tested different methods of execution, settling finally on a chopstick-pincer arrangement, spoon below, fork on top.

"Won't it break?" asked Agneau.

"Scotch tapes," said Rosenbloom, "hold the worl' together. She look pretty, how you call him, stolid."

"Solid," corrected Fitzgore, hands over his eyes, peeking between the fingers.

"Thas the one," said Rosenbloom, making contact, lifting the gargantuan object free, raising it perilously high, one end dangling over the spoon, straining, but showing no signs of fracture.

"Man," said Heffalump. "Just look at it."

"Oh, the bloody indignity! Tidal waves, earthquakes, solar eclipses!"

Delicately Rosenbloom lifted the flexible object over the plastic bag as Heff arranged the opening. It fell with a wet plop and shoved out the sides of the bag.

Gnossos stared, unbelieving. "I disown it. It's not mine. Must have floated up from downtown. It belongs to Fat Fred or somebody."

They filed out of the bathroom one at a time, Gnossos glancing at each static face, Judases all, failing to know me, making off with their cargo. "Wait," he called. "A boon. Grant me a boon, you guys."

"A what?" asked Heff, wheeling. "What the hell did you call me?"

"No, man, a *boon,* a favor."

"Certainly," from Agneau.

"When you're finished, you have to bury it, okay?"

"With full honors," said Youngblood.

"Militaring funerals," said Rosenbloom, still holding the ebony fork and spoon. "Let's do it."

They all marched through the living room in step, and out the front door. Fitzgore did an about-face on the porch and returned wearily, still looking exhausted, to his bed. Gnossos heard the cars start and drive off but he refused to go to the window. Fitzgore avoided his menacing eyes.

"Butchers," he hissed. "Maniacs." And returned to the bathroom, where he looked at the empty toilet bowl. It seemed there was nothing more to do. Remembering Kristin, he turned the hot water on in the tub and compulsively emptied every bottle of oil and salt into the billowing steam. The fumes impregnated each nook of the apartment with the sugary odor of nectar and honeydew. Sweet perfumes for the flesh, drive away the demons.

Provided they're ready to go.

10

Two nautical hours in the oceangoing tub, half emptying then refilling the water, turning the tap when the temperature fell below a critical level; the periscoping tool a thermometer. He watched it absently, foreshortened as it was by the plane of soapy liquid, some new genus of lily pad, a blind, muscular fish, single hollow eye socket hidden under catholicized skin. On the final filling he added the blue cosmetic crystals of Prince Matchabelli bubble bath, aerating the multiplied froth with his knees, using the periscope to lift a weightless clump of sixty or seventy spheres. He slipped on Fitzgore's skin-diving goggles and descended, looking for treasure, a tiny Poseidon or Aphrodite clip-clopping along in the microcosm. All gods and muses tiny, the length of a thumbnail or smaller; primitives wrong to make them monumental. Find them in peanut butter jars, under bottlecap cork slices.

He caught sight of an unlikely movement and plunged forward to examine a cluster of partially dissolved crystals. He had to wipe the fog from the goggles in order to see. But instead of Hermes he found the reflection of Fitzgore, immaculately dressed, distorted like a fat man in a sideshow looking glass. *"God,* Paps, you're not still in the goddamned tub?"

"No, as it happens I'm not."

"What are you doing, anyway?"

"Man, how come you guys have such a talent for slipping worms in the image?"

"Worms?"

"Later, Gore, I'm busy."

Fitzgore nodded, straightening his tie in the mirror. "That girl's coming over, isn't she, that one in the kneesocks, what's her name?"

"Why don't you flee, man, before you get some bath oil on your nice John Lewton suit?"

"Brooks Brothers, Paps, please. Only wanted to know 'cause I can hang around D.U. or someplace after house meeting."

"That *would* be kind of you, yes. Unless of course you plan to fall by and watch, take seconds."

"Speaking of which, you don't know anything about Pamela and Mojo, do you?"

"Will you get *out* of here?"

Fitzgore shrugging, looking as if he might have something more to say, then dabbing after-shave lotion under his ears and leaving with a diabolical, "Have fun." Gnossos slid into the froth to be alone, submerged his head, and looked up at the glittering underside of the surface. He talked out loud into the bubbly liquid, his mouth flooding with perfume: *How can those terrified vague fingers push the feathered glory from her loosening thighs?*

By five-thirty he was out of the tub and she had not come. His stomach was warm with the discomforting incalescence of anxiety. He sang nonsense lyrics to himself and jumped around the apartment with an oil rag, dabbing at already spotless ashtrays, mantels, hunting horns, record jackets, rucksack buckles, window sills, door handles, pots and pans, and the ominous Blacknesse painting. The dolma lay simmering in an exotic sauce on the stove, wine chilled in the baby refrigerator, olives waiting on one of Fitzgore's Wedgwood plates. Chunks of seasoned lamb were impaled on coathanger skewers, marinating, ready for the flame.

He tried Mose Allison but lost patience and turned him off in favor of the Hohner F, which wouldn't work. The C note had been blown out during his morning walk. Man, still the same day. Cycles of the sun the wrong way to measure time. Crusting of the cells was how, little vessels aging, collapsing at the temples, inching you along without your say.

At six she still was not there. Why? She couldn't have forgotten, surely. The whole thing just a tumble for the evening, chitchat with a maniac Greek, quaint little animal tales to share with the dorm?

Six-thirty.

He curled into a ball on Fitzgore's clean bed and peeled back the cover in order to feel the algid pillow. Sleep seemed unlikely while he counted minutes, but he found it

all the same, a gloomy, humid breed of semiconsciousness.
The well-lubricated lid of his mind's additional eye lifted on
a winter clearing, where the silently driving wind made
powder of the snow, cosmetic talcum storms dusting the
pines. A disemboweled wolf offered a Cheshire grin at the
gates of perception, its presence only partially sensed, never
explicit. Then a faint odor of animal ammonia, the landscape changing form and dimension, the wind abating, the
talcum receding, spiraling backward into a panoramic vista.
The scene was viewed from a high-altitude plateau, a mesa
perhaps, but with the mouth of a cave gaping on the surface.
An unimaginable creature stirred within the cave, prepared
to reveal itself, scuttle lewdly out. The vista beyond was
Oriental. But why? A sound of quarter tones, a muted tam-
bourine, the chanting of an Amane: . . . *Ela ke si ke
klapse. Ke par to ema mou, ke ta mallia sou vapse.*

"Gnossos."

"Unh?"

"Are you awake?"

"Un."

"You were dreaming."

"What?"

"You were talking something. It sounded foreign."

"Unh. Hello. How long have you been here?"

"About half an hour. Hello yourself."

"Man," stirring, rubbing his eyes with a fist.

"The door was open. I knocked for a while."

"Ummm. C'mon in, sit down."

"I've been watching that whatever it is on the stove. It
was nearly burned."

The dolma. Forgot about the sauce. Sit up. Oomph.
Green knee-socks still. "I'd better go look—"

"It's okay, I turned it down. And I put that shish kebab

business in the oven. I hope you don't mind, but you looked comfortable."

"Sure thing." Could have been Pamela. Leave the door unlocked, find an icepick in your temple. "I've got a rug for a tongue, man."

"Drinking?"

"Talking is all. I looked comfortable, did I?"

"Was the dream bad?"

"Neurotic, baby, full of warning. You hungry? How about a Salonika pepper?"

"When you wake up, you have to talk them out. Right away, otherwise you forget."

"Yeah, well it's not really worth it. No overt sex, just a lot of symbols, loose ends. You want an hors d'oeuvre, little something to chew on?"

She shoved back the sleeves of her denim blouse, shook her hair loose, and called after him as he padded into the kitchen: "Listen, I'm sorry I'm late. I had that seminar I mentioned last night and Judy was supposed to take me down to the infirmary."

"Don't sweat it, baby."

"She's off somewhere with that one-eyed creature."

"Heap?"

"Whatever it's called. The bald one that snaps its fingers."

Gnossos patting his pockets for cigarettes, Kristin giving him one from what looked like a silver case with a bear on the hallmark. Quick puff, stain the lungs. "Anything wrong? The infirmary, I mean?"

"Only a friend with mono, an old roommate. I tried calling you but the number's unlisted or something."

"Under Pamela's name, nobody can get it. Have an endive?"

Her eyebrow going up as she munched. "Pamela?"

"Watson-May. Girl who used to have the pad. English."

"Oh."

"Alone, baby, not with me. You want some resin wine? Vitamin D, good for metabolism."

She kicked away her loafers as she crossed the room and had one knee-sock off when she returned with the bottle. She eased the other down with her toe as she stood on a single foot and poured. Her grace was astonishing. Gnossos put a finger to his lips instead of taking the offered glass, indicating that she should be silent a moment, as if some sound required their attention and in order to hear it they had to remain motionless. The neck of the bottle was poised, tilted in one hand, and his waiting drink in the other. She glanced from side to side, still on one leg, and looked at him. But it was a trick. All he wanted was time. The last of the sun's spectral color was refracted from the far side of the valley. It filtered through the bamboo slats that served as shades, lining her face in orange, ocher, blue, and brown, teasing the nap of her skin, polarizing the otherwise invisible down on her forearms, cheeks, and legs, pollenating the soft hairs into erotic dimension. The sleeves on her denim blouse were rolled high, her suede skirt was luxurious with texture, a knee was cocked, poking below the hem.

Blood pulsed into his groin and she probably knew. She took the brass ring that bound her hair and tossed it across the room, where it landed on the couch. "You haven't had any wine yet," she said.

He slaked the urge to touch her then and there. Talk food. "You dig stuffed vine leaves, all like that?"

"I guess. Try me."

Half a foot of Greek sausage, just the thing. "Why don't you turn on the machine? There's some Miles, a little J.J.

You said you were hungry, right?" He pogo-sticked into the kitchen in bare feet and whisked out the new Kresge's table-cloth. Powder-blue linen trimmed with white, little touch of nationalism. Must send a silver dollar to Makarios, buys two kilos of goat cheese. He reduced the flame under the egg-and-lemon sauce, squeezed a lime on the sizzling kebab, moved the plate of olives and feta nearer the stove, and took the chilled Pouilly-Fuissé from the refrigerator. Nod to a for-eign culture, liberal touch for the second course. Back in the living room he spread the linen cloth over the plywood table and arranged the knives and forks. He'd scrubbed them in Bon Ami and dried with cheesecloth. Kristin sat watching, bare leg tucked under her bottom, free foot tracing a pat-tern on the floor. Again in the kitchen he turned up the oven, extra lick of crust to the old sheep, and brought in more hors d'oeuvres, chilled, on a pewter platter. "You want a cushion for the floor?" Kristin smiled at the mussel fantasy, sliding a foam rubber pumpkin beneath her, and asked, "What's in them?"

"Treats. Little *moules farcies* thing, secret recipe, brought with Momma Pappadopoulis from the old country. Eat up, they make you grow."

She sat cross-legged, the skirt high but not high enough. Gnossos wondering about the dimension of her thighs, hop-ing for slimness, resiliency to the touch, tiny blond hairs, immaculate bevel. They touched glass rims and began. Si-lences then. Meal sounds: dishes clattering, knives scraping, wine gurgling out of bottles, toasted onion rolls opening, vine leaves sliding in sauce, broiled tomatoes squishing off skewers; Gnossos rising once to flip the record and bring in a salad chilled crisp with icecubes. The romaine and cucum-ber were dovetailed in a Radcliffe wastepaper basket, specially Brilloed for the occasion. Kristin watching every gesture, every step. Approving? "You know where meals are at, man?" he asked. "They're what they leave out of flicks. The commonplace."

"Like going to the bathroom?"

"You care for an insight? Life is a celluloid passion."

"Pooh, honestly, you're so busy thinking. Doesn't it get you tired?"

He looked around the table he had been so careful to keep tidy. Each dish neatly stacked, each course in its place, no crumbs, no peelings, no bones, no slops. The blue and white tablecloth as immaculate as a foreign minister's flag. He winked at Kristin, who was watching him carefully. Then lifted an urn full of salad dressing in his left hand and the nearly empty bottle of Greek wine in his right. A storm of cloudy residue swirled in both. With a flashing grin he turned them slowly upside down. He poured their heavy fluids all over the unviolated linen, painting like Jackson Pollock.

Later they waited by the fire. Cherry logs sputtered from the damp, hissed with wet little whispers that comforted their already humming ears. They sipped Cointreau from Wedgwood demitasse cups, nibbled chunks of feta from plastic toothpicks. The tablecloth was nailed over the plywood window, its fermenting images fixed in place by a quick coat of shellac. Gnossos had found the can in the hall closet and used it once before, to seal the sprung Captain Midnight Code-O-Graph against the mortal insult of rust. The dishes were abandoned in the shallow kitchen sink, a surprise for Fitzgore, payment for his wise-guy remarks. Pewter, china, stainless steel, glass, silver, and greasy lettuce.

Kristin puffed with languid abandon on an after-dinner

cigarette. Gnossos lay on his back, boy scout shirt open at the throat, watching shadows flutter on the ceiling. Hybrid animals leaping among shadow and flame. *How can those terrified vague fingers,* came the thought, just an instant before he found them in his palm.

Again, she was actually holding his hand.

Marriage, whispered the specter of some unwanted self. And right behind it, almost as if this self were implicit in the decapitated face above the fireplace: Beware the monkey-demon. Instead he measured her body with the fleshy calipers of his mind's vicarious eye, matched it against the feral silhouettes of his Radcliffe muse, of Southside five years earlier in the basement full of inner tubes under the Black Elks, of the girl with a forgotten name on the coast, who wore white silk stockings and red high heels. Faceless figures in the back seats of cars, on tabletops, rugs, afghan-covered beds, couches (with parents dozing in adjacent rooms), windy seashores on the sand, once up against a field-stone wall in Kansas City; bathtubs, showers, lakesides, river-banks, bushes, woods, grass, gravel, cobblestone, a garage, a summerhouse, a rocking chair; all the forearms, thighs, breasts, vaginas, kneecaps, tongues, fingers, skin, hair, and loins he had ever numbered or known. But always pulling for the big alternative, an intersection of the arcs, co-ordinates plotted by some cosmic hand, a circle enclosing the tip of his parabola in the ozone-tinted quadrant of Fulfillment. He measured, and nothing seemed wanting. For the nth $+$ 1 time the keeper of the wanton flame tried the mortal suggestion: Now or never.

One sock had yet to be removed. It lay collapsed around an ankle. He placed his hand over the green wool, hesitated gently, then went underneath to the vulnerable sole of her foot. She smiled with the sensation, not trying in the slightest to avoid his eyes, offering a subtly reinforcing sound of careless pleasure. At the same time, by way of magnificent surprise, of sudden, stimulating bonus, she brought her knee to her chest. The periscope rose with as much purpose as a surface-shattering Polaris missile.

But her expression changed when his hands slid under her buttocks. He pulled her closer against him, pretending not to see the sudden anxiety, and slipped his fingertips beneath the elastic, scuttling toward the front. Nice, springy around the navel, no fat, all firm. C'mon, baby, keep it going, no left turns.

"Gnossos."

"Right here, Piglet." Stopping not allowed.

But she went stiff just the same. Her smile faded and her eyes closed. "Could you wait a moment?"

Coax her, man, no slowing down, remember past failures. Go.

She jerked away just as he would have found it; the searching finger detoured uselessly, trapped under the elastic. "Really, Gnossos, wait."

Her period, of course. What the hell, do it anyway, no risk. Red corpuscles good for the 'scope, make it grow.

"It's just," she began, "oh, it's never easy to say."

Be kind. "I understand, man, happens all the time, every month in fact—"

"No you don't, either. It's just—Gnossos, wait, could you move your finger a minute? It's only—oh damn."

Kiss her, make it easier, little neckrub, supply confidence, be a husband. She twisted away, her eyes seeking the fire for distraction, then heaved an uncomfortable sigh, blurting out the news, "It's not my period, it's just that I'm a virgin."

And I'm Popeye the Sailor Man. Back down—

"No, Pooh Bear, really. It would be horrible with your

fingernail or something." She was still watching the fire. "Please."

"Check," he said, brushing her eyebrows. The short hairs were bristly and electric, people never dig eyebrows enough. Try the thighs.

"Gnossos!" She wheeled around. "Oh all right, but you'll know soon enough." Could she mean it? Too good to be true.

"You're putting me on?"

"If you mean I'm trying to fool you, no."

"No, man?"

"There's no reason, don't be silly."

"Virgin, baby?"

"Piglet genus."

"Membrane, and like that?"

"I guess."

"O wow."

"You can't tell me you didn't half expect it?"

Gnossos rolled over on his side and bumped against her rib cage. He gave a short, meaningful giggle. She waited a moment before coming after him.

"Don't make fun, Gnossos."

He waved his hand to tell her it was anything but, yet he couldn't stop the recurrence of the giggle. His forehead finally came to rest on the rug. His brain reeled from the potential significance of the fact, the extraordinary coincidence. "Me too," he said, "me too, man," and threw one arm around her waist, as if it belonged.

"You *are* making fun!"

"No no, really, not at all. Come on, Piglet, you must have known."

"Known what? You're all so cryptic, Pooh, and this is getting embarrassing."

"Intact, unviolated. Virgin, baby. Me."

She gave him back his arm and made a face. "Oh, Gnossos, come on."

"It's true, man, dig it, it's a real fact."

"I'll bet it is."

"Honest to Jesus."

"They even talk about you in Chevy Chase."

"No they don't, man, what is it?"

"It's where I live, near Washington."

"Never been there, must've been someone else."

"What about that Radcliffe junior who carries used things around in a musette bag? And the coed who went into a nunnery last year."

"What kind of things?"

"You know, those rubber things. She carries them in a bag like your rucksack. They talk about it all over the ivy league."

Jesus, saving up her Gnossos seed. "Don't believe it, all innuendo, cats need something to jaw about, spice up their day."

"Gnossos, really. And in the first place, it doesn't matter that much."

"Come on, man, you know it does. I laid them was all. What's that got to do with being a virgin?" He tried taking her hand. "Seriously."

"Oh, now you look intense. I said it didn't matter. Please, I couldn't bear to have you somber."

"But I'm telling you true, man. Membranes are spiritual. I mean, in the last analysis. Even vestals made it with priests when they weren't diddling around."

She moaned. "I don't *care* what vestals did, and men aren't virgins, anyway. You can't just throw the word around like that."

"Vestals kept the *flame,* you've got to care a little. And in *this* country, baby, men are virgins."

"Gnossos, you practically admitted you slept with all those girls—"

"Laid," he said, pointing with a finger. "It's not the same. You never masturbated on a seesaw? No, wait, don't look away."

"That's plain not nice."

"Flagpoles, man, monkey-bars? C'mon, everybody masturbates."

"Do they? Oh even if they do, it's different."

"I'm hip it's different, that's where it's all at. It's balling, not love-making, right? Man, you can hop-off on another individual just as easily as you can on a motorcycle, say."

"Well, maybe I'm just thinking of it physically, then. After all, if you're inside them—"

"Hey, I could be inside the nozzle of a vacuum cleaner. It's only what you surrender, a question of choice. If you're passive, what the hell happens? Nothing, right?"

"Listen, if this turns into a word game I'm going to lose out. Anyone can talk circles around me, even my father."

"Surrender is the critical factor, dig? The will imparts permission. And if you don't mind, leave your father out of this."

"But what is there to surrender?"

Gnossos poked the embers with an engraved andiron and thought for a moment. A charred log collapsed into a puff of new flame. The room was comfortably warm, on the verge of becoming hot. "Your head, for one."

She shook her hair free of her eyes, then nodded slightly. "Then you've never, I'd suppose you'd say—given yourself? I mean, the way you're describing it?"

"Check."

"And you expect me to understand why, just like that?"

Gnossos shrugged and took her other hand. "You know already, man. The conventional reason. Lose it and it's gone."

She watched the irony change his expression, then smiled a little more. "But girls have their own reasons. They worry about liking it too much, not being able to stop."

"Get the clap, never marry, ruin and scandal in Chevy Chase."

"Well yes, since you mention it."

"So?"

"Oh hell," she said, getting up. "Will you wait a moment, then. While I go to the bathroom?"

He grinned, and watched the fluttering air over the ash as she tiptoed across the room. He picked up her discarded knee-sock, rolled it into a ball, smiled, tumbled over on his back, drained both glasses of Cointreau, and filled again. Some Ouzo next time.

Then he noticed the record propped next to the pillow on his bed. It was tied with a green ribbon and had a note attached. It must have been there all evening. He crawled over curious and read the message:

> A thank you for the party, Pooh,
> and the Black Elks. Isn't it funny
> how a bear likes honey?

Well, how do you like that? Groovy old chic actually came bearing gifts. He looked, and it was a morning and evening raga by Ravi Shankar. The needle was dropping into place when she came back into the room.

"You found it," she said.

"Hey, man," looking for words, slightly embarrassed, "you buy gifts."

"Now and again," she said, strolling over. While she was still standing, he came up on his knees and reached under the suede skirt. It was open to the thigh like a wonchai dress. He meant to take down whatever was beneath, but amazingly nothing was there.

Behind her back she held the beige nylon panties she had removed in the bathroom. Gnossos looked up just in time to see them leave her hand, ripple through the air, and land lightly on the smoldering coals. After a moment they blossomed into flame.

"That seems to be that," she said.

Still on his knees, he parted the heavy material of the skirt and looked. Kristin's hands took him behind the ears. The hairs glistened umber from the flame. Her legs moved apart and her knees bent slightly as his fingers closed on the backs of her legs. One knee-sock was still collapsed around an ankle.

"Very excellent tasting in music."

They both jerked around.

George Rajamuttu was standing in the open door, toasting the phonograph with a glass of gin and grenadine.

"Superb improvisation," said Irma, materializing at his side. Under her arm were a number of 78 records. She was dressed in gauze.

"You will of course enjoy," said George Rajamuttu, moving clumsily into the room, setting down his drink on the plywood table, "these other recordings from our country."

"Ali Akbar Khan," said Irma.

"Pandit Chatur Lal," said George.

Kristin's knees had straightened and locked. Her skirt fell closed. She reached down self-consciously and pulled up the sock.

"The continual repetition of seven beats," said George;

"Corresponding to the Western measure," said Irma;

"As marked by the time of the tabla," said George;

"A kind of drum which can be played through an unusual number of octaves," explained Irma;

"Is worth your respectably particular attention."

They removed the Ravi Shankar, replaced it with an Ali Akbar Khan, clinked the icecubes in their glasses to punctuate the change, and went to the Navajo rug, where they squatted in the full lotus just inches away from the immobile couple.

"Cheers," said George and Irma Rajamuttu together, smiling their red-toothed smiles, lifting their glasses.

Under the blinking warning light of Circe III, Gnossos gave the finger to the sign-in girl.

"Pooh Bear!"

"I don't give a shit."

"It's not her fault. I'm sorry, really I am."

"Then stay out with me. It's not your fault either."

"It *is* my fault for getting you started and then having to come back. You know what would happen if I stayed."

"Fuck it. So you get booted. We'd flee."

"Listen, Pooh Bear. Are you listening?"

"I'm listening."

"And stop giving the finger to that girl, she's getting all upset. Are you listening?"

"Right."

"Do you know why I said okay tonight? I mean, before those people came in."

"Those were not people. Those were Oriental maniacs and I'm going to kill them in their sleep."

"You're not listening to what I mean."

"Go ahead."

"Do you know why I said okay?"

"What okay?"

"Gnossos, honest to God, would you put that finger in your pocket or something. We only have another minute."

"Another minute, that's right."

"People are watching you."

"Do you know what I'm going to do to those wogs? Do you have any idea what terror I'm going to bring down on their nodding, alcoholic heads?"

"Gnossos, listen to me!"

"I'm listening. What the hell makes you think I'm not listening? Just because those idiots stayed there and got smashed and grinned at us for two and a half hours."

"I said okay because I want you, does that make any sense?"

"They're going to fear the sound of my footsteps, man."

"And because of everything you said tonight."

"Torture, mutilation, the death of a Thousand Cuts. And who the hell are you kidding, baby? Whenever I talk, I talk to the old wall, right? Twenty times, maybe, I told them to clear out, you were there, you heard me. All's we got was that inscrutable crap they come on with."

"I have to get inside, Gnossos."

"I'll bet they practice it. I'll bet they stay up in front of little mirrors from Poona or someplace and rehearse Detachment."

"I'm talking about what you said to *me*, not them, or the wall. Oh Christ, the light is out. Hurry and kiss me." Her arms flew around his neck and held on for nearly a minute. The girl from the sign-in desk came to the door with a huge key and said officially: "Miss McLeod."

Gnossos wiggled his finger back and forth. His baseball cap was on the back of his head, his boy scout shirt was buttoned at the throat, tied with a red bandana, his tennis shoes were full of holes, and his corduroy trousers were too short.

"Tomorrow," she whispered, and was gone through the door. He could see her pronouncing the word goodnight as she paused in the vestibule, and his heart sank. He gave the Greek horns to the sign-in girl, who was pale with hatred, then turned back to the empty courtyard.

In his shirt pocket was a rolled-up piece of paper. Irma Rajamuttu had inserted it mysteriously when Kristin was in the bathroom, fixing the brass ring on her hair. In an alarming moment of sober exemption from betel, gin, and grenadine, and with the professional air of a secret lover at a cocktail party, she'd said to him, "Much caution."

Now the paper was in his hand, and he kept it there until he reached the street. The first warm wind of spring was still blowing strongly, and all the fraternity automobiles were gone. There was no moon, so he shuffled under a lamppost to read, easing the baseball cap forward on his eyes. Indian pinheads, all into their own little thing. Much caution of what? Spooky, those red teeth, like a nutria, younger than I thought.

The message was written in indelible purple ink. It said:

the statement on the other side is false

He turned it over cautiously. The paper had a faint odor of incense and rosewater.

the statement on the other side is true

He thought about it only as long as he had to, then looked up, across the campus, at nothing in particular.

Tell me all about it.

BOOK
THE SECOND

11

G. Alonso Oeuf, also a paradox.

But not without a plan. Old corpulent jelly foxing the outside world for ten years, playing the game in enemy territory. Impossible to elude, like Muzak in Las Vegas. A subliminal breed of animate slogan, owl features and horn rims grinning at you everywhere. Textbook illustrations, Oeuf doing titration; billboards, Oeuf drinking Red Cap; campus calendars, Oeuf talking to summery coeds under sycamores. The Kodak blowup in Grand Central Station, his technicolor form expanded eighty times, gazing past a row of binocular microscopes, YOUNG AMERICA AT WORK. A *Daily Sun* supplement on faculty achievement, in sweatclothes with a medicine ball, endorsing Dean Magnolia's calcium remedy for athlete's foot. Testimonial posters in the student union, wearing his black knit tie and olive shirt, shaking hands with candidates, bright-eyed androids who never lose. Wire photos, standing just behind President Carbon at groundbreaking ceremonies. Newsreels, always prominent in the spectator footage; parades, football games, state funerals. People remember but don't know why. Who was that young man with the umbrella, Miss Pankhurst, don't we know him from somewhere?

Gnossos finally clomped down the hill to check Oeuf's condition. The belated visit was coaxed by Youngblood's early-morning call, a smell of unrest in the thermal air, and a taste of ferment and revolt. Heffalump had once returned with a description of the private infirmary room. Odors of antiseptic and Old Spice toilet water, he'd said, the university's only Hollywood sack, topped with the inflatable mattress they kept for inflamed-prostate cases, sons of South American dictators. Something about an office atmosphere, file cabinets on casters, swingaway bookshelves with political science texts, electric typewriters plugged in and humming, an abacus, an adding machine, a dictaphone, mimeograph stencils, chrome-plated photostat devices, empty peanut jars of sharpened pencils, shorthand pads, small combination safe, addressograph machine, three telephones. One with a red panic-bulb, padlocked.

He wandered through the antiseptic Victorian building, opening ward doors, peeking into out-patient waiting rooms, stumbling upon blood tests and urine analyses, feeling his way. Too much of a drag to check with the desk, forms to fill out, questions to answer, maybe get a no at the end: Sorry, young man, Mr. Oeuf is not allowed visitors, will you just sign this loyalty oath and try again in the fall?

But he was approached mysteriously by a red-haired nurse in orange spike heels. She looked him up and down and said, "Room one-o-one. Follow me, please."

"Who're you?"

"Nurse Fang. This way, please, last door on the left, Alonso has been expecting you."

She walked ahead of him, ass swinging, nearly six feet tall. At the door she used a four-inch key, nodded, and waited for him to enter.

Oeuf lay propped up in the huge bed, wearing baby-blue pajamas. There was white piping on the lapels. He was shorter and fatter than Gnossos remembered him, chubby little-boy fingers, trimmed cuticles, new goatee. His attention was momentarily fixed on a pack of playing cards. Systematically he was cutting kings and aces. Not realizing who had entered, he motioned for a moment's silence before making a final part in the deck. The pause gave Gnossos an opportunity to locate the padlocked telephone on a bedside table. Around Oeuf's neck were a platinum chain and key.

Cough. Two owl eyes blinked up.

"Pappadopoulis, well!" They blinked again. "I was beginning to despair. You find me *in extremis* and somewhat *en deshabillé*." The whites of his eyes were cloudy yellow, not white. His expression changed from preoccupied intensity to pleasurable interest.

"Hello, Oeuf. Long time no see, buddy."

"Chacun à son goût. Did you get my message?"

"Youngblood called at seven in the morning, man. Said you wanted to see me before you died, or something."

"Splendid fellow, Youngblood. The perfect *particeps criminis,* I should say." His horn rims slipped down on the tip of his tiny nose, fingers continuing to cut money cards. "Little poker, five-card draw?"

Gnossos shaking his head, patting the rucksack where the few remaining silver dollars clinked weakly. "Heff said you thought I was frozen, man, how'd you find out?"

"Oh, an *obiter dictum* here and there. How was she, anyway?"

"Who?"

"Your Radcliffe muse?"

He paused a moment. *"Obiter dictum,* my ass.

"*Sotto voce,* Gnossos, *sotto voce.* There's a nurse's aid or two suspicious of my presence here."

"Can't blame them," turning over a card, getting the queen of spades, sliding it back into the deck. "How's your frame doing?"

"Bedsores, Gnossos. You wouldn't believe them. Sometimes I wonder if it's all worth it. And look at my eyes."

"Jaundice?"

"Convincing, isn't it? That's what they thought *ab initio.*"

"What've you got, anyway?"

"It's all unlikely. The whole thing is extremely unlikely. Speaking of which, I hear you're in love."

"Jesus Christ, Oeuf."

"Venus is really more worthy of the invocation. Aphrodite, in your case. Cloud is her name? Christmas Cloud?"

"Kristin McCleod. And what do you mean 'convincing'? Isn't it still jaundice?"

"Never was, old boy. Not even mono. Didn't have a thing, actually, till I caught the clap from Ian."

"Clap? Who's Ian?"

"I didn't really catch it from Ian, but I said I did. He was their prostate surgeon here. Not a bad fellow at all, Canadian, I think. We shared a bathroom before they gave me these private accommodations, you see."

"You don't have the clap?"

"Oh, but I do. I caught it from Nurse Fang on this very same inflatable mattress. God knows where she got it. Perhaps from you. A great deal of *noblesse oblige,* Nurse Fang. Very *au fait.* Runs my addressograph machine, all kinds of special skills. You didn't give her the clap, did you, Gnossos?"

"What the hell is this all about, you scheming maniac? And why are your eyes yellow?"

"You know Rosenbloom, certainly? Splendid fellow. *Agent provocateur* type. A chemical engineer, extremely useful, he prepares the inert ocher compound I'm obliged to use."

Gnossos watched him carefully with a measured sideways glance. Then moved around the room slowly, cautiously, touching all the office machines to establish their presence, picking up pads to test for weight, listening to dial tones on the two unpadlocked telephones, trying the space bar on the electric typewriter. Oeuf watched with a considerate smile on his pale lips, continuing to shuffle cards on the pink silk quilt, cutting aces and kings. Gnossos finally stopped, after checking half a dozen names on the addressograph plates.

"All right, man, what's up?"

"Whatever do you mean, Paps?"

"You know what I mean. All this organization crap, this private room, your not being sick and the whole goddamned campus thinking you were ready to die with hepatitis or something."

"You do me an injustice, Paps. Like I said, I'm *in extremis*. I've got the clap. It's very uncomfortable. Drip-drip-drip."

"So get some penicillin. I want to know what's up."

"Penicillin no longer kills the Athené clap bug. Got to use one of the mycins."

"Use one, then. What're all the phones for?"

"They suggested aureomycin, but it might have cured me, and we cannot afford to let that happen. Too much harm would come of it. I'm safe here, Gnossos. We're all safe here. Would you care for a drink? Metaxa perhaps, ice, twist of lemon, dash of angostura?" Oeuf cut the ace of diamonds as he leaned over toward the intercom and snapped a switch:

"Double Metaxa, *à la grecque;* the usual for me. And hurry, please." He smiled again at Gnossos, then flicked the entire deck, a card at a time, from one palm to the other over a distance of nine inches. "Would you be surprised to learn, Paps, that with a minimum of risk and the vaguest co-operation on your part, you could earn precisely enough Exemption Status to keep you Immune, Secure, and Non-ionized, say, for the next generation?"

Gnossos watched the cards shuffle in the opposite direc-tion like the folds in a collapsing concertina. He had not answered by the time Nurse Fang pranced into the room with a glass of Metaxa, a half pint of *piña colada,* and a small silver pail of icecubes. Her orange spike heels sank luxuriously in the wall-to-wall weave of the Kerman rug. Her pinstriped uniform was skintight.

"This is Mr. Pappadopoulis, Nurse Fang," continued Oeuf, carefully watching both of them for signs of recogni-tion. "He is not the man who gave you the clap you gave me, is he? The truth, now."

Nurse Fang examined Gnossos with a clinical once-over from baseball cap to borrowed combat boots. "No sir," she said.

"Very well. See that we're not disturbed by anyone ex-cept the Junta."

"Junta?" asked Gnossos. The nurse had walked across the rug and was closing the door behind her. She wore fish-net stockings.

"Sit down," said Oeuf. "Let's talk *en famille.*"

Gnossos eased into the empty leather chair by the side of the bed. Play it through, go along, who knows? There were no windows in the room, just the single door. His stomach rolled, but it could have been an intestinal hangover from the trauma of the previous afternoon's bowel evacuation. He sipped at the Metaxa and forced a clever, "Try me, man."

"The *ancien régime* is about to fall, Gnossos."

"Oh yeah?"

"The *beau monde* is ready to topple."

He nodded.

"There is going to be a *coup d'état*. The *bête noire* is doomed."

"The *bête noire?*"

"President Carbon."

"Oh."

"Why just 'oh'?"

"I've heard about it."

"Youngblood?"

"And I'm not interested," standing up, looking for an uncluttered surface on which to set down his drink. "I'm a-political, dig?"

Oeuf with a look of supremely confident patience: "Gnossos?"

"What?"

"Do you want a Ford?"

"A what?"

"Fellowship. Ten grand. Private secretary, research office?"

"Don't put me on."

"A Guggenheim to Paris, Firenze, some groovy place like Tangier?"

"Tangier?"

"You want the Nobel Peace Prize?"

"The what?"

"I'm willing to pay. You help me, I help you."

"Oeuf man, anything I have that's tangible, you don't want."

"*Au contraire*, old sport, *au contraire*," Oeuf releasing a window-style shade above the bed. Underneath, on the wall, was a map of Athené, studded with miniature paper flags of different colors. "You can get me Lairville," he said.

"Lairville?"

"*Entre nous*, Gnossos, in case you were previously unaware of it, you are the *jeunesse dorée* of Lairville. A figure. An anti-hero."

"Bullshit, man, I'm immune to that kind of crap."

"Just *entre nous*, Gnossos, you are far from immune to it. Consciously or otherwise, you attract it."

"Look, man, I'm Exempt as it is. On my own. I don't like people getting too close. Especially maniacs who want a piece of my ass for something. Now, what are you getting at, 'cause I've got things to do."

"Yes, I know. Speaking of which, how are your grades? Good, I imagine?"

"Why?"

"Mustn't have you coming up before any academic review boards. They're always good, Gnossos; your grades, I mean. It's just that no one ever expects them to be. You have a way of giving people to think you never study, wouldn't you say? Like your orphan syndrome."

"I don't follow, man, be explicit."

"This quality you exude of having no parents. Who associates you with Brooklyn?"

Gnossos put down his glass, feeling an insidious threat to identity. "Look, Oeuf, old buddy, Youngblood called me in the middle of the goddamned night to get me over here," starting for the door, "and the whole scene is just a little too tenuous and middle class for my—"

"The door is locked, Gnossos, from the outside. And you're not being quite yourself."

"I'll knock it down, baby."

"Be reasonable or unreasonable, whichever you prefer, but pay attention. You want to stay in Athené. Without the ultimate hangup of having to be in school, correct? You want Immunity. I can fix it. You want Exemption, I can fix that too. Look at the map."

"I'm looking. And I'm Exempt anyway, just keep it in mind."

"Only in a subjective sense. You're not truly protected, you see. The important color on the flags, of course, is red. At heart I'm a traditionalist. *Ex post facto,* it will be changed to blue."

"*Ex post* what *facto?*"

"The *coup d'état.* At the moment you'll notice the coed dormitory areas, in particular the Siren group, denoted by the palest pinks. The same for Lairville. Faculty compounds, men's dorms, downtown apartments, most fraternities—with the exception of the Southern brotherhoods— these are scarlet to vermilion in hue. The immediate concern, however, remains Lairville. It wants conversion."

Gnossos pushed his orange-peaked baseball cap over his eyes and absently fondled the photostat machine. "Come on, Oeuf, really. Me?" He slung his rucksack over his shoulder, as if to leave. "Are you out of your mind?"

"The independents in Lairville hold you in high esteem. You are in a position to alter their inability to think collectively."

"That's why they're independent, man, not in the goddamned fraternities. Little anarchy action never hurt anyone. And who the hell ever figured me for the political-vanguard type, to begin with? Now no shit, give the word to whoever works that door or I'll heave your IBM typewriter clean through it."

"Think of Miss Cloud."

The point slid in, sensibility still injured by having to rush her back at curfew, her very presence in the pad making her subject to dismissal. But there were other ways. "Leave her out of it."

"And Carbon. His is *non compos mentis,* Paps. He is going to tear down Ovid Hall."

"What?"

"Ovid Hall is the testicular aesthetic extension of the tall Clock Tower. The buildings belong together. Emasculation as a policy should never be condoned. He couldn't do it without the consent of the Architectural Advisory Committee of course, but as you know, he's refused to reappoint them."

"I read that in the *Sun.*"

"Youngblood's editorial; yes, I know. I did the first draft. The architecture building, if you'll refer to the map, is represented by a bright red flag."

Gnossos glanced, picked up his Metaxa, drained it, and said nothing. Oeuf pressed on:

"Carbon has too much *amour-propre.* You couldn't be expected to know, for instance, that he is about to be considered for a Cabinet post in Washington."

"Oh come on."

"Secretary of State, Gnossos, bite your tongue."

"Of State?"

"Another Dulles. Now prepare yourself. Are you prepared? Susan B. Pankhurst is a Daughter of the American Revolution."

"No."

"A descendant of John Adams."

"It's not true."

"And we all know about John Adams."

Gnossos sat down.

"Should Carbon leave, for any reason—say, to accept this Cabinet position—she would become President of the university."

"Stop."

"It's in the bylaws. There's a copy at your elbow," Oeuf cutting the ace of spades from the deck and showing it to Gnossos. Then speaking into the intercom again:

"Nurse Fang. Another double Metaxa." After putting the cards aside, he sighed deeply into the temporary silence. "Calvin Blacknesse is on our Junta. So is your composer friend Grün.

"You're lying."

"Ask them."

Nurse Fang entered quietly and filled Gnossos' empty glass, adding an icecube with a pair of surgical tongs from the bucket. She touched Oeuf on the pulse, "Some of the Junta waiting to see you, sir. And I'm available for the addressograph, effective eleven hundred hours."

"In a moment."

She left, ass-bouncing, and Gnossos said, "No."

"No what?"

"I still couldn't. It's not my scene. Too political."

"It's been that way *de novo,* old sport."

"I don't give a shit."

"Miss Cloud is with us."

"What?"

"So is Fitzgore. And your ace buddy Heffalump, at least until he leaves for Cuba. We will win, Gnossos, and *vae vic-*

tus when we do. You want a Prix de Rome? A Pulitzer Prize?"

"What about grass? I'm only asking, mind you."

"We've got a trustee who just won the proxy fight at Sandoz."

"Sandoz?"

"The lab of the same name. Largest manufacturers of synthetic mescaline in the world. You want to do research?"

"Stop!" Gnossos jumped up and paced the carpeted floor from one wall to the other. He turned his baseball cap back to front, sideways, then forward again. Finally halting, he flicked a couple of beads on the abacus. "You're evil shit, you know that, Oeuf?"

"Au contraire, Gnossos, I'm doing good." Oeuf squirmed into a sit-up position and took off his glasses. "The closed community is our refuge, our salvation. The answers to questions of immediate comfort, as you know, are valid in the microcosm as well. Nearly by definition, *nicht wahr?"*

"Enough. I'm going."

"Think about it."

"I'm too busy. Goodbye. Get a streptomycin jolt, stops the dripping. Clap's affected your mind."

"That's as may be. *Sholom aleicheim,* Gnossos."

The door swung open and Nurse Fang stepped in, still wearing her pinstriped uniform. But in place of her nurse's cap she wore a bun, which sported a number of freshly inserted pencils. She sat down at the addressograph machine without a word, efficiently inserted a tray of plates, and stepped on the starter pedal. Behind her came Judy Lumpers in a turquoise angora sweater, Drew Youngblood in white shirtsleeves, Juan Carlos Rosenbloom under an oversized Stetson, and Dean Magnolia in a wrinkled seersucker suit. "Mawnin', Mistuh Pappadopolum," from Magnolia with an uneasy smile.

Gnossos could not speak. George Rajamuttu strolled behind the dean, carrying a transistor radio against his ear and a thermos jug under his arm. There were icecubes tinkling in the thermos.

When the entire group had entered the room, Nurse Fang surprised them all by pronouncing with reverence the words:

"Condition Red."

The lightbulb on the padlocked telephone was going on and off, and apparently had been doing so for some seconds. Oeuf unhooked the platinum key from the chain around his neck. He paused and transferred a pregnant glance from Gnossos to Nurse Fang, who said, "You'll have to leave, Mr. Pappadopoulis. Sorry."

He was shown summarily out.

Heffalump was waiting in a wheelchair in the corridor. He got up when he saw Gnossos and skipped over, checking his pocketwatch. "Hurry up, Paps, there's not much time."

"Christ, what now?"

"No chitchat, c'mon, I got the rice an' everything."

"Rice?"

"For the wedding, man."

The word gave a sense of appalling vertigo. The infirmary surroundings slid into an ether of madness around his senses. "Not you and Jack, man, not the dyke?"

"Keep your cool, Paps."

"I don't feel very well."

Heff helped him into the wheelchair and pushed him down the hall to the exit. "It's that English chic, what's her name? That Pamela girl."

"Watson-May?"

"Yeah, we'll just about make it. Jack's got Fitzgore's Impala."

Gnossos rubbed his eyes with thumb and forefinger and allowed himself to be hustled out the Victorian doors into the sunshine. The car was at the curb, top down, and Jack helped him in, smiling, asking no questions. As they pulled away he grumbled, "Maniac bitch. Told me Simon had taken the gas pipe."

"He did, man," from Heff in the front seat. "This is someone else."

"Someone else?"

"You haven't heard? Fitzgore didn't tell you?"

"Who, goddammit?"

"Mojo."

He heard the name and repronounced it softly to the space beside him, as if another Gnossos were sitting there. "Mojo."

"He wanted you for best man, the way I heard it, but you couldn't be found."

"Mojo?"

"He's using that Heap kid instead." Then, as they turned up Academae Avenue, "Come on, Jack, move it, it's probably started by now."

Gnossos closed his semifeverish, guilt-heavy eyes, slid down into the ersatz leather seat, and held a forefinger cocked against his temple like a Smith & Wesson .38. He thought, just before he pulled the trigger, how

plucked petals, by any other name

would be as beat.

Another one loves me not.

Bang.

12

And bang again.

One for good measure. Can't be too careful, bullets reputed to have lodged in harmless wads of little-known tissue, fiber just adjacent to mortal veins and arteries. Wouldn't do to have a leadlump in the temple, filling in a useless tooth. Bang bang. Bangbang bang. How many, six, seven? Mustn't violate the unities.

The Impala rounded the sweeping uphill entrance to the campus and braked to a jerking halt before the university Gothic of Coprolite Hall. When Jack turned off the engine they could hear the electronic harmonium, dissonant Schoenberg frequencies, metallic fifths rattling the stained-glass windows. The sun was hazy-bright, the crocuses and jonquils poked pointed heads through the freshly cut lawn. Crowds of curious students, apparently tipped off, gathered under trees for a look at the new bride and groom, eager for a glimpse at one of the epochs of mortality. But everything seemed to be over. The microbus waited at the curb like a mechanical afterthought in Mojo's dreamy mind. The whipping scars had been inked in with red lead, the fenders and lights were decorated with white roses and little silver bells, and the happy couple was just leaving the chapel door.

They were accompanied by a beaming Monsignor Putti and half a dozen zombi attendants. Gnossos, in his mind's eye, seeing an arch of crossed bullwhips.

"Goddamn," said Jack, "we missed it."

"I've got lentils," from Heff, "in case you don't dig rice."

Gnossos glared at them, his instincts receiving a number of unmistakably aggressive impulses. "You got any rocks?"

"Bitter," said Jack casually, "mustn't be bitter."

There was a sudden, collective indrawn hush as the ensemble reached the car and Pamela, in ivory silk, freed her throwing-arm of confining lace. She was holding a bridal spray of St.-John's-worts and about to fling. Flashbulbs popped. She paused, then tossed the flowers high into the air. A collective "Ooooooo" of approval as they tumbled over and over, almost in slow motion, arching above knots of hopeful fingers, sailing through the warm breeze, down toward the open Impala. Gnossos watched horrified as they plopped into his lap, petals popping loose like butterflies. "Ahhh," said the crowd, endorsing.

Pamela recognized him. She whispered something to Mojo, then waved and giggled insanely before turning and skipping away. Heap was right behind, rolling up the bridal train, donning a chauffeur's cap. He ushered everyone into the microbus with an extraordinary lack of confusion, then leaned on the horn. A few people cheered, tin cans clattered, Heffalump threw his lentils with a shrug, and the machine eased casually away from the curb. Two of Proctor Slug's motorcycle campus police met them at the corner and led them away down the hill, sirens wailing.

Gnossos, a little daffy, looked at the spray of St.-John's-worts. He felt a breed of sugary nausea enveloping his sensibilities, nearly as if he'd eaten a porridge of sweetmeats and custard while looking at French postcards. The crowd on the lawn continued waving, and Jack and Heff turned around and asked together: "Where to, sport?"

He closed his eyes and sighed. What could one say? "Fresh air, babies. My tubes need cleansing."

"How about a Dairy Queen?" from Jack. And if he could, he would have poached her with his stare.

As they drove along Harpy Creek, Heff finally whistled and said, "All that money. Wow."

"Just think of it," from Jack, accelerating. "You'd need a Univac."

There was a full minute's silence. Then Gnossos asked, "All what money?"

"Really out of the question, when you give it a little thought." She was coming out of a curve and couldn't hear with the top down.

Gnossos was busy stuffing flowers into the rucksack, his hair whipping in the wind. "*What* money?" he tried again, louder.

"Real spooky," said Heff, who also couldn't hear. "Like bread was the only thing keeping him in the small time. He's really home-free."

"Where'll they go?" asked Jack.

"Fitzgore figured Monaco," from Heff, while Gnossos moaned and pounded his knees. "No tax problems, close to international borders, easy access to Switzerland, mountain hideouts, all like that."

Gnossos controlled the tantrum, waited for Jack to brake, going into a curve, then leaned over the front seat between them and screamed, "What money, goddammit?!"

Heff looked back. "Her oil bread, man. What do you mean 'what money'?"

"Her oil bread," repeated Gnossos weakly.

"Didn't Fitzgore tell you? He introduced them, you know."

Silence.

"The Watson-May Holdings," explained Jack, accelerating again. "She's the only heir."

"Heiress," corrected Heff.

"Eighty billion dollars," from Jack.

"Something like that," from Heff. "In gold."

"Think of it," from Jack.

Gnossos near collapse on the floor of the back seat, his fingers kneading the almost moneyless rucksack, musing idiotically to himself:

I'm thinking.

Boy, am I thinking.

13

Still, he was in love.

And love was a consolation. Like a sideshow panacea for symptomatic ills, it soothed anxiety, pain, and doubt; eased fear and insomnia, purged the more accessible demons, and apparently acted as a mild laxative. Above mach 1, of course, control systems were likely to reverse. Anxiety might come clawing back on six prickly legs, pain might return with a prodigal scream to the inner ear, fanged demons might drop from the darkness, doubt might creep whispering from a mildewed closet, insomnia might collapse weeping between his eyes, constipation might close insidiously in. But speeds were still relatively moderate and Gnossos liked it down where he could hear the sound of his own exhaust.

Dreaming, but still tangibly aware of the Epiphanal Defloration to come, he wandered in the country alone. The Impala had long since continued to the Dairy Queen without him, and he walked along the swollen, puffy mudbanks of Harpy Creek. In the air were odors of increase. In the wind were sounds of narcosis. He continued on an invisible arc of magnetic flux, more ionized than he had a mind to be, until he found the swampy, stump-punctuated acreage behind the Blacknesse house. Even with the bright sun above, the land was somber and chilly under the pines, and one of the stumps turned out to be not a stump but Calvin Blacknesse in the full lotus. He was under a tree, gazing at nothing, his eyes turned over in his brooding head. The creek, still charging from the thaw, roared and gurgled twenty feet below, carrying branches, bits of spongy sod, erosion, and stone. Gnossos approached him quietly, tired from his walk, not wanting to disturb, but there was no reaction. He sat down nearby and ate a flower, waiting. In a while, the silence of the surrounding was overwhelming.

"Calvin," he tried.

But in his trance Blacknesse failed to answer. A small circular weight was attached by cord to his head. It pressed against his brow where the third eye would be. His fingers were formed in graceful loops and ellipses, palms up, and he made a humming sound. This sound was in harmony with the extraordinary silence, it was the frequency of a thousand insect wings. When Gnossos looked, there were bees and wasps falling from the buds, dropping stunned out of the sky, winging dizzily from an infinity of directions. They swarmed and collided, they bumped pleasantly together, they swam in the modulation of their own flight, they hovered in a fluid dance until Blacknesse broke off with a sudden shriek. Then they scattered and vanished. Two eyes came leisurely open.

"No," he said, his fingers making circles of the ellipses. "It is not right."

Gnossos leaned forward, his mouth hanging open, to ask what. But Calvin's eyes had again revolved and the blind whites stared at nothing.

Another sound commenced, a chirping inflection, a feathered clack. The head rolled slightly, describing small curves, and Gnossos feared (but only remotely) for the man's sanity. Then two kingfishers came, answering the sudden call. They whirled about one another, they spun as if hinged to some common center, fluttering on the circumference of an invisible pinwheel. Before they could be drawn to the vortex, Calvin's voice faltered and broke. The birds dropped like stones into the rushing creek, splashed furiously, then rose with gleaming fishes wiggling in their beaks.

When their cries could no longer be heard and the earlier silence again commanded the air, Blacknesse shook his head slowly, opened his hands in a gesture of futility. Something seemed to have failed. Gnossos, not daring to move, waited for him to speak.

"No," he said finally. "It seems useless." His eyes returned and he removed the weight from his forehead. An oval indentation remained, fading.

"What's going on, man?"

"Useless," repeated Blacknesse.

"Useless?"

"How long have you been here?"

"Not long. Since just before the bees."

"Ah." He dropped the weight into his shirt pocket.

"Calvin, man?"

"Umm?"

"You're okay?"

"What?"

"Are you all right?"

"What do you mean?"

"Never mind, it'll keep."

Blacknesse looked momentarily at his hands, paused, then said, "Don't blame yourself." He spoke the words as if they were part of some longer, more complex conversation, and not out of context.

"Hunh?"

"For Mojo."

"What?"

"It was none of your doing, Gnossos. Evil," he paused a moment, nearly sighing, "evil needn't be conjured to be manifest. It often functions on its own. You'll see."

"I'll see what?"

Another long, quivering pause.

But when Gnossos arrived at the house with the Swiss drolleries and entered the apartment, he found Fitzgore with his red head in the commode.

Scattered all over the floor were pewter pots, brass plates, copper hunting horns, and nineteen empty bottles. The bottles had until recently been filled with aspirin, Bufferin, Anacin, NoDoz, Miltown, milk of magnesia, mineral oil, paregoric, rubbing alcohol, Coricidin, Super Anahist cold pills, Pepto-Bismol, calamine lotion, baby oil, Bromo Quinine, Lavoris, Old Spice toilet water, after-shave lotion, and Dr. Brown's Cel-Ray tonic. Fitzgore was wearing his Navy ROTC uniform and had left a note. It read:

> How I hungered for her touch.
> Her darling hand enclosed in
> mine. There shall be weeping
> and gnashing of tee

The place stunk of vomit. Fitzgore was still semiconscious.

A dull moment of panic. "What the hell did you *do?!*," bellowed Gnossos, jerking the head out of the commode. "Did you *swallow* all that shit?"

A limp-necked nod: "Rrrggffd," came the answer.

"Holy Christ," he implored the ceiling. He let the head snap back and rushed to the baby refrigerator, whipping up a horror of egg whites, mustard, and warm water. When Fitzgore saw and understood he was meant to drink it, his eyes swam. He closed his hands over the top of his head in numb protest. His once white ROTC hat was inverted next to him on the tile floor, already full of regurgitated, semidigested suicide stew.

"C'mon mother, drink it, drink it up!"

"Rrrggffd."

Gnossos forced the unwilling head back and poured the slimy mixture into its mouth. When he was satisfied with the amount swallowed, he ran to the phone and called for an ambulance, impressing the terrified switchboard operator with the false fact that the victim had turned blue and was hemorrhaging. She failed to doubt him and promised instant action. When he again returned to the bathroom Fitzgore was retching with astonishing violence. Gnossos held him so he wouldn't choke.

After a while the spasms subsided and he tried speaking, but the words emerged in a soapy mumble. "I . . . grrfrder . . . unnerstans? I've never . . ."

"Shut up and vomit. Christ."

". . . Squeeeze . . . rrI wanna squeeeeeezee . . ."

His stomach muscles contracted violently and he threw up again, this time returning better than a dozen of the

Miltown. Sure thing, thought Gnossos, keep her coming.

". . . betrayal . . . all atime awake . . . you jerk."

"Quiet, man, just heave."

"And me affer . . . her . . . ass . . . anall that . . . rrmonieeeee . . ."

"You could've killed yourself, you cabbage. Come on, upchuck!"

". . . an I hadda innerduce em . . ." he went on, his face the color of the bathtub, his hair matted, without life. "Me . . . meee. I hadda innerduce em allright . . . allright . . . hehehe." He began to laugh, then stopped abruptly, went cross-eyed, and threw up again.

"Easy, baby, there you go, zippo-bang."

". . . married . . . hehehe . . . just like that . . . urp."

"Married, man?"

"Urp."

Something devious occurred to Gnossos.

"Introduce who?" he asked. "You feeling any better?"

"Hehehehehehehehehehehehehe . . ."

"Go slow, man, stay loose. Who do you mean?"

". . . rrgfdallatime . . . awake . . . an you thought I was sleeping . . . hehehehehe."

For a moment Gnossos stopped trying to help. It's not possible, came the thought. What I think he's talking about could not truly be possible.

"Hehehehe . . . an I heard every . . . fuckin' word he said, Paps . . . him an that one-eyed creep. Egh."

"You mean Mojo, baby?"

"Hehehehehe . . ."

"That morning when he was here?" Gnossos held the pale head up by its ear.

"Ggrrfd."

"When he was in *here?*"

"Hehehehe . . . youdumbjerk . . . yousweetdumbgreek-greekjerk . . . hehehe . . ."

Gnossos looked at the bare wall, slapped his forehead, and whispered to himself, "The loft party. How else would everyone have known?" Then he considered the vomiting figure, who was as limp as a marionette with the strings cut away. Fitzgore somehow managing to grin and nod, finally blurting:

"Oh, she's beautiful, Paps . . . allbeautifultwat an no boobs, I know, but beautiful, wow . . ."

Gnossos in his mind's eye looking again at the small door in the loft, through which had come so many sounds of wet flesh. A delicate phthisic hand reaching across the threshold to guide the drooling Mojo; but this time pegging its owner, zeroing in like a Zoomar lens on those same fingers which had once wrenched the enema bag. Pamela.

"You scheming little bastard," he said softly.

"Hehehehe . . . I wanna die . . ."

"You fetid, mangy bastard."

"Ggg . . . but I loved her, Paps, see? . . . egh did I love . . ."

"You fixed it all!"

He belched.

"The whole contaminated scene, man."

Fitzgore nodded, gulping for breath, trying to look up, the serge lapels of his ROTC uniform smeared with drool. "Only way . . . I could make her, Paps . . . Paps baby . . . Paps man . . . the only way she wanted . . . little orgy action . . . little lucky Pierre thing . . . me on bottom, man . . . beautiful, oh so beautiful. But how could I have known, sweetheart . . . tell me . . . oh, lemme die, man."

"I'll let you die in a minute, mother. Just tell me what you couldn't have known."

"Couldn't know, man . . . how could I? . . . ol' Mojo on top with his bullwhip, man . . . just rollin' around . . . oh, Paps baby, she went for it. She liked him an' that bullwhip, man. Oh, she liked it all, man . . . gone now . . . all gone." Fitzgore began to weep pathetically. "She went away. Gonegonegone . . . all gone. Rrrgffd. Pamela-honeybaby . . ."

Gnossos felt revulsion like a moldy bacterial growth in his mouth. "Oh, you corrupt little bedsore," he said. "Die, why don't you? I mean, just go rancid and expire." He let the head clunk down against the inside of the commode, then searched frantically in the medicine cabinet for bottles that could be saved for another try. But everything had been used. He stormed into the living room and called the infirmary.

"That's right, lady, cancel the goddamned ambulance."

"But it's on its way, Mr. Pappadoo."

"I don't give a shit, right? Intercept it, stop it, he's okay, believe me. Not a thing wrong with him."

"But he had a hemorrhage not twenty minutes ago."

"Amazing recovery, all better, all cool. Don't worry. He's not here, anyway. Out having a drink to celebrate."

But it was useless. The ambulance came while he was still talking, and a team of attendants led by Nurse Fang carried Fitzgore away, weeping, giggling, vomiting on his uniform with brass buttons.

That very same night, to atone, he abandoned his body without care to the girl in the green knee-socks. The time for

Epiphanal Defloration seemed to be upon them and there was no use fighting the metaphysical weather.

"Really," she said, disrobing. "Pretending to be asleep."

"It brought me down, baby. Do I look down?"

"And then he just planned the whole thing with Mojo?"

"I'm sick, dig? I'm sick all over."

"Was he really in love with Pamela? It's a bit difficult to believe."

"And I never saw it, not a bit of it. Rub my back a little, will you?"

"I brought a book along, a special one."

"Read to me, baby, put a little something in my head."

"God though, when you think of it. Just to be in bed, couldn't he have asked her? I mean, some other way?"

"American, baby. The country is diseased. Little lower. To the left more."

" 'Wherever I am,' " she read, " 'it's always Pooh,

It's always Pooh and me.

Whatever I do, *he* likes to do,

"So what are you doing tonight?" says Pooh:

"Well how very nice, 'cos I am too . . ." ' "

Yet to his cataclysmic surprise—when he had her ready and waiting, when he cautiously eased her knees apart with his own, when he hand-offered the sacrifice of his periscope's blind eye, when she leaned nervously away and uttered a moan of exquisite surrender—to his cataclysmic surprise there was no membrane to stop him.

He was within her as easily as a plug in a socket and nothing had happened, nothing whatever. But they didn't stop to discuss it and neither did they come together when they came. She was a full minute ahead.

As they were drinking Dairy Queen root beer floats in

Fitzgore's Impala she explained that it could only have been a Tampax accident. Gnossos said he didn't understand; he was having trouble with the empty, drawing feeling in his loins. Well once, she told him, sipping, she had mistakenly used a second Tampax without removing the first. There had been this sudden, ugly pain. Probably when she'd applied force, since as she said she'd forgotten about the first one, well, there you were.

There who was, came the thought, but he tried laughing anyway, and believed her.

'What's two times ten?' I said to Pooh.
(Twice who? said Pooh to Me.)
'I think it ought to be ten times two.'
'Just what I thought to myself,' said Pooh.

Now, a month and a day later, with the fume of lilacs in the outside air, he lay naked in David Grün's blossoming greenhouse, his back on a bed of Irish moss, his hands locked behind his head. Kristin, not exactly naked, crouched with both of her delicate Cashmere Bouquet arms wrapped around his legs. She wore green-tinted nylons, a beige lace garter belt and mauve high heels because she'd learned what he liked. Now and again she pulled up some of the damp, glistening moss and scattered it over his belly. Gnossos, Immune, Exempt, partially transported, knowing next to nothing beyond the sensation of her lips, the patient exhilarating warmth. Around them were heady soporific odors. Fig trees, poinsettia, wild tulips, windflowers, foxgloves, bearberries, pink carnations, sweet sultans, marsh mallows, fuchsias, candy tufts, tiger lilies, rhododendron, sweet williams, the pot of Pot, and a clay vase which once had held St.-John's-worts. The foliage rustled with the motion of toads and snakes.

She chased him into the barn. The smell of horses, hay, and grain restored them. They tumbled on the oats, clothes flying, fingers searching. From the meadow beyond, they heard children's laughter, shouts, yells, distant cries. Kiwi, Towhee, and Sparrow were home from school, prematurely building a maypole. Gnossos and Kristin sat facing each other, thighs straddling, bodies high, hands propped behind for balance. They made sounds belonging to no one language but common to all.

And again in the saddle of the sidehill, where he'd shattered the head of the galloping rabbit. Now he knew only Kristin. He watched her ecstatic expression, measured her rhythm, and ran out of protein. Drink chocolate milk, eat eggs, raw beef. Oh la.

"So," asked David Grün in baggy pants, red-faced, hands covered with green paint. "When is the date? When do you fix the wedding?"

"June," said Kristin.

"Traditional," said Gnossos. He was whittling a mackerel for a mobile. Three other balsa fish, smaller, lay beside him on the floor, tiny screw eyes for dorsal fins.

Not so certain, Catbird shrugged. She was mixing small tins of black and electric-blue enamel for the mackerel. Tern and Bobwhite prepared brushes. Robin, the baby, growing stronger by the hour, crawled around the fluffy rug like a kitten, chasing something no one else could see. Kiwi and Towhee combed Kristin's brown hair with translucent tortoise shell, picked out pieces of hay and oats. They tried braiding but it was too short. They wove a fantasy of colored bows instead, made curls with rubberbands, brushed and combed, then combed again, sculpting, building secret tunnels. "Enough," said Catbird, in calico, "she'll have no hair left. Come and help paint Gnossos' fishes."

He pared and whittled with David's honed tools, chipped rough edges, planed the scaleless flanks, beveled the backs, shaped the obtuse angle of the tail, a graceful V. It was a time of building. Already they had made another music room by knocking through the kitchen into the old storage loft. They had salvaged ancient plans of the house and charted accordingly, locating beams, reinforcing supports, demolishing plaster, changing familiar space. Now Grün had washed his hands with Lava and turpentine and was carrying a tray of coffee and Cordon Bleu, milk and cookies for the girls. "So," he said. "Some nourishment finally. You enjoyed the day in the woods, Kristin, you saw the greenhouse? The pointsettias still come, it's amazing. Some brandy in your coffee?"

Tern and Bobwhite, wary of the grown-up talk, left the room and became actresses, returning in feather boas, sequined gowns, high-button shoes, rouge, velvet hats, patent leather belts. "We have a trunk," whispered David, to explain. "I'll remember," said Kristin, maternally. "Do," from Gnossos, touching the back of her neck.

While they drank and watched the actresses dance, they prepared the wooden fish, painting black stripes on blue bodies, looping wire through screw eyes, bending sections of coathangers into suitable curves. When the mackerel balanced, Gnossos pinched the mobile between thumb and forefinger and climbed a stepladder to fix it to the ceiling.

The smaller fish dipped and swung around the larger. Kristin only watched with a cigarette, sipping her coffee.

"Gnossos," asked Sparrow, "can fishes fly?"

"Special ones," he told her. "Some birds even swim."

David, standing on a chair, tapped the largest mackerel on the tail. It spun around, paused, and returned. "To change media is not so hard,' he said. "Only dangerous."

"Oh, Daddy," from Sparrow, mock-teacherlike, "fishes don't drown."

"If they leave the water," with a pregnant pause, "they drown."

Not ready for parables Gnossos shook away the reference and hung the new piece of sculpture, using a large thumbtack. Along with the herons, to no one's great surprise, it swam and flew. The children made sounds of gentle pleasure.

But in the lull of watching, as the moment was suspended, Catbird turned to Kristin and caught her putting out a cigarette.

"It's government you study, isn't it?"

Kristin, her arm extended, hand empty of the butt, off balance, answered, "Yes."

"It's all right for you?"

Glancing at Gnossos for support. "I guess so. I mean, I like it, is that what you're asking?"

"She does very well, man."

"Phi Beta Kappa," David informed them, putting the stepladder in a closet, pronouncing the name with a surprising tincture of cynicism. "A Greek organization."

Catbird moved the plate of macaroons and uncovered a dish of strudel, apples in a syrup of nuts and maple sugar. "Your father's work is Washington, I think you said before?"

"He's an advisor," she said carefully. "To the President."

Trying to ease the discomfort, Gnossos added, "Very conservative cat. Free enterprise for the privileged, and like that." He was testing his brandy with a middle finger.

Catbird gave an intimate "Oh."

"Well, he is," said Kristin. "Militant, paranoiac, just about everything."

"He thinks there's a Negro-Jewish plot, man, to take over the republic."

"He called last week to warn me."

The actresses did pirouettes, the beauticians made a French roll. "Some more cognac?" asked David, finally sitting with them.

Kiwi was doing a headstand to get their attention. One of her button shoes had toppled off and her costume was upside down.

"He knows Gnossos, of course?" continuing slyly.

"O *God,* no. Even the name would give him some kind of attack. He'd probably itch to death."

David's eyebrows raised again, his body motionless for a second, his brow hinting at a frown. He poured a little more brandy into their cups, picking up a spoon to stir, saying nothing.

"Live near us," said Tern, sitting cross-legged on the floor beside them, picking up the baby, Robin.

"Oh yes," said Kiwi and Towhee, "live here, even."

"So," asked David finally. "What will you do?"

"Me, man?"

He nodded seriously.

"I don't know. Research. Grants and stipends."

"Awards," said Kristin.

"So. You have a field of study?"

"Who knows? Little Consciousness Expansion. Not

enough work being done on hallucinogens, for instance. And the mechanics of probability, man, they haven't dented it yet."

"No, I imagine they haven't."

"Some more strudel?" asked Catbird, touching her hair. "Why, man? What's the pitch?" talking to David.

"It gives a living, that? Hallucinations?"

"A what? I don't follow."

"His grades," said Kristin. "They're better than you'd think."

"A living. Enough for a family to eat."

"Man, *no*body makes a living. Are you serious?" He looked at the ceiling for effect but found his mobile instead. Robin began to cry. "It's safe here, right?" he went on, "nice little microcosm."

"Cozy and warm," added Kristin, quoting. The baby wailed again and looked for her mother, who leaned over and took her. But she wouldn't stop and Catbird had to take her out, muttering "Excuse me" through a forced smile.

Kiwi and Towhee ran behind to change costumes, Sparrow going with them. There was an uncomfortable silence, at the end of which Tern sighed, imitating an adult, and began gathering plates and cups. "Let me help," said Kristin, and together they went to the kitchen, carrying trays. Gnossos tried offering a wink, but she failed to see it as she disappeared.

He was left alone with David. He stretched back on the fluffy rug and watched his mackerel dangling in the gentle convections of late-spring air. Absently he counted strings on the autoharps, dulcimers, banjos, and guitars. Cleanup sounds came from the kitchen, little-girl noises from upstairs. The sun was beginning to set, and only silence reached them through the open windows.

"What's the old poop, David? You've been hinting."

"Oh, we shouldn't be too serious here, yes? Pedantic talk could alter my function." Grün put his glasses on and talked over the rims. "This Immunity business. We worry how you mean to co-ordinate Marriage and Immunity."

"Hey listen, it's just the next thing for me to do, take it in stride, why don't you?"

"Perhaps you could live together?"

"They'd throw us out, man, they've got rules and I want to stay. Don't give me hurt looks either, I know it's a little paradoxical, but nothing is ever simple."

"But in such a place you choose to live? From five years old, except for summers, you've been in institutions. This is life? Here, in the microcosm, with what you know, you are a waste. Lost, but truly lost."

"Exempt."

"We share a dissipating current, Gnossos. Like transformer coils, you see, we mistake induction for generation. Vicarious sampling is all that remains; the sour evening game of the academies."

"Man, I've been to where the legions go. They go to Las Vegas and I've been there. I watched it all happening one morning and, man, it was bigger than the fucking sun and I don't want any part of it."

"No. No, you're talking about the bomb you saw and no, it was *not* bigger than the fucking sun. Believe me, it was most certainly *not* bigger than the fucking sun!"

Coming from David, the language surprised him. "In my head it was bigger."

"So, the inside again, always the inside." Grün eased his grip, looked around the room for something to identify with, and found the mobile still again. He pointed, shaking his finger. "To ease suffering, the method is easy. Simply weaken the bond with reality." He put the finger down and swallowed the remaining brandy in his cup. "What is sin but an attack upon the third dimension?"

"Sin? What sin? What are you talking about all of a sudden?"

"It's getting late," murmured Catbird, strolling into the room with jackets. "We'd better get going, David."

"Sin, man? Like guilt and expiation?"

"Or perhaps not," he told him, rising with a heavy grunt, taking one of the jackets. "As the case may be." He picked up the remaining tray and waved it in the air like a fan. The disturbance caused the wooden fish to clatter and collide.

When he left the room Catbird was still standing against the doorjamb, arms folded, staring at Gnossos. After a moment she added:

"How do you know? Perhaps we love you. Should we be silent?"

Two hours later, when the Grüns were gone off to their local Shakespeare reading with the farmers, and the girls were safely asleep under quilts, and the house was humming with its own breed of comforting silence, the lovers again lay naked. This time they had snuck into David and Catbird's four-poster bed. The sheets had a faint scent of lavender and freshly cut grass.

But it was impossible for Gnossos to have an erection.

Instead, Kristin offered comfort.

Holding his woolly head against her pale breast, she read:

" 'Bump, bump, bump,
here comes Weary Bear . . .' "

14

In the cobalt night he dreamed of disaster to come and cursed her sweetly into the sulfur cauldrons of hell. Intimations of imminent loss, the cruising monkey-demon biding time, ammoniac odors threatening doom. Sometimes Grün's idyllic landscapes, loamy hillsides sown with seeds of doubt; sometimes his Taos sleeping bag, surrounded by masked pachucos. Subconscious symptoms of festering disease in the core of a country's opulent flesh. Come on, kids, be the first in your neighborhood to crash-dive in your own atomic submarine. Twenty-five cents and the top from your mother's convertible. Wheee.

But always he woke in a sweat of mortal fear. One morning there came the usual gentle rapping at the door. The Mentor *Daily Sun* should have slid across the threshold, the rapping should have ceased, yet this time there was no mystery. He listened as the noise came again and still again. It seemed that the silent messenger of some months was about to make himself known. But Gnossos was only half surprised. The weeks before spring vacation were an anxious season, and even without portentous dreams, the mornings promised uncertainty and revelation. He mopped his body with a pillowcase and said, "Come on in, man."

But no one came, and again the rapping: delicate, importunate.

"Come in, goddammit, I'm in the sack. Who is it?"

He threw back the covers with a moan and shuffled naked

across the room, unable to find Fitzgore's bathrobe. When he unlocked the door, Irma Rajamuttu, in gauze, smiled back through red teeth. In one hand she held the usual glass of gin and grenadine, in the other the *Daily Sun*.

"My particular congratulations," she said.

Gnossos covered his groin and blinked spasmodically.

She handed him the paper, raised her drink in a mock toast, and glided off silently on bare feet, one two three.

"Hey, wait a minute," he called, but she was gone. Only the sound of tinkling icecubes.

His nearly forgotten letter was on the front page, and he had to steady his head before sitting down to read with a nervous twitch.

April 1958

Our Dear Miss B. Pankhurst:

To the issue, yes?

The presence of women in Lairville apartments is not to your taste. You suggest registration and chaperons. A coed would be denied access to gentlemen's quarters unless accompanied by another coed and two protective couples. One over thirty, the other married, right? Me, for instance, if I wanted a coed over for dinner, I'd have to ask her roommate, a graduate student couple, and someone like you and your husband, if you were married, which I believe you are not.

A dinner party of eight. All of whom would have to be out before 10:30 on weeknights, weekends at 11. But surely enough time to eat, you'll agree. The hassle, Miss B. Pankhurst, is like so. We don't entirely believe you're worried about dinner conversation. Again to the point, you want to prevent the occupation of a Lairville apartment by a coed and a, well, man.

Why?

We assume you're worried something will happen. Handholding, kissing? Fondling perhaps? Something more critical. Plainly, we'd like to know *precisely* what you object to. We would like this objection made public. If in fact you object to the possibility of sexual intercourse, be good enough to say so. The implications of such an objection may well transcend the breed of action you are considering.

It is spring. See the forsythia; Athené is blessed with its abundance. Smell the pollen in the air. Observe the birds and beasts of the realm.

Love,
Gnossos Pappadopoulis

The phone rang immediately, and it was Heffalump.

"Holy shit, Paps, are you serious?"

"Ain't never serious, Horralump, just do things to pass the time. An' why are you up so early?"

"Packing for Cuba, man. But how come? I mean, what—"

"Kristin."

"The knee-sock chic?"

"I'm involved."

"Wow, I know you're involved, but this is like politics or something. She talked you into it?"

"We discussed it, man. Anyway, Oeuf did most of the final draft. I only really wrote the last paragraph."

"But you signed it, baby, I told you you'd get dosed. Jesus."

"Keep your cool, it's all right. Oh, and make it over here about three. There's a meeting."

"A *meeting?* You serious, or what?"

"Bring Jack, the rest of the crew, little Red Cap."

"Man, you *know* what this means."

The phone rang again and it was Juan Carlos Rosenbloom.

"You are my general," he told Gnossos, voice shaking emotionally.

"Crap. Just make it at three."

"I die for you."

"Bring potato chips, some Fritos."

"You want a Sten gun? Air-cooled job? Special from my country."

The third call was from the infirmary.

"*Verbum sapienti*," said Oeuf. "We're home-free."

"Don't put me on, man, I did it for Kristin."

"Keep your *sang-froid*. The word has proceeded *ex cathedra*, sport, we're under way."

Gnossos hung up uncomfortably, brushed his teeth with hair cream, screamed oaths, and in order to dissipate a fraction of his culpable energy, padded next door about the paper. He could hear them murmuring secrets, yet no one answered his heavy knocking. Goofy Benares maniacs. He stormed back and waited for Kristin to call, but the next voice belonged to Judy Lumpers.

"It's *fabulous*, Paps, my God, the dorms are going *wild*."

"Is Kristin in her room, baby?"

"*Really*, I've never seen anything like it. It's just too great to be *true*, can you hear them?"

"Kristin is all, man. She there?"

"Golly no, I don't think so. She signed out last night and didn't come back."

His heart sank. "What?"

"I mean, isn't she at your place? Can you *hear* them? They're all jumping around in their underwear. Oh, I wonder if there'll be a panty raid?"

This time he sought diversion in the cosmos. Hours went by in the drab Quonset astronomy building as he considered the relative motion of the stars and became hideously depressed. Two separate methods of calculation told him that if the universe had been expanding at a given rate, it had had its beginnings in a coagulated mass of—call it crap— some ten thousand million years before. So much for that. But after one thousand million years of expansion the crap had settled into clusters, all of which had been moving away from one another ever since. The separate answers were the same, so the universe seemed to be exploding, but Gnossos was hardly in a mood to worry about it. Just the same, to set concerned minds at ease, the weasel of a lab assistant drew sine waves on the blackboard and argued for another theory.

"The expansion of the universe is slowing down," he pronounced in a sexless monotone, one hand grasping his technician's lapel. His teeth were bad. "Eventually it will cease and be followed by contraction. Assuming that even though one kind of matter changes into another and produces or destroys energy in the process, the total amount of energy and/or matter in the universe does not change. Enough energy is thus left at max contraction to start the clusters moving together again under the force of their own attraction. Gravity, as it were. Your calculations ought to show that a whole expansion-contraction cycle takes about thirty thousand million years and that at present we're two thirds of the way through an expansion phase. How about it?"

A positive murmur from most of the class. Gnossos checked his figures desultorily. If they were correct, it meant the universe had a center and an edge and that with the right instruments he might even get a look at this edge. But again, it didn't seem worth the effort. He had a craving for pickled watermelon rind.

He tried to forget it in the mechanics of a steady-state theory. Clusters of crap expanding outward, new crap being born at a rate providing for constant density in space. Individual crap clusters changing shape, evolving, but the whole crappy system (viewed objectively) not changing at all. No beginning, no end. Every individual piece of crap, yes, but the system, no. The assumption being that permanence of matter and energy was also a lot of crap. Gnossos, sitting miserable on his stool, reconsidered the Las Vegas fission, the drunken movie star, the two strawberry blondes, the Oklahoma oil-cowboy and his Radcliffe muse—all in the relative luminosity of the new information. Subjectively, then (viewed even as an integral piece of crap), his own end was assured. I mean, why the hell bother to burn the candle at both ends when you can use an oxyacetylene torch on the middle. Less aesthetic, but more people see the flame.

Armed with this suicidal confidence, he made his way back down the hill after lunch and rolled a needle-thin Black Elks hipster joint. He wore it over his ear to tempt the secular fates, but his stomach still churned at the meaning of Kristin's all-night absence from the dorm. Something distant, irreverent in her attitude ever since he'd penned the letter, bowing to her coy insistence, the promise of lewd, extraordinary pleasures. An improbable whisper of betrayal, came the thought, but Love was said to conquer all.

Jumping up the freshly painted steps to his pad, he reflected that it ought not to. Hope you've been stewing, baby, Daddy's home from school.

Nonetheless, at the three-o'clock meeting she was missing.

"Panghurts," said Rosenbloom, in his cowboy hat. "We break her."

"She'll answer the letter," from Youngblood, "that much is certain. Jack, can you take care of posters?"

"Where the hell is my woman?" asked Gnossos.

"I think so," said Jack, staring at the angora Lumpers breasts. "There's all that paint in Polygon Hall. As long as we know what to say."

"There's a whole lot of stuff written down somewhere," from Heff, working to distract her, handing over an unopened Red Cap.

"In three weeks, a revolutiong. Esmash."

"*God*, can you imagine? I mean, do you really think it will work?"

"The guys at the house are already writing chants," from Agneau, in a crewneck sweater. "Some of them are *incredibly* good."

"Hey, Jack, you seen Kristin?"

"Got to keep momentum over spring vacation," from Youngblood, with his sleeves rolled up. "Can't let it slide. Students go home, change roles, come back and have to readjust."

"Maybe some kind of mailing list," suggested Jack to Lumpers, sliding a hand over her thigh.

"No mercy," tried Rosenbloom, pulling his finger like a straight razor across the jugular vein. "We eslit them oping."

The phone rang every two or three minutes, Youngblood

always first to answer, hushing the rest of the room with a gesture, sometimes laughing with excited satisfaction. Agneau sent cables, Judy Lumpers took shorthand, Juan Carlos Rosenbloom studied Gnossos with unbridled admiration, and Heffalump tried without success to keep Jack's attention from the Lumpers anatomy. "Make some corn bread, baby," he said.

When Kristin finally arrived, she was out of breath, accompanied by two renegade officers from the women's undergraduate judiciary board. She was wearing her kneesocks, and she touched the lobe of Gnossos' left ear as she passed him, knocking the joint to the floor. "Any progress?" she asked officially.

"Where you been?" from Gnossos, on his hands and knees.

"Tons," said Youngblood. "Most of it since the letter this morning. You'll be pleased to know, Oeuf reports a pink flag on most of Lairville."

"Red predicted by the weekend," added Agneau, taking off his glasses for emphasis.

"God, I wonder how they're taking it over at the administration building?" from one of the debutantes in a denim skirt.

"Really," said the other, also in denim, 'I'll bet old Pankhurst is crawling up the proverbial wall."

"I called the dorm five times," said Gnossos, "where the hell were you, baby?"

The phone rang and Youngblood hushed them with an air of importance. While he talked, Kristin briefed the others: "There seems to be some question at headquarters about the optimum time for direct action. We need a morning dead hour, when everyone's at the Ramrod for coffee, but statistics aren't clear on the number of students free between ten and noon."

"I'd guess eleven," said Agneau.

"Kill them," said Rosenbloom.

"Will you answer my question, baby?"

"Shh!" commanded Youngblood, listening to the phone.

"What about instructors?" from Lumpers, lowering her voice.

"Most of them," said Kristin, her fingers in a clutter of lists, "have agreed to dismiss their classes if we get a crowd into the arts quad. The idea is to make noise."

One of the debutantes added: "God, it's inspiring how the faculty are finally coming over. All their latent antagonism toward the administration is revealing itself."

"Really," said the other one, "their hitherto-unspoken opinions are bubbling to the proverbial surface."

Unable to evoke response, Gnossos murmured, "Holy shit," and made his way to the bathroom. He locked and bolted the door, took down the *Anatomy of Melancholy* from the commode bookshelf, and lit his joint. For fire he rolled up the letter on the front page of the *Sun* and started it with a match. There's a time in the lives of men, came the thought, which taken at the tide you're liable to fucking drown.

He had attempted to singe Kristin's knee-socks with the temperature of a parting glance as he passed, but she failed to notice. Punish her with my absence. That Tampax story, man, got to get things a little bit clear, knowledge of the taut membrane ought to stay in front. Celebrate the passion with blood is where it's at, closest they come to crucifixion, atonement for the old forbidden fruit. He purged the pockets of carbon dioxide in his lungs and sucked a little pure ambrosia, Mixture Sixty-nine, cut with the remains of a paregoric Pall Mall. All natural goodness, no carburetion. He kept it down until his temperature changed, a vague swelling at the temples. Then he stuffed his ears with Q-tips to keep away the outside world and read for an hour, not even rising when he sensed a pounding on the door.

Later he realized he'd been scanning the same paragraph two or three hundred times, so he stumbled into the kitchen and called Fitzgore. He was slightly higher than an Indian elephant's eye.

"What's the matter with you?" came Kristin's voice. "Fitzgore's been in the infirmary for weeks." She was searching in the refrigerator for food, and everyone else had gone.

"Hey, Piglet, where you been?"

"Well, I couldn't get into the goddamned bathroom, so I had to use the Rajamuttus'."

"That's not what I meant, man, where you been, anyway?" He teetered slightly and his lids were annoyingly heavy.

"Getting my thing. It always comes early when something exciting's going on like this. Is there any of that Greek cheese?"

"Your *thing*, man?"

"My period."

"Oh, that's lovely. Really sweet."

"Am I supposed to apologize or something?"

"You signed out last night, man, what's going on?"

She had taken off her knee-socks and was barefoot in a summer dress. "Who told you that?"

"Never mind, baby, just don't put me on."

She paused with a marinated artichoke heart. "You're not jealous, honey? I mean, how flattering—"

"An' cut out that honey stuff, okay? Sounds like a god-damned housewife."

"I thought you liked it. Say, these things are good."

"Lot of shit, that honey business. Sweetie pie. Lambkins."

"Are you drunk, Gnossos?"

"Honey bunch. Angel."

"Are you?" In her free hand she was holding a list of faculty names.

"C'mon baby, you got a nose."

"Oh, Pooh, dammit, I thought you'd stopped that."

"Yeah, that's right, it's the new me. C'mere, wanna feel you up." He tripped and crashed against the refrigerator door, giggling.

"Don't be so rough, please. God, if you could only see your eyes."

"What, man?"

"I don't like it."

She doesn't like it. All of a goddamned sudden she doesn't like it. "Why are you looking at me like that?"

"Are you going to get all paranoiac now?"

"Paranoiac? Who the hell is paranoiac? And where the hell were you last night, what's going on round here?"

"In the dorms of course, silly. Did Judy Lumpers tell you I'd signed out? I was making posters for the demonstration, that's all."

"Oh yeah? Well, dump the demonstration, right? All that Junta business, Ladies'-tea-society crap, meetings, what are you, some kind of Florence Nightingale under Oeuf, man?" Her expression changing. Ha.

"I thought you were *interested* in what we're doing!"

Don't get her too twisted, be cryptic. "You've been putting me on is all."

"I'm not putting you—"

"Fool with me, I'll break your arm, right?"

"Gnossos," putting down her list where he couldn't read it, "what in heaven's name is wrong with you?"

"Nothing, right? Just c'mere, got a little something to give you."

"You're not being at all nice just now."

"Cyclical phase, periodical, speaking of which—"

"Here I was, so pleased that they printed the letter verbatim, and everything—"

"Fuck the letter."

"Gnossos, bite your tongue. I really wish you wouldn't curse so damned much, really. Do you have any cigarettes?"

"No. And double-fuck the letter. Not like me, see? Where the hell were you this afternoon at three, and what's going on with all these scheming maniacs? I don't like any of this organizational thing happening, see, I mean how the hell did it get to be everybody's big hangup all of a sudden?"

"It wasn't sudden, silly. When I suggested it, you—"

"Look, I wrote the letter, right? Rest is up to all the gung-ho troopers. You and me are Exempt, perfectly Immune. C'mere."

"You're too high for that, please."

"You telling me no, man?"

"Please, Pooh Bear."

"I have to ask now?"

"Gnossos, stop."

He took a long drag on the remains of his reignited joint and tossed the roach into the sink. In the slippery gray coil of his intestines he felt a coming ugliness. He wondered, in actual fact, what he was doing.

Still later, of course, when she had electrified his mind's eye with subtle hints of post-period pleasures and their bellies were swollen with stuffed lamb shoulder and braised Salonika peppers, he read to her in the narrow, gray-sheeted bed. To oblige him, she had taken off her clothes, and sure enough she had her thing. The farther he could travel from the letter in the *Sun* the better, and he read in an apologetic, childlike voice, trying to conjure up the whole Pooh Corner syndrome with inflection alone. " 'Chapter Four,' " he continued. " 'In Which Rastus Loses a Tail and Pooh Finds One.' "

"Will you show me the good pictures when you come to them?"

"Sure thing, ducks," still high, but coming down. " 'The Old Brown Workhorse, Rastus, stood by himself in a thorny corner of the woods, his front feet sort of pigeon-toed, his head to one side, and considered the Situation. Sometimes he thought oddly to himself, Nowhere, and sometimes he thought, Later . . .' " He read on, tilting his own furry head from side to side, using different voices for all the animals, showing her the drawings of Rastus staring back through his front legs, looking for the missing tail.

" '. . . And so at last, down and somewhat out, to the Thousand Acre Plantation. For it was on the Plantation that Topsy . . .' "

Yet it was nothing like a workhorse or a Topsy—nothing either of them could name except in the dimmest, least accessible part of his consciousness, the semisweet darkness where its warning had been so insidiously whispered. It came at the moment when Immunity was surrendered and no guard or shield held out against its force. It came swooping in through the windows and doors, through fissures in the wall, out of the septic breath of the commode. It came with the force and intention of violent death, and its malevolent presence could be no less ignored. They lurched bolt upright in bed, twisting every which way to find it, holding out their hands for pathetic protection, the book falling to the floor and bouncing shut. Sounds of untempered fear fled their throats, primitive cries they might have uttered in their sleep, being thrown awake by some jarring, physical horror. Yet they were awake.

Pooh, honest to God, she murmured, clutching him fiercely, I felt something come into the room.

The blood chilled instantly in Gnossos' loins, his scalp cringed, as if being crawled over by scaly centipedes. The room might have been torn loose from underneath, pushed up into the night by the force of some titanic hand, sent slowly revolving through the etherous void.

Who's there? he called, his voice faltering. Who is it?

Yet the doors and windows were shut, had never been opened, and the question, like the presence which coiled itself so suddenly into the blackest corner of the room, was absurd.

Oh my God, Pooh, I think it's sitting right there.

An odor mingled with the cooking smells, a stench of decomposing fat, a fetor of ammonia. It stung their mucous membranes, singed their sinuses, choked them with a foul opprobrium. While they coughed and rubbed their eyes, some tentative mortal pressure came to their chests. They held each other, staring into the room, terrified.

Then Gnossos, in the same mind's eye which had been appealed to so sensuously moments before, saw superimposed a malignant vista. A wild, impetuous scream gathered strength in his lungs but wouldn't escape, and he shuddered spasmodically.

What, she asked, twisting her hair and trembling, what is it?

I saw something, baby, Holy Christ, man, I saw it all right there.

Oh God, Gnossos, in the room?

He spoke barely loud enough to be heard, his pupils distending fiercely. In my head, baby, but it's really there. Oh shit.

Listen, Gnossos, listen to me, are you listening?

He tried to nod but nothing happened.

I think I saw it too, really, oh God, was it a cave, tell me, because I think I'm going crazy.

He touched his lips together and said: A monkey.

Oh my God, yes, coming out of a cave.

Like a mandrill, came the thought, heinous, rabid, depraved . . .

I don't feel well, Gnossos . . .

An Oriental vista, mountains vanishing in color and smoke, a plain, a mesa . . .

She sank against him in a half swoon, her body going clammy and limp. The smell in the room was overwhelming. All at once he could no longer bear it.

"*Annhh!*" Gnossos leapt free of the bed and grabbed an andiron, flicking on the lamp in the rice-paper globe. Then another light and still another, until the apartment was brilliant, shadowless, overt. He jumped all around, pants falling down, wielding the andiron, his hair standing on end, his flesh glistening with goosebumps. "C'mon. C'mon, goddammit, c'mon—"

But there was nothing, only the odor. He ran to the kitchen, prancing, lifting his heels like a terrified satyr, then to the bathroom until no light was left turned off. Finally to the record player, where in a compulsive seizure he put on the overture to *La Traviata*. But it failed to help. Kristin revived with a lanquid moan and he searched closets vainly for some liquor, always glancing back over his shoulder.

"Ohhhhh, Gnossos," she called, and began to sob. "What

in God's name is it? Let's get out of here, please . . ." He
tossed her shoes and knee-socks onto the bed, then pranced
back into the kitchen: Don't be hysterical, baby, I'll go out
of my skull if you get hysterical. Under the sink, maybe it's
there. In the commode. Oh go away, for Christ's sake, leave.
Eeeee.

He turned on all the faucets and flushed the toilet, but
still it wouldn't budge. "It wants us out, Gnossos," Kristin
wailed from the other room, "it really does, can't you feel
it?" He pulled on his baseball cap, took the rucksack from
its nail, and grabbed her by the hand, never for an instant
putting down the andiron. They ran across the room, tripping over a fold in the Navajo rug, then had a moment of
panic as the lock stuck on the door.

"Oh God, what's the matter, can't you get it open, let me
hold the andiron."

"Easy, for Christ's sake, don't go crazy, just take it easy."

George and Irma Rajamuttu were cowering in the hall,
obviously aware of the demonic invasion, their faces pale,
their eyes aghast, their jaundiced fingers clutching robes at
their throats. Kristin screamed unmercifully when she saw
them.

Fitzgore's Impala was at the curb and he helped her in,
seconds before she fainted on the seat. He dropped the keys
on the floor, nearly ruptured a blood vessel searching, inserted them upside down in the ignition, stalled the engine
twice, and finally drove to Guido's Grill at eighty-seven
miles an hour.

When they were calm enough to take a table the waitress
did not want to serve them.

"I said, get her a double bourbon, baby, or I'll cut out
your polluted kidneys, right?"

"Disgraceful, where's her shoes and socks, anyway?" Kristin had forgotten to put them on. Gnossos lifted an empty bottle with a candle in the neck and aimed it at the window. The waitress ran.

After the bourbon, color seeped back into Kristin's face, but with the return of familiar surroundings came intensified fear. She began to weep uncontrollably and everyone stared. "The monkey," she sobbed passionately, "it wants to kill me." And with a vehement shriek she went hysterical. The waitress came waddling over, waving towels.

"What the hell's the matter with the girl, anyway, is she nuts or something? Why is she laughing like a maniac?"

"Get out of here, man, go away!"

"I'm gonna call the cops, this is ridiculous."

Gnossos slapped Kristin on the cheek. She stopped laughing, started again, then began to cry. He carried her to the car, staggering under the dead weight, and drove back to the dorms. At the entrance to Circe III she lost all control, wet her pants, and he could no longer handle her.

The coed at the sign-in desk came running out, full of alarm, rubbing her hands on her hips. "Is anything wrong? What's the matter with her?"

He had her call Judy Lumpers, who after a nerve-wracking pause came skipping into the courtyard with Jack jumping along behind.

"Later," he told them, to avoid a discussion, "just take care of her, okay?"

"What's the matter with your place, for Christ's sake?" asked Jack, suspecting that the girl had been screwed half to death. Judy was slipping an arm around Kristin's waist, feeling her head for fever.

"Please," he said. "I'll come by in the morning."

When he turned back to the dormitory parking lot, there was a prowl car waiting. Proctor Slug, in a fedora, was getting out one door and a police sergeant out the other. Behind them was the Impala, with two wheels up on the curb. The tires were hot and rubbery, and the brakes smelled of scorched lining. Gnossos was barefoot, his corduroys were down around his hips, his shirt was torn open in half a dozen places. He also reeked of bourbon. Slug and the sergeant approached him from both sides.

"We've been meaning to talk with you, Pappadopoulis," said the sergeant, "about a little matter of stolen Italian statues from the Christmas manger last year."

"Sacrilege," said Proctor Slug, sliding his bear-paw hands into the outside pockets of his jacket.

Gnossos closed his eyes and sighed wearily, a sigh of indignant hatred. Measuring his words, using a sonorous low voice, he said:

"Not now. Any time but now."

The barely audible statement stopped the two men. Embarrassed, the sergeant told him: "Funny boy."

Gnossos pointed a trembling finger at the man's Adam's apple, his arm rigid. "If you touch me now," he said in an even lower tone, "so help me Jesus, one of you will get a testicle torn up."

"Watch that talk," said Slug. But he backed off.

Gnossos walked between them to the Impala, got in, and drove away. Of all the noplaces he could go, one was better than most.

15

Blacknesse listened silently to the story, moving nothing but the tips of his paint-stained fingers. He was fondling an orange and fuchsia ping-pong ball. He wore a faded linen Nehru jacket, mandarin collar, white cotton trousers, and buffalo-hide sandals. He maintained the full lotus on a cobraskin stool. Next to him was the small colony of carnivorous plants, each of which had grown a number of inches. A single ultraviolet light burned palely from a socket in the eye of a nickel toad, bringing to life the dormant creatures in the depths and planes of the wall paintings. Sprung from the surface of their canvas, they dipped and swung in the medium of short-wave light, as fully dimensional as the mackerel on David Grün's ceiling. In this same visible intensity Gnossos' face looked electric baby-blue, his lips maroon. He was barefoot, naked from the waist up, although Beth had silently draped a paisley shawl around his shoulders as he entered the house, shivering. He had stepped gingerly over the tiger-shaped flagstones, and shielded his eyes from the enamel masks hanging in the pines. When he finished the story the muscles were twitching in his cheeks and his gaze shifted continually from windows to closet doors.

Blacknesse made no sound but he listened to Gnossos' breathing long enough for both of them to become conscious of the silence. Finally he raised the ping-pong ball, cocked it by his ear, and flicked it gently into the cushioning air. The distorted light on the falling ball brought the memory of another arching sphere within the field of uneasy vision. A pearl, small and gleaming, plunging through the opaque abyss of a nearly eternal Adirondacks night.

But this time it landed gently on the warmer weave of a saffron rug. "It all seems quite familiar," spoke Blacknesse, reflecting.

Gnossos exhaled carefully, the way he might have tested for residual paregoric fumes, but he said nothing.

"Her and not yourself," continued the painter. "That much ought to be clear."

"Sure thing, man."

"Do you know what I'm talking about? The monkey. It wanted to kill her."

"So why not? All the signs were there." The hair stood on the back of his neck and he smoothed it down, at the same time catching sight of an evil specter creeping from under the ocher muff, which turned out to be Apricot, the cat.

"Yet I fail to understand precisely why."

"You've got company."

"No. I mean, why her and not yourself?"

"Well *some*body knows, man, only don't look at me, I've got my own problems. Here, Apricot, nice pussy."

"It came from a cave?"

"Yeah, a cave, a hole, some kind of opening, you know, full of smells."

"It seems so familiar."

Apricot sniffed his feet and crawled away. "And cut out that familiar crap, all right? You're scaring the shit out of me."

"I'm sorry, I didn't mean to."

"Goddamned demons aren't bad enough, the cops have to shag after my ass, cat won't come near me . . ."

"But there *is* danger, Gnossos."

"Right, boogiemen all over the place. Now tell me something I don't already know." He covered his toes with the shawl. "Here, Apricot, c'mon, baby."

"I'd be afraid too, if it's any consolation."

"You wouldn't either, man, you'd know what it was all about. And why kill her, anyway? Where'd this kill business come out of? She's got squat to do with that kind of shit. Straight old government major, no schemes, no anything. Here, Apricot, goddammit."

"It always implies death, this breed of vision. You've felt its presence before, you know the odor, certainly."

"But then why not me, man? Why all Kristin out of the blue? She's really not *into* any of that scene. And what the hell's the matter with this cat anyway, doesn't he dig old buddies?"

"If it were you, the experience might have been paralyzing."

"It wasn't exactly a picnic in the country."

"But you feel better now?"

"Less threatened, but no better. Liable to crap my corduroys any minute."

Blacknesse again grinning slightly. "I was thinking of your apartment. You wouldn't want to go back there tonight?"

He reconsidered the stink of ammonia and decomposition. "Man, I'm not going *near* it."

"That's not precisely what I meant—"

"Bet your ass. Goddamned feenies scratching around, looking for veins to eat. Might get their wires crossed, fall on the wrong throat."

"I only wondered if there may have been something additional, even causal, lying around."

"In the pad? To make the whole thing happen?"

"Something, say catalytic."

Gnossos thought a moment and without much comprehensive scrutiny answered: "Your painting, maybe." The figure cutting off its head, holding the severed self with a hesitant hand.

"A picture of mine?"

"I don't know, I just said it without thinking. It fell on top of me the night Pamela came by with that knife."

Blacknesse eased forward on the cobraskin stool. He slid one leg out of the full lotus and sighed wearily, pinching the ridge of his nose, rubbing his eyes. For a moment he considered the ping-pong ball, then looked up. "Who knows? Perhaps. One way or the other, you'll be safer here tonight. We'll put you in Kim's room."

"It's okay with Beth? I mean, she digs what's happened?"

"I told her only what you said on the phone, no specific details. I'm afraid it might upset her."

"Hey, man, shit, this is my hangup. I'll stay with Heff or someone. I just thought you'd be able to straighten my head a little—"

"Don't be foolish, Gnossos, you could be in danger. If there's any chance of error, you're better off here. I have good reasons."

He wrapped the shawl around his shoulders again and shuddered.

"Take this candle. I'll look for a match. And would you trust a suggestion?"

"Maybe."

Blacknesse was loosening his mandarin collar as he crossed the room. "Should it come back, for any reason at all, don't turn away."

"Again, man? It comes again, it can have me."

"No, please, that would gain nothing. You must try to defy it, stand up and make it go back into the cave."

"Shit, man, it's after *her*, remember?"

"Just in case."

"No promises, I'm liable to fake it. You got a shotgun, old butcher knife you're not using?"

Blacknesse frowned and lit the candle. "Beth has probably put out extra blankets. If you need anything else, I'll be down here in the studio."

"It's late, man, don't you ever sleep?"

"There's a book of photographs I want to look through."

"I just don't want to go up alone, man, it's dark."

"Not that dark, Gnossos. I told you you'll be safe here."

Thanks a lot. Maybe call Rosenbloom, get a Sten gun. Little flame-thrower action, whoosh, monkey-cinders.

In the middle of the night he woke up talking. Over and over again, first in sleep and then in semiconsciousness, he had been saying "fuck you" out loud. Not that the monkey had returned, because it hadn't, but why take chances. Stakes are terminal, play your hand, lose, and zap, no more stakes. (When it made its move it had seen them both. Across the ether regions in their dovetailing mind's eye, it had chosen her. Yet should it change its plan, he was lost, and Calvin's final suggestion boiled protectively through his dreams.) So he found himself on his back, again soaking from head to foot, trying maledictions for defiance. It was Kim's room, and the candle flame flickered on her twelve-year-old things, ivory figures, ballet shoes. She lay next to the window, blond hair cushioning her cheek, body covered by an Indian robe. Waking, he knew why he was there. Her company had a fragrance of Innocence.

"Fuck you," he said anyway, arms around his shoulders. He watched the shadows fluttering on the wall, then gathered enough nerve to glance beneath the bed.

But no monkey came. He lifted his fist free of the covers and shook it at the window to court his fear. "Come on, how about it?" Suppose it did, though. Yellow, rabid fangs, cross-eyes, leathery blue face, gnarled claws searching for his jugular. He sat up in bed and shook both fists together, the blanket twisted around his chill-damp legs, bare feet sticking out. "Come on, if you're coming. I'm right in the old sack, come get me."

As it dawned on him that the challenge was one-sided he became exhilarated. He jumped up on the cot, waving his arms. But the blanket tangled around his ankles and he lost balance, teetered, and fell over sideways on the floor. He thrashed his fists wildly as he went down, and screamed, "Fuuuuck yoouuu!!"

"Gnossos," came the voice.

He jerked around, the blanket now over his head like a cowl, and remembered he was naked. He peeked through a fold and found Kim crouched on her bed, knees up, holding the Indian robe for protection. She was watching him in sleepy surprise. He had an appalling erection.

"Is that you, Gnossos?"

He covered himself quickly but not quickly enough. Her eyes had time to fix the object forever in her mind. "Go back to sleep, man, it's only me."

"Daddy said you'd come, I remember now. Were you dreaming? Why are you on the floor?"

"Shh, go to sleep, see you in the morning. You're really having a nightmare, bad for your nerves. One, two, three, count sheep, four, five—" He got up and made for the door.

"Where are you going?"

"Seven, eight—little walk, moonlight exercise, gather mushrooms, it's all right. Go to sleep now, all a bad dream, nine, ten . . ." He picked up his paisley shawl and tied it around him like a Sramana's loincloth, prancing into the hall on goat feet, a finger to his lips for silence, doing the antic hay.

Outside the moon was full. It gave him a feeling of partial possession as he leered at the stars with his imaginary horns. He wove his way through the somber Blacknesse swamp, flicking fingertips at the dangling masks, hissing at purple and vermilion stumps, muttering nonsense oaths and allegiances, spitting curses at whatever phantoms might be hovering over his spine like monster malarial mosquitoes.

At the stream he could go no further, and he sat down to tear up handfuls of grass and watch the water. Calvin had charmed the bees and the kingfishers here, had rolled his eyes and reiterated for Gnossos his surprisingly fundamental ethos.

What kind of ethos, man?

A simple kind.

So tell me.

You'll listen?

I'll try is all.

So I could dwell in alternative forms.

Forms, man?

Objects.

How?

I had to learn. If a bird flew past, a heron or a crane, I could take it within me, fly over rivers, dive for its food, suffer its delicate pain. If a stone waited in the desert, I could enter its fiber, take the heat of the sun, cool in the dawn, feel the wind etch my features, collapse into dust, mingle with the wind. If a cobra lay killed, I could enter his flesh, decay, have the skin shed from my pulp, be eaten by flies, turn back to the earth.

That's pretty spooky, man.

In those same ways, my soul would be troubled. You relieve the mind of the burden of image, Gnossos. You put aside experience. Guilt or fear. Even hunger or love. Can you see that, perhaps?

Maybe, man, I don't know. Keep talking.

You lose what you are, you go into other things. Flesh, marble, skin. Rope, hair, and bone. There's the ethos.

I don't understand.

Rebirth.

Ah.

It's a simple one. It only takes the telling.

"No."

"What?"

"It's wrong."

He turned his attention from the gurgle of the stream and found Beth standing behind him, barefoot, in a sari. Her body was clearly outlined against the night but her features were obscure and the wind blew her hair across her eyes.

"It's wrong that you're here. You'll do yourself harm."

"What are you doing, Beth? It's the middle of the night. Did you hear me get up?" He was shaking from the cold and was suddenly uneasy that he'd been followed without his knowledge. She lifted a cautious finger for answer and pointed in the direction of the house. There was a furious tension implicit in the gesture.

"Nothing," she told him. "Not even the suspicion of a meaningful answer will he give you. Nothing, Gnossos."

Gone mad. Raving under the moon. "Who? What time is it? What are you walking around for, anyway, dressed like that?"

She looked at his loincloth and laughed sarcastically. "So pathetically blind."

"What blind?"

"About Calvin, you little fool. My Brahmin specter of a husband."

The wind tossed the hair over her cheeks, her mouth, but she made no effort to arrange it. Her sari blew back and her legs gleamed quickly in the vague light. When it happened, Gnossos could not keep from looking. They were the color of talcum. "What specter?" he asked, to cover the glance. "What's going on?"

"You're opening a wound in your side."

"Hey please, Beth, go way, all right? I'm trying to get into a little something."

"Oh damn him," she whispered cruelly, closing her eyes. "Just goddamn him, anyway."

He rubbed the prickly flesh on his thighs. "What's up, man, I'm just trying to hang around by the water here, figure things out."

"You'll kill yourself, that's what."

"What kill? Everybody's talking kill all of a sudden. Listen, there's a maniac monkey cruising around tonight, case you haven't heard."

She shook her hair back over a shoulder and dropped to her knees beside him; then suddenly, impulsively, with the same quick gesture Grün had used to grab his arm, she took his head between her hands and stared directly into his eyes. For a moment there was no sound but the wind and the murmur of the stream.

"Why are you here?" came the question. "I mean now, sitting on this bank, why? Tell me."

Don't lie. "I don't know."

"Yes you do."

"To get into something, then."

"What?"

Don't lie. "Forms. Objects, creatures—"

"Stone," she interrupted, mocking. "Herons and fish."

He took her hands away gently, but with gnawing anger. "Hell, man, you asked me, right?"

"Calvin's ethos."

"Yeah. So what?"

Again she held him, moving her fingers instead of remaining so intensely still, pushing his hair back over his ears. "It drives you away, Gnossos. It forces you away from what you are."

He was embarrassed but he let it go. "Look, Beth, really, man, it's the middle—"

"Listen to me. You can't stay wherever it takes you, you have to come back."

"Leave me alone, will you?"

"You have to come back, are you even listening?"

He blushed furiously, "Yeah I'm listening." Then, after a suitable silence, "Say it again."

"Go into as many pebbles or artichokes as you choose, but you have to return to what you are. The torment is inside you to begin with."

"*Tor*ment?"

"He's sitting up all night looking through pictures of monkeys, did you know that, did he tell you?"

"Oh wow, man—"

"But goddammit, Gnossos, he's simply not going to find

yours because, if you'll pardon the intrusion on your solidarity, you've made it yourself!"

"It's after Kristin, hey, it ain't after me. It's her goddamned demon as much as mine."

"You've made it yourself, Gnossos, you," still holding him. "He'll never find it in occult compilations."

"What are you putting him down for, what the hell's this all about? You're supposed to be into the same things, he's your goddamned husband!"

"I'm sick of him," she hissed in a forced whisper. "I'm sick to death of him." Her hand pulled his own into her sari, into the fold that had blown suddenly open in the wind. She pulled it over her belly, down under her navel, down where she had something to say.

Oh no, man, dear sweet Mary, I'm holding her thing.

But almost as quickly she gave the hand back and stood. The sari closed over the fold. Gnossos was still sitting in the full lotus, his hand held foolishly in the air.

"Pebbles and bones?" she asked him, still mocking. Then turned and went back through the swamp, disappearing in the somber darkness of the trees.

Until he could no longer see her, Gnossos remained on the damp grass, staring, not able to move. For a delicate moment he considered going after her, yet the part of him that wanted to dwell in bees and fish faltered, and he passed.

It was not a simple matter, getting up and staggering back across the country fields and roads to the apartment on Academae Avenue. But the menace had gone by degrees out of the night; the demon seemed comfortable, if frustrated, in his cave; and there was really very little else to do.

When he got there, exhausted and feverish, Proctor Slug was waiting in his prowl car, asleep at the wheel. He awoke as Gnossos shuffled up the flower-lined path in his loincloth, but only wrote something on a pad and failed to utter so much as a cynical good morning.

That's right, baby, from under the drowsy lids. Later. But much later.

16

The anonymous typewritten letter barely questioned Kristin's fidelity, but Gnossos sat like a cross section of pre-occupied stone on the floor of Oeuf's antiseptic salon. She stood tenuously by his side, leaning away from him, wearing gray, summerweight knee-socks.

Nurse Fang waited at bedside attention with a Pitman notebook under her arm. Juan Carlos Rosenbloom guarded the reinforced door, playing with a straight razor. Heff paced a carpeted zone of neutrality between Jack and Judy Lumpers, keeping them apart. Dean Magnolia occupied a plushy red-leather loveseat, which had not been there before, fingering silica marbles. Byron Agneau, wearing shades, gazed longingly at Nurse Fang. George Rajamuttu mumbled incoherently in the corner, sipping from a sixteen-ounce glass of gin and grenadine, through double heavy-duty soda straws. Fitzgore, twenty pounds slimmer, lay on a stretcher along one wall, eating honey. And Oeuf—under his tailored John Lewton pajama tops—wore a sea-island shirt and English challis tie.

Gnossos, however, gave most of his extrasensory attention to the red-leather loveseat, the very presence of which provoked a discomforting suspicion.

But before he could identify its cause, there came a coded knocking on the door and Rosenbloom sprang to act as sergeant at arms. Drew Youngblood was waiting in brown loafers, sweatsocks, pressed chinos, and a clean white shirt (the sleeves held up by rubberbands). He smiled at the group of nervously expectant faces, nodded the silent affirmation they'd been waiting for, and produced a damp proof of the following morning's *Sun*, which he stretched across his chest. The pages smelled of printer's ink and Youngblood looked like the cat with the key to canary headquarters:

"I think Gnossos ought to be the one to read it."

"God yes," from Lumpers.

But Pappadopoulis eased his crumpled baseball cap forward on his eyebrows and pulled up his knees. "I pass, gang. Try Juan Carlos, why don't you?"

Rosenbloom saluted and waited for the go-ahead from Oeuf. He got it from Kristin instead, took the proofs, swept away his ten-gallon hat, scanned the room for attention, and tried valiantly to be intelligible.

"'*Miss Panghurt's Stateming.*' Thas the headline only."

"Whart?" asked Rajamuttu.

"The statement," translated Agneau, turning away from Nurse Fang, fingering his shades to get her attention.

"Thas only the headline," said Rosenbloom.

"Whose pang hurts?" asked Fitzgore feebly from his stretcher. "I've been ill."

"Come on, you guys," from Jack, "we ain't got all day, Heff an' me have to pack."

Gnossos watched Kristin with microscopic intensity and read anxiety into her every gesture.

"Undor the headline," continued Rosenbloom, "he say, 'The adminestrating has approve with two-thirds majorities the new proposing for apartmings in Lairvilles.' "

"Whart?"

" 'We feel tha' the presence of coeds in excess of the new restrictings would be conducive to pettings and inter-course.' "

There were murmurs of satisfaction from Magnolia and Oeuf.

"Thas the en' of the paragraphs. Then he go to say—"

"*C'est assez,*" from of all people Kristin, half under her breath. Gnossos' mouth dropped open.

"He go on to say—"

Heff stopped pacing and looked at Rosenbloom, "Con-ducive to what, man?"

"Pettings and intercourse. But like I say now, thas only the firs' paragraph. Affer that he still go on—"

"Sounds like you're in the money," said Jack to Judy.

"*C'est ça,*" added Kristin, absently tapping Gnossos on top of the head.

"Hey you are," came Rosenbloom's protest, "that ain' the end. He go on more to say—"

"Quite all right, Juan," from Oeuf. "We really don't need to hear any more." He was fingering the platinum keychain around his neck. "Miss Pankhurst has unwittingly become our *particeps criminis.* Wouldn't you say, Kristin?"

"I don't really understand," from Fitzgore weakly. "I haven't been very well, you know."

Kristin crossed the room to get the paper and lit a ciga-rette, explaining: "How could we talk undergraduates into conflict without some kind of moral issue?"

"The seeds of agitation are sown," said Oeuf. "*Ab initio* at least. But spring is the season of rebellion. If the weather is warm and eyes are on the sparrow—"

"—very few will watch the dove," finished Kristin, blowing a smoke ring.

Gnossos fumed at the air of conspiracy. Nurse Fang had begun taking shorthand in her notebook. Rajamuttu whispered secrets to the wall. Fitzgore shook his head: "It's all Greek to me. Will someone pass me that other jar of honey there?"

Nurse Fang had ceased writing on her shorthand pad and was lifting her pencil skyward, as she might have a torch. "We really can claim," she intoned reverently, blinking back the tears, "to have God—"

"—on our side," said Heffalump, seeing it all.

"*Dios mío,*" reinforced Rosenbloom, blessing himself quickly, kissing his Saint Christopher.

From under the bedclothes Oeuf produced a piece of three-ply cardboard with a window in its face. He handed it to Youngblood, who had remained respectfully quiet. The window opened on a group of rotating numbers.

"Today is D-day," he told them, moving the numbers ahead one digit, "minus nineteen."

Juan Carlos Rosenbloom manfully choked a sob; Nurse Fang recorded it in shorthand; and Agneau watched her with unabating desire.

Alone in the surgical silence of the infirmary john, Gnossos stewed in his own Aegean juices. But he tried to reason, because clawing not all that remotely at his forebrain was the possibility he had been jockeyed. Oeuf, he could maybe understand, a regular Tammany Hall Santa Claus, suffering the jaded drip-drop of his tool while charting constituencies in a political hamlet. But Kristin, man, turning off like a cold-water faucet, you'd think the monkey had nibbled on her ass. All that pedantic Mickey Mouse chitchat.

He stuck out his most malevolent tongue, showing it to her ghost on the bathroom wall. There was a pair of stainless steel scissors looking back from an open medicine cabinet, giving off a suggestion of potential energy. He ignored them, buttoned his fly impatiently, brushed maple seeds out of his hair, and headed for the door. Maybe some time at the local funny farm would help.

But just before he slid the bolt, an uncanny bit of protective strategy took him by the ear. It returned him to the cabinet, where he picked up the scissors. What the hell, baby, if the fault isn't in the stars, it may as well be our own. *Mea* most *maxima culpa.*

He reached into his rucksack and removed one of the foil-sealed Trojans. Between his thoughts and the physical experience of what he was doing, there was no distance whatever. He unrolled the rubber, peeled it back the entire way, and blew it up like a balloon. When it was almost eight inches in diameter he flicked at the special receptacle which protruded like an erect nipple. He played with it momentarily, pushing it inside out with his forefinger, chuckling wickedly. Then he snipped it away with the scissors. The rubber collapsed.

He rolled it back carefully and reinserted it in the foil package. Finally he dropped it into the rucksack, turned his baseball cap back to front, and returned to the salon.

The room was nearly emptied out. Heff and Jack were waiting at the door, Fitzgore was being wheeled across the threshold by Nurse Fang, and Kristin was getting up from a whispered conversation with Oeuf. "Are you ready?" she asked.

"We got a cab waiting," said Heff. "Come on, man."

As they turned to leave, he paused and tried a sudden question on Oeuf. "What's my cut, baby?"

"What?"

"I just want to know if you've figured out my cut."

"Why, Gnossos, I'm surprised at you. I thought we discussed all that."

"Come on, Paps," from Jack.

"Immunity, baby, that's what we discussed."

"Certainly. However much you need."

"It may not be enough is all."

"You want more?"

"I might, Alonso, who knows? Have a good vacation."

"Thank you, no. Some flags are still too green."

In the cab Kristin pretended to ignore him and made small talk about going home to Washington during the coming week. She was crowded in the front seat with Rosenbloom and Jack, who chatted busily about Cuba, and she directed her conversation at Judy: "So you and Juan will only be going along for the ride?"

"If you can call it that. We're hitchhiking in couples to make it easier. I mean, Fitzgore won't let anyone use his car, and buses are really too depressing for words."

Gnossos crouched next to a rear window, waiting for an appropriate silence, then said, "I know a guy. No sweat."

Heff had been making notes on distances between Southern cities. He looked up, "A car, man?"

"Who do you know with a car?" from Kristin.

"There's a guy is all."

"Wow," said Jack, affectionately touching Heff's shoulder, "anything to get us through Georgia."

"We were already off schedule," from Heff, "I'm supposed to meet Aquavitus on the ferry from Miami."

"Oh God," said Judy Lumpers, "a ride. All four of us together. How perfectly 1920's." Then to Gnossos and Kristin: "Really, you guys ought to come along."

"Got to study the stars, sweetheart. We also serve who stand and wait. Send me a postcard." He winked at Heffalump, who winked back and crumpled up his notes.

"There you go, Piglet, no more menace."

They were looking at the large dustless space above the mantel where the Blacknesse painting had been. Kristin sniffed the air tentatively and moved around the apartment. All doors and windows were open to the outside, and gentle breezes blew.

"That's not what I wanted to talk to you about, anyway." She put on an actresslike expression and cocked an eyebrow. "I wanted you to come and meet Daddy over spring vacation."

Gnossos choked on his chewing gum and she had to get up and slam him on the back. He coughed hoarsely for nearly a minute and his face turned purplish. "You what?" he finally got out.

"I've written him about you, nothing to do with your wanting to get married, just your name and everything. I thought it would be sort of nice, don't you?"

How well she lies. He coughed again and was silent.

"What do you think, Pooh?"

He said nothing whatever.

"Well, come on, you must think something, it's not that difficult a problem."

"You know damned well what I think."

She slammed him once more on the back and stormed over to the couch. "Really, Gnossos, please, for God's sakes, instead of us going and having a huge thing over it, couldn't you just somehow manage to come because I'm asking you to?"

"What are you talking about, man, come? No, of course I couldn't come just because you want me to, since just because you want me to doesn't make it cool."

"Cool," she told the ceiling.

"Yeah, cool."

"That's all you're worried about, is how cool it would be. It doesn't occur to you for a minute that I might want to do it out of, oh, some traditional respect for my family!"

"Hey, what are you talking about?"

"Respect for my family, that's what."

"Family? Where's that at? Man, a regular Bavarian Nazi for a father and you call it a *family?*"

"Oh, what's the sense anyway, what the hell do you know about families, you never so much as breathe a word about your own, I don't even know if you've got one."

"You bet your ass, man, so why go? You want me to wear tails?"

"Oh, just forget it, would you please?"

"What? Are you getting guilty now all of a sudden?"

"I said please to forget it, it was apparently the wrong thing to ask. I didn't expect such a traumatic reaction."

"Traumatic ain't the word. Baby, if he even *looked* at me one of his peptic ulcers might hemorrhage right on the floor. And that French crap in Oeuf's pad, where'd you pick that up, anyway, that *c'est assez* crap?"

"Really, forget the whole damned thing, please, would you?"

"A regular Molly Pitcher, stoking the guns."

"Go to hell."

"*S'il vous plaît.* C'mon hey, where'd you get shit like that?"

She lifted the martini pitcher by the handle and glared. It occurred to him how close she was to throwing the remaining contents in his face. Little motion picture histrionics, dash the crystal in the fireplace. Why not, man, get her feeling sorry, slip her into the sack. Take hours otherwise, too much temperature up.

He stuck out his jaw and said, "*Chacun à son goût,* sweetie pie."

She removed the stirring rod as a warning but said nothing. He got up from the butterfly chair, crossed to within an arm's length of her shoulder and tried, "*Rien à faire.*"

She threw the liquid at his mouth. But he ducked and leaned forward. Their movements worked together, and surprisingly the glass shattered over his eye. He gasped and they jumped apart. Kristin dropped the broken handle as a line of dark red bulged, then flowed down over his nose. Almost instantly she cried his name and burst into tears. Gnossos sitting on the floor from the force of the blow, waiting for the blood to run down his face and off his chin before getting up with exaggerated dizziness.

"Oh no," she said, rising with him, terribly alarmed, looking for a handkerchief to stop the bleeding, "I'm sorry, I didn't mean—"

He waved her aside casually and wandered into the kitchen, testing the semisweet trickle with his tongue as he went. She followed at first, then ran ahead to turn on the cold water. Let her do the Nightingale, fall into your stricken arms. Try limping.

She dampened a dishtowel and made him sit on a stool as she sponged away the blood and gently patted the gash. "Does it hurt you, Gnossos? God, I'm terribly sorry."

He shook his head stoically and tried to look at nothing.

"Oh dear, it's deeper than I thought. Now wait right there, don't go away." She ran to the bathroom and returned with a vial of merthiolate, unscrewing the dropper. "Hold still. Does it sting?"

He winced despite himself, but shook his head, and she blew on it softly.

Within ten minutes the tepid evening breezes were puffing quiet gusts across their bodies. Kristin wearing only her summerweight gray knee-socks and a pair of high heels he'd insisted she keep in the closet for just such emergencies. Gnossos wearing only a bandage over his eye. Fingers of penitent passion made tunnels in the tangle of his curls. Atoning lips traced the hairline down his belly.

When she was more than ready, he selected the altered Trojan from his rucksack, rolled it on where she couldn't see the insidious hole, and climbed on from behind. He wanted it good and deep. As the semen left his loins he bucked with disquieting force and wished it Godspeed, helping it on its way home.

That night he wrote an explanatory note and left it with the sign-in girl at the dorm. Since Fitzgore had had the audacity to demand his car keys back, he hot-wired the Impala with Pamela's stiletto and drove directly to Heff's.

"Call the whole gang, baby, see if you can get them to the student union in half an hour."

"Half an hour?"

"Bags packed."

Heff went to the phone as Gnossos lit a straight Chester-field and picked up an old copy of *Ebony*. He leafed through it and was in the middle of an article on the mulatto model in America when the last call was finished. "What's up, Paps?" came the question, "you're looking a little weird."

"You got any shit, man?"

"Yeah, quarter ounce maybe."

"I want it all."

Heff watched his eyes. "All right."

"Any lush?"

"Some Irish whiskey left, Powers, I think."

"Lovely, let's go to Cuba."

"You're *coming?*"

"I'm coming, man."

"Oh wow."

"I'm also coming back, but let's say I need a change of view."

"Don't explain, man, it's all cool. Rosenbloom even said something about a *credit* card. What about the chic?"

"Fuck her. For the time being, so to speak."

"Right. You got any luggage?"

"You're looking at it."

Heff sat between Jack and Judy Lumpers in the back seat, Juan Carlos took the first driving shift, and Gnossos put away the remaining paregoric, Mixture Sixty-nine, and Irish whiskey, in that order. He did not wake up until Dela-ware, and he said to Heff, "Hey, baby, where are we?"

Heff was driving by then. "Delaware, man," he said.

"That's pretty funny."

"It's even funnier when you look at it."

"Oh yeah? You got any shades?"

"Jack, give Paps the shades."

"And hey, man, when I finish digging it, wake me up in Washington. I gotta make a call."

In Washington, Kristin's father was in conference with the President of the United States. But Gnossos got him on the line by telling them that Mrs. McCleod had just been machine-gunned by the Soviet cultural attaché.

"My God," said Mr. McCleod at the other end of the phone, "how did it happen? Have you notified the Pentagon?" He had a voice like a radio announcer's.

"It didn't happen, baby, just get yourself a glass of milk and sit down." It was eight o'clock in the morning and Gnossos was standing in a gas station booth, watching the others stretch by the side of the car. The breeze already had a foreign, exhilarating odor.

"Who is this? What's happened to my wife?"

"I already told you, man, nothing, but I had to talk to you, dig? You cats are difficult to reach."

There was confused muttering at the other end of the line, extensions being clicked in, delicate whispers, then: "Would you mind telling me—"

"I probably knocked up your daughter is all. I wanted you to know."

More whispers. "What did you say?"

"But I'm planning to be big about it, and you shouldn't lose your cool."

"What?"

"Ought to be a good-looking kid, actually, Greek, lots of curly hair, dark. My name is Pappadopoulis."

"How do you do. What's this all—"

"I can't talk much longer, man, I'm low on coins and we're off to Cuba."

"To where?"

"Later, right? Tell the President we're all pulling for him."

He hung up and returned to the car, climbing in with Judy Lumpers. "You got any Clorets or anything, baby, my breath is a little swampy."

In Maryland he found a postcard that showed a girl in a polo shirt and short shorts, having trouble with a cocker spaniel. The dog had run circles around her and the leash was tangled on her thighs. Her mouth was open in a sensuous oval of surprise and she wore a sailor hat. Gnossos sent copies to everyone he could think of, including Louie Motherball at the old Taos address, with a Please Forward on the front.

God, they say, is love.

And someone's got to pass the word.

17

When his head was straight, Gnossos drove. Once he got the rhythm he couldn't lose it and no one could take it away. The Impala did 111 miles an hour on the straight, 120 coming out of a downhill grade. He took them from the gas station on the perimeter of the city, over the freeway, across the mall, to the Washington monument. He stopped the car and asked them each to pay homage. Crowds of tourists strolled on the grass and ate ice cream, gazing myopically at the towering obelisk.

"Look at it, man," he said. "It's George Washington."

Jack was being trusted alone with Judy in the car. Juan Carlos stood at his side with Heff. "Where?" they asked.

"I'm not exactly sure, but around here somewhere. I feel him."

"He's all yours, Paps baby. Fat white father."

"Now now, Heff, mustn't be bitter."

"General Washingtons," said Juan Carlos militantly, placing his cowboy hat over his heart. "I salute him."

"Phooey," said Heff. "He was a fascist."

"Notice the architecture, good Heffalump. The clever lines. The way they travel—how shall we say—up. And down as well. The devilish simplicity."

"Stuff it."

"Our spiritual heritage? You can't be serious. So proud. So erect."

"He had holes in his face."

"But he walked on the water, chopped up cherries, something like that."

"He wore a wig, man."

"Façade, old sport. Fox the Tories, that was his ploy." Gnossos shielded his eyes from the spiritual light, turning away speechless, in humility.

"Hey come on, man, let's split, we got a boat to catch."

"The valor. Do you dig the valor part?"

"Valors," echoed Juan Carlos, again nearly weeping.

"Martha Washington, wife and mother."

"Ecch," said Heff.

"Only Batman is closer to the heart of an American boy." The girls were calling from the car but he went on. "Only Mark Trail has more cool."

In Richmond, Virginia, they wandered optimistically into Mother Fischer's Kountry Kitchen for hush puppies and shakes, but no one came to offer service. Gnossos pounded on the table. After breathy whispering behind the counter

Mother Fischer herself placed a sign under their noses, which said in effect that Heff was a nigger. Gnossos went and sat on top of the refrigerator and had to be carried to the car by a deputy sheriff.

In Emporia, Virginia, they tried again and this time the waiter, a blond weight-lifter type, laughed until he drooled.

"Let's go, man," said Heff, "it hurts."

"Just like that? You serious?"

"Let's just go."

Judy Lumpers looked at her watch for diversion. "God, is it eight-thirty already?"

Gnossos stole two sugar jars, full to the brims, and dropped them heavily into his rucksack. Later, while the others nibbled salami and cheese in a Safeway parking lot, he sat under the Enter sign and studied the incoming drivers. He picked a teenager with a long grocery list and a U. S. Olympic Drinking Team sweatshirt, stole his yellow Lincoln, drove past the restaurant, and lobbed both jars gingerly through the plate-glass window. He went back to the parking lot, ate a piece of block provolone, and eased away in the Impala just as the police arrived, located the Lincoln, and arrested the bag-carrying, surprised-looking teenager.

In Fayetteville, North Carolina, Judy Lumpers awakened to find Jack semiconsciously massaging her toes, and the hairy undersized hands of Juan Carlos Rosenbloom exploring the area where the hem of her bermudas joined her thighs. The experience left the poor girl distracted.

On the shores of the muddy Santee River they feasted on hush puppies, grits, corn pone, deep-fried shrimp, and chilled tap beer. The restaurant was Negro, the service was extraordinary, and during a dessert of lemon sherbet and honeydew melon, Heff went into the men's room and wept quietly by a window. But only Gnossos saw him.

In Charleston they wandered out to dig Fort Sumter and Gnossos recited what he could of The Star-Spangled Banner.

" '. . . we hailed at the twilight's last gleaming . . .' "

"He'd just better keep his hands off the material, that's all," from Lumpers, still in a snit. Juan Carlos Rosenbloom was bursting bombs in air and failed to hear.

" '. . . the rocket's red glare . . .' "

"Jack brings me down with that toe fetish, Paps." Heff was trying to light a cigarette in the wind. "I mean, who needs her when she gets like that? Do I need her?" She slept in the front seat, wrapped in a blanket, withdrawing.

" '. . . gave proof through the night that—that'—somebody clue me, please, I always go to pieces in the tough parts—'that . . .' "

In Savannah, where the hibiscus was beginning to flower and the air grew tropically heavy, Jack, still sleeping, began to moan and caress the chrome door handle at her side. Now and again she lifted her spine free of the seat, arched her pelvis, and shuddered. Heff leaned over and whispered to Gnossos, "She's in heat, man."

"How can you tell?"

"I always know. Doorknobs, candlesticks, all that bouncing around. It's seasonal, probably the warm weather."

"Will she wake up?"

"She never wakes up," he whispered intimately.

"You serious?"

"Never."

"Not even—"

"Nope. It's her thing."

"It sure is."

"But I love her."

They stopped at a motel with beds that vibrated when you put in money, and Gnossos gave them a handful of change. Heff carried her in and told them to come back in half an hour.

In the meantime the keeper of the flame went down to look at the sea, where, alone, he was able to wonder about the ominous drawing pain in the lower part of his intestines.

In Woodbine, Georgia, Judy Lumpers went hysterical. The car was littered with bits of Oreo creme sandwiches, Burry's chocolate chip cookies, empty beercans, stale-smelling laundry, used tissues, old Q-tips, rigid socks, crumbled paper bags, fudgicle sticks, salami rind, Snickers wrappers, sandals, sneakers, fractured hot dog rolls, cheese Danish crumbs, seashells, sand, a palm frond, hair, chicken bones, milkshake containers, peach pits, orange peel, two *Blackhawk* comic books, torn *Time* magazines, broken sunglasses, postcards, Juan Carlos' maps, and a limp, nearly full, knotted Trojan which had belonged to Heffalump. It was the Trojan that touched her off. She had been trying for six hours to maneuver Rosenbloom into an inert position so she could curl up and get some rest. When she finally did, something tacky touched her cheek. She leapt up, and the unspeakable thing was sticking to her ear.

"What'll we do with her?" asked Heff. She was giggling insanely and twisting her hair.

"Give her some provolone, man."

Heffalump popped a piece of block provolone into her mouth and she wolfed it down compulsively.

In Jacksonville, Florida, her giggles subsided into whimpers and her eyelids looked heavy. In St. Augustine she fell suddenly asleep and dropped into Rosenbloom's patiently waiting arms. To celebrate, he recited Ramón Pérez de Ayala:

"En el cristal del cielo las agudas gaviotas,
como un diamante en un vidrio, hacen una raya."

"St. Augustine, old Horralump, dig it."

"Old people's homes?"

"Right. Retirement schemes, shuffleboard tournaments."

"Nordeste y sol. La sombra de las aves remotas
se desliza por sobre el oro de la playa."

"MMmm," said Jack, awakening to the sound of a foreign language and the smell of salt air. "Where are we, you guys?"

"She's moving, man, just look at her."

"She thinks we're in Havana," from Heff. "Speaking of which, I've got a little business on the boat. What's the date?"

"¡ Oh tristeza de las cosas vagas y errantes,
de todo lo que en el silencio se desliza!"

At Titusville they began to believe where they were.

At Vero Beach, Heff and Jack sang Peggy Sue.

At Fort Pierce they slept on the sand and woke up thirsty. Gnossos went creeping into an orange grove off the highway and returned, rucksack bulging.

At Lake Worth they got a traffic ticket for using the horn and Gnossos took up an hour collecting as many stubs as he could find on the windshields of other cars. He mailed them all to the local fuzz, in a large manila envelope with no return address.

In Fort Lauderdale the stomach pain grew worse. It spread, in fact, into his groin and he pretended it didn't exist.

In Miami there was an ecstatically painful burning sensation when he went to the bathroom, and he had to lean against the wall to steady himself. But by the time they drove down Collins Avenue it was not so bad. They dug the ankleless women in pink straw hats, the faces dripping of Coppertone and cacao butter, the men in Dr. Scholl's sandals, the off-duty busboys playing Aga Khan. Judy and Juan Carlos had been given the back seat to themselves and seemed, incredibly, to have found true love.

On the P and O pier they parked the Impala, bought tickets with the magic credit card, were given Series B tourist cards, drank a pitcher of ice-cold *piña colada,* and boarded the S.S. *Florida.* In the quayside world of salt air and quick expectancy, Gnossos was neither Here nor There. Pelicans stood on poles, cormorants dove, black-backed gulls waited for swill. Oil slick, leather, rope, squeaking timbers, the Caribbean. Water eddied in translucent pools, blue and pale green. The color of her spring stockings. Found the note by now, doing what, I wonder? Too late to douche, wait and see is all, count the days. Gnossos seed too tenacious and single-minded. Old ovum doesn't have a chance.

"But why, Paps? Holy shit, man, there must have been other ways."

"It was going a little sour on me, right? Not exactly rancid, but a little buttermilk odor."

"So what? It goes bad, it goes bad, man. Then it's over, bang."

They were standing with the other tourists at the rail, watching the ship ease past the narrow peninsula of quarantine huts toward the open water. The sun had set and the sky was turquoise and saffron. The girls were taking showers and Juan Carlos was looking for plots.

"I'm not up to the bang is all."

"You? Come on."

"I'm just not up to it, baby. I've been down too long, dig, all those asphalt seas behind me, all I want is to go like home to the hill. Maybe she turns me on."

"She's starting to smell like buttermilk, and she turns you on? Tell me about it."

"Nothing's simple."

"You keep saying that."

"Yeah, well it was true before I started. Look at you and Jack anyway, man. You catch her practically in Lumpers' pants and five hundred miles later you're back in the vibrating sack, ready to go looking for Castro."

"That's different."

"I guess it is."

"I mean, she's a little bit sick, so it's different."

"Yeah, and you're a little bit boogie, and I'm a little bit Greek. And Kristin, man, is a little bit American, but if she thinks she's gonna use me for some doublethink university politics, her head is twisted!"

"Her head is twisted?"

"I will not be done up, sport, it cuts my Exemption. And that shitty letter warning me she might be out fooling around. Man."

"So you knock her up?"

"Check."

"To teach her a lesson, I suppose?"

"To bring her full circle, man, to have her nearby."

"That's where you lose me, right there, that circular stuff. I mean, why the hell do you want to keep anybody who's going to hate you, man?"

"She won't hate me is all, the kid will turn her on."

"Oh wow, you *do* need a vacation."

"The American mother-syndrome takes over, just like changing gears. Overdrive, dig?"

"I also don't see why she wanted you to meet her old man."

"She didn't, baby, she knew goddamned good and well I'd say no. She only brought it up to cover all that scheming in the infirmary. I've been *used* by the bitch."

Heff watched one of the heavy pelicans pause in its lazy flight, fold its wings, and drop like a bag of stones into the water. "Listen, Paps, dig what I have to say. For the first time since I've been hanging out with you I think maybe you're in trouble. Usually you can talk your way around a hangup and I end up seeing a little where you're at and it's mostly pretty cool, see; but right now you're into something very private and from here it looks spooky. I've got no rational insight for you, man, but the spooky feeling is there just the same and you ought to know."

The steam whistle sounded as they passed a winking lighthouse, and Gnossos turned to watch the line of pink and white hotels beginning to fade on the Miami horizon. "You're not into the monkey is why," he said wearily.

"What monkey?"

"Back in Athené."

"Wow, man, you've been shooting up horse?"

"No, baby, it's a different breed. Or maybe not, I don't have it all figured out. Blacknesse is looking for a picture, dig?"

"You feel all right?"

"Beth says he won't find it, and Kristin's afraid she's going to see it again."

"O man—"

"It was trying to kill her, right?"

"Let's go have a drink."

"It smelled like ammonia."

"Little Johnny Walker, just the thing for your head, white Bacardi, maybe."

"It wouldn't come to Kim's room, though. Smell of Innocence there. She caught me with a boner, dammit, bound to stick in her memory, get her all screwed up."

"Little birdbath martini?"

They drank the martinis from a wicker table in the small ballroom amidships. A four-piece band played mambos and cha-chas, passengers in paper hats waddled around the floor, lights from the Keys glowed occasionally through the portholes. There was a pleasing vibration from the engine throughout the hull, and the fragrance of the warm Caribbean. Heff waited impatiently for his business connection to show, and Gnossos, soothed after the potent alcohol, watched him with a growing feeling of nostalgia.

"What are you going to do with Jack, anyway?"

"I'm not sure. Tell me more about your monkey."

"To hell with the monkey."

"Listen, man, you don't go around digging demons and tell me to forget it. What am I, just a passive ear or something?"

Gnossos tossed him a cigarette and smiled, "It's only your frame I'm worried about. You might get it bent, running around those mountains."

"My frame stays straight, you can tell just by looking at it."

"Those cats don't use water pistols is all, they can shoot through trees."

"I know about guns, man, I went to school in Harlem."

"Don't get racial, baby, all's I want to know is whether Jack is really going with you."

"We'll know in Havana, there are people we have to see, get the firsthand word."

"The Buddha? Pick up a little bread?"

"Maybe. I'm not supposed to talk about it."

"The Scarlet Heffalump."

"Shove it."

"They play finders-keepers, baby."

"I know all that, so what? I'm fed up with hanging around, everybody jawing, nobody doing anything. This cat in the Sierra is stepping out, so now's no time for you to bring him down."

"He's high in my eyes, baby, he swings, I dig him."

"He has class, man, he's on his own. Whole Batista army looking for him and he makes it anyway."

"If he makes it alone, then learn a lesson." Gnossos streaking the moisture on his glass. "Jack is better off out of it."

"She can handle herself."

"Maybe. That doesn't mean you shouldn't step away clean. Just split, zippo-bang, you don't need fans along for the ride. You especially don't need anybody to send reports back to Athené."

"That isn't fair, man—"

"You know what I'm laying down."

"Maybe."

"There's something else too, important, are you listening?"

But before he could tell him, their attention was distracted by a small commotion on the dance floor. A figure like a Zeppelin was cutting a path through the waddling couples, pushing everyone out of his way. He wore a silk double-breasted suit, a maroon fedora, brown and white shoes, and smoked a black Italian cigar.

"I think that's my man," from Heff, shifting weight.

He apparently was making his way to their small table, walking flat-footed like an elephant. One of his teeth was missing and a lethal-looking bump protruded beneath his jacket. He smiled broadly when he saw them, ignoring the whispering tourists. Gnossos checked Heffalump's slackening jaw and said: "Aquavitus."

"Gnossos," from the man, quite loudly, extending jeweled fingers. "An' you mus' be Hippalump?"

Heff's cigarette fell clumsily out of his mouth into his martini.

"I join you, yes?" asked Aquavitus. "We talk business." He sat down just as the violinist detached himself from the bandstand and began wandering around the tables. A waiter came over and smiled cautiously. "For me," he continued, "Brolio Chianti, '47, cool, not too cold, if you follow. These guys, what they got?"

"Birdbath martinis," said Gnossos. "No olive, wipe the rim with lemon peel."

"Don't take all day, either." The waiter gathered up the glasses and ran away to the bar. Aquavitus noticed the approaching violinist and cursed under his breath. He whispered perilously to Gnossos and Heffalump, "He will stay away from here. He come near to our table I have him killed, okay?"

Heff put a handful of peanuts in his mouth all at once.

The man's cigar had gone out and he fumbled in his pockets for a match. A waiter appeared with a candle. Aquavitus took it away, blew out the flame, broke the wax in two and dropped the pieces on the table. "You gotta keep them jumpin' alla time," he explained to Gnossos with a wink. "They ain't jumpin', they don't come through. How you doin', Hippalump, pleasure to make you acquaintance, you ready to make the run all right?"

Heff coughed on his peanuts but Gnossos smiled. "This guy working for you, Giacomo? Little bread on the side?"

"Shoo," said Aquavitus. "Everybody work for me. Giacomo, he espreading out, goin' worldwide, if you follow. How you doin' anyway youself, Gnossos, take a little vacation? Those guys come to see you in Atheené, those Heap guys?"

Heff's eyes widened and he ate another handful of nuts. The first waiter arrived with the drinks and the bottle of Brolio. Aquavitus tested it against his cheek, pointed a thumb and said, "Maybe I put out my cigar in you eye?"

The waiter jerked up but managed to ask, "Too cold?"

"You, *Farabutto!*" came the hiss. "What you mean 'too cold,' he's too hot. You want to be a lampshade? Cool him."

"*Sí, señor.*"

"Drink you drink, Hippalump, little martini, anh? Strong estuff. Then to Gnossos, "He drink pretty strong estuff, this Hippalump, you know him pretty good, he do nice work?"

"He's all right, Giacomo, spiritual Italian."

"Oh yeah, he that way?" In a sudden intimate whisper,

leaning over the table, breathing garlic and eggplant fumes: "I got him going into new territory. He breaking ground, this kid. Heap, he recommend him."

Heff and Gnossos looked at each other. "Heap did, man?"

"Heap, he say Hippalump go to Cuba anyway, ha ha, maybe use some bread on the side like you say, make a little run, ha ha."

"Heap," said Heff, amazed. "That spooky little ghoul."

"Conspiracies, man. It's all getting pretty zany."

The waiter brought back a new bottle of Brolio and stood trembling until Giacomo savored the bouquet and nodded condescending approval.

"Maybe we make a toast to Palermo, okay?"

"How much you paying him, Giacomo?"

"What do you want to talk money alla time? Drink up."

"How much?"

"Come on, Paps," from Heff, slightly embarrassed.

"He make what you used to get, fixed rate a kilo, little shit fo' private use."

"Uncut?"

"Shoo uncut, you think I'm in olive oil?"

"Double it, then."

Aquavitus rolled his head back in laughter, blubbery jowls shaking; his hat, held by a complex of rubberbands, failing to fall off. Phony old Capo, came the thought, never been closer to Cosa Nostra than the New York *Daily News*.

"I look like a Christmas tree, Gnossos?"

"He's my buddy, man, you don't want him bending his frame for coins. Who's your connection anyway, Heff?"

"I don't know, some spook, big cat with an opal in his forehead."

"Meester Boodah. He okay."

"Buddha, man, are you serious?"

"He open up a whole new territory."

"Hey, man, nobody's ever seen the cat, let alone do business with him. Heff, no fooling, you're better off getting your ass straight into the mountains, what do you want to fool around with maniacs for?"

"I don't have any bread, man, this whole trip's on credit already."

"Shoo, okay, I give some more money. But no double, double's not in the question. We gotta have a little profit showing."

"Who laid out the credit?" from Gnossos, again suspicious.

"But suppose I really can't get in touch with this opal cat. Mojo and Pamela seem to feel he's very unpredictable."

"*Pamela?* What the hell has she got to do with any of this?"

"This man Boodah, he unpredictable like Meester Mojup describe. But in Palermo if he has function, then we make him exploit, if you follow. He don' wanna be exploit, we tie anvils to his feet and go swimming in the beach. You understan' how I intend."

"Pamela paid the bill, man," from Heff, sideways.

Gnossos stopped the drink halfway to his mouth. "No, man. Don't say that."

"Anybody work for Mafia," continued Aquavitus, straining off his chair, "got something to offa. They remove the offa, we remove them. Very simple arrangement. Gnossos, you excuse me an' Hippalump. Or maybe you wanna make a little run youself, pick up a couple dolla?"

Gnossos shook his head.

"Then you excuse us fo' a little while, okay? Here, have a guinea stinker. Special tobacco, cured in Torino."

Gnossos took the cigar, clamped the acrid tip in his molars, and stormed across the dance floor. He stormed back a moment later, finished his martini, and stormed out again, nearly colliding with a whirling Juan Carlos and Judy Lumpers. They seemed oblivious in their *paso doble* world.

Out on deck the music and din were lost on the warm seawinds and he walked off his agitation during twenty laps around the smokestack. He was finally able to slow down enough to pause at the railing and watch a school of flying fish. They broke the surface at the hull and skipped away toward the stern like flat-backed stones. Phosphorescent amoebas swirled in their wake, tropical perfumes blew. Now and then a porpoise loomed out of the depths, shot steam through its blowhole, arched, and vanished.

He thought of Heffalump. Enterprising little maniac, chip off the old Greek block. But Mrs. Mojo he still couldn't accept. And then there was old Oeuf. Finger in every insidious pie, clapping hands, getting what he wants. Clap, bring me Lairville; Clap, bring me Pankhurst's head; Clap, bring me—

Wait.

In a comic strip the light would have gone on over his head, emitting little wavy lines of illumination. But while he was standing there with one hand on the railing, the bulb shattered somewhere between his eyes. He closed them quickly. There was a palpebral singe against his pupils and the feeling that the rest of his body was a corpuscular complex of plastique and TNT.

Clap.

He tried it under his breath, softly.

He whispered it aloud to another school of flying fish. They flashed their fins and dove.

He spoke it to the sky, and the stars for answer blinked. Clap.

He pulled the baseball cap down around his ears, folded his arms across his stomach, and tried to disappear. Say the magic formula, blend with the nautical woodwork, who would ever know? He spun around in a slow circle and again began walking, this time slowly, with great care, measuring the intensity of sensation in his groin. Drip-drop, drip-drop, there was no denying the appalling symptom. He paused while two Cubans with Zapata mustaches strolled past. He shrugged his shoulders helplessly and said, "Clap, right?"

"*Salud*," they smiled together.

Jump, came the sinister suggestion at the bow.

Jump, this time at the stern. Propeller stew.

Jump, on the port side. Lead belaying pins to help you down.

Jump, on starboard, maybe porpoises eat Greek.

In his next incarnation he might be Oeuf and everything would come out even.

He was inspired to court the abyss. He climbed over the railing and crawled out on the metal lip that had nothing beneath it but the sea. Salt crackled under his boots, wind blew through his ears. He had only to straighten his protectively bent knees, let go with his hands, and lean backward.

He stayed there for almost an entire hour, chilling slowly, trying to anaesthetize the insistent pain. Finally Heffalump and Aquavitus stepped out of the ballroom for air, exchanged some kind of envelope, and shook hands. Gnossos watched them part about twenty yards away, then Heff began strolling in the opposite direction. What the hell, man, little audience never hurt anybody, call him.

"Pssst."

He failed to hear.

"PSSSSST!"

"What?"

"Heff?"

"Who's there?"

"Over here."

"Paps, that you?"

"Over here, man."

"I can't see you, where are you?"

"Off the deep end, baby, dig me."

Heff gasped and went rigid. "Paps, holy shit!"

"Dig me, Heff, it's all over. Wheeee."

"Get off that thing. You want to get killed? How'd you get out there?"

"All over, man, drip-drop."

"What the hell are you doing anyway?" He started forward to help but Gnossos' voice interrupted.

"Stay there!"

Heff looked around the deck. There was no one to help. "What are you doing, man?"

"Don't come near me. Drip-drop. Wheee."

"What's wrong, anyway? You drunk, Paps?"

"Diseased is all, dig me."

"What are you talking about?"

"Syphilis, man. Leprosy, general paresis."

"Come on over on this side, I'll buy you a drink. You want another martini?"

"I'm dosed, baby. Clap, if you dig. Look, one hand."

"Paps, cut that out, man. What are you doing, for Christ's sake?"

"I've got Oeuf's clap, baby. Drip-drop right out of my

joint. Cramps, the whole scene. Stay back, come near me and I hit the pool."

"Oeuf's clap, are you serious or what? How could you get Oeuf's clap? Come here, why don't you, Giacomo gave me some of the mixture."

"It's a long story, man. Wheeee."

"You didn't catch it from Oeuf, for Christ's sake?"

"Not directly, right? Dig me, baby, I'm dripping to death."

"Hey, man, come on back here and let's talk about it. There's evil things swimming out there."

"They wouldn't come *near* me, man, I've got leprosy. Goodbye, baby."

"Hey, Paps, cut that shit, will you? What's wrong, you've really got Oeuf's clap? How'd you like some nice Mexican grass?"

"I got it all right; boy, do I have it. Right through the hole in the old Trojan, zippo-bang."

"What did you say, man? I can't hear you in this god-damned wind."

A number of tourists had gathered around Heff and were murmuring suggestions, some of them fixing flashbulbs in their cameras.

"Goodbye, man, tell them I sank like a lamppost."

Jack, Judy Lumpers, and Juan Carlos joined the growing crowd and stared incredulously while the flashbulbs began going off and people snickered.

"God," said Lumpers. "What's Gnossos doing now?"

"He's got Oeuf's clap."

"How groovy," from Jack.

Gnossos studied the rushing water for a brief instant, then tried balancing while letting go with both hands. When he looked back, Juan Carlos, all-purpose master of passionate bravado, had dashed out of the crowd like Speedy Gonzales and was now holding him under the arms and dragging him to safety.

"Noooo!" he bellowed, "get out of here!"

"You are my leader," from Rosenbloom, dodging fists, sitting on his chest.

"Get his hands," said Heff, pinning down the thrashing knees.

"What's he screaming about, anyway?" asked Judy. More flashbulbs went off.

"Yaws!" yelled Gnossos, "pellagra!"

"You must survive," said Rosenbloom, using leverage.

"Oh, Thanatos baby, kiss my wicked tongue."

In the morning the S.S. *Florida* made her way at walking speed past the shell-pocked Morro Castle into Havana Harbor. In the cavity of Gnossos' soul was a soggy depression. The others sensed it and left him alone, except for Juan Carlos, who never strayed far. Together they watched the men and boys who'd swum out to dive for American coins. One of them was slower and weaker than the others and when Gnossos tossed a silver dollar it hit him on the head.

On the pier they were met by a maraca band in festooned shirtsleeves. A smell of saffron and fried bananas everywhere, roast pork, chicken, garlic, paella, chorizos, peppers sizzling in oil. But Gnossos held his nose. He brooded on the gonococcic pus that trickled through his stomach, and the very thought of food made him gag. Pictures of Kristin and Oeuf formed in his mind's eye, unspeakably lewd intimacies, sadistic positions. He wanted to beat the living shit out of her. But guitars strummed, cláves clacked, flutes trembled, and he planned a more terrible retribution.

In the taxi the driver informed them that their hotel was in colonial Havana, but safe. Bags were strapped onto the roof, windows were rolled down, and Gnossos rode in front, staring at landmarks and bodegas. Automatic weapons pumped nervously from the distance but no one seemed to mind. When they stopped for a light along the seawall, swarms of undersized children climbed over the cab. They wiped the windshield free of spray, polished the chrome, cleaned the headlights, and yelled words in English: "Lucky Strike," from one. "Hooray, Eisenhower," from another. The light changed and they crowded in front of the grille. The driver spoke to Juan Carlos in Spanish. He wore a hat with gold braid and a silver eagle.

"He say, if we don't tip the kids, they stay there."

"God," said Judy Lumpers. "I mean, if they *stay* there, how will we get to the hotel?"

The driver put the car into gear and again spoke to Rosenbloom.

"He say he is obliged to run them over."

Gnossos scattered silver dollars out his window and they drove on. But there were swarms of children waiting at each of the lights and when they got to Calle O'Reilly he had no more money at all.

"You mean, you're entirely out of bread, is that what you mean?" Heff was searching through the rucksack while the others untied the bags.

"Don't bug me, baby, I've got credit. I feel it coming."

The Calle O'Reilly was narrow and cobbled, free of tourists. At the end of the street was an open square with an adobe church that looked like the Alamo. There were palm trees and mimosa, but Gnossos dreamed dreams of blitz-krieg vendetta.

Their hotel was called Casa Hilda and they shared what Hilda herself called the Penthouse, a large room with three double beds. It opened on a balcony overlooking the square, but Gnossos locked himself in the bathroom.

"Come out," they pleaded, "we'll find some penicilin."

He sat in the tub and plugged fingers in his ears. Later, when everyone had finally decided to explore the city and trust him to the fates, he sent down for a bottle of dark Bacardi, a bowl of icecubes, sugar, and half a dozen limes, all to ease the pain.

He was half finished with the bottle, just getting a rolling buzz, when an unsalutary thought of wet diapers came bubbling back through childhood memories. He went to the tiled balcony, made a miniature funeral pyre, and burned his saturated underpants. From hotel towels he improvised absorbent pads.

When the bottle was gone, he rolled paregoric Pall Malls, dried them in the afternoon sun, went to bed, and watched the cracks in the old foreign ceiling. But as he expected they had very little to say.

18

The lymphatic grottos of Limbo.

For three days he stayed in bed, serving a self-imposed penance, rising only to change absorbent pads. He burned the old ones, yellow and fetid, and tried to keep his bladder clean. The pains, excruciating and caustic, were too severe to coax, so he drank no more. Instead he watched the ceiling, ate fatty links of chorizo, and wondered occasionally what had become of his Immunity. There was also the continuing spatter of gunfire for diversion. Small arms in the morning, machine guns in the afternoon, tiny bombs at cocktail hour. After the bombs he listened for the flat echo of wings, pigeons frightened half to death by the shudder in the air. Dust blew through the window.

Near the end of the seventy-second hour he rolled over and found a damp oval on his pillow, reminder of his open-mouthed night. The sallow bag of doom, spilling over. With a stubby pencil he scratched above his bed:

A plastic sack, twisted at the ends and sealed.

Yet we can set small cells to gnaw,

to tear and puncture of our own accord.

"Handwriting on the wall?"

Jack was standing in the doorway, smiling.

"Not really, man, more on our foreheads. People need mirrors is where it's at."

"It'd get all backward. What about you? Incubation period up?"

"I guess so, any minute now. C'mere and comfort my decaying frame. Where's Heff?"

She was wearing khaki shorts, a polo shirt, and a black beret. "He says for you to meet him in the square if you're ready to face the world. We found this groovy little bodega, full of absinthe. Did you know they still make it right here in Havana?" She tossed him his boy scout shirt. "You'll turn into a cauliflower or something, just lying around like that."

"No more drinks. Got to avoid liquids."

"Why the hell don't you see a doctor? Juan says two injections do the trick. Hey, you ought to dig Juan, he's really in his element."

"Not the Oeuf genus of clap, sweetheart, it's way ahead of penicillin. Anyhow, I want to wait for Athené. What day is it?"

"Wednesday, believe it or not." She was adjusting her beret and stepping into sandals. "You've been in bed three days, about time to rise from the tomb."

"Nobody to roll the stone away, baby, where'd you say Heff was?" Gnossos sitting up dizzily, unshaven, looking around him, Jack helping, smoothing the hair back over his ears.

"You can see him from the balcony. You want your baseball cap?"

He splashed cold, sulfurous-smelling water on his face as she held the cut-up towel. "I burned it, man, it's the end of an era."

"The baseball cap? Oh, Paps."

"Used it for kindling, man, scattered the ashes, zippobang, all gone. What's happening with you guys, anyway? Heff found the Buddha?"

"He's been doing a lot of creeping around on his own, for that Mafia guy, I think. We're really rolling in bread, he probably wants to talk to you about it."

He paused while twisting a towel corner into an ear. "He's going through with it?"

"Tomorrow, in fact. It's all pretty exciting. I think I'm going with him."

"To the mountains, man?"

"Why not?" She was on the balcony now, looking over the tops of the buildings, toward the harbor. "There's a whole lot happening."

"Jesus, man, there must be."

Embarrassed, she smoothed her polo shirt and shuffled her feet. "It's a little bit spooky too."

He crossed the room, not wanting to sow any more doubt seeds, and kissed her softly on the forehead while she made a face. "You're stepping out is all."

"Mostly, I'm sick of school."

"Just don't look back, you'll turn into salt, something terrible like a fire hydrant."

"No promises, okay? I might need to peek now and again."

"Right, no promises. How do I look?"

"Shitty, you need a shave. Hurry up, why don't you, he's waiting down there."

He paused at the door, watching her sort out her baggage on the bed. Maniac little dyke, who knows her, anyway? "Hey, man—"

She looked up and he had the feeling she was waiting for him to leave so she could sit down and cry. "What, Paps?"

"Nothing. Shit, it's on the wall now, anyway."

They chewed stalks of sugar cane, lounged in the shade, and watched the people going by. The kids from the seawall, who had apparently fallen in love with Gnossos and his silver dollars, were waiting across the square, where they seemed to have been for some time. Heff talked with his hands, laughed excitedly, snapped his fingers, jumped up, and down flashed his new bankroll. "Six months, man, that's how they figure. A full-scale offensive by the New Year, do you dig what I'm saying at all? You've got to make it with us."

"Wow, baby, you really believe it."

"Look at this bread, American dollars. Shit, what do you want to go back to Athené for? I've already even talked to a guy about you; they're taking anybody who has eyes to join."

"You need some lush. Where's this absinthe place Jack was talking about?"

"Come on, Paps, make it, they'd even let us all stick together. You want some more sugar cane?"

"What about Lumpers and Rosenbloom?"

"They're involved, man, forget it. They've got all that Mickey Mouse stuff with Pankhurst back at school."

"Can't see my way clear, that's all. Lost my old Exemption button, have to look around a little."

"Hey, I don't think you really know what I'm talking about. These guys are going the whole *way*. It ain't just raids and sabotage any more, they're moving out, man. They're into things that could straighten your skull for life."

"Not my skull, man. Where do they sell that cane stuff, anyway?"

In a whisper, pulling him under a tree: "Man, they're going to be coming all the way, clear across the island, smack down the middle, right from Oriente!"

"You've been talking to somebody, baby, you ought to watch who you hang out with."

"Batista's going to *lose*, Paps, he's going under, bang, like that."

"Listen, you know what I want to be when I grow up?"

"You've got to make it, man, we'll be in the goddamned mountains Friday morning, afternoon at the latest."

"A maker of mirrors, that's what. Is it maybe too much to ask?"

"You've even got a beard started, let it grow out, man."

Gnossos began to tell him that it was all right, to go in peace, and like that. A similar blessing had been on his lips when Aquavitus interrupted them on the ship. Only, this time it was the Buddha.

He glided out of the shadows, across the square, a seven-foot Negro with an opal in his forehead. He stepped briefly through a patch of sunlight, grinned, and vanished into a bar. On the back of his orange robe was the single word:

MOTHERBALL

"Hey," from Gnossos, pointing a quick finger. "Did you see that?"

But from nowhere an armored car clattered into the street. Three helmeted soldiers rode the roof with automatic weapons, and everyone in sight dove at doorways. "Gang-busters," said Heff, jerking around. Shutters banged shut, store fronts rolled down, tables overturned. They were the only people left without cover. The soldiers pivoted and opened fire madly at the entrance of the bar. Bottles splintered, windows crashed, and Gnossos tugged at Heffalump, first one way, then the other. The firing stopped for a moment but bullets sang and ricocheted through the tropical air. A palm frond snapped on the tree above them and tumbled to the ground. There were screams and more slamming shutters. The soldiers fired again, this time laughing. Gnossos dropped his remaining sugar cane, said, "Fake it, baby," and ran with his hands cupped over his ears, yelling insanely as he moved, "Lalalalalalala . . ." Heff stumbled by his side, grabbed for a leg, but said not a word.

Again the firing paused but Heff stayed down. Gnossos had reached a splintered mimosa by the curb and was crouched against its trunk, rucksack tucked between his legs, body shielded from the armored car. Something on the façade of their hotel caught his attention and he glanced up to find Jack standing by the balcony, looking on as curiously as an opera-goer in a box seat. He waved her away as the soldiers began shooting up anything that moved. First a terrified cat, then a flag, finally the balcony. Gnossos' stomach twitched. The glass around the window flew to pieces. He scrambled back to Heff and again tugged at his sleeve, pointing at the window, screaming crazily above the noise. But nothing happened. He tugged again.

Heff had a hole the size of a thumbtack in his Adam's apple. His eyes were wide open and twisted crosswise. There was blood soaking his kinky hair. Gnossos threw up his arms and wailed a single, faltering cry that rang in the afternoon like the peal of a shattering bell.

19

HEFFALUMP DOWN said the cable. One to an address in Harlem, the other for Beth Blacknesse.

Jack, her face bandaged from flying glass, rocked the body in her arms, hummed a private atonal tune, whispered mortal secrets into the sealed and swollen ears, and kept from crying until the police arrived two hours later.

When it happened, Juan Carlos Rosenbloom had been soothing the gun-shy Judy Lumpers with Cuba Libres in Sloppy Joe's. He took a cab to the crowded scene, looked at the distorted face, choked on a tepid surge of liver bile, and ran away to search out a priest.

Judy Lumpers crept into seclusion at the elegant Hotel Nacional. She locked the door and turned off the phone, after wiring her Larchmont parents for emergency bread.

She felt a compulsive need to visit the continental foyer and play the slot machines.

Gnossos, standing in the square, warned no one to touch so much as an eyelash of the souring body. He finally ignored the scorching gonococcus in his urinary tract and drank two frosted tumblers of straight Bacardi. The priest administered Extreme Unction and inquired, via Rosenbloom, if he should arrange some ground. There came a terrible throb of transcendent memory, a palsied vision of Monsignor Putti purging a hangover, annointing toes.

But the Harlem cable returned unacknowledged. A long-distance call through the confusion of the neighborhood bodega told disquieting tales. Nobody know no Heffalump here, you trying to put us on? Boy used to go by, fit the description all right but that Abraham Jackson White, scholarship boy, he gone to college. You talk to the settlement house, man, he don't have no family. He in trouble? He in some kind of mess? Everyone at the bar of the bodega stopping to stare as Gnossos wailed again. He had never known the name.

Abraham Jackson White. Of all the ridiculous combinations.

He left Juan Carlos as collateral for the telephone charges and went back to the hotel just as the rum began to etch. Yet incredibly, Jack had split for the mountains. In an envelope with a coconut palm on the flap were two hundred dollars in American Express traveler's checks and a note which said she had copied his words from the wall and he would understand.

But he didn't understand.

In the residential section of Vedado the priest wiped an oily face with a linen handkerchief and explained to Rosenbloom that no finer grave site was available at the price. The loose beads of perception seemed to be falling through a hole in the tangible surface of the world and spilling all over the four-dimensional floor. Gnossos rubbed his stubble wearily and asked if anyone was liable to bomb the grave-yard.

"The priest say every leaders like to live here when the shooting stop. Vedado survive all revolutiong."

He nodded, and helped the workers dig the inevitable cavity while an ebony casket rested in the shade, waiting. The silver-dollar kids from the seawall appeared again and stood behind trees. When the workers had trouble with the ropes and rusty pulleys, they came forward and helped, and silence was the password that brought them all together. The priest took out a book to offer prayers over the lowered body but Gnossos told him no. Instead he unfolded paper from his rucksack and wrote with the same stubby pencil he'd used in the hotel:

> This is Heffalump, coming back.
> Maybe, only I doubt it,
> the ashes of his tinted Innocence
> will annoint us all.

The paper fluttered into the grave like a nearly weight-less, injured moth. Behind it went the last of the severed rabbits' feet, a bottlecap from Dr. Brown's Cel-Ray Tonic, a piece of moldy feta, loose pot seeds to flourish in the tropical heat, a vial of paregoric and his Hohner F. He placed the harmonica above the buried head, and planted the pot seeds in a circle around it. You're all through, baby; what can I say?

Juan Carlos came over with his face down, skin still a

little green. "The priest, Gnossos, he want to know about the stone."

Beads were still dropping through the hole, but with less frequency and clatter, and Gnossos only shook his head silently.

"He tell me she importang."

"What's that, man?"

"He say, what kind of stone you want? For marking the graves."

The workers were sprinkling water on the clay to make it settle. "No stone, man."

There was more conversation in Spanish, much polite singsong inflection, then, "He say everyone got stones."

"I don't want it marked is all, let's skip the small shit, okay? It's over. It doesn't matter, man." Gnossos stamped firmly on the remaining loose earth, fighting the sensations of excessive heat and exhaustion. "Tell him there's no more. He can bill me at Casa Hilda." He began to walk away but remembered something and went back with the keys to Fitzgore's Impala. "You can drive, can't you?"

"Who me? You kidding?"

"I'll see you in Athené. You can leave in the morning. Take Lumpers."

"Where you going?"

"Out."

"What you talking about? You okay?"

He made a sign that he was, then motioned for the silver-dollar kids to follow. They hesitated, chattering among themselves, and finally marched after him in a long column, coins jingling in their pockets

Gnossos the gnu and his gnomes.

Hup, two, three, four . . .

●   ●   ●

The bar across the square from Calle O'Reilly was decimated by submachine gun fire and boarded up. A rusty rainspout, however, embedded in the caked adobe, spilled a torrent of water at his sneakered feet. Just about where we left off, buddy boy, but it won't be too long.

The gang of kids approached in twos and threes, breaking ranks, following his gesture, and heard him speak the single word "Motherball." They smiled, poked one another, and he had to try again:

"Señor Motherball, babies. C'mon, *dónde?*"

They shook the money in their pockets for polite reference and started back across the square until he leaned against a lamppost, drawing dollar signs in the sky.

Casa Hilda was where they took him and where it seemed to be. But then it only made the usual maniac sense. Like backtracking in the snow, where you're going is where you've never been but it looks like you were there already, so everybody hunts the other way. They marched through the front door, down the narrow tiled corridor, into a damp courtyard, where a girl in a red dress was learning to play castanets. The kids shuffled about, sat in twos and threes, and pointed to a heavy wooden door that swung from the wall at a perilous tilt. "Thas him," said one as another drew a dollar sign in the dirt, grinned, and indicated they would wait. All month, I'd bet. He hesitated by the door, sniffing, adjusting the rucksack on his shoulder, looking at the girl, who motioned him to go on. Bottomless pit on the other side, rodents in a typhoid pool, hear my falling scream.

Inside, he could see nothing. Too much gloom after the bright pastels of daylight. A smell of musk and heroin, movements in the dark, tempt them not.

"It's only me, gang," he tried, straightening up.

"Flame," said a familiar voice, by way of reply, and a hand lit the wick of a kerosene lamp.

The light came up on a decrepit pock-marked bar and a pall of narcotizing smoke. Like the visage of a Cheshire cat was Louie Motherball's benevolent grin. He stood without a shirt in fuchsia suspenders, sweatlines trickling across his hogshead belly, wiping glasses, breathing clouds of sen-sen fumes into the room. The flame-providing hand belonged to an emaciated Chinese-Cuban woman with a mustache. She sat in a faded maroon dress, sipping from a gallon bowl through a length of surgical tubing. A large sign said TO-NIGHT ONLY: GENERAL WILLIAM BOOTH ENTERS INTO HEAVEN. Gnossos with lockjaw, staring.

"Long time," said Motherball, indicating a stool. There was a pause. "Sit down, why don't you."

"Down, why don't you," echoed the woman.

Gnossos moved carefully, nodding, and said nothing. Another silence, this one longer.

"You endure so well," from Motherball. "Your vigor inspires."

"Vigor," from the woman.

The huge man leaned forward intimately, lowering his voice. "We heard of troubles. Monkey bites."

The woman turned down the flame, and hollows danced in her cheeks, flickering.

"I'm all right," said Gnossos.

A towel which read "Havana Hilton" was used to mop up the lines of sweat, leaving the belly momentarily dry. "You don't look it, but then we all know about appearances."

Gnossos shifted weight as the woman giggled. He leaned his head over to ask who.

"Mrs. Motherball. I'd forgotten you were strangers. The second Mrs. Motherball."

"Charmed," from Gnossos, avoiding her breath.

Louie touched his eyes mournfully with the towel and said, "Poor Maude."

"Maude," giggled the woman.

"My first wife," he explained, going back to the glasses. "Deceased. A violent end in the River Taos, perhaps word reached you. Pliers and acid. Fishhooks. Have a little Summer Snow?"

The beads were falling singly now, but the hole through which they fell had narrowed, so that some of them missed the mark and bounced back up into the tangible world. "Why not?"

"Why not, indeed?" Sen-sen fumes blew into the black, musty room. Motherball opened an icebox in the shadows and lifted out containers of milk and white rum. He blended them in a battery-driven mixer with crushed cubes, fresh heart of cactus, confectioner's sugar and shredded coconut. Gnossos' personal mug was served with a froth of chopped peyote buds, and he tested for bitterness as he heard, "You're of course familiar with the works of Vachel Lindsay?"

"Sooooon," said Mrs. Motherball, mysteriously.

"Little reading thing happening later. Like the sign says."

"Into Heaven," came the giggle.

"I've got business, Louie."

Motherball pausing in the glass-wiping to cast a suspicious glance. "Naturally, a little business, good for your head. Drink up, man, you want some surgical tubing, cuts the oxygen, gives a little side kick."

Gnossos took the length of rubber and said, "I want to see the Buddha is all."

"Business keeps the cells together, buys a little soul time, yes? Take Lindsay, now, the fellow had a great deal going for him."

"Just tell me about the Buddha, man."

"Peddled a pamphlet on the road, see, little thing called *Rhymes To Be Traded for Bread*. Cool, but functional, yes?"

Gnossos put down his mug and set the rucksack on the bar, breathing deeply. "Where's he at, Louie, I'm up-tight."

"He's right behind you, Gnossos, stay loose and all. He's always right behind you."

Before he turned around, he knew that Louie spoke the truth. The presence was ominous and sudden. A faint rustle in the shadows, a motion accompanied by the swish and whisper of heavy silk. Again the smell of heroin.

The Buddha laid a serene, bangled hand on his shoulder. A voice with timbre mellowed by draughts of honeydew and ambrosia spoke the words: "Pretty eyes."

Gnossos chilled from nose to pubes as the impossibly gelid fingers froze the shoulder through his boy scout shirt. The touch of a year-old corpse, turn around.

A massively robed personage towered twenty inches above his highest hair and offered a munificent smile. It had perfumed, nut-brown skin, flawless and taut. An impeccably wrapped turban contained its head and an iridescent opal flashed in the middle of its brow, gleaming, hypnotic. Its eyes shimmered like stygian moons. Stoned. Ossified beyond belief, corpuscles swimming in saturated horse. Say something.

"Hello, man."

"Motherball, he got them pretty eyes. He want everybody to See what he See." The Buddha lifted the entire punch bowl of Summer Snow in one hand and elevated it gracefully to his pursed violet lips. The castanets rattled in the courtyard, beads began to fall once more through the hole.

"Jingle-jingle," said Mrs. Motherball in a private reverie. "Bang-bang."

"I'm a long time coming, Buddha," from Gnossos, turning cautiously on the stool. "Gimme some skin."

"It's on you, baby."

Sure enough, it was. "Fat Fred says hello."

"He free to talk."

"That's the Buddha," from Louie Motherball, digging him, shaking his head.

"Jingle-bang," said his wife, sucking noisily through her empty tube, hinting for a refill.

"Like I said, I'm a long time coming."

"I hear you, Gnossos."

"And a long time gone," said Louie.

"That right."

"You think it's right?"

"He told you," said Louie, digging, "I heard him say it."

"Okay then," from Gnossos, "maybe you can give me a little word, right?"

The Buddha dipped his huge head reflectively, put down the bowl of Summer Snow, and replaced his hands in the folds of the silk robe. "I try, baby."

"Dig him," from Louie.

"Bang-bang."

"If you got them big ears," said the Buddha.

"He's down," said Motherball, mixing again, chopping buds.

"How long, baby?"

"Long enough," from Gnossos.

"Tell me."

Gnossos said, "It looks like up is all."

"That right," said the Buddha.

"In Taos," added Motherball, "he was already down."

"Ting-a-ling, jingle-bang."

"That was fifty years ago," said Gnossos. "You know about Heffalump?"

The Buddha touched his opal with a manicured index finger, nodded his idol-sized skull, and said gently, "We saw him *go* down."

Gnossos remembered the Adam's apple, gaping, dumb. "It made a sound."

"We heard the sound," from Motherball, pausing.

"Ting-a-bang, Bang-bang."

"Some people are going to hear it yet."

"That true," said the Buddha, waiting.

Gnossos scooped up some of the leftover froth with a spoon and munched on the buds. "Straighten me then, man; I'm looking to be straight is all."

The Buddha smiled and moved his elbows in his robes, Motherball pushed a new batch of liquid toward his mesmerized wife, but none of them spoke a word.

"Somebody has a plan," Gnossos went on. "You dig what I'm saying? I see the signs."

"Tell us," from Louie.

"Monkey signs, babies, signs in the Adirondacks—"

"Heap signs," said Motherball. "Pachuco signs."

"That's right. Signs in Nevada you wouldn't believe."

"We believe the signs," said the Buddha.

"But mostly there's the Mojo sign."

"Yeah," from Motherball, "we know the Mojo sign."

"Aquavitus-jingle-bang."

"Giacomo too, check. Where's he at?"

"Giacomo on the payroll, baby."

"What payroll, man?"

"He on the Mojo payroll, baby."

The lockjaw hit Gnossos again, this time from the bottom up.

"Mojo movin' out," continued the Buddha. "He goin' big."

"He's looking around, all right," from Motherball. "Listen to the Buddha."

"Mr. Giacomo, dig, he only on the payroll."

Gnossos traced little figure eights on the moisture of the portable mixer, first one way, then the other. Everyone was silent, and in the pause, he fancied he could hear the visceral seepage in his gonococcic cells. The fantasy brought with it a fleeting sensation of mortal danger, blowpipes hidden in crevices, belladonna in the Bacardi. He measured his situation, the three improbable creatures who made up his company, the squadron of cannibal kids who waited outside, the uniformed assassins who cruised the streets, the moneyless rucksack with the dwindling remains of his identity shredded among the fluff. "You guys," he finally asked, "what about you?"

A pause before Motherball answered with a grin, "Independent."

"We in the shadows," said the Buddha.

"No more franchise," said Motherball. "We have our own little thing. We can't be bought."

"Man," said Gnossos, "I want to believe you."

"You been down too long," from the Buddha. "You got to have faith."

"Ring-a-ding-dong, Mojo-bang."

"I know what Gnossos needs," said Motherball practically.

"Bread," from the Buddha, again touching his opal.

"Let's us talk a little bread, baby."

That night Louie Motherball wove his magic circle, spun his rhythmic words, hypnotized his psychedelic legion, spoke to opiated faces. Gnossos sat with taxi drivers, prostitutes, refugee Taos Indians, and the recently paid-off gnomes. Each of them sucked at a private surgical tube connected to a regulator which pulsated in the contents of a cyclopean bowl. The megaphonic voice spoke out:

"Booth led boldly with his big bass drum—
(Are you washed in the blood of the Lamb?)
The Saints smiled gravely and they said, 'He's come.'
(Are you washed in the blood of the Lamb?)"

In the shadows behind Motherball, on the tops of a dozen antique barrels, the girl in the red dress from the courtyard worked with her assistants. They unscrewed the hollow shells of castanets by the hundreds, they opened the secretly hinged gourds of embellished maracas, they filled the waiting pockets with sweetly smelling horse.

"Unwashed legions with the ways of Death—
(Are you washed in the blood of the lamb?)
(Banjos)"

A phonograph needle was dropped into place by the swimmer who'd been hit on the head by one of Gnossos' silver dollars, and a percussive chorus of marching mummers rendered the smoky air.

"Sages and sibyls now, and athletes clean.
Rulers of empires, and of forests green!
(Grand chorus of all instruments.
Tambourines to the foreground)"

Mrs. Motherball directed the packing operation as eunuchlike coolies stacked the castanets and maracas in vending trays and stuck little name tags onto their sides. The Cubans and the Indians strained forward, sucking intently on their tubes while the milk machine chugged and the Buddha reclined on his beatified side, smiling on everyone with an expression of inscrutable and abundant love.

The next four days found Gnossos selling souvenirs. He hawked on corners, buses, the backs of trolley cars, under palm-frond huts at Varadero Beach, to old fishermen setting off in marlin dinghys from Cojimar, to couples walking the *paseo* in Santa Clara, to cabana boys at the Havana Hilton, to Batista army sergeants dressed like field marshals, to bearded law students lurking under sewer plates, to Superman between acts at the Little Theatre, to croupiers at the Nacional, to every genus of lewd stateside pedestrian panting the alleys.

He paid the priest for the funeral, arranged a CARE package for Jack in the Sierra (Hersheys and khaki socks), got three heavy jolts of aureomycin to check his clap, and won nearly fifteen hundred dollars from a near-sighted Palm Beach masochist who couldn't have seen the double deck anyway. The tide seemed to be turning but Gnossos took no chances.

He bought a first-class ticket on the executive flight to Idlewild. The Motherballs came to wave goodbye with the squadron of gnomes, and a Congo band. From the steps leading to the waiting plane he threw a handful of new dollar bills into the air, and the terminal was chaos. A hostess emerged through the curved door and offered him a bouquet of American Beauty roses. He wore rope-soled sandals, white linen trousers, a freshly starched Cuban boy scout shirt, his bulging rucksack, and a campesino hat for the sun. He carried the quota of liquor in the form of four quarts of Summer Snow, V.S.R. From his woven Pueblo belt were strung six pairs of clacking castanets. He kissed the hostess under the ear, and flashbulbs popped. He waved a blessing to the control tower, and they popped again. Mrs. Motherball fainted, it seemed from the heat and the sudden exposure to daylight.

In his rucksack was a pinch of clay from the grave of Abraham Jackson White.

As the aircraft revved its engines above the sound of the frenetic band, he rolled the grains in his palms and wailed again, this time silently, in his heart, with an anguish of ironies.

Help help, a horrible Heffalump.

Horr Horr, a heffable Horralump.

20

109 Academae Avenue
Athené
May 13, 1958

Selected Friend:

In your hour of sorrow I am imbued with a spirit of agapē. Please to accept humble apologies and felicitations.

The mandrill was of course an error. Conjurations were only practiced on behalf of Mr. Oeuf's demise. Yet one's requisite disciplines are perforce compromised by the juniper berry, and my husband was lax in gleaning coherent information. I am shamed. Please to convey amends to your Miss McCleod, who it seems was terrorized in error. Neither was your own person spared tiresome dangers. Alas.

George, having completed factotum studies in the college of hotel administration, has accepted a position with The Dorchester in London. In that sober atmosphere perhaps we will temper our tastes. As you read this, we are on the seas. Please to forgive. Should the demon continue advances, a daily enema of Lux and warm ale is recommended. I love you.

Extreme and fervent condolences,
Irma Rajamuttu, D. B. E.

There was the feeling he might lose his diluted Aegean mind. He put some Corelli on the record machine, drank a warm glass of Summer Snow, and listened to the duel of tutti and ripieno. It did no good. The spongy fibers of his agitated innards sucked up the stimulation and burned it off directly, leaving nothing behind but the subtle fumes of anxiety. Every so often he belched them out.

The letter had been rolled into the neck of a blotched grenadine bottle on the floor of the empty Benares pad. Window shades flapped in the evening breeze, dustballs blew across the vacant floor. Furniture, books, pots and pans, zoom all gone.

But in his own apartment, things had been happening. The Navajo rug was littered with lists of names, ashtrays were piled high with filters, beercans lay crushed on their sides, four electric typewriters stood plugged into an extension, and a Pitney-Bowes mailing machine hummed in the corner. Hunger gnawed at his stomach but the refrigerator was empty of everything save lint, and the Proctor Slug prowl car that had followed from the airport was waiting patiently by the curb.

There was also a hastily scrawled note from Rosenbloom telling him to get to the campus the instant he arrived, but when he used the phone to find out why, no one answered. Even Kristin's dormitory number, kept for last, rang a mysterious ten minutes. He drank three more fingers of Motherball's brew, took a bath to pass an hour, slipped his hands into a pair of discarded loafers, clomped about on all fours, did a handstand which knocked a brass plate off the wall, rang the weather bureau, chatted obscenities with the recorded operator, fondled his old pillow for Kristin's jugular, hung the horse-filled castanets from a copper hunting horn, and checked the ever-present fuzz. When it was dark he crept furtively through the Rajamuttus', climbed out a window, and made his way to Guido's Grill. The place was empty of anyone he knew, so he bided time with a pizzaburger and cherry malted, finally calling Fitzgore's fraternity as a last resort. The houseman told him all the brothers were at the Demonstration.

The Demonstration. Dear sweet Mary.

Approaching the arts quad he could hear the swell of massive shouts and cheers, the throb of bass drums muffled by a milling crowd. Here and there a figure darted out of a building, carrying a torch. Madmen ran in the direction of the girls' dorms, screaming warcries. The sky beyond flickered with violence, the undersides of clouds danced in reflected flame. He ambled toward the noise, rucksack on his shoulder, *campesino* hat squashing his curls.

A skyrocket shuddered, burst into sulfurous fragments,

and inspired a deafening roar from the ground. From the law school, the ag quad, the engineering buildings, rose strong echoes. It sounded as if they were out in the hundreds.

But when he arrived there were thousands. Cars blocking the Harpy Creek Bridge, students standing on hoods with megaphones, banners fluttering colorfully in the wind, torches smoking, coeds surging back and forth on the lawns, whole fraternities shouting slogans. Men with microphones stumbled along, pigeonholing whomever they could. Photographers loaded cameras with frantic fingers. Reporters ran in circles, jumping between centers of activity, taking notes on little pads. One of them bumped into the rucksack as he was screwing in a bulb, and there was a moment of quick recognition. "My God," he said, "it's Pappadopoulis!"

Around him came a crush of Leicas, Rolleis, Speed Graphics. "Hey, babies," was the startled reaction. He tried elbowing free, feeling the first muggy symptoms of panic. "C'mon, get away—"

They pressed closer, whispering, gaping at his clothes, shouting questions. "Look this way, please." Pop. Click.

"Hey really, get out of here—"

"The wire services estimate seven thousand people, Mr. Pappopoulis—"

"How do you plan to manage them? Will there be a speech?"

"I'm from *Look,* buddy, hold still, be intense—"

He jerked the Cuban hat over his ears and barreled clear, taking refuge in a galloping cluster of students. But as they ran along they began nudging one another and whispering his name.

"That Greek," said one, "the nut from Lairville."

"Where's the platform? Get him to the platform!"

They galloped right past Juan Carlos Rosenbloom, who was prancing on top of Fitzgore's Impala, waving his arms, whipping the air with his cowboy hat, leading a cheer. Gnossos did an about-face and tried to get his attention, but he was jostled out of sight.

We bemoan the chaperone
We would rather be alone . . .

Still another chant began, merging with the first. When he tried creeping under the legs of the mob, he was lifted off the grass by anonymous hands and thrust across the shoulders of a trotting phalanx.

Gno-ssos . . . *Gno*-ssos
Gno-ssos . . . *Gno*-ssos

He used his rucksack to pound ferociously on their skulls, but all across the campus the demonstrators saw it as a signal and began to pound in kind.

A crimson banner rustled past, flying the cry MOTHERS' MARCH ON SEX. And behind it Judy Lumpers in a frenzied flash, dancing in fishnet leotards, high heels, a cheerleader's sweater, holding Byron Agneau by the hand, both of them yelling, "Ying-Yang, Ying-Yang, Ying-Yang . . ."

More skyrockets, Roman candles, cherry bombs, sparklers, fireworks, sirens, bass drums, bugles, *GNO*-ssos . . . *GNO*-ssos . . . He was being hustled toward an elevated platform, which rose above the bobbing heads at the far end of the mob. There were loudspeakers, spotlights, blood-red flags, and two figures side by side who seemed—impossibly enough—to be Oeuf and Kristin, Oeuf in a wheelchair. NON LOCO PARENTIS, read a sign at their backs. They wore serene smiles and looked upon the crashing multitudes.

Gnossos squirmed helplessly for a moment, trying to twist

free of the hands that balanced his teetering weight, then threw out an enraged fist, howling without mercy at his betrayers, mustering the blend of outrage and hurt that tore at his senses, "Vennndettaa!"

But again he was misunderstood and the object of his cry was taken as the cue for wilder yearnings. Fists by the thousands jammed skyward, and the thunder of the vengeful word went up:

"VENNNNNNNDETTTAAAAAAAA!"

Right behind it came the rhythmic marching of an approaching legion, Dean Magnolia leading a chanting column of rebellious faculty:

One-two, what d'we do?
Three-four, smash the door.
Five-six, pick up sticks
Seven-eight, abdicate . . .

Hosts of anarchists everywhere, itching to blow things up, tear things down, cave things in. A now steaming Pappadopoulis was rushed through their midst, handed over the heads of the denser crowd, flipped along like a sack of limp kidney beans. He held his rucksack between clenched teeth, the hat over his ears. As he spun nearer the platform the cheers grew more expectant, less purposeless, blending together in the single, lilting utterance of his name. Then, when the motion faltered and ceased, he found himself tipped forward, standing unsteadily, skipping a little from the momentum. For an instant Oeuf and Kristin were directly in front of him; but Youngblood appeared from a ramp, stepped quickly between them, and seven thousand people fell astonishingly silent.

Find a heavy weapon, man, strike the mortal blow.

Youngblood spoke in a forced whisper before he moved,

side-stepping the podium microphone, gesturing for good sense. "Gnossos—"

But Greek teeth gave a malevolent hiss.

"Gnossos, take it easy. You may find this difficult to believe, but everything is for the good."

"That's right, baby, tell me all about it—"

"Don't be rash, try to control yourself—"

An apprehensive clapping began when he failed to recognize the crowd. People picked it up in threes and fours.

"Gnossos," from Kristin quickly, motioning Youngblood aside. "We can settle our differences later. I promise."

"People are watching us," said Youngblood.

"Speeeech," came a distant call, echoed by the clappers. "Speeeeeeeeeech!"

He hissed once more, glancing around like an exhibited captive Apache. Oeuf leaned forward in his wheelchair, speaking under his breath. "Stop that ridiculous noise. Where's your *amour-propre?*"

Speech, came the call again. Bass drums picked up the clapping, claxons hee-hawed.

Speech-speech-*speech*-speech—

"They've heard us all," from Youngblood desperately. "They just *won't* be satisfied. You're the only one left."

Ven-detta . . . *Ven*-detta . . . *Ven*-detta . . .

Gnossos shifted weight to cover his flanks, but the crowd's collective acumen picked up the subtle change and thought he might be about to speak. They sent forth a spectacular cheer. In the midst of the din, as confetti blossomed skyward and showered over their heads, Oeuf tried an importunate whisper, ignoring the pickup of the mikes.

"Bread, Gnossos. Immunity. Sex. Name it quickly, what in hell do you want? There's no holding this goddamned crowd."

Knuckles under the nose, came the thought. Stiff fingers in the larynx. But the Slugmen were standing at corners of the platform, Mausers in their coats. He felt his shirt pocket for the little white box he'd prepared in the Idlewild pharmacy, and "Kristin" was what he finally said.

At the sound she looked up, catching her breath.

Speech-*speech*-speech-*speech*—

Oeuf's glance caught her parted lips, but returned to Gnossos all the same. "Kristin?"

"Check baby."

Ven-detta . . . *Ven*-detta . . . *Ven*-detta . . .

"How long?"

"Half an hour."

"Too long."

"Forty minutes."

"Jesus, Gnossos."

"Sixty."

"Hurry," said Youngblood.

"You mustn't harm her."

"That's right."

Kristin began to protest but Oeuf motioned her into silence. "I have your word?"

Gnossos' hand was on his heart.

VEN-DETT-*A* . . . VEN-DETT-*A* . . .

A short pause. "Forty minutes?"

"Okay, man."

"For Christ's sake," said Youngblood, perspiring fiercely, "Hurry up!"

GNO-SSOS . . . *GNO-SSOS* . . .

He grinned openly at Kristin, half concealing the menace that trembled on his lips. Then he threw up his arms for the crowd, palms facing, as if he were signaling a touchdown.

For fully five minutes he was Lindbergh at Orly, MacArthur on Wall Street, Ulanova at the Bolshoi, Sinatra at the Paramount. The cadence of stamping feet shook the campus as if it were an island on a seismic fault. Through the deafening rumble he motioned to Youngblood for words.

"Say something, Christ, it couldn't matter."

"What, man?"

"Oh God, Pankhurst, free love, *any*thing!"

GNO-SSOS . . . GNO-SSO . . .

The touchdown arms came slowly to his sides. The chants subsided gradually, hushing noises ran through the mob like the whisper of doom itself, heads came up to listen. He stood, waiting for the periphery of the crowd, ignoring the urgings of Kristin and Oeuf, holding out for complete control. For a moment a lone bass drum continued booming, then nothing but embarrassed laughter, odd shouts from distant stragglers, the sizzle of sparklers burning in the dark.

Seven thousand ivy league smiles flickered and gleamed. Two hundred and twenty-four thousand calcium-white incisors, canines, bicuspids, premolars, eyeteeth, and molars, anxious to bite, ready for the bacchanal, hungry and drooling. A tremble of despotic power shuddered in his loins. A flood of adrenalin buoyed up his blood. He could do worse than give them provender for a night of romping abandon.

With exquisite deliberation he made two loose fists, held them up, and gave everyone the finger.

And they loved it. If he'd called for the carnal defloration of Susan B. Pankhurst in Macy's window, the ecstatic concourse would have been no less inspired. They went rabidly giddy, they danced up and down, they pounded one another on the head, they gave irrational screams, they wandered amuck.

Placards tumbled in the air, skyrockets tore through trees, automobiles rolled on their backs, brassières were raised on spikes, and fuel was added by the bushelful to an impetuous bonfire of male underpants.

Kristin wheeled Oeuf quickly to the microphone, and into the maelstrom of the frenzy he slipped the name of the university President.

"Carbon," swelled the echo.

"Down with Carbon," he said, again with hardly subliminal intent.

"Down with Carbon," they repeated.

Through the crowd inched Fitzgore's Impala, shooting off pinwheels, backfiring, horn blowing. Someone who looked like Heap was at the wheel, Juan Carlos Rosenbloom straddled the back seat, wielding a banner like El Cid.

"DOWN WITH CARBON!" was the cry.

Rosenbloom lowered his banner, and the car swerved suddenly toward Harpy Creek Bridge in the direction of the President's mansion. The crowd parted as if it were the Red Sea. There was a moment's pause. Then torches in hand, all seven thousand of them followed with a bloodcurdling bellow, stampeding like the Pharaoh's army.

"Come on," said Youngblood, "let's go."

Someone fired a ceremonial cannon.

"Hurry," said Kristin, "we'll miss it." She was starting to wheel Oeuf to a ramp at the edge of the platform.

VENDETTA * VENDETTA * VENDETTA

"Easy, baby," from Gnossos, blocking the way.

"Hey," yelled Youngblood, "move it, will you, the fun's just starting!"

BOOOOOOOM, went the cannon again.

Gnossos was smiling, pointing at Kristin.

"Now?" she asked.

Oeuf glared back, looked at his watch, and said, "Forty minutes."

Chi Psi's fire engine clanged by, sirens wailing, a bikini coed sitting on the hood.

Gnossos had Kristin firmly by the hand.

"Later," he said.

"Where?" from Oeuf.

"The Dairy Queen," said Gnossos.

A nod from the departing Oeuf. The Slugmen fell in behind; and the sounds of night intensified, as if someone had turned up the volume on the entire televised scene.

It was precisely the place where Mojo had watched the flogged microbus. They sat once more in Youngblood's Anglia, listening to the engine cool after the drive. Time was a-wasting, but Kristin turned on him suddenly, looking for the advantage. "If I'm pregnant," she said, "I'll just have to do something about it. You must have known that, Gnossos, for God's sake."

He reached into the rucksack and lifted out the open bottle of Summer Snow. "You want a drink?"

"It was such a damned *adolescent* thing to do. Do you realize it gave my father eczema from head to toe?"

He drank off two inches and smiled insanely, saying nothing.

"As if everything were so simple! I mean I *cared* for you too, you know, I could hardly have done all those things if you weren't so damned attractive."

He reached into his boy scout shirt pocket and removed

the small white box, fondling it absently, still failing to speak.

"And Heffalump," she tried, on a different tack, sighing, looking at the window, "I was sick about it."

"Were you?"

"Don't be foolish, Gnossos, of course I was."

He slid the rubberband away, paused, then offered the bottle again. "Come on, man, have a taste. It's good for you."

Her mouth twitched fearfully from the menace in his inflection and she said, "No, thanks."

He showed her the box. "Got a present for you. Little something for your head."

The clearing was under the trees at the end of a roughed-out parking lot. The Dairy Queen was closed, there were no other cars in the lot, the only sounds came from the distant campus, unreal and remote. She reached casually for the door handle but he caught her arm with unmistakable pressure. "Gnossos, don't!"

"All the way from Cuba, compliments of the Buddha."

"Please, you're hurting me."

"Don't you want to know what it is? Sweetie pie."

The pulse in her throat was tapping wildly, but she kept her free hand on the door. "Oh God, Gnossos, what are you talking about? Wasn't the damned monkey enough? Will you let go of my arm?"

He tightened the grip and slid the lid off the box with his thumb. "That's right, baby, keep talking."

She twisted around violently, her back against the handle, tears coming into her eyes. "For God's sake, please, Gnossos. I didn't have to come here."

"But you did, man, what can I say?"

"You promised Alonso. You said you wouldn't hurt me."

He watched her eyes close against his snarling smile and took out a handkerchief. "It won't hurt at all. Believe me."

"Oh *please*—"

There seemed to be nothing more to talk about. He jerked her suddenly away from the door, pulling her across his lap. She fought to sit up as he moved from under the confines of the wheel, but he took her by the hair to keep her still. It was perfumed, bound by a brass band; she wore a short-sleeved blouse, pressed denim skirt, and gray knee-socks. Then he patted her bottom. "Get them off," is what he said.

Her mouth dropped open with a gasp. "What?"

"And don't be all night."

"Oh Jesus, you don't want—"

"Man, I wouldn't touch you with a windowpole, you've got the clap."

"Gnossos, really, for God's sake—" she gathered her breath to scream but it was all over. He used the handkerchief for a rolled-up gag and undid his woven Pueblo belt. With it he caught her flailing hands and bound them behind her. There came a hideous, muffled gurgle. She tried to kick and he let her. He forced her face-down on the seat, moving clumsily, having to kneel around her, then took the hem of her skirt. He was sitting on the small of her back as he opened the box. Inside was a glycerin suppository filled with Motherball's uncut horse. He poised the pellet like a small torpedo between thumb and forefinger, then used it precisely as it was meant to be used, adding little for old times' sake but tender care.

He counted to fifty, gave a couple of playful pats, and rolled her over. She was ghastly pale and trying to lose consciousness.

"Feel good?"

The whites of her eyes were etched with furiously constricted little veins. He watched them until the pupils dilated and the lids grew heavy. Occasional booms from the distant cannon filled the silences. After a while she began to shiver, stopped thrashing, and withdrew. Welcome to Limbo, hope you enjoy your stay.

He helped her out of the car, took away the gag, in case she might be sick, and untied her hands. She began an uncontrollable giggle.

He lit a cigarette, checked her watch, and took a deep breath. "Don't forget to write, baby."

He hiked the rucksack onto his shoulder and walked away through the woods, leaving her alone on the grass, not even pausing to look back.

You never know just who might turn you into salt.

21

Actually he might have spent more than seven days on David Grün's idyllic hill, had Tern and Towhee not brought up the *Daily Sun*. His little camp was well made, sheltered, utilitarian, free from any but the most natural distractions. Songbirds came to breakfast, squirrels shared his lunch, raccoons cleaned up the dinner scraps. His bedroll lay on a cushion of pines, the sun warmed porous stones that radiated heat in the night; there were blackberries, water cress, rose hips, sour grass, cherries, and a mineral spring. He might have abandoned all hope for differential equations and theories of solar origin. The microcosm was beginning to look pretty good. Only once had he been interrupted, the time David came to ask whether he cared to receive any

phone messages. But Gnossos was making herbal mushroom soup at the time and only asked where the rosemary
grew.

In fact, he was reheating this same brew with green ore-
gano when the girls brought the paper and began picking
wildflowers. He watched them for some time, chewed on
one of Tern's violets, showed them where the fairy lanterns
hid. It was the black, alarming headline tilted on the clover,
that caught his unbelieving eye.

G. ALONSO OEUF ACCEDES TO PRESIDENCY
Decision Follows Death of
President Magnolia in Freak Landslide

"What's the matter, Gnossos?" asked the girls when they
heard the curious grunt. But he was reading on, tracing
lines word by word with a weak finger:

> Falling shale in gorge crushes ex-dean on final
> field trip. Magnolia's mangled form was recov-
> ered by Alastair P. Heap of Cambridge, Massa-
> chusetts, who was rock-scrambling nearby at the
> time of the event. The tragedy marred the an-
> nouncement of Dean Oeuf's bethrothal to Kristin
> F. McCleod, daughter of G. Kenneth McCleod,
> special assistant to President Eisenhower . . .

But when Gnossos stormed through the door of his Lairville apartment, Proctor Slug was waiting on the Navajo
rug. He had a dossier under his arm and was rattling the
heroin-filled castanets. There was an unmistakable odor of
monkey-fumes in the air.

"Hold it," came the order.

And to make sure he did, two sergeants stepped in behind him, closing the door. "Hello, Pappadopoulis," they added, smiling.

"Sit down," said Slug.

Gnossos glanced at the castanets and felt decidedly faint. But he remained standing and shook his head. "What's happening?" he tried. "Little cop convention going on?"

"Why waste his time?" asked one of the sergeants. "Give him the business."

"We know all about you," said Slug, in a fedora. "We've got it all written down."

"Those statues," from the second sergeant. "Last Christmas."

"Magnolia's office," from the first. "Vandalism."

"That party in the loft," said Slug, moving closer. "These castanets. Gnossos, I'm afraid you're in a lot of trouble."

"Don't call me Gnossos, man."

"Not that it matters. You're hardly a local problem any more." He handed him a white envelope that had PERSONAL stamped on the front in red letters.

"Open it," said the sergeants, together.

GREETINGS was the first word he read. And underneath, the usual invitation from the United States Army. It was signed, of course, by the chairman of the Athené draft board, and although Gnossos had never seen Oeuf's pudgy signature before, he reflected how like him it was.

The Slugmen took away the rucksack.

Old keeper of the flame, it seemed as if the asphalt seas were calling.

Oh la.

Bump bump bump,

down the funny stairs.